THE MAKING OF A HERO

Allenson fired a single shot at a renegade aiming a weapon. He missed, and cursed his poor marksmanship. This was hopeless.

Hawthorn and Destry fired coolly and steadily, dropping renegades as if they were shooting targets on a practice range.

Allenson's gun shut down with a click. He gave up on it and charged toward the renegades.

He was the only man standing when he reached the fire.

Hawthorn fired his rifle at the wood below the window ledge. Wood exploded in a shower of splinters. The gunman screamed and reared up, pawing at his face. A burst from Destry's carbine lit up the renegade's chest.

"Got you," Destry said with satisfaction.

Allenson turned to thank his friends. He flushed when he saw the strange expression on their faces.

"Hawthorn, should I ever chance to risk being called out by our friend here, pray do not hesitate to remind me of this day," Destry said.

"You can be sure of it," Hawthorn replied. "I suppose we should bind up our hero's wounds before he bleeds to death."

Blood ran down Allenson's arm, soaking into his jacket.

"I thought that last renegade had missed me," Allenson said.

"He did," Hawthorn said. "The one in green winged you. Destry put him down before he could correct his aim."

Destry shrugged. "O⸻ ⸻ ⸻ ⸻ their full attention. You took one hel⸻

Allenson examined ⸻ his forearm.

"It doesn't hurt," h⸻

"It will," Hawthor⸻

INTO THE HINTERLANDS

DAVID DRAKE
JOHN LAMBSHEAD

Copyright © 2011 by David Drake & John Lambshead

A Baen Books Original

Baen Publishing Enterprises
P.O. Box 1403
Riverdale, NY 10471
www.baen.com

ISBN: 978-1-4516-3842-4

Cover art by Bob Eggleton

First Baen paperback printing, October, 2012

Library of Congress Control Number: 2011020559

Distributed by Simon & Schuster
1230 Avenue of the Americas
New York, NY 10020

Pages by Joy Freeman (www.pagesbyjoy.com)
Printed in the United States of America

For our late friend Jim Baen,
whose idea it was.

Speak not of doleful things in a time of mirth or at the table; speak not of melancholy things as death or wounds, and if others mention them change if you can the discourse; tell not your dreams, but to your intimate friend.

—George Washington

· CONTENTS ·

INTO THE
HINTERLANDS

· CHAPTER 1 ·

The Continuum

The Continuum was angry.

Sometimes you could see forever through its violet tints. Today, turbulent currents spilled colors with such energy that Allenson could not keep Jem Hawthorn's frame in sight. He was reduced to following the silver track of its wake.

Allenson pedaled a similar frame, a machine not unlike an exercise bike in appearance. It had a central column with pedals at the bottom and a seat on top. A control panel and a display screen were slung between handlebars projecting between his legs. His rucksack was clipped to the back. The entire machine was made from paper-light ceramic and carbon composites.

Thin filaments of carbon enclosed him; balls of green and blue light rolled slowly along them. If Allenson concentrated he could see the faint shimmer of the interface between his reality bubble and the raw energy of the Continuum. That delicate bubble was only maintained by constant pedaling, as the frame had little capacity for storing energy.

The bubble field could be phased to move the frame through the Continuum. It was tuned to leak light in the visible frequencies, so the pilot could navigate, but was otherwise impervious. It was unsafe to allow too much interaction between reality and the Continuum. Inevitably, heat build up became an issue on long trips. The harder you had to pedal, the more saunalike it got. Allenson had to work very hard to push his frame through the turbulence.

Hawthorn reappeared suddenly, his frame materializing out of a boiling purple mist. Allen Allenson twisted his hand throttle forward to brake. Colliding frame fields could produce unpleasantly terminal interactions.

He kept a wary eye behind for Royman Destry. Destry had spent fifteen years of his youth on the home world, highly civilized Brasilia. He had taken a degree at Blue Horizon College, part of the prestigious University of Freelanding.

Allenson thought highly of Destry's education but the downside was that Destry had neither the physical fitness nor the wilderness skills of the other two men.

The Continuum lay outside of reality—our reality, where mankind evolved. The universe was a 4D-membrane floating in the Continuum. There might be other universes, the mathematics suggested the possibility, but no one had ever discovered one. The Continuum's infinite dimensions twisted and changed scale, folding in to nothingness before uncurling in an endless dance. Its drag on elements varied according to their subatomic properties. Metals were particularly troublesome.

Frame technology offered mankind the means to

cross interstellar distances, but at a price. Frames were delicate and transportation of goods, especially metals, was difficult in anything but small quantities, or in very large ships. The Continuum heaved, tossing frames like coracles in a mighty ocean. Some currents were strong and persisted, allowing easier travel in certain directions. One of the most important was the Cutter Stream that crossed the worldless Bight to the galactic west of the Home Worlds. This stream made possible Brasilia's five Cutter Stream Colonies, situated as they were on the far side of the Bight.

Allenson, Hawthorn, and Destry had the task of surveying the Hinterlands to the west of the Cutter Stream Colonies for the Harbinger Project. This area was thought to be rich in exploitable worlds. There was already a trickle of migration into the area. Brasilia had agents keeping an eye on one or two of the faster growing colonies. Most of the Hinterlands was unexplored and known only by hearsay and traveler's tales.

Hawthorn looked around and made an overtaking gesture. Allenson glanced at his watch. Surely it was not yet time for him to take point? The position of the minute bar confirmed that Hawthorn was requesting to be relieved early. It was most unlike him not to serve his full shift. The leader of a column of frames created a wake that eased the path for those following. The "going" at the front of their small column must be very difficult indeed.

Allenson raised a hand to signal acknowledgement and steered his frame out of Hawthorn's slipstream. It rocked in the turbulence and he had to press harder on the pedals to maintain speed. He checked the charging bar, which showed that his frame's small capacitors were only at three-quarter storage.

Allenson was a fit young man of twenty-two. He was tall, strong, and healthy, but he nevertheless felt compelled to adjust his frame's power flow such that it all went straight to the frame's energy field. This fractionally eased the loading on his pedals. Out here in the wilderness, that could mean the difference between survival and destruction.

Destry was the Chief Surveyor of the Harbinger project, as befitted his social rank as a member of the Brasilian aristocracy, but it was understood that the Assistant Surveyor, Allenson, would lead the team.

Allenson considered his options. Normally, he would have consulted his friends but discussion from frame to frame was not possible so he had to make a decision for the whole team. He would probably have gambled on pedaling on through the turbulence had it been just Hawthorn and himself but he had Destry to consider. Destry was struggling to keep up. It would go ill for the Allensons if he lost a member of the Destry family tree, even such an unimportant colonial twig as Royman. To Allenson's credit, this was not at the forefront of his mind. Destry was his friend and, more importantly, his responsibility.

Allenson decided that they had no choice but to land and rest while the gale blew itself out, but that was easier said than done. The survey team was in uncharted wilderness, so choosing a direction to find shelter was problematical.

Large gravity fields projected shadows in the Continuum that were usually visible for great distances, but not today. Allenson ran blind, peering helplessly at the swirling energy. He was tempted to initiate a search pattern but the danger was that they would become confused and pedal round in circles.

Pilots tended to see things in the Continuum's colored patterns. Experiments with cameras had shown that the visions were at least partly hallucinations caused by some unknown direct interaction between the Continuum and the human mind. Many an academic and mystic had topped up their pension fund by speculating at length about the meaning, if any, of these phenomena.

Allenson kept seeing an image of his stepmother. She smiled at him with love in her eyes, holding out her arms and eagerly beckoning to him. This was an intensely irritating fantasy, all things considered. He shook his head to clear his mind. This was not the time to get distracted.

Allenson slowed to check that the rest of the team were still with him. The Continuum gale had not blown out; indeed conditions were deteriorating. Allenson noted that Destry's pedaling was increasingly erratic. They were fast running out of options.

Hawthorn blipped the phasing on his frame causing it to flash to attract Allenson's intention. He gestured exaggeratedly to his left. Faint orange coils spun lazily into the distance. That meant only one thing—Rider tracks!

Riders liked storms no more than did people, but they knew the Hinterlands intimately. Allenson swung his frame behind the dissipating coils and followed. He had been pedaling for what seemed a lifetime and his vision was blurring. When he first glimpsed the shadow ahead he thought it was just fatigue, but it was a star's gravitational field distorting the continuum. He pedaled with renewed energy and soon spotted the smaller shadow of a planet. They were saved. He followed the Rider's spiraling trail right down to a point on the world's equator.

Allenson carefully and slowly adjusted his frame's phasing until reality became visible as a ghostly monochrome image. He could see out of the Continuum tolerably well, but he would still be quite invisible to anyone in the realspace. Long shadows showed that he had materialized in the twilight zone between night and day.

The Riders had set up camp in a clearing surrounded by a forest of tall, cone-shaped trees covered with needle-like "leaves." Something fleshy cooked on a spit over a fire. Fat dripped, flashing when it caught alight in midair. Allenson noticed a dozen or so near-naked Riders huddled around the flames, suggesting that the weather was cool even on the equator. Riders were more or less human. They were short—most were less than one and a half meters—and thin, with long greasy hair that hung around their shoulders.

The group was mostly male with a few scrawny girls. The genders could only be distinguished by the scrubby beards on the men.

Large crystal boulders were scattered around the campsite. A flickering shadow showed where one moved, twisting around before settling like a dog in a reed bed. Where there were Riders, there were inevitably Rider beasts. Long crystals on the beast slid against each other and opened. A Rider jumped out and made his way toward the fire. Riders got their name because they rode crystal beasts through the Continuum, protected in some way by the crystal latticework around them.

Hawthorn's frame gently solidified into half-real. Allenson pointed at the Riders and then gestured that the team should move around the planet into the night zone. Hawthorn nodded in agreement. Riders were capricious and could be dangerous even when unprovoked.

Destry's frame flickered briefly into view before vanishing back into the Continuum as he over-compensated on the phasing slider. Destry then reappeared, his frame dropping fully into the material universe with a flare of energy. He was too exhausted to achieve the delicate control needed to examine the Riders unobserved.

Several of the beasts stirred, phasing in and out of the Continuum like frogs sticking their head out of a pond to check on the surface world. The beast's agitation attracted the Riders' attention.

Allenson was not the type to waste time cursing over events. His mind clicked coldly through the options. Fleeing was the least attractive. The Riders could easily chase down tired men and flight suggested weakness. Riders despised weakness and they attacked what they despised.

There was only one realistic course of action. Allenson phased fully into the real world. He descended to ground level in the Riders' clearing by slowly deenergizing his frame, allowing gravity to take hold. His legs trembled slightly when he climbed off.

He busied himself with unloading packs and breaking down his vehicle. A single-pilot frame was designed to fold up into a small load that could be slung over one shoulder. He made a great show of ignoring the

Riders, although he took the precaution of unclipping
his lasercarbine and swinging it over his shoulder.

Hawthorn followed him in, swinging a leg over his
frame's saddle to drop to the ground almost before it
had landed. Allenson greeted his friend with a slap on
the shoulder. Hawthorn was a tall man, so he could
meet Allenson eye to eye, but Hawthorn was lean and
rangy whereas Allenson had a burly physique that had
won him a place as anchorman on the school tug-of-
war team. Hawthorn had a shock of blond wavy hair
and deep blue eyes. These were untypical for Cutter Stream colonists and gave him a distinctly unfair
advantage with the fairer sex.

Allenson had the dark brown hair and eyes that
were the human norm. He gave an impression of
clumsiness that translated to unastute people as lack
of intellect.

Hawthorn casually swung a powerful laserifle in
his left hand, as if he had forgotten it was there.
The laserifle was a big game hunter's weapon. Several of the Riders rose to their feet, clutching spears
and divers close-quarter weapons. They were clearly
undecided how to respond.

Hawthorn's laserifle was made of a gray polymer
that was indistinct in the twilight. Hawthorn stretched.
He tilted the rifle barrel so that firelight reflected
off the synthetic focusing crystal at the muzzle. The
Riders sat down again.

"I'm so, so glad to be off that saddle," Hawthorn
said. "Another hour of that and the ladies of the Red
Lantern would have cause to sue the frame's manufacturer for loss of earnings. You'd think they could
pad them a little more."

Destry finally made it down beside them with a thump caused by a failure to time de-energization with ground level. Still, every one that you walked away from was a good one—as the old saying went.

"I'm sorry, Allenson..." Destry began.

Royman Destry was a small slender man with narrow features and a long, sharp nose. He had the jet black, curly hair typical of Brasilian aristocracy. He made quick movements with his hands when he talked, accentuating his likeness to a bird.

"Say nothing, but look haughty," Allenson said, in a tone of great respect.

Fortunately Destry grasped the situation quickly. His family was not noted for their foolishness. He waved a hand languidly at Hawthorn.

"Deal with my frame, there's a good chap," Destry said.

Destry sported the clothes that a Brasilian gentleman wore when visiting the wilderness to "take the air," which was usually a euphemism for slaughtering the local wildlife or an illicit assignation. His attire was brightly colored in blue and yellow. White lace ribbons floated in the slightest breath of air. He carried this outfit off to the manner born, or should that be "manor born"? Allenson made a note to check the etymology of the phrase when he returned to civilization.

Hawthorn and Allenson were gentlemen, meaning that their families had sizable land holdings in the Cutter Stream, so they were theoretically Destry's peers. However, some peers were more equal than others.

Allenson and Hawthorn wore the functional toned down dress in the autumn camo-colors of colonial country gentlemen. The clothing material was hard

wearing and tight fitting, the jacket short to the waist
to free the legs for pedaling. Both jacket and trousers were generously equipped with sealable pockets.
They also wore webbing, to which more pouches and
equipment were attached.

Destry's close friendship with the other men would
have puzzled a Brasilian, but social ranks were relaxed
on the frontier. The Cutter Stream branch of gens
Destry had adopted the Allensons. Destry's sister,
Linsye, had married Allenson's brother, Todd. That
made the Allensons family, not clients.

Allenson and Hawthorn were friends because they
had grown up together, attended the same schools,
kissed the same girls—well, Hawthorn had done most
of the kissing—and fought the same battles.

The Riders could not help but notice the distinction in dress between the men, and they would draw
the obvious conclusion. Destry was a "chief," and the
other two his warriors.

"Certainly, Sar Destry, your worship," said Hawthorn,
touching his forelock. He made a rude gesture with the
other hand, masking it from the Riders with his body.

"Quite right, my man," said Destry, grinning. "And
be quick about it."

"Don't push your luck, pal," said Hawthorn, in a
tone of respect.

Allenson could not help but smile at the familiar
exchange. The wilderness was like a fire that boiled a
man's personality down to core essentials. There was
little room for pretense or prevarication. The Cutter
Stream residents described a sound man as one "to
go into the Hinterlands with." Both his friends were
sound men, in their different ways.

Destry stood with his hands on his hips. He finally deigned to notice the Riders, observing them with the expression of the Lord of a Terran Manor on discovering a caravan of gypsies setting up home in the corner of his estate. Allenson hid a smile; the first rule of dealing with Riders was never, never to show fear.

Allenson shivered. The abrupt transition from the sauna-like frame to a cool climate was bracing.

"There's plenty of kindling wood around," said Hawthorn, noticing. "I'll get a fire started."

The survey team walked to the treeline. The bottom third of the trunks was bare and there was no ground vegetation. Branches touched above to form a continuous canopy. Nothing moved under the trees and the only sound came from the Riders around their fire. The ground was covered with the detritus of slowly decaying leaves and wood.

"The trees must shed their branches when stressed," Destry said.

He picked up some twigs and rubbed them between his fingers before sniffing at them.

"Odd smell. I'll warrant there's something toxic in the sap. That would explain why nothing seems to inhabit the trees."

Allenson and Hawthorn exchanged a grin. Destry had read natural science at Blue Horizon.

The dead wood lit easily so they soon had a fire going. They warmed themselves, heating ceramic-wrapped ration packs in the flames. The Riders had a massive blaze roaring in the center of the clearing. Every so often there would be a squabble and the loser was dispatched to chop down another sapling at the edge of the treeline and throw it on the fire. The wood caught fire immediately. It spat yellow flames that shot out violently with explosive cracks.

"Interesting," Destry said. "The tree sap contains inflammable oil. That must be the toxic agent."

He wiped his hands carefully with a scented handkerchief.

"I wonder if it would be cost-effective to extract as a fuel," Allenson said, jotting down a note on his datapad.

"Not much to power around here," said Hawthorn, sweeping his arm to encompass the wilderness around them.

"It may not always be forests," said Allenson, mildly.

This was a variation of a routine argument between them. Hawthorn knew just how to needle his friend, but his grin was infectious, so it was impossible not to smile back.

"We might as well take some notes. We are not going anywhere until the storm passes," Allenson said, aware of how pompous he sounded but unable to emulate his friend's irreverent style.

"True," Hawthorn replied. "And Brasilia's money spends as well as anyone's, even if they are wasting it. This place won't make a profit in my lifetime."

"It isn't just about immediate profit, although financial returns are necessary to placate backers," said Destry. "My family invested substantially in the Harbinger Project partly for strategic reasons. Trance takes the long view."

Trance was the paterfamilias of the Destry gens and so had considerable political influence, including a seat on the Brasilian Council. This body was nominally merely advisory to the People's Representative Committees who had legislative power, but its advice was rarely ignored, partly because of prestige, but mostly because the majority of Committee Members were clients of one or other of the paterfamilias who made up the Council.

"Terra is extending across the Bight on each side of the Cutter Stream colonies. Brasilian expansion into the New Worlds will be blocked if these arms link up. Terra is trying to surround and strategically strangle us," said Destry, gesturing with his hands to illustrate encirclement.

Destry seemed unconscious of a dichotomy developing in the Cutter Stream between those who still considered Brasilia "us" and those who tended to think of Brasilia as "them." It was a small distinction, but one that cut across class boundaries.

"I have to admit that the Project has been a useful source of ready cash," Destry said, with the candor of a man who had unassailable social status whatever his financial standing.

The Cutter Stream Legislature had appointed Royman's father, Brasman Destry, to the Project's Presidency in an effort to curry favor with the paterfamilias of Gens Destry back on Brasilia. Did Trance care about what happened to the cadet branch of the family across the Bight? Not very much, Allenson suspected, but he was glad at what the appointment meant for his friend Royman. The Cutter Stream Destrys had no money of their own. Their aristocratic connections brought them status and expensive social obligations, but little in the way of hard cash.

It was entirely proper for Brasman to appoint his son Chief Surveyor and natural that Royman would select an associate to do the actual work. Thus Allenson acquired the title, duties, and honorarium of Assistant Surveyor. The fact that Allenson was competent to do the job was a welcome bonus.

The packs in the fire changed color. Hawthorn hooked them out with a stick and the survey team settled down to eat. Destry spooned out a helping of something resembling yellow ocher porridge and blew on it. A trail of water vapor condensed into the air. He tasted the concoction and grimaced.

"Ready meals aren't getting any more palatable."

Allenson nodded politely. Actually, he had few gastronomic pretensions. He made little distinction between one dish and another provided it was hot and nourishing. The complex sauces used by Brasilian chefs merely muddied the flavor of the food in his opinion. But it would not be politic to voice such a view, as it would label him a hopeless colonial peasant. Brasilian nobility already tended to assume that their Cutter Stream colonists had barely lost their tails and were still striving for the evolutionary level achieved by *Homo erectus*.

The Riders and survey team surreptitiously kept an eye on each other while ostentatiously pretending indifference. While they were still eating, a Rider made a great show of standing. He approached the survey team with his spear reversed in his right hand.

Allenson and Hawthorn rose to meet him. The Rider offered Allenson a piece of burnt meat. It smelled of charcoal and blood. Allenson made a gesture of polite refusal. He was too far from home to risk food poisoning. He offered the Rider a spoonful from his ration pack in return. The man sniffed at it suspiciously, shuddered, and mimicked Allenson's refusal.

The Rider spoke to Allenson in Kant, a simplified universal trade tongue. Each Rider Clan seemed to have a distinct language so they all used Kant when talking to outsiders. It now included a smattering of English words. These were usually connected with industrial trade goods, as the Riders had little indigenous technology higher than Palaeolithic.

Allenson could understand only a few words of Kant, but Hawthorn spoke it fluently. The Rider said the word "tonk" emphatically to Hawthorn, who shook his head firmly. "Tonk" was the slang name for Tollins Superior Berry Distillation, a cheap gin found throughout the Cutter Stream. Allenson noticed the word because he was expecting it. Hawthorn waved a hand dismissively and made some sort of counteroffer. This set off a voluble exchange between the two that went on for some time.

"He demanded a gift of a bottle of joyjuice," said Hawthorn, using another Cutter Stream colloquialism. "I refused, of course, and asked him what he had to trade. We agreed on the use of one of the women in exchange. I could probably push him for two, if you like," said Hawthorn, flashing the ready smile that so impressed the girls.

Allenson blushed, turning a cold eye on his smirking friend. "Thank him politely for the generous offer, but tell him that Sar Destry has taken a vow of abstinence until he has killed a special enemy and we as his loyal followers are bound by the same oath. Tell him that the Sar will honor the principle of the trade even if we have no use for the women."

"Shame, some of their girls are really quite inventive," said Hawthorn. He rattled off a speech in Kant to the Rider.

Allenson was fairly sure that Hawthorn was winding him up—the man regularly teased him for being po-faced—fairly sure, but not absolutely certain. The Rider's near-naked body was stained with dirt and his long hair hung dankly, greased with some sort of animal fat. He was small, twisted, and had bad teeth. His body showed the result of dietary deficiencies, parasites, and a hard life. Pock marks, scars, and sores covered his skin.

Allenson thought that artists from the central worlds who idealized Riders in the currently fashionable "noble savage" poetry would find the reality a great disappointment. The smell from the man's body was overwhelming even in the open air. The thought of coupling with a Rider woman in exchange for alcohol was not only morally unacceptable but physically repugnant.

Allenson disliked the use of prostitutes. His friends considered this another example of his eccentric romantic leanings. However, a gentleman was permitted to be eccentric but not preachy, so Allenson usually kept his own counsel on such matters.

"Ask him where he got those," said Allenson, pointing.

The Rider had a soiled strip of cheap trade-cloth wrapped around his loins. A twisted vine served as a belt. A stone knife was thrust into the vine, but it was the two human hands that attracted Allenson's attention. Dried blood showed that they were not long separated from their original owner.

The Rider responded to Hawthorn's query with a long tale involving expansive gestures and leaps into the air. Hawthorn interrupted the Rider's flow with occasional interjections. The Rider finally wound down and Allenson looked expectantly at his friend.

"I'll give you a summary of the highlights," said Hawthorn.

"Yes, the shortened version, please," said Allenson.

"This group is from the Purple Star Clan. They were traveling to a moot, a sort of neutral sacred place, to trade girls with the Soft Foot Clan when they came across a hunting party of Sharp Spears. Our friend here made a kill and has taken trophies."

"Why?" Destry asked.

Hawthorn shrugged. "They have no current truce with the Sharp Spears. Enemy and stranger are the same word in Kant."

"No, why has he chopped off the hands?"

"To make a necklace from the finger bones. Riders believe that the possession of a man's amputated hands binds his soul to serve whosoever wears the necklace in the afterlife," Hawthorn explained.

"I see," said Destry.

"What do they do to bind women's souls?" Allenson asked.

"You don't want to know," Hawthorn replied.

"Congratulate him for me and give him his tonk," said Allenson, changing the subject.

Hawthorn dug a bottle out of his pack and tossed it to the Rider, who caught it one-handed. Allenson noted that the Rider dropped the meat rather than his spear to make the catch. The Rider returned to his compatriots, whooping and dancing with glee.

Destry examined another food pack with deep suspicion. He snapped the tab open and the pack flash-chilled with an audible snap. Destry handed ceramic spoons out and passed the pack to Allenson who tried a spoonful. The iced pudding had a sharp, bitter taste that he didn't recognize. It was not unpalatable, but Allenson suspected that a little would go a long way.

"Greenberry ferment," said Destry with approval, when the pack came back around to him. "It's a tad sweet. They probably didn't age it long enough, but it's not bad for all that. Pater must have slipped it into my stores as a surprise treat."

Greenberry plants were native to a Brasilian colony on the other side of the Bight. They could be grown artificially on many worlds but some combination of minerals and climate on their home planet gave the wild berries a distinctive flavor that resisted replication. This rarity made them highly desirable, and hideously expensive by the time they reached the Cutter Stream.

Conversation stopped as the team gave the pudding the respect that politeness demanded of such an outrageously generous gift.

Allenson found himself thinking about the Rider's trophies: not because the severed hands particularly bothered him, but because they didn't. They were the sort of thing that a human born and bred in the Cutter Stream came to take for granted.

He glanced at Destry. *Perhaps we have slipped to the level of beasts. But this is our land, not Brasilia's.*

· CHAPTER 2 ·

The Riders

Raucous laughter indicted that the Rider's party was getting into full swing. One Rider had surreptitiously pushed the end of his neighbor's loincloth into the fire. The victim of the practical joke shot up with flames licking around his genitals. He ripped off the burning garment. The practical joker shook with mirth. The outraged Rider drew his knife and leapt on his tormentor. The two rolled over and over on the ground, slashing, kicking, and biting like wildcats. The other Riders yelled encouragement to the combatants.

Allenson half rose to his feet with some vague idea of intervening, but Hawthorn grabbed his arm and pulled him down.

"They won't thank you. Let them sort it out their way," Hawthorn said.

The Rider's leader carefully stoppered the bottle of tonk before driving the fighting men apart with kicks and blows from his spear haft.

"They sure do go on a bender real easy," said Hawthorn.

19

"Allelic differences in their alcohol dehydrogenase genes, compared with those found in true humans, severely limit their body's capacity to break down alcohol," said Destry.

"I suspect that's more or less what I said," said Hawthorn, dryly.

Allenson envied the education that Royman Destry had obtained at the Home World. Allenson was a keen reader of popular books and journals but he considered that an inadequate substitute for proper learning. A place had been reserved for Allenson at a military academy on Brasilia, but his stepmother canceled the arrangement after his father's untimely death, citing lack of funds for such unnecessary luxury. This killed his hopes for a career in the Brasilian military since he had neither the patronage nor the funds to buy a commission.

"Does that mean that they split off from our species before we invented alcoholic drinks?" asked Allenson. "That would be—what—more than ten thousand years ago at the dawn of the First Civilization?"

"Much more than ten thousand years," Destry replied. "Riders aren't exactly keen to supply DNA so we have only analyzed a limited number of specimens."

Destry had slipped into abstract academic thinking, where people became specimens. He probably had not given much thought as to how the specimens' DNA had been collected.

"You know the calibration problem with molecular clocks, Allenson. Fossil evidence has given us a rough time base for most human gene clusters, so we can calibrate the *Homo sapiens'* molecular clock rather well, but it's clear that the mutation rate in

Rider DNA has not followed the same patterns. The molecular biologists are still arguing about when the Riders left Old Earth," said Destry.

"They are definitely human, then?" Allenson asked. Many in the Cutter Stream denied the humanity of the Riders despite their close physical resemblance to people. These were usually the same people who advocated a solution of genocide to "The Rider Question."

"They were human once," Destry replied. "The Lord knows what they are now."

"Riders aren't so different from people," said Hawthorn.

The Riders, fighting over, began to sing a harmonically complicated epic dirge where various warriors took turns to stand and sing solos.

"The Rider DNA tested so far has been incredibly similar from specimen to specimen. There's very little variability in human DNA, too, but it looks as if all Riders are descended from the same group. That suggests that their ancestors left Old Earth in a single event," said Destry, raising his voice above the noise.

"Did you notice with which hand the Rider caught the tonk?" asked Destry.

Allenson concentrated, replaying the event in his mind. "The left, but that was because he held his spear in his right hand."

"He had his spear in his right hand to indicate his peaceful intentions," said Hawthorn.

"All Riders are left-handed," said Destry. "They are an extreme example of a 'bottle-necked' population. You get the same effect in the DNA of Old Earth animals recreated since the fall of the Third Civilization.

The original Rider population was probably less than a hundred people."

"Not all Riders are left-handed," said Hawthorn. "And speaking of tonk..."

He rummaged around, coming up with a bottle of brandy. It was a local brand made from the fruit of modified plum trees. Brasilian grapes would not grow on any of the Cutter Stream worlds, and no one had bothered to engineer the necessary modifications. It still tasted a damn sight better than tonk, and plum brandy had the advantage of not causing blindness. Hawthorn poured three generous glasses.

"That'll keep out the cold, gentlemen," Hawthorn said.

"I was taught that all Riders were left-handed with no exceptions," said Destry.

"But had your professors ever talked to a Rider?" asked Hawthorn.

"Shouldn't imagine so," Destry replied.

He giggled; Hawthorn stiffened in response.

Destry held a hand up, palm forward. "Sorry Hawthorn, I wasn't laughing at you. I just had a mental image of Professor Hackenheim in a Rider encampment. He is very keen on the noble savage ideal. The reality might be a bit too much for him."

Hawthorn relaxed, mollified by the apology.

"Barbarism must look more appealing from a comfortable armchair in the senior common room," said Allenson.

"A Rider infant occasionally shows signs of being right-handed," Hawthorn said.

"So why have we never heard of right-handed Riders?" asked Destry.

Hawthorn shrugged. "Kant isn't the best language for exchanging philosophical ideas, even if the Riders were inclined to talk about such matters. I do know right-handed Rider infants are called 'messengers to the spirit world.' You can make what you like of that."

"I have read in the *Geographic Journal*," said Allenson, thoughtfully, "that First Civilization peoples sacrificed children for religious purposes. I think some of them were considered to carry messages to the Gods in heaven."

This observation had the effect of killing conversation, as each person mulled over the implications. It was typical that the irrepressible Hawthorn was the first to break the silence.

"The party is hotting up," he said, glancing toward the Riders.

A couple of Riders were banging sticks together to create a rhythm and a third produced a wooden flute. The rest of the men danced wildly. They threw themselves down on the ground when exhausted, but rejoined the dance as soon as soon as they could. The handful of girls present clapped in time to the stick beats but did not dance.

A Rider ran over to a beast and climbed between its crystals. The beast shimmered, bouncing in and out of reality. It worked its way over the camp fire in a jagged dance. More Riders mounted and took to the air in a complicated display. The beasts looked like bundles of crystalline rods, bound in the center and flaring out at the bottom and top. The rods slid against each other as the creatures flexed. They shone like rubies in the light from the flickering bonfire.

"Amazing, aren't they?" asked Destry. "They are the only silicon-based species ever discovered, the only species able to traverse the Continuum, and the only species to have domesticated human beings."

"Surely that's an assumption rather than a fact," said Allenson. "There's no evidence that beasts took the first Riders direct from Terra. I find it difficult to believe that Rider beasts are intelligent enough to plan the domestication of anything, let alone people. Surely Riders domesticated beasts rather than the other way round."

"Perhaps," Destry conceded. "But in regard to the exodus of Riders from Old Earth, any alternative to the beast hypothesis demands a two step process. First, something takes people off world, and then these primitives are let free and encounter Rider beasts. We have no evidence either way, so philosophical parsimony suggests that the simplest process is more likely to be correct. There is other evidence that may or may not be significant."

"Really?" asked Allenson, intrigued.

"Hmm," said Destry, poking the fire. "If you take a median of the various estimates for Rider molecular clocks, you get a figure for the exodus of around sixty millennia before the formation of the first civilization. You realize the significance of that time period?"

Destry looked expectantly at his colleagues, who stared back blankly.

"No," said Hawthorn, succinctly.

"Well, the date coincides more or less with the Toba supervolcano eruption," said Destry. "That was a massive bang. The resulting ice age nearly drove our own species to extinction. Fewer than ten thousand people on Old Earth survived. That's why all human DNA is so similar."

"Are you saying that the beasts had something to do with the explosion?" asked Allenson.

"It's difficult to see how," Destry replied. "They have no technology, after all."

"Maybe the explosion attracted the beasts to Terra," said Allenson. "The gravity disturbance must have set up waves in the Continuum."

"Perhaps," said Destry. "That would be the most parsimonious explanation."

"I'll guess we'll never know," said Hawthorn. "And it doesn't matter much anyway. The universe is as it is."

Destry opened his mouth, presumably to argue the value of knowledge for its own sake, but was distracted. A Rider had mounted one of the women, and was thrusting away vigorously. Other girls were taken and a full scale orgy started.

"I thought you said that they intended to exchange these girls with some from another clan?" asked Allenson, studiously examining his drink.

"Sure," said Hawthorn, watching the floor show. "But clan honor demands that they do their best to impregnate them first. You can be sure that the other lot are doing the same."

"Inbreeding must be a real danger for Riders, given their small social populations," said Destry.

"Yah, just like Mudball," said Hawthorn.

The failing colony on Muhbal, better known as Mudball, was notorious for its complicated inter-family relationships, and for the concomitant genetic diseases.

"I suppose swapping pregnant women exchanges more genes," said Destry.

"That may be true, but the real reason for the custom is that Riders are nasty bastards," said Hawthorn. "As I said, they aren't so different from people."

A Rider not occupied with a woman staggered over to the bottle of tonk and took a swig. He looked puzzled and raised the bottle to his mouth a second time before shaking it upside down. Nothing came out. The Rider furiously flung it into the fire and started toward the survey team.

He staggered up to Hawthorn and yelled something in Kant. Hawthorn smiled lazily and answered with one word. The Rider's eyes bulged, his face reddened, and his hand dropped down to the hilt of his knife. Hawthorn's smile widened. He moved casually, but the focusing crystal of his laserifle painted a red sighting spot on the Rider's chest.

The Rider froze, sobering in an instant. His eyes narrowed as if properly seeing Hawthorn for the first time. The moment stretched out. The Rider was probably in his early twenties, although he looked older. That made him a long-term survivor in a society where stupidity was a terminal condition. He took his hand off the knife and backed away very slowly, his hand raised in a conciliatory gesture. That made him a better judge of character than many a man in the Cutter Stream who had taken Hawthorn's easy smile at face value.

That night, the survey team scattered motion detectors around them. Even so, Hawthorn and Allenson took it in turns to sleep.

In the morning, the Riders were gone.
Faint wisps of gray smoke from their campfire hung lazily in the still air. Hawthorn prepared breakfast

while Destry wandered around their clearing, poking at the ground with a stick.

"What's he up to?" asked Hawthorn, shielding his eyes against the rising sun.

Allenson finished slotting his frame back together and straightened up.

"I expect he is looking for evidence of natural history phenomena," said Allenson.

"Why?" asked Hawthorn.

"Because he finds it interesting," replied Allenson.

"I see," said Hawthorn.

Clearly he didn't see at all, but a gentleman did not comment on another gentleman's harmless eccentricities, no matter how peculiar they might appear to onlookers.

"I was a little concerned when he announced he was coming with us on this trip," said Hawthorn.

"It can be a problem if figureheads insist on getting involved and start making decisions," said Allenson, "but Destry is just curious about things."

Destry knelt down, talking animatedly while recording images of something on the ground.

"Better take this to him before it goes cold." Hawthorn handed Allenson a sausage wrap.

When Allenson reached Destry, the man was talking quickly into his datapad.

". . . more supporting evidence for Wittenham's symbiosis hypothesis but it still doesn't entirely refute the domestication—"

Allenson tapped Destroy on the shoulder and pushed the wrap into his hand.

"What? Oh, thank you, Allenson. Take a look at this."

He gestured toward a beast-hole. Allenson had seen

similar remnants around ancient Rider encampments in the Cutter Stream, but this was newly formed. The topsoil had been scraped away in a meter circle exposing a spur of slate. Pink-tinged crystal seams laced the gray rock.

"Is that rose quartz?" asked Allenson.

"Good question," replied Destry. He made an adjustment to his datapad and waved it over the rock.

"The pink color is certainly caused by rutile needles, but the titanium-iron ratio is unusual," said Destry. "There are also traces of cobalt in an uncommon molecular structure."

Allenson made a note on his own data pad. Good quality rose quartz was a high value-to-weight commodity and was easy to transport through the Continuum. The crystal had been removed in a number of places, leaving empty pipes except for traces of liquid. Intrigued, Allenson reached down.

"No!" said Destry, grabbing his arm. "That chemical cocktail includes hydrofluoric acid!"

"Thanks, Destry," Allenson was angry with himself. How stupid to allow curiosity to overcome common sense. He must be getting tired. The team carried a medical kit but it did not include bone regeneration gear.

Mass or volume of cargo had only a slight impact on a frame's performance. The subelectronic structure of the load had a far greater effect. Metal created an enormous drag, which was why equipment on the frontier tended to use ceramic or organic materials.

"Where in Hades has hydrofluoric acid come from?" asked Allenson. "It surely can't be natural?"

"Hardly," Destry replied. "It's highly reactive and

lethal to nucleic acid based life. It can only be made by a fairly sophisticated industrial process."

"That rules out the Riders," said Allenson.

"Quite," said Destry. "I think the Rider beasts have been feeding. I suspect they dissolve the minerals with corrosive saliva and then absorb the ions they need. Flies feed much the same way."

Beasts must build up their bulk somehow, so Allenson supposed it made sense, although he did not usually associate hydrofluoric acid with spit.

"You know," said Destry, in between bites of his breakfast. "I think I can see how the relationship between the Riders and the beasts works. What do you think keeps this clearing free, Allenson? When we landed, I noticed that the forest stretches for miles in all directions. Why is a clearing located here, where unusual mineral formations lie just below the surface?"

Allenson considered. "It could be just coincidence, or maybe something about the soil inhibits tree growth. The topsoil is very shallow here."

"Yes," said Destry. "But there should be tree shoots. The soil should easily support saplings." He threw his arms out expansively. "It won't do, Allenson. Consider this: the beasts couldn't get at their minerals if the Riders didn't chop down trees for firewood, and who brings the Riders to this exact spot, hmmm?"

"Beasts," replied Allenson, supplying the expected answer.

Destry beamed at Allenson like a professor acknowledging a favored student.

"Precisely, the beasts choose the location and the Riders keep it clear. It's a symbiotic relationship, so asking which of the partners is dominant and which domesticated is irrelevant. I am so glad I accompanied you on this venture. I have enough material for a paper that will blow Gefton away."

Destry waved his datapad for emphasis. Allenson was not convinced. You could use a similar argument to demonstrate that chickens had a symbiotic relationship with people, but he did not have the heart to crush Destry's enthusiasm. Other scholars, notably Gefton, would do that well enough without his help.

Allenson steered the conversation back to the matter at hand after they had eaten. "I took a short trip into the Continuum this morning. The storm has blown out, so I think it is time to return home."

Hawthorn opened his mouth to say something, but Allenson forestalled him.

"I know that we had intended to survey further but I have decided to curtail our enterprise early. Come, gentlemen, we have done handsomely."

"I was about to agree," said Hawthorn mildly. "I was also about to suggest we return on a route that takes in Paragon. It's on the way."

"Not entirely on the way," said Allenson, a sense of honesty causing him to correct his friend.

"Nonsense," said Destry. "I had every intention of visiting Paragon to see my sister."

"It would enable us to look in on the developing colonies at Kalimantan and Laywant. It is a bit outside our brief, but I confess a curiosity about how they are faring. Well, if you are of one mind, gentlemen, then Paragon it is," said Allenson, throwing the remains of his coffee into the grass.

Allenson could have hugged his friends, but that would only have embarrassed them. His brother, Todd, was with Linsye, and he was dying. The clinic at Paragon was Todd's last chance. Allenson was desperate to see his brother. His friends knew that and made sure that his sense of duty did not get in the way. How well they understood him, and how decent they were.

· CHAPTER 3 ·

Paragon

Allenson hovered in the Continuum, a vibration removed from realspace. He knew that Paragon was a blue and white ball resembling Old Earth's appearance before the collapse of the Third Civilization but, to an out of phase observer, Paragon was merely a blur of gray patterns.

Psychics claimed that they could see a cleansing violet aura streaming out from Paragon. Allenson had never seen it, no matter how hard he looked. He would have liked to see tangible evidence supporting Paragon's reputation as a Healing World.

Allenson rephased back into the Continuum and pedaled to retrieve Hawthorn and Destry. A soft chime sounded when his frame picked up a landing beacon. Allenson flicked his frame's guidance to automatic. Finding isolated settlements without beacons was like looking for a pimple on a breakwater. Beacons served the further purpose of guiding a frame into an approved materialization slot, one that would not trigger an automatic point defense system.

The beacon drew him onto a flat island built up

from accumulated sediments lodged in a species of tangleweed. Nowhere on the island was more than five meters above sea level. Paragon lacked a satellite large enough to cause tides. The world was also tectonically inert, lacked strong climatic banding, and had a guardian angel in the form of a gas giant that swept up debris from the system's Kuiper Belt. The low-lying island was therefore as safe from natural disaster as anything could be in an unpredictable universe.

Allenson's frame phased into a small paved courtyard surrounded by white walls. The air outside was much the same temperature as within his frame, but Paragon's low humidity made it feel less oppressive. Stillness filled the courtyard with an almost physical presence. The bright sunlight on the walls made him squint. A bell tolled irregularly in the distance, as if it were tied around the neck of a grazing animal.

Allenson shook his head to clear his mind. He left the courtyard by its only exit, stooping to avoid bumping his head on a stone archway made from vitrified sand. The smell of a hundred fragrances overwhelmed his senses. Flowers, bushes, and low trees crowded around in a seemingly random, but no doubt carefully contrived, pattern designed to imitate a wilderness.

A tangle of climbing plants decorated the garden walls, displaying a blaze of purple flowers. Allenson stooped to inhale the musky fragrance. Small flying creatures danced in profusion amongst the petals, zipping from flower to flower in dense swarms.

Allenson could just detect the high-pitched whine emitted by a million tiny wings. The insectoids tubelike anatomy and multiple legs eliminated Old Earth insects as their ancestors. They could not be indigenous, as Paragon had no terrestrial life. The land surface area was tiny, and the quiescent planet had never experienced a biodiversity crash sufficient to kickstart the rapid evolution needed to produce ecologically marginal species.

People had moved many organisms from world to world, often significantly modifying them in the process. Only the ancient Heritage Museums on the Home Worlds made any effort to keep track of all the twisted phylogenies.

Allenson pushed a low-hanging willow branch to one side and selected a path across the garden that followed the course of a small slow-flowing stream. Circular ripples marked where lemon-colored fish vied with pond-skaters to feed on the insectoids trapped in the water meniscus.

Walking deeper into the garden, Allenson heard a soft female voice. A woman appeared to be talking to herself. He caught a glimpse of her through a gap in the greenery. She wore a simple short tunic that showed bare legs. The clothes had a cut suitable for a female worker, but the quality of the dazzling white material suggested an employee rather than a servant.

The woman moved slowly, pushing a man in a wheelchair. The occupant slumped down, unmoving, but the woman chatted to him nevertheless, pointing out plants and features of interest.

Allenson turned into a subsidiary path to avoid intruding on the couple. Disturbing their walk would feel like interrupting a religious service. There was a sense of ritual in the woman's manner.

A few hundred meters on, he emerged in front of an extensive two-story villa with white plastered walls. Laser point-defense cannons disguised as classical decorations were mounted on the flat roof. He spotted them because the sun reflected off their focusing lenses.

The outer walls of the villa were completely blank and windowless. A red tile-roofed walkway ran around the outside of the building. He gratefully stepped into the shade.

A V-shaped portico supported by white columns framed the villa entrance. Black marbled letters over the lintel spelled out *Palencia Oceania*. Allenson entered through the open doorway into the villa's atrium, welcoming the sharp drop in temperature and brightness.

Eight tall, fluted columns supported the roof. A large square opening in the middle acted as a light well, filling the atrium with indirect sunlight that sparkled off a pool. A woman in a white tunic sat on a tall upright stool beside an office screen shaped to look like a broken column. The black snake and staff logo of the medical guild was emblazoned on the tunic over her left breast.

Allenson's footsteps on the marble floor slabs echoed off the bare stone walls. They looked like marble, but that material was not found on Paragon. If the slabs were synthetic, a highly sophisticated process must have been employed. It would probably have been cheaper just to pay the extortionate shipping costs to import the real thing.

The woman looked at him inquiringly, but did not otherwise move or speak. He focused on the matter at hand, rebuking himself for his wandering mind. His stepmother had often found herself forced to comment on his inability to concentrate.

"My name is Allen Allenson. I'm here to see Sar Todd Allenson. I believe he is in the Destry Gallery," he said.

The woman ran her finger down the screen, her conservative flat purple-colored hair flopping slightly around the headband that almost kept it away from her face.

"Yes, Sar Allenson. Sar Destry said you would be here shortly. Do you know the way?"

He nodded and moved past her. There was no sign of any security other than the petite receptionist, but Allenson had no doubt that armed guards waited close by. They had probably watched him on concealed cameras from the moment his frame materialized in the courtyard. The *Villa Palencia* offered its wealthy clientele quiet serenity and ensured their privacy with top quality, unobtrusive Brasilian security.

The large square archway into the peristylium was open. Allenson could see the lines that marked where concealed blast doors could be slid out on magnetic fields. He passed into a large formal garden with dwarf trees, fountains, and sculpted waterfalls. He turned along the covered walkway that ran around the inside of the peristylium until he came to a door marked with the Destry logo—a cockerel crowing at a star.

Allenson paused for a moment, took a deep breath, and knocked.

A servant girl, marked by her short light-brown tunic and work-calloused hands, opened the door and ushered him along a hall into a reception room that was decorated with blue mosaics of Brasilian sea life. Destry and Hawthorn sat inside, with Allenson's sister-in-law, drinking scented tea from ornate ceramic cups. Linsye motioned for the servant to refill their drinks. She stood to welcome Allenson, slits down the length of her heavy ankle-length dress opening and closing to show teasing glimpses of her body through gossamer-thin petticoats.

He held her hands and she kissed him lightly on the mouth, the proper greeting that a lady made to her husband's male relatives. As a Destry, Royman's sister Linsye did everything properly.

"You look well, Linsye," Allenson said.

In truth, she looked worn out, as if she had been stretched too thin. She had always been an angular woman, but now her face was gaunt with projecting cheek bones. Ironically, grief had lent her an empyreal beauty that had been denied her in happiness.

She waved a hand as if brushing at an invisible web. "I look terrible," she said. "I do my best, for Todd's sake."

"Is there any change?" Allenson asked.

"No," she replied. "He slips further away from me, day by day. The genesurgeons and doctors have tried everything, but all they can do is slow the process and make him comfortable. His cell lines are aging at an ever accelerating rate."

"So they have not identified the cause?" asked Allenson.

She shook her head. "The best guess is that he came into contact with an unknown dormant virus weapon left over from the biowars."

"How could he be attacked without the rest of us also falling victim?" asked Allenson, skeptically.

"The genesurgeons suggest that he must have some unique vulnerability hidden in his genotype. One even speculated about a unique combination of bioweapon and alien DNA or even an alien bioweapon," Linsye replied.

She snorted dismissively, as well she might. Mankind had never discovered an alien capable of making a flint knife, let alone a bioweapon—if you allowed that the Riders were essentially human. Offering alien bioweapons as a diagnosis was the medical equivalent of throwing one's arms in the air and blaming black magic.

"Right!" Allenson took a deep breath. "I will go up and see him."

Todd sat wired into a medical monitoring chair positioned so he could look out onto the garden. He had lost body mass since Allenson's last visit and his hair had thinned to the point that a bald patch was visible on the crown. Allenson paused, composing himself so his brother would not notice his disquiet.

Todd had a book propped on an anglepoise. He struggled to turn the page manually, refusing to use the remote. That was so like Todd. Allenson's older half-brother had indomitable determination. After Allenson's father died, Todd became his guardian and instructor. Todd had been the strong one, full of fire and wind, endlessly energetic. Most of all, he had been Allenson's best friend.

Allenson reached over Todd's shoulder and turned the page for him.

"Hell's teeth, you startled me, Allen. How long have you been there? For a big man, you have an annoying habit of sneaking around. I recall threatening to hang a bell around your neck when you were young; too late now I suppose."

"Far too late," Allenson said. "You won't be hanging bells on anything until you get better."

"Cut the bollocks, brother," Todd said. "You and I both know that I will leave this place in an urn. They will insist on cremating the body in case of infection. There was some reluctance to let you in to my room given the level of paranoia about my condition. I told Linsye that I wanted to see you if you came, and I expect my wife made my wishes crystal clear to the clinical staff."

He grinned at Allenson and winked, just for a moment looking his old self. Linsye was notoriously formidable in defense of her family's interests and would have left the staff in no doubt as to who called the shots.

"Pull up a chair and tell me your news," said Todd.

Allenson did as he was bid. Clearly there was nothing yet wrong with Todd's mind, despite his physical deterioration. After dutifully repeating family gossip, Allenson related the more interesting events from his expedition into the wilderness. Todd listened intently, asking probing questions. For a while, his eyes were alight with the old fire, but eventually he slumped back exhausted, struggling for breath.

"Maybe I should let you rest," said Allenson, alarmed.

"No, wait. The machines will soon revive me," Todd said.

Todd rested his eyes, breathing shallowly. Allenson waited patiently until his brother recovered.

"See, I am much better already. I want to talk to you about the future. The great powers are in the mood to flex their muscles. The four horsemen are set to ride, and I fear that the Cutter Stream is on their itinerary."

"I know the situation is tense but..." began Allen.

"Here to the galactic west, the conflict will be between Terra and Brasilia, of course. They daren't try to strike at each other directly, so the Cutter Stream and Hinterlands colonies will be the arena." Todd ignored Allen's interruption. He spoke impatiently, like a man who needed to convey an important message but only had a few moments before he had to be on his way.

His forward impetus was stopped when he coughed: once he started he couldn't stop until he hacked up thin spittle. Allenson wiped his mouth and considered what Todd had said. It was nigh impossible for one Home World to successfully invade another. The logistics were insurmountable. The invader had to haul equipment and supplies laboriously through the Continuum while the defender could focus a massive counterattack within minutes of detecting a landing. Of course, one could sneak in agents to spy, assassinate, and commit sabotage, but these were pinpricks, mere gestures that had little strategic value.

It would be terrifyingly easy to infiltrate an agent with a bioweapon capable of decimating a Home World's crowded population, but two could play at that game. The biowars of Old Earth presented a terrible historical lesson for even the unimaginative.

The Home Worlds, in a rare display of touching, brotherly solidarity, had declared such weapons to be immoral, inhuman, and against the Word of God. Mass destruction weapons were banned and Interworld

Bailiffs enforced the Home Worlds' will, delivering severe reprisals against offenders.

The sentence of genocide against the Terran colony of Prospero stood as a demonstration to all that the Home Worlds really, really meant what they said.

"Do you know what caused the collapse of the Third Civilization?" asked Todd.

"What!" Allenson said, confused by the abrupt change of topic. He started to order his thoughts. More academic sweat had been devoted to this issue than all other events in human history combined. "Well..." he began.

"I don't want a list of incidents," said Todd. "Let's try something simpler. Why did the First Civilization fall?"

"The Monument Builders? That's common knowledge," replied Allen. "They created huge populations in climatically favorable periods, but could not withstand a few bad harvests when conditions changed. The resulting mass starvation and disease demonstrated to the people that the ruling classes' magic had failed. The inevitable revolts caused organizational collapse, and hence more degradation of resources in a downward destructive spiral."

"Exactly, and so civilization collapses," said Todd. "The Second Civilization must have thought that better technology would insulate them. The chariot warriors built great palaces with cyclopean defensive walls. They had vast storehouses of grain reserves and fresh water. The people might starve, but the aristocracy intended to survive—and yet the palaces fell."

He paused to catch his breath. Allenson felt completely helpless. It was pitiful to see the wasted remains of his elder brother. Todd's condition was all the more disturbing because it hinted at Allenson's own mortality. You are fit and strong now, was the subliminal message, but one day you will be like me—as you are, so I was; as I am, so shall you be.

Allenson noticed the odor of Todd's room, the chemical smell of hygienic purifiers spiced with the plastic tang of new high-tech equipment. He forever after associated that as the scent of death.

"You were about to give me an academic account of how the Third Civilization fell," said Todd, with a smile. "No doubt you would have discussed the trigger events to war such as the assassination of the Turkish Prime Minister or General Chou's declaration of independence for Shanghai. Then you would have moved on to the underlying processes of collapse such as the Water Wars or the proliferation of bioweapons?"

Allenson smiled back and nodded his agreement.

"It's so much simpler than that. All civilizations fall because human beings are bacteria."

Something must have shown on Allenson's face, because Todd snorted. "Don't look at me like that, little brother. My brain is not quite addled yet. Tell me, what happens when you put a dab of bacteria in a new Petri dish of agar?"

"The culture grows," replied Allenson, happy to revert back to their old relationship of tutor and pupil. It was like wrapping himself in a warm blanket.

"The culture grows exponentially," Todd said. "Until it fills the dish, uses up the entire agar, and dies in its own toxic waste. Human civilization is like a bacteria culture. It expands until it has exploited all resources, and then it collapses at the first shock. All technology achieves is to create a bigger Petri dish and a larger population so that the crash is all the more disastrous when it finally happens."

"But surely this is of historical interest only," said Allenson, playing Boswell to Todd's Johnson. "It can have no relevance to the modern world."

"Oh, why not?" asked Todd.

"Because we have broken the historical boom-crash cycle with our improved political and technical skills," replied Allenson.

"Just like the Second and Third Civilizations," Todd said.

"But we really have," Allenson protested. "However skilled they were in some disciplines, the Third Civilization was trapped on Old Earth by their peculiar superstitions about the nature of the universe. Humans now live in many Petri dishes, not just one, to use your bacteria analogy. We have access to the galaxy."

"We have access to one small corner of the galaxy," Todd said. "Let's assume for the sake of argument that you are right about our technology, although I think you delude yourself about our supposed political superiority. Do you know how much of the galaxy we occupy in realspace?"

"Realspace," repeated Allenson, to give himself time to consider. He was more used to thinking of distances across the Continuum. The dimensions between reality and the Continuum did not exactly match, and energy currents made some regions in the Continuum easier to traverse than others. It was an energy current flowing across the Bight that made the Cutter Stream colonies economically viable, albeit barely. "I don't know, maybe a couple of thousand light years."

"All the Home Worlds fit into a single thousand

light year bubble. Just one supernova in the wrong place could knock out human civilization. Do you recall what the Ordovician supernova did to life on Old Earth?" asked Todd.

"The gamma-ray burst wrecked the biosphere," replied Allenson.

"Exactly, and the resulting ice-age drove half of all life into extinction. That nova was at least six thousand light years from Old Earth," said Todd.

"Supernovas are very rare," said Allenson. "The chance of one occurring across the Home Worlds must be incredibly low."

"It is a finite possibility, and it's only one of many doomsday scenarios," said Todd. "The only sure way to protect civilization is for it to grow to such an extent that it cannot be destroyed by a single chance event. Ideally, we should expand in all directions, but habitable worlds to the galactic north and south are rare and The Golden Path controls the route to the east. I hope that frozen theocracy does not represent the future course of human civilization. That only leaves the west, so the worlds across the Bight are our best chance for new living space and the Cutter Stream is the gateway. Whether we like it or not, politico-geography decrees that we will be at the center of the struggle. The Cutter Stream colonies need leaders, by which I mean leaders drawn from our own people who will concern themselves with safeguarding our own interests. I had hoped to be one of them, but fate decreed otherwise. You are now the head of our family, Allen. You must do what I cannot, brother."

"I will, brother," said Allenson, somewhat confused, but unwilling to contradict Todd.

Todd relaxed and shrank into himself. "I'm tired now."

"I'm sorry. I kept you talking too long. I will come back later when you are rested," Allenson said.

"No," Todd said. "We shall not meet again."

"Goodbye, brother," said Allenson, agreeing to nothing.

Todd had already closed his eyes. There was nothing left to be said, so Allenson kissed his brother on the forehead, scorning the risk of infection. Then he left, the positive air pressure outside the room pushing at his clothes before the door shut behind him.

Linsye waited at the bottom of the stairs.

"Will you take a turn with me along the shore?" she asked. "There is a shell beach nearby. Todd and I walked on it when he was still mobile."

A servant showed them to a side door leading outside. Linsye waved away the girl when she showed signs of accompanying them. Palm trees shaded a path down to the ocean where the sharp salt-tang was a welcome relief from the clinic's filtered air. Low waves burst rhythmically onto a shell ridge that marked the shore, retreating back into the sea with the sucking rustle of moving shell flakes.

They stood in silence for a moment, watching sunlight sparkle on the water. Allenson picked up a likely looking flat chip of shell and spun it horizontally across the water with a snap of his wrist. It bounced twice before turning sideways and plunging into a wave crest with a plop.

"I am out of practice at skimming stones," said Allen. "Todd taught me how to play. He was always better at it than me. I saw him throw a fourteen once."

He looked around for another flat piece of shell.

"Todd often talked of your childhood," said Linsye. "It sounded as though you had such fun." She sounded wistful. An aristocratic girl's childhood would have been much regulated.

"How long?" Allenson asked.

"Soon," Linsye replied. "The doctors won't commit themselves, but Todd will die soon. I feel it."

"Then I'll stay," said Allenson.

"Todd would hate that," Linsye said sharply.

More gently she said, "He would rather you remember him with his mind intact. Leave him some dignity, please. It is my responsibility to oversee his nursing, not yours."

They walked on in silence until Linsye stopped abruptly. She studied Allenson carefully, like the chair of an interview board eyeing a potential recruit. She seemed to be turning something over in her mind. She gave a little nod as if confirming a decision that she had already made.

"Have you ever wondered why I married Todd?" asked Linsye. "And why my father permitted a marriage beneath my social standing?"

"It had not occurred to me to consider the matter," replied Allenson, stiffly. "I assumed it was a love match."

"Love!" Linsye said. "What has love to do with marriage?"

Allenson could not think of a suitable reply.

"Don't look so shocked, brother-in-law. You should have progressed beyond romantic notions fit only for giggling schoolgirls. Come; let us have frankness in our dealings. I respected and admired Todd. That is a much sounder basis for a marriage than some childish crush." She indicated that they should resume their stroll.

"My father intended that I should marry into a Brasilian ruling gens to improve our family's opportunities for preferment. However, I persuaded him that our future lay in the Cutter Stream and that any return to prominence in Brasilian society for our branch of the family was a pipe dream. I considered our interests better served by an alliance with the right local family." She stopped walking and waited until he met her eyes.

"Brasman Destry's grandchildren, my children, were not born to be hewers of wood or drawers of water in someone else's enterprise," she said. "My father's influence with our cousins in Brasilia will die with him. My brother lacks the drive to secure our position; his time in Brasilia proved a disappointment."

Linsye shrugged angrily. Allenson thought she caught her lower lip in her teeth for an instant, but her voice was frigidly calm as she resumed.

"Todd is no longer in a position to provide for the family, so that leaves you, brother-in-law. Todd has always had great faith in your abilities and I trust his judgement. Todd's position as Inspector of Military Forces for the Cutter Stream will soon be vacant."

Linsye made a flicking motion with her left hand. "You must move fast to secure the title before his predicament becomes common knowledge," she said.

"I think it unseemly to be discussing this before Todd is cold," said Allen. "Let other people do as they may."

"Grow up, Allen!" Linsye didn't raise her voice, but her tone stabbed him like broken glass. "You, not

Todd, are now head of the family, so *act* like it. You do your best for Todd by shouldering his burdens. Otherwise, all he worked for will be lost. You can't play the hero-worshipping little brother any longer."

Linsye turned on her heel and started back the way they had come, head and body erect, every inch a Destry.

· CHAPTER 4 ·

Rafe

The Continuum was placid the next day. That spared Allenson the temptation to rationalize staying on Paragon. They made a fast crossing and reached Rafe ahead of schedule after five hours pedaling.

Allenson considered: they had made good time and the next possible rest point after Rafe was a good two hours away. It would do no harm to take a break and allow the air recyclers on the frame to refresh. He was surprised to hear a chime and see a directional beacon indicator light up. Rafe was supposedly uninhabited. There had been talk of setting up permanent hunting lodges on various Hinterlands worlds, as a commercial enterprise to attract wealthy Brasilians, but Allenson had paid little attention. The Hinterlands inspired madcap schemes but nothing came of most of them. The little amber light triggered his curiosity and crystallized his decision; they would land at Rafe.

The beacon was a simple reference point type without automatic guidance. Allenson phased in about a klom from it. The team broke down their frames and hiked the rest of the way on foot. The climate was hot and humid, and they soon had sweat running down their faces and necks. Tall, well-spaced trees spread an almost continuous blue-green roof over their heads. The light leaking through had a purple tint. In contrast, browns and reds dominated the bulbous ground-level vegetation.

"I think that maybe I should have taken us in a little closer," said Allenson, wiping the moisture from his forehead with a handkerchief.

"No, you were right," said Hawthorn. "It never hurts to be careful."

"Brown and red pigments provide the most efficient utilization of the limited purple light under the canopy," said Destry, prodding a podlike plant with his datapad.

The plant made a popping sound and deposited orange powder all over his legs. He brushed it off absentmindedly while flicking through his pad readout. He seemed not to notice that the spores had stained his clothes.

"But it's unusual to find different photosynthetic pigment colors evolving from the same genetic stock," Destry said. He pressed his datapad against some leaf litter that had fallen from the forest canopy.

"The vegetation is monophyletic but not closely related. You know, I suspect the ground cover is more like a fungus than a true plant," Destry said, more to himself than the other members of the team.

"This way," Allenson said, tuning his datapad to the beacon's frequency.

❖   ❖   ❖

The team moved easily between the trees, turning aside when the ground fungus was heavy enough to block their way, but they could not see ahead for more than twenty meters or so. The forest seemed endless, and it would have been difficult to hold a course without the beacon.

Allenson continually checked his datapad. It not only showed the direction of the beacon, but also gave an estimate of distance. He checked the modulation and frowned.

He said in a loud voice, "We are within half a klom of the beacon, but I don't see any sign of a settlement, Destry. Do you think there is something wrong with the receiver?"

"What's that, Allenson?" Destry said, honestly puzzled. "I don't see how there can be. It either works or it doesn't."

"I guess you two must be on the level," said an unfamiliar voice. "Bandits normally do more sneaking around."

A man stepped out from behind a tree trunk. He was dressed in cheap, coarse clothes colored in neutral purple-browns. He sounded friendly enough, but he kept a shotgun leveled, and his forefinger was on the trigger.

"I am Sar Destry, Chief Surveyor for the Harbinger Project," Destry said.

"Is that so?" asked the man.

"Yes," Destry replied. "We are on our way back to Wagener. These gentlemen are my associates." He turned and waved a hand at Allenson.

"Gentlemen? I see only one," said the man, suspiciously.

"That's because I'm standing behind you," said Hawthorn.

The man stiffened, fear flicking across his face.

"Hell's bells, man, relax," said Hawthorn. "You would already be dead if I wanted to kill you. Humor me and break that gun over your arm. Lethal weapons make me nervous and we don't want any accidents now, do we?"

The man considered. Clearly he was not the type to make quick decisions, but eventually he accepted the reality of the situation. He flicked the catch that lowered the barrels, rendering the weapon harmless.

Hawthorn sauntered into view, laserifle across his shoulder.

"I see you let me play bait again," said Allenson, without rancor. "One day you'll get me shot."

"Possibly, but you should accept that risk to prevent a greater tragedy," said Hawthorn.

"Like what?" asked Allenson.

"Like *me* getting shot," Hawthorn replied. "Imagine the tragic impact that news of my death would inflict on the good ladies of the Cutter Stream. No gentleman could tolerate that."

It was an old piece of repartee, but it had the desired effect of giving the local a moment to compose himself.

"What is a beacon doing on Rafe?" asked Allenson, finally turning to the man.

"That's Lakeside, our settlement," replied the man.

"You couldn't have been here long," said Allenson.

"No, not long," the man said. "But the town is growing fast. We have nigh on fifty people now, with more arriving every week. My name is Gupper, by the way."

He shook hands with each of them as they went through the formal introduction process. This seemed to transform the survey team in Gupper's eyes to a known quantity.

"Have you folks eaten? It will be dinner soon and Fara, my wife, would enjoy offering you hospitality. She likes to hear news of the outside and we don't get many visitors."

"That would be most kind," said Allenson. "I think that I speak for everybody when I say that we are heartily sick of packed food."

"Absolutely!" Destry nodded vigorously. "Tell me, Master Gupper, is there much seasonal change in the plants?"

Calling Gupper "Master" was stretching a point, as the title was usually reserved for artisans or smallholders and a Hinterlands settler was neither. Allenson nonetheless approved of Destry bumping Gupper up a social scale. Politeness was seldom wasted, and he approved in principle of encouraging settlers as a way of spreading civilization. Unfortunately, Cutter Stream residents reserved the same social contempt for settlers that they themselves received from Brasilians. "Mudtrotter" was one of the more polite labels by which settlers were known.

Almost everyone this side of the Bight was Destry's social inferior, which had the odd result of causing him to treat strangers of all classes with the same cool politeness.

"Very little, Sar Destry. In truth, there is little seasonable change here. It rains to excess at times in the summer, making the ground swampy but nothing too untoward," said Gupper.

"This is summer now?" Allenson asked, mopping his brow.

"No, indeed, sar," Gupper replied. "We have just passed the winter solstice."

Allenson thought that Rafe must be distinctly unpleasant come summer. He made a note on his datapad to that effect. Any tourist-based enterprise would be limited to polar winters only.

"This way, sars," said Gupper, leading the way.

They left the treeline after only a hundred meters, emerging into a cleared area. Large fleshy plants fully two meters high with large yellow-ocher lobes grew on either side of the path. They were laid out in neat rows, so were clearly a crop. Destry reached out with his datapad to take an analysis.

"Careful, Sar Destry," said Gupper. "Gunja plants sting and leave a nasty rash."

Allenson examined the nearest lobe. Hairs, almost too fine to see, stuck out from brown nodules on the lobes.

"You grow them for food, or can you extract something useful from them?" Allenson asked.

"Naw, they taste like shit," said Gupper. "And I never heard of anyone harvesting gunja for anything. You can't even smoke it."

"Then why cultivate the crop?" Allenson asked.

Gupper grinned at his bafflement. "Bless you, sar. Rooters won't come anywhere near a gunja field. Gunjas work better than a shock fence, and there's no maintenance or running costs once you grow them."

"Rooters?" Allenson asked, patiently.

"Native animals," Gupper replied. "Big buggers. They

feed on giant worms and they have these tusks under the jaws for digging 'em up. A herd of rooters can create an almighty mess of a settlement. They spook easily and charge off, trampling everything underfoot."

"I see," Allenson said.

"No you don't," Gupper said. "You have to be there. Rooter herds smashed up the first few settlements on Rafe. Killed quite a few people, too." He ran his fingers through his beard, contemplating the gunja crop. "I doubt whether we would have survived here if we hadn't discovered gunja. Rooters are the reason I was carrying old Henry here when I bumped into you."

Gupper patted his battered shotgun.

"That will stop a charging rooter?" asked Hawthorn, skepticism clear in his tone.

"Most times, sar," Gupper replied. "Especially if you give it both barrels."

He pulled a cartridge out of the gun and gave it to Hawthorn, who whistled and showed the round to Allenson. The cartridge held a single, large-caliber lead shot with a hollowed-out nose that would stop a bull and tear the leg off a man.

"I would have taken your shotgun more seriously if I had known what you had loaded," Allenson said.

Allenson made a record of the conversation, adding a note that big-game hunting was a possibility on Rafe.

The gunja crop was only a few meters deep, but the safe path snaked to present an impossible wall of plants to a large clumsy animal. Allenson had to maneuver with care, burdened as he was by his packs.

They emerged into cultivated fields of more recognizable crops. Women and children moved up and down the rows with hoes and spray guns. The women wore cheap, high color-saturated utility clothing. They favored russet reds, greens, and yellow ocher, colors that would not easily show stains. The locals all stopped working and stared when they noticed the survey team.

"We don't see much in the way of visitors," said Gupper, somewhat defensively.

"I would jump at any excuse for a break from such backbreaking work," said Allenson. "Do you do all the farming manually?"

"At the moment, we do," Gupper replied. "But we hope to buy some fleeks as soon as we have a surplus to sell on. We may eventually be able to get some autos."

"Good for you," said Destry.

"Cash crops are the only sensible way to fund colonization of the Hinterlands, but automotons take a great deal of maintenance," said Allenson, quietly. "In their own way, so do fleeks. What do you envision would make a profitable cash crop?"

"Then us Lakesiders can live properly, like gentlefolk," said Gupper. He did not appear to have heard Allenson, who did not push the point.

Hawthorn smiled at a girl gaping at them and half lifted a hand in salute. She blushed and recommenced frantically hoeing, head down.

The Lakeside settlement was based on a variant of the square-grid pattern, modified to follow the contours of the slope down to the water. Most of the buildings followed a traditional settlers' design of a single story with a sideways sloping roof. Gutters funnelled rainwater down to a storage tank. The buildings sat on rafts of plasticized soil, the lower walls being made of the same material. The roof and upper walls were constructed of wooden planks. A single two-story building dominated the group.

Wooden shacks built directly on the soil were scattered higgledy-piggledy around the edges of the settlement. Many were in poor condition, with rotted-out planks and tacked-together repairs. Allenson assumed that they were storage sheds but a woman emerged from one as they passed, pushing aside plastic strips that hung down across the doorway as a makeshift door. She jiggled a baby who was suckling at her breast. The woman watched them pass without expression and did not reply to Allenson's greeting.

The roof had collapsed inward on the next shed. Someone had effected a repair with a stained tarpaulin. A filamentous purple growth ran through the wood.

"That's a nasty case of fungal rot," said Destry. "Don't you use fungicides?"

"We had some," Gupper said, shrugging, "but they never seemed to work. Contact with the ground makes the problem worse. The strands grow straight out of the soil. That's why most people build the bottom of their houses out of syncrete."

"Fungal spores must still infect the wooden structures, even if they are a meter up. Would it not help to avoid the use of wood at all?" asked Destry.

"I guess so, but plasticizer is expensive and the wood is free," said Gupper.

Destry examined the rotten wood, waving his datapad over the purple filaments.

"The fungus has an unusual mix of detoxification enzymes that would break down most off-the-shelf fungicides, but it should be possible to design something that would work," said Destry.

"No doubt that would be a pricy business," Gupper said.

Allenson gave Destry a warning look and was pleased that he took the hint and let the matter drop. There was no point in winding Gupper up by dangling unattainable luxuries in the man's face. A single consignment of a few liters of specially tailored fungicide that would probably have to be imported across the Bight could cost more than the capital value of Lakeside.

"That's funny," Allenson said, consulting his datapad. "Your beacon seems to be coming from the lake rather than the settlement."

Gupper chuckled. "The beacon's on that little island," he said, pointing across the water.

Allenson shielded his eyes and looked in the indicated direction. A handful of scraggly trees clung to a gravel bank that barely cleared the water. He could just see an orange canister tied to the trunk of the largest.

"That's so uninvited visitors materialize far enough away that we can get a look at them. We have a detector that warns us when the Continuum is disturbed. That's how I picked up your arrival."

A detector, Allenson thought, but no automated defenses. That was not ideal; it depended on the warning being acted on faster than a raiding force could swamp the defenses.

"I'm an alderman so I have a property by the Meeting House," Gupper said, proudly.

He pointed out a single-story dwelling that stood opposite the two-story building. It was in decent condition. The wood was new and decorated with yellow stain.

Gupper ushered them inside. The doorway opened

into a single spacious room that occupied a good two-thirds of the ground floor. Allenson unclipped his boots and left them by the door. Mats in a variety of clashing colors and patterns were scattered around the syncrete floor.

"Fara," Gupper yelled. "We have visitors."

A small rotund woman bustled through hanging strips of weighted cloth that separated off a kitchen. Gupper made the introductions, and Fara was suitably wide-eyed at the rank of her guests. In particular, she paid great deference to Destry and insisted on removing the orange powder from his trousers by vigorous strokes with a clothes brush that she took off a hook by the door.

"She makes me go outside to clean up," said Gupper.

"You are not a gentleman, Gupper," said Fara.

"But the dirt is the same," said Gupper, teasingly.

"Thank you, mistress," Destry said, breaking up what was clearly a ritualized husband and wife squabble. He inclined his head, politely.

Gupper pulled a long table out from where it stood against the wall. He arranged benches on each side and placed a wooden armchair at each end.

"Perhaps you would like to sit," Gupper said, gesturing that Destry should take the chair.

"Yes, but not at the head of the table," Destry said, swinging his legs over the nearest bench. "That seat is reserved for the master of the house."

Gupper looked surprised, but pleased. He did not argue the point.

"Some tea, gentlemen?" Fara asked.

"That would be delightful," Destry replied on the behalf of the whole team.

"A bevy would go down a treat, love," said Gupper.

The tea, when it arrived, was a herbal infusion of a type that Allenson had not tried before. It had a characteristic minty flavor that was not unpleasant. He glanced at his friends to assess their reaction. Destry sipped at his mug in between pumping Gupper about the natural history of Lakeside. Hawthorn had slipped into a detached state. He stared unblinkingly forward, his mind lost in thought.

Hawthorn had a mercurial personality that veered abruptly from driving optimism to labyrinthine despair. He would emerge when he was ready. For their different reasons, neither of Allenson's friends paid much attention to their palette, and that was a shame because the drink was real tea. The strain was unfamiliar to Allenson; it might even be novel, but it undoubtedly was genuine tea from a genetic ancestry that traced back to old Earth.

Tea was a luxury food in the Cutter Stream. It was transported across the Bight from Brasilia and subject to substantial import taxes. Only imported Brasilian tea could legally be drunk in the Cutter Stream, so the drink was eye-wateringly expensive.

This was an arrangement that suited everybody, at least everybody who mattered. The proprietors of the Brasilian tea plantations and merchant shippers enjoyed high profit margins and prospered. Import duties raised the monies that paid for the Governor's office and other Cutter Stream officials. The only other sources of tax in the Cutter Stream were the real estate taxes on compounds of the local gentry and the sales taxes on transfer of indentured servants' contracts, which amounted to taxing much the same people, since only the gentry used servants. There was only so much that could be squeezed out of the gentry before they stopped cooperating with the colonial authorities.

All aristocracies needed some way of spending money pointlessly to demonstrate their status. Brasilian politicians organized vast entertainments for the masses. Terran landholders sponsored baroque and decadent arts whose subtleties appealed only to other aristocrats. Cutter Stream gentry drank tea.

Allenson now knew why Gupper had met them and guided them directly to the compound. Somewhere, hidden in the forest, the Lakesiders were growing tea cultivar. This was the cash crop on which the community based their hope of prosperity.

Taking tea took some time, as the more important members of the community managed to find some reason to visit Gupper's house and be introduced. Allenson suspected that Gupper himself had put the word out that he was extending hospitality to Sar Destry and two friends.

Dinner was fortunately a quieter matter. They were joined by Gupper's three sons and a daughter. The boys ranged from about ten years old to late teens, with the daughter somewhere in the middle. Destry was in fine form, entertaining the table with stories about his time on Brasilia. Fara was keen to hear about the balls and fashions, as well as gossip about the private lives of the ruling families. Destry was a polished raconteur who brightened any dinner party. Allenson sometimes found that irritating, but today he was glad of the fact, as he had much to reflect on after his conversations with Todd and Linsye.

❖   ❖   ❖

The survey team left the next morning after breakfasting on a locally made porridge. Gupper came to see them off. Allenson intercepted him so that he could talk to the man in private.

"Thank you for your hospitality, Master Gupper, and thank Mistress Gupper for the tea," Allenson said.

"Ah yes," Gupper replied, his expression suddenly blank.

"Expensive stuff, tea," Allenson said.

"Fara had been saving it for a special occasion," Gupper said, defensively.

"Indeed," Allenson replied. "People do serve it when they have guests. It would be much cheaper if we grew it here in the Cutter Stream, but that would threaten the Governor's monopoly."

"Yes," said Gupper, obviously wondering where the conversation was going.

"That's why the law against illegal tea plantations is so rigorously enforced," Allenson said. "One of my family's tenants was tempted to grow tea in secret. He cleverly hid the crop inside a sunflower field, but the problem with selling illegal tea is that it is enjoyed publically. What is the point of taking tea if you can't impress your friends with a cup? Someone always gets jealous and talks. When it comes down to it, everyone informs on the person higher up the chain in return for immunity from prosecution."

"What happened to your tenant?" Gupper asked.

"One day the Lictors came and burned his fields. They sized his goods to pay the fines and import taxes. Of course, he had little of much cash value, so they arrested his family and sold their contracts as indentured servants to make up the difference."

Allenson looked across the settlement to where Fara was shepherding her children out to the fields. Gupper went pale.

"But this is an unhappy conversation," Allenson said, mounting his frame. "Be thankful such a disaster will never happen to you or me, Master Gupper."

Allenson pedaled vigorously for a few moments to charge the systems. Gupper retreated to a safe distance. Allenson waved to him and switched on the frame, phasing into the Continuum on the way to Kalimantan.

· CHAPTER 5 ·

Kalimantan

Allenson was pleasantly surprised by the sheer number of beacons tagged by his frame's navigation. The Kalimantan colony must be prospering. Many of the beacons were simple location identifiers, but a few had recognition systems with auto-landers. He locked on to one of the latter, identified as KPS19, and let it guide him in.

The team phased onto an extensive grassy area outside a substantial high-walled compound. Bushes planted in straight lines stretched away in all directions toward the horizon, except for one small area that seemed to be a mixed farm surrounded by green hedges and low stone walls, which is what they headed for. A cool wind blew steadily over the flat ground, offering some relief from the yellow sun that shone unrelentingly from a cloudless sky.

Guards patroling along the top of the walls watched the team dismount. They wore wide-brimmed hats that left their faces in shadow. Their body language oozed boredom. Possibly they were more effective than they looked, but Allenson rather doubted it.

"Visitors from the Cutter Stream to see the manager," he said to the guard who lolled above the gate.

"Door's open," the guard replied laconically, his attention focused on lighting a cigarette.

"That sod would get the toe of my boot if he worked for me," Hawthorn said, none too quietly. The guard must have overheard, but he chose to ignore the comment.

A small doorway was cut into the larger wooden gate. Allenson pushed and it swung open. Inside, the compound was laid out according to a classic Brasilian colonial pattern. One-story buildings lined the walls, their flat roofs providing a parapet for the guards. A three-story villa dominated the back wall. An array of communication equipment and a multi-barrelled automatic cannon were built into the roof.

The center of the compound was clear of buildings except for a nodding derrick. Various stores were piled up in crates and there were tractors parked haphazardly. Men and women in servant's clothes hurried about various chores, largely ignoring the survey team.

"This is amazing," Destry said. "We might almost be back in the Cutter Stream itself. I had no idea how well this colony is capitalized."

"Indeed not," Allenson agreed. "I suppose we should try the main building, as no one has had the courtesy to greet us."

Up close, it could be seen that the villa was roughly finished, although robustly built. It had the feel of a commercial building rather than a family home. This impression was reinforced by a sign on the wall that sternly ordered visitors to report to reception. An arrow indicated that they should enter through the main door.

Inside the portico, Allenson walked through a cold air curtain that significantly lowered the temperature. A desk to one side sported a sign boasting that it was reception. Allenson dinged a bell. Nothing happened, so he dinged it two or three times more. Finally Allenson noticed a middle aged woman with an impressive moustache walking as slowly as possible down the corridor. She seated herself behind the desk and made a great show of adjusting the display on her screen. When she was quite satisfied, she deigned to raise her eyes.

"Sars Destry, Allenson, and Hawthorn of the Harbinger Project," Allenson said. "Who is in charge here?"

"Sar Fullbrite is the General Manager," she replied reluctantly, as if the information had been tortured out of her.

Allenson kept a grip on his temper. He recognized a middle management bureaucrat when he saw one. They only got more mulish if you leaned on them. The trick was to bend them to your will with the minimum effort.

"Then kindly inform Sar Fullbrite that we are here," Allenson said.

"Do you have an appointment?" the receptionist asked, playing another obstructionist card.

"We do not, but I fancy he will wish to see us," said Allenson.

The woman sniffed as if to say that she thought it unlikely, and touched her screen. After a few seconds she spoke into it and listened to a reply. Allenson could hear nothing, which meant that the screen must be equipped with a sophisticated tight sound suppressor, not something one would expect to encounter in a Hinterlands colony.

The woman rose, "Follow me," she said.

She guided them up the corridor to a door, which she opened without knocking. An astonishingly young man in expensive casual clothes stood up behind a desk and gestured them in.

"Come in, sars. Would you like some refreshment after your journey?"

"That would be welcome," Allenson said.

"Gladys, make some cafay," Fullbrite said.

"Who, me?" Gladys asked.

"Yes, you. Are you my bloody secretary or not?" Fullbrite asked in frustration.

Gladys seemed to consider the question. "Personal assistant, not secretary," she finally replied.

Fullbrite wiped his forehead. He said, "Just get us some cafay, Gladys."

"I thought you told me to check the Arundel invoices?" Gladys asked.

"And now I am telling you to make us some cafay," Fullbright replied, wearily. "Just do it, Gladys, and stop giving me a hard time."

She exited the room, her expression indicating that she considered drink preparation well beneath her dignity.

"Sorry about Gladys, gentlemen," Fullbrite said. "She's the only person who properly understands the accounting system." He sighed as if that explained everything, and perhaps it did. "Competence is at a premium in Kalimantan. Gladys would not have to work here if she boasted social skills to match her administrative talents."

"And what brings you here?" Destry asked, rather rudely. He was obviously a bit nettled by their cavalier treatment.

"Very large bonuses," Fullbrite replied, spacing

the words for emphasis. He spread his hands as if to indicate the generous scale of the remuneration. "I'm the younger son of my father's second mistress, which means I inherited good breeding, but damn all else."

Destry laughed, good humor restored. He gave a rueful smile of empathy with Fullbrite.

At that point Gladys ushered in a servant, whose role was to carry the tray. She passed around the refreshment while Gladys supervised. Fullbrite winked at Destry. Allenson made the introductions after the staff exited.

"I didn't notice a name over the compound gate." Allenson said, more to make conversation than anything.

"We are officially Kalimantan Product Supply Number 19, or KPS19 for short, of the Feel Rite Health Cooperative, a division of Home & Colonial Supplies, which is I believe is currently owned by Macrakrunch Arms & Riot Control. You know their motto—'Don't just stop'em, MARC'em.' It's all a bit of a mouthful to hang over the door, and no one gives a damn what the compound is really called."

"No doubt the staff have their own version," Hawthorn said.

Fullbrite smiled. "They think I don't know."

"I still don't understand why Brasilian corporations have poured so much capital into Kalimantan," Allenson said.

"To farm kali bushes. The fibers fluoresce in a magnetic field and emit light," Fullbrite said.

"So I understand," Allenson said, "but there are many processes that produce light far more cheaply and efficiently than kali fibers."

"Yes, but synthetic machines produce synthetic light," Fullbrite said, "not like kali fibers that produce bluish natural light thought to have psychic healing properties and to enhance sexual potency. It's the latest fashion in Brasilia."

"And does the light have recuperative properties?" Destry asked, delicately.

"It's certainly tinted blue," Fullbrite said, with a cynical grin.

"I wonder if we might make camp here for a night?" Allenson asked, politely.

"Most certainly not," Fullbrite replied. "You shall stay as my guests in the management suite. It will be a pleasure to have gentlemanly conversation for a change. You can tell me the latest gossip."

"That is most civil. We accept with pleasure and we shall certainly sing for our supper, but I fear we are some weeks out of the Cutter Stream so our gossip will be out of date," Allenson said.

"You can't be more out of date than we are here," Fullbrite said, with feeling. "If you listen carefully you can still hear the echoes of the Big Bang from KPS19. I can't wait for my contract to finish so I can get back to civilization."

Allenson noticed that there were two hand drawn wall charts in the office. One showed KPS19's production figures; the other ticked off the number of days before Fullbrite could go home to Brasilia.

"If you will excuse me, gentlemen, I had better go over those invoices with Gladys or she will sulk with me for days. Would you like a guided tour of our operation here?"

"Very much," Allenson replied.

"So be it. I will arrange it."

The wheels jolted over a pothole. Allenson gripped the handrail tightly, feeling slightly nauseous. The four-wheeled trailer was designed to carry weight, and its suspension was woefully underloaded with just the survey team aboard. They sat on a bench clamped longways onto the flatbed. Their guide drove the four-wheeled tractor unit. He had a sprung bucket seat that bounced up and down.

The tractor was powered by alcohol, judging from the smell of the exhaust. The motor spun at high fixed revs, emitting a constant whine that got on Allenson's nerves. He was not used to engine noise. The tractor's large balloon tires appeared to be independently powered by torque units in the hubs, as they often ran at different speeds as each one gained and lost traction.

To Allenson's relief, the guide pulled over when they reached a small clearing in the rows of purple kali bushes. The team climbed gratefully off their transport. Hawthorn rubbed life back into his buttocks and grimaced. Allenson would have loved to emulate him, but thought it unseemly.

In the center of the clearing, a derrick pump nodded away. Allenson pointed to it. "What are you pumping?" he asked their guide.

"Water, Sar Allenson," he replied. "Kali plants like their heads in the sun and their feet in the water. There is no free water on the plateau so we pump it up from the ground and it runs out along underground pipes. We have a pump every tenth of a klom or so. When they dry up we sink a deeper shaft."

"The water table is dropping, then?" Allenson asked.

The man shrugged, "I guess so." It was clearly not something that concerned him.

Destry wandered over to the derrick and poked around it, flipping over covers. He had a curiosity about technology. The supervisor looked a little alarmed. "Is there anything I can help you with, sar?"

"I just wondered what this outlet did. It seems somewhat complicated for a tap." Destry said.

"Ah," the supervisor said. "We have sprayer machines to keep the bugs and weeds and suchlike down. That box there controls them. The machines dock on that spigot to fill up with water and stuff. Something was wrong with the controller on this derrick, and the sprayers started to run wild."

"The plants look healthy enough," Destry said.

"We have hand sprayers. Spray duty is used as a sort of punishment for the field servants. It's hot, unpleasant work. Truth is we never have enough working sprayer machines to go around anyway. Shall we move on? There's a station nearby with a water cooler."

They reluctantly climbed back aboard their makeshift carriage and lurched up the track into an area where the bushes were taller and bluer. They looked as if they had been bleached. Long fibers hung down, flapping in the continuous wind. Teams of female servants cut them down using long-armed shears, catching them and dropping them in sacks slung over their backs. Noting Allenson's interest, their guide stopped their tractor.

"We harvest the plants' pollinators for processing into kali fibers," he said.

A tractor and trailer moved slowly between the harvesters. A female servant took the opportunity to empty her sack into a bowl on the side of the trailer. A screen briefly flashed up some numbers before the bowl emptied into the trailer.

"The servants have daily targets to achieve. They get bonuses for exceeding their targets that can be put toward paying off their contracts or used to buy small luxuries from the company shop," the guide said.

"Do any of the field servants pay off their contracts?" Destry asked.

"It is theoretically possible," the guide replied.

"The female workers all wear the same ankle bracelet. Is that some sort of Kalimanatan fashion?" asked Hawthorn.

Allenson had not noticed because he thought it ungentlemanly to pay too much attention to the servant's legs, but now that Hawthorn had raised the issue, he studied the ornament on the leg of a nearby girl. It was made of thick silvery cables twisted into a braid. The girl, noticing his interest, tossed her head and turned her back.

Allenson felt his cheeks burn. He hastily turned his attention back to their guide. The man had twisted on the tractor seat and put his right foot on one of the wheels, causing his trouser leg to hitch up. Allenson saw that he also wore one of the bracelets.

The guide chuckled, "Not exactly; they're servants' tags. Sar Fullbrite likes devices to be pretty as well as functional."

"I understand that kali plants are native to Kalimantan," Destry said.

"Yes, but the wild ones grow around streams and ponds and are usually smaller than this. There are independents who harvest them. Some servants run away with the intention of wildcatting, but they have no way of getting the fibers off-planet. Food is also a problem. The native plants and animals lack stuff that people need. Your teeth and nails fall out if you don't get proper food."

"Do you have much problem with servants running?" Allenson asked.

"Not at KPS19," the guide replied. "Runners are easily tracked by the identity tags, and Sar Fullbrite prefers to use a reward rather than a punishment system. He sells the contracts of servants who run to other compounds that have rougher ways of making people work."

"I see," said Allenson, quietly.

"Enough, sars?" asked the guide, starting the tractor.

The station was a larger clearing around one of the ubiquitous derricks. It had half a dozen shelters made from orange plastic sheeting. A dispensing machine in one offered a selection of sticky flavored waters and food bars filled with glucose. When they returned, Allenson opted for a simple mug of water.

He took a stroll around the shelters to stretch his legs. The constructions contained various sacks and drums of chemicals, but mostly they were filled with machinery. He stopped to examine a mechanical harvesting machine that had clippers on long vertical arms. It looked functional but its moving parts were covered in a thick layer of dust.

In one shelter, there were so many automatic sprayers that they were piled one on top of the other. At the back of this shelter were three tractor units. Scorch marks indicated that each had one of its wheel hub motors burnt out. It occurred to Allenson that this was not so much an equipment store as a junkyard.

Allenson signaled for the guide to join him.

"Are these machines beyond repair?" Allenson asked.

The guide shrugged. "Suppose so, sar."

"But these tractors seem to have minor faults in the single drive unit. Don't you have spares?"

"I guess not, sar."

"Could you not cannibalize one tractor to obtain spares for the other?"

The guide shrugged again. He seemed puzzled by the question.

Their guide drove them through the farm on their way back to the compound. Allenson was astonished by how small it was. It was divided into rectangular gardens by hedges creating green rooms, sheltered from the wind but open to the sun.

The smell of spice filled a garden full of herbs. Another was filled with flowering plants. Allenson recognized many of them as Brasilian. A lady carefully cut selected flowers and passed them to a servant who walked behind with a basket. She wore a fashionable casual dress and a wide-brimmed white hat held on by a blue ribbon tied under her chin. A second servant carried a spray gun which he deployed as the lady directed.

A raucous cry drew Allenson's attention to a male bird perched on the roof of a shed. It spread its tail into a fan of iridescent green eye spots. Allenson realized that the small brown birds running around were the females of the species, not some sort of free range fowl as he had assumed. There were vegetable plots and orchards, but they could not have fed many people. Allenson was intrigued. He leaned over and tapped the guide on the shoulder. The man stopped the tractor.

"Sar Allenson?" the guide asked politely.

"What is this farm for?" Allenson asked. "It could not possibly feed the staff of a facility the size of KPS19."

"Oh no," the guide replied. "The kitchen gardens are for the management and their wives. Some of the ladies like to grow fresh herbs and vegetables or flowers for their apartments."

"Flowers from home," Allenson said quietly.

"Sar?" the guide asked.

Allenson indicated that he should continue.

"There are also walks and summer houses and suchlike."

"So do you grow food elsewhere on the site?" Allenson asked.

"Not at all," the guide said astonished. "All available growing soil has kali plants. We import food from other worlds in the Hinterlands."

"I see," Allenson said, thoughtfully.

Dinner with Fullbrite and his senior managers was pleasant, but Allenson was disappointed that the Kalimantans were uninterested in discussing their colony. He made several attempts to steer the conversation but desisted when it would have been ill-mannered to persist.

The Kalimantans wanted to hear the latest society gossip from Brasilia, or at least the latest that had reached the Cutter Stream. Destry was far better at that type of conversation than Allenson. The locals also talked endlessly about their plans for the future when they returned home.

Destry and Allenson retired early after brandy,

leaving Hawthorn dancing with the bored young wife of a middle-aged manager who was on night duty. They discussed the colony in the quiet of their guest apartment.

"I don't understand your reservations," Destry said. "This colony is a great success."

"You think so?" Allenson asked. "They don't even grow their own food."

"Fullbrite explained that," Destry replied. "It's not in anyone's interests to grow food when kali fibers are so much more profitable."

"They use complex equipment but lack the infrastructure to maintain it," Allenson said.

"Fullbrite explained that as well," Destry said. "Servants don't have the skills and technicians earn too much in Brasilia to want to bury themselves out here. The company would have to pay them so much that it is cheaper to scrap failed equipment and bring in replacements."

"Kali fibers are a fashionable health fad," Allenson said. "How long does the average health fad last, Destry?"

"Who knows?"

"It will end, and then the companies and wildcatters will abandon the world. In a few hundred years there will be no sign that once human beings lived here. Kalimantan will be another failed colony, like Mudball."

"But it won't have been a failure," Destry said, puzzled. "It will simply have served its purpose."

"Its purpose for the home world," Allenson said.

Allenson smiled at his friend. He was a good chap and there was no point in arguing. Destry saw things from a certain viewpoint. Allenson had once shared that viewpoint, without thinking too much about it, but lately events had challenged his complacency. He sipped his drink and contemplated his conversations with Todd, and with Linsye. He had much to think about. His thoughts kept returning to one point: Kalimantan served Brasilia's purpose well enough, but what use was it to the Cutter Stream?

CHAPTER 6

Laywant

The Continuum was in a forgiving mood. It was one of those times where one could see deep into violet. The frequency of light in the Continuum varied according to distance. Photons absorbed energy with distance traveled. This manifested itself in shortened wavelengths, as light stubbornly insisted on moving only at its set speed.

The survey team made it straight through to Laywant in a single trip, stopping only once at an uninhabited world for rest and refreshment. Laywant was in the grip of an ice age, with most of the land area of the single continental mass under ice at its north pole. An archipelago on the equator enjoyed a cool temperate climate, perfect for agriculture, so a semi-self-sufficient farming society had spread over the islands.

Laywant Town was a market center built on a medium-sized island exceptional only in that it was the first place colonized. It boasted the beacon of a Brasilian Agent. This luminary was not exactly a governor, as Laywant was not officially part of the Cutter Stream, but he was the nearest thing. The team followed the beacon's signal down to the surface, arriving about noon local time. They emerged in a compound that served as the business center and port.

Allenson broke and packed his frame with his usual efficient care. A tan-colored mongrel wandered over and sat down to watch. It scratched its neck reflectively with a back leg. Nobody else took the slightest interest in the arrival of the survey team. Nearby, three men loaded a transport frame with wooden cases from a flatbed trailer.

The laborers moved with painful indolence, two lifting and one supervising the rest, a duty that involved lying on the flatbed and smoking. The laborers dropped a case and started a squabble over who was to blame. They exchanged feeble blows without much enthusiasm. The supervisor ignored them and the quarrel ran down quickly. The men gave the impression of actors who were bored with their roles.

A laborer examined the case and discovered a crack, so he called to the supervisor. That worthy made a great show of rising, stretching, and scratching before climbing off the flatbed. He examined the case and then kicked it, staving in the damaged plank. Olive green vegetable matter spilled out. The supervisor chalked a large red cross on the top and gestured wordlessly to the laborers. They placed the damaged case in the foot-well of the flatbed's tractor unit and pulled a tarpaulin over it.

Allenson tightened his lips in disapproval at the pantomime. Everyone in the Cutter Stream's economic system took a top slice off the movement of goods or services as a perk of the job. The pervasive low-level corruption made the system horribly inefficient, but the rich and powerful took the largest slice of all, so there was no incentive for change.

The loading team stopped work and ambled toward the perimeter fence. Theoretically, the compound was sealed off by a three-meter-high fence but the fence was in such a poor state of repair that it served more as a boundary marker. The workers wandered off and disappeared down an alley between two of the low syncrete buildings that surrounded the compound. The mongrel, worn out by all the excitement, rolled over on his side and went to sleep.

Allenson kicked the compound floor, dislodging a fragment of stabilized earth. The plasticized layer was so thin that the wheels of loaded flatbeds had broken through the surface. Some desultory attempts had been made to fill in the worst potholes with spoil.

"What a dump," Destry said.

"I suppose we ought to report to the Agent as a matter of courtesy," said Allenson.

"Yeah," Hawthorn said, with a distinct lack of enthusiasm.

Allenson looked around in an effort to locate an office. Wooden sheds and barns were scattered around the compound without any noticeable logic or pattern. One otherwise undistinguished hut boasted a sign above the door whose message had long since faded but might have once read "Office."

A thin man in ratty clothes sat asleep on the ground with his back against the hut wall. Allenson could smell him three meters away. Hearing their footsteps, the beggar held out an empty cupped hand, palm up. He did not bother to look at them or even open his eyes.

Destry spun a silver threepenny coin onto the ground. The polygonal coin bounced from side to side. The beggar was startled into frantic activity by the ching of metal. He clearly had not really expected alms.

"Thankee, sars, thankee kindly," the beggar said, retrieving the coin. He hobbled off with a shaky but determined gait toward the fence.

"Buy some food," Destry said to his retreating back.

"Yes, sar," came the reply.

"He will convert that straight into a bottle of tonk," Hawthorn said, sourly.

Destry shrugged. "His choice."

The hut was no better on the inside. There was a single room half separated into a public and private area by a counter. Faded notices tacked to the walls announced customs duties and other local regulations. One poster invited clients to experience the delights of the Rooster Gentlemens Club where "Yure plesure is are plesure." Silhouettes of girls with cat ears, whiskers, and tails illustrated the pleasures to be had. Another poster advertised the delights of Taproot's Tavern. A handwritten notice offered a bounty of a half-crown for each pair of Rider hands brought in. It was signed by a Sar Rimmer, Agent.

The ambiance of the hut was brown. The wooden floor and walls were brown. The brown counter was decorated in lighter brown cup rings. Even the light filtering through the stained window was brown.

A fly made a half-hearted attempt to butt through the glass before settling on a pile of desiccated bodies on the ledge. They were brown as well.

A man dozed in a chair on the public side of the counter. His soiled T-shirt almost covered a prominent belly. He had the wooden chair rocked back on its rear legs, leaning against the hut wall. An empty bottle of tonk lay on the counter. The man snored raspingly, stomach quivering with the effort of drawing air through a broken nose.

Allenson slapped his hand on the countertop. He regretted this immediately, as the surface was sticky with something organic.

The man woke with a start at the noise, emitting a final nasal splutter. He looked at the survey team with incurious eyes.

"Where would we find the Cutter Agent, my good man?" Destry asked.

The man looked Destry up and down, sneered, and shrugged his shoulders. He raised a buttock to emit a thunderous fart. Closing his eyes, he settled back in his seat. Pink spots formed on Destry's cheeks. He was not used to such incivility and was clearly unsure what to do. After all, he could hardly call the man out without compromising his own dignity.

Hawthorn was less inclined to stand on ceremony. He kicked out the chair legs, depositing the man on the floor with a crash that made Allenson wince. Hawthorn pulled the man up by the grubby shirt and slammed him against the counter so hard that its retaining brackets ripped from the hut wall, exposing corroded screws.

"Listen, scum. When Sar Destry deigns to ask you a question you will reply promptly and civilly. Do you understand, or do I have to reinforce the lesson?" asked Hawthorn.

"No sar," the man replied.

"Well, where is the Agent?" Hawthorn asked.

"Sar Rimmer will be in his villa. It's by Southgate," the man said. He pointed, indicating the direction, his finger shaking.

Hawthorn dropped him without further comment.

"Thank you, my man," Destry said, politely.

Allenson approved of the civility. Just because an oik had no manners was no excuse for gentlemen not to behave properly. Conversely, he also approved of Hawthorn's reaction. Lines must be drawn or society would descend into anarchy. The oik in question frantically pumped the lever on a 'phone as they left.

Southgate was more of a concept than an actual structure. Twisted pieces scattered beside a hole in the wire fence indicated where a gate had once stood. Something very heavy had crushed it into scrap metal, and not recently either, judging from the state of corrosion of the wreckage.

On the other side of the dirt road, a syncrete building stood out from its fellows, partly because it was two stories high, and partly because it was painted shocking pink.

"Somehow, I fancy we have found our quarry," Hawthorn said, dryly.

The front door opened straight onto the street. Allenson was about to knock on the paneling when it flew open. He had to check the motion, or he would have struck the nose of the short, rotund man of middle age who shot out like a hamster from its bedding. The man was preoccupied with adjusting an official-looking scarlet sash that passed over his right shoulder and under his left arm. Somehow he had tangled his right wrist in the folds.

The man hopped up and down, struggling with the recalcitrant item of clothing. His face turned a shade of beetroot purple that contrived to clash horribly with both the scarlet sash and the pink walls.

"Allow me to assist you, sar," Allenson said. He unhooked the sash where it had caught on large ceremonial gold cufflinks that the man sported on the cuffs of an immaculate cream shirt. The effect was slightly spoiled by the buttons being done up in the wrong holes so that one of the stiff collar wings jutted higher than the other.

"Sar Rimmer?" Allenson asked.

"I apologize for being late to meet you, Sar Destry," Rimmer said to Allenson. "That idle fool Ruget only just informed me of your arrival."

Allenson made the correct introductions and Rimmer invited them into his villa. The front door opened into a corridor with a cobbled floor that ran to an exit at the far end. Rimmer ushered them through a door halfway down the corridor. It opened into a large sitting room that occupied one whole wing of the property. It was tastefully furnished in modern colonial minimalist style. Allenson revised his opinion of their host.

"What a comfortable spot," Destry said, approvingly. "You indulge yourself most shamefully, Sar Rimmer."

Rimmer wriggled in embarrassment, adding to his comic appearance.

"No doubt you assumed that the interior design would mirror the vulgarity of the exterior," Rimmer said, ruefully. "The locals demand a show, unfortunately."

The furniture was a good copy of classical Brasilian red shinewood antiques. One end was dominated by a dining table and chairs. The other was set up as a lounge. Leather reclining chairs were arranged in a semicircle facing a master chair that concealed office interfaces. A handpainted artwork depicting a stylized meeting of the Council of Brasilia hung behind. Allenson walked over to examine the painting more closely. A paterfamilias in traditional dress was depicted in the act of hurling a datapad onto the assembly floor.

"You are familiar with the scene, Sar Allenson?" asked Rimmer.

"Possibly," Allenson replied. "Is the paterfamilias not dressed in the colors of Gens Rodrigez? If so, this painting records the Ovidean Declaration."

"The—what?" Hawthorn asked.

"It is little remembered now, but it was an important event in the early days of the Republic. Terra made unreasonable financial demands, but The Rodrigez persuaded the Council to reject them. Terra backed down. Historians dated Brasilia's rise as an independent power from the event."

"Indeed," said Rimmer, clearly pleased. "My family are clients of Gens Rodrigez. Of course, the gens is not quite so prominent as it once was."

Rimmer hesitated before choosing the word "prominent," steering a middle course between precision and loyalty. The Rodrigez wielded little power in modern Brasilia; their glory days had long expired. Their illustrious name was now their primary asset. They stayed mostly on their estates and wrote academic theses on obscure history. That was why their clients like Rimmer failed to get plum positions and were obliged to accept lesser positions like Laywant Agent.

A painting of a narrow-faced woman in severe formal dress hung in a dark corner. She surveyed the room with pursed narrow lips. Allenson was reminded of the old joke about the painting whose eyes followed you around the room. The woman in the picture gave that impression and her eyes disapproved of what they saw.

"My, ah, wife," Rimmer said, following Allenson's gaze.

"Has she joined you here?" Destry asked.

"Ah, no," Rimmer replied. "She elected to stay in Brasilia." He adopted an expression that suggested resilience in the face of hardship. "But I forgot my manners, gentlemen. Sit and I shall order tea."

He sat in the master chair and tapped an interface. "Tea for my guests, Fleur," Rimmer said.

The group made small talk until a petite brunette of perhaps twenty years pushed the door open with her bottom, her hands being occupied by a tray. She wore the short sleeveless tunic of an indentured servant. The girl arranged the cups for the guests.

"Thank you, Fleur. I think we shall have rich tea biscuits as well," Rimmer said. "And some garibaldis."

"You told me not to bring you any more biscuits for the rest of the week," Fleur said, scolding him. "You said you wanted to eat more healthily."

"Yes, yes, well now I am telling you something different. Just this once, and then I will be good. Now scoot; there's a good girl," Rimmer said, slapping her bottom playfully. He darted a half-guilty, half triumphant look at the portrait of his wife.

"Hmmf," Fleur exclaimed. She pouted and headed for the door, wiggling her rear as she went.

"We are, ah, quite informal here," Rimmer said.

"Indeed," said Destry, neutrally. "No doubt that is because the house lacks its mistress."

Hawthorn put his hand across his mouth and turned a laugh into a cough. The house undoubtedly had a mistress. Fleur was no doubt the reason that Rimmer could bear the disappointment of his wife's absence with such fortitude. Being scolded by Fleur was likely to be a lot more agreeable than being chastized by the sour-faced woman in the portrait.

"Is there a suitable hotel or hostel nearby?" Destry asked.

"I think not," Rimmer answered. "You must stay in my guest wing."

Fleur showed them down the central corridor of the villa and out of the door at the end into a rectangular dirt courtyard enclosed by one-story buildings. Chickens and servants scattered before the party, bustling about various errands. Hawthorn chatted with the girl, who flirted outrageously with him, flashing her eyes and patting her hair.

She showed them to their rooms, shrewdly sorting her guests by social status so that Destry had the first and, presumably, the grandest accommodation, Allenson was next, and Hawthorn last.

Allenson was pleased to see that his room contained all essential utilities. He dumped his gear and poured out a basin of water from the jug provided. Giggles and a squeal sounded from Hawthorn's room next door. Allenson sighed. His friend was a fine fellow with many sterling qualities, but they did not include discretion, at least not where women were concerned. To his relief, he heard Hawthorn's door slam. Fleur's silhouette was briefly outlined at his bedroom window as she went about her duties.

Allenson splashed water on his face. He threw himself on the bed and was almost instantly asleep.

That night Rimmer took Allenson, Destry, and Hawthorn to Taproot's Tavern. The noise through the open door hit like a gust of wind, almost physically pushing Allenson back. The Taproot's sound system sacrificed clarity for sheer volume. The room smelled of too many warm bodies and not enough ventilation.

"Perhaps we should go somewhere quieter," Allenson said, hesitating.

"You cannot possibly leave Laywant without visiting Taproot's," Rimmer said, firmly.

"Time we let our hair down with some old fashioned fun," Hawthorn said, pushing his friends further in.

The main area of the bar was clear of furniture so that customers could cluster around pedestals where girls in cages, who were more or less wrapped in wispy thin cloth, wriggled in time to the music. Tables in three-sided cubicles around the walls gave more discerning patrons a degree of privacy. Rimmer ushered the friends to an empty cubicle.

The noise levels precluded conversation, so Allenson looked around the bar. People always interested him. Allenson was not the sort of young man who was the life and soul of a party, but he liked to observe. When he was younger, he used to imagine the back stories of strangers, a harmless game that had honed his powers of observation and judgment of character.

The dancer nearest them had managed to get her nipple tassels rotating in opposite direction by dint of dexterous torso gyration. Men in working clothes clutching glasses of tonk cheered and tossed coins into the cage. The woman's eyes flashed and she preened at the attention. A handful of slatternly women of indeterminate age moved among them, exchanging kisses for drinks.

The sharp dressers were in the cubicles. Some observed the dancers, while others entertained hard-faced young women who wore too much makeup.

Other men negotiated with each other, exchanging sharp glances and, in one case, a small bag. The man receiving the bag must have felt Allenson's gaze, for he looked up and their eyes locked. Allenson held the man's gaze until he looked away first. It was just like dealing with Riders. Never show weakness.

A brunette in a spangly one-piece, cut up to the waist, appeared. She placed a damper on their table and slapped the top. The background noise subsided from impossible to merely inconvenient.

"What can I get you sars?" she asked, remembering to grimace in imitation of a smile.

"A flagon of beer," Rimmer said. "Imported."

The waitress nodded and moved to take the damper.

"Leave it," Rimmer said, intercepting her hand. He passed her a half-crown, a rectangular jet-black Brasilian coin that flashed indigo as it passed from hand to hand to demonstrate its authenticity.

This time the waitress's smile was genuine. "At once, Sar Rimmer."

She bustled through a door into a back room, pointedly ignoring seated customers who tried to catch her eye.

"That's better," Rimmer said.

"The damper does make conversation possible," said Destry. "Now we can hear each other."

"As could a concealed microphone," said Hawthorn, cynically.

Rimmer winked at him.

The waitress reappeared with a three-liter container of beer and three glasses. She showed the unbroken seal to Rimmer, who nodded approval. The waitress cracked it, setting off an endothermic reaction that chilled the contents. She poured a glass of sparkling liquid for each of them.

"Enjoy," she said, with a bob of the head before leaving to deal with the increasingly impatient customers in the next cubicle.

Allenson sipped the beer carefully. He suspected that its alcohol content was near wine strength. "This is exceedingly smooth, Sar Rimmer. I am not familiar with it."

Destry turned the flagon to examine the brand. Beads of water had already condensed on the outside.

"Savara Plain," he said, approvingly. "This is a premium brand even in Brasilia. How odd to find it out here."

"Taproot has a taste for fine living. He imports some for his personal use and generously allows me to lay down a tranche in his cellar for my own use," said Rimmer.

"Taproot being the proprietor?" Hawthorn asked.

"Of Taproot's Tavern, yes," Rimmer replied. "Speak of the devil. Here is the gentleman."

A bald man of middle age approached their table. He was powerfully built, but had run to seed with a pronounced paunch produced by too many beers and not enough exercise. Nevertheless, he still exuded an impression of strength. The two minders who flanked him at a respectful distance showed no such physical deterioration.

"Agent Rimmer. I had no idea that you were coming in tonight or I would have prepared a private room."

"Not at all, Taproot, I wanted my guests to experience the full flavor of your establishment. Can't do that in a private room, can we?"

Rimmer played a fat little official exaggeratedly aping the manners of a gentleman awfully well.

"Ah yes, your guests." Taproot looked expectantly at the survey team.

Rimmer made the appropriate introductions.

"Will you not join us, Taproot?" Rimmer asked.

"Well, perhaps for a moment," Taproot replied.

He clicked his fingers and a minder pulled a chair back and seated him at a table. The waitress materialized with an additional glass, into which she poured beer from the flagon. Taproot stopped her with a gesture when his glass was but a quarter full.

"Bring some sweetmeats from my personal stock," Taproot said.

The waitress bowed so low that her hair fell over her face and hurried away.

"What brings such gentlemen to our little backwater?" Taproot asked.

"A little sightseeing," Allenson replied. "It is interesting to see how civilization is spreading into the Hinterlands."

"We do our best," Taproot said.

The waitress returned with a wicker basket. She passed it around, starting with Taproot. Allenson selected a twisted spiral of candied fruit covered with honey. It was a little sugary for his taste, but he expressed his enjoyment for form's sake.

"Master Taproot is quite the central pillar of our little community," said Rimmer.

Taproot waved a hand in a depreciating gesture that was belied by his smug expression.

"Sar Rimmer insists you own the best establishment in Laywant Town," Allenson said, politely.

"And many other businesses beside," Rimmer said. "There is the Gentlemen's Club and the Supply Stores for starters. I think there is hardly a business of any size that Master Taproot has not invested in at least to some degree. You must have increased your capital a thousand fold in the few years you have been here."

"The fruits of hard work and a little luck, sars," Taproot said, shrugging.

"I keep telling him that he is wasted in our inconsequential colony," Rimmer said. "A man with his business acumen deserves a bigger stage."

"I am content," Taproot said.

"Is not Taproot a Terran name?" asked Destry.

"Is it?" Taproot replied. "I really could not say."

He finished his drink in three gulps and rose. "I won't disturb your evening any further, sars," Taproot said. "I have obligations to attend to."

"Dianah," he said to the waitress. "See that these gentlemen have whatever they desire. Charge it to my account."

"Yes, master," Dianah said, bobbing her head.

"Most generous," Destry said. "I hope your business is profitable."

"It normally is," Taproot said. With that he left, minders in tow.

"An impressive man," Destry said.

"Indeed," Rimmer said. "I rely on his support to enforce Cutter Stream regulations. The town watchmen are next to useless."

"If that specimen who greeted us in the customs shed was typical, then you have my sympathies, Sar Rimmer," Hawthorn said.

"Typical? Hardly," Rimmer said. "Ruget is one of the more reliable ones. At least, he turns up for work even if he does not actually do any. Most of the rest just draw a salary. I am not sure some of them even exist."

Rimmer finished his drink. "I must also leave you, sars. I have to go over some figures with Fleur."

Hawthorn and Destry waited until Rimmer had gone before bursting out laughing.

"He has a very rounded set of figures to go over, to be sure," Hawthorn said.

"Gentlemen, no unseemly comments about our host, if you please," Allenson said, suppressing a chuckle. "I am sure his motives are entirely..."

"Understandable." Hawthorn finished the sentence for him.

"I was about to say 'unimpeachable,'" Allenson said.

"Always the romantic," Hawthorn said, shaking his head. He refilled his glass from the flagon. "This beer slips down remarkably easily." He demonstrated.

"Why do you say that?" Allenson asked, somewhat nettled.

"Because it does; don't you like the beer?" Hawthorn asked.

"Why do you say that I'm a romantic?" asked Allenson, refusing to be deflected.

"You've started a new poem," Destry said.

"What makes you think so?" Allenson asked.

"We saw you writing on paper," Hawthorn replied.

"Paper is organic," Allenson admitted. "One can't write poetry on a datapad. It has no soul."

"Will you give us a reading?" asked Destry.

"I don't see why I should," Allenson replied.

"Of course not, if you are embarrassed," Hawthorn said.

"I am not embarrassed," Allenson said.

He pulled out a notebook and selected a page.

"I have only put a couple of lines together, so far," Allenson said.

"From your bright sparkling eyes, I was undone,

"Rays, you have, more transparent than the sun,

"Amidst its glory in the rising day,

"None can you equal in your bright array,

"Constant in your calm and unspotted mind,

"Equal to all, but will to none prove kind."

There was silence.

"Well!" Allenson said, a note of challenge in his voice.

"It has a charming allegory—a lady as the rising sun," said Destry, finally.

"It rhymes," Hawthorn noted, helpfully.

"Is it about any particular lady, or an ideal of womanhood?" Destry asked hurriedly, quelling Hawthorn with a glance.

"It's an acrostic," Allenson said. "Or it will be when it's finished. That's why I haven't got very far."

"F-R-A-N-C-E," Destry spelled out. "So the next line has to start with an S."

"Frances Alexander," Hawthorn said to Destry. "He danced with her at the Smethwick ball."

"She was so poised, so regal," Allenson said, wistfully. "So innocent, so pure, a friend to all, but giving her favors to none."

Destry and Hawthorn exchanged meaningful glances when Allenson was not looking.

"We are getting maudlin," Destry said, refilling their glasses. The flagon was empty when he came to fill his own so he signaled to Dianah for another.

"I am not entirely clear why Rimmer brought us here." Destry said.

"He wanted us to meet Taproot," Hawthorn said flatly.

"Yes," Allenson said. "I wonder why?"

· CHAPTER 7 ·

Greenfey Island

Allenson heard the cry at the edge of his consciousness. "Ayoh, ayoh."

He attempted to ignore it, but it got louder, tugging him from sleep.

"Ayoh, ayoh."

Allenson drifted in that dream-zone when one was not truly asleep but not yet properly awake. A child cried out and a woman's voice scolded. The slow metallic scrape of someone cleaning a pan marked time.

He opened his eyes, taking a moment to orient himself. Dust sparkled in a ray of light thrusting through a chink in the curtains. Focusing on the clock on the wall required rather more effort than was usually necessary. He sat up, immediately regretting the sudden movement when a dull pain struck him between the eyes. For some reason, the pan-cleaner elected to beat the utensil. Allenson's head rang in sympathy with each blow.

He poured himself a glass of water and used it to push down a detox pill. He then filled the wash bowl and thrust his face in. Either the pill or the cold water worked, because the thudding pain in his head faded to the point that he thought it quite likely that he would survive the next twenty minutes. Completing his toilette, he went out into the yard.

The pan-cleaner turned out to be a mechanic making subtle adjustments to the motor of a tractor unit with a hammer. In one of the buildings in the compound, a pig squealed and grunted, throwing its body against the wooden door. A startled chicken shot off with an alarmed squawk. It clucked in anger when it was safely away, ruffling its feathers like an indignant dowager duchess.

Spotting him, a servant began to set up a breakfast table outside the kitchen wing of the villa, where a small area was paved and separated off by a low wall.

Allenson knocked on the door of Hawthorn's room. "Yes, come," Hawthorn said.

When Allenson went in, his friend was sitting on the edge of the bed running his fingers through his hair. His eyes were bright and alert. Allenson was exasperated. Hawthorn had consumed two drinks to his one and yet still managed to look as if he had spent the evening reading an uplifting book.

There was a groan behind him from the outline of a body still abed. Hawthorn turned and Allenson saw a spread of brunette hair on the pillow. Not Fleur, he prayed. Please don't tell me he has bedded the Agent's favorite.

Hawthorn pulled the sheet back revealing a face, that of Dianah from the tavern. Allenson tried to work out when Hawthorn had arranged the liaison. The three friends had been together all night, though admittedly his memory of the end of the evening was a little hazy.

"Ah, breakfast is served," Allenson said.

He beat a quick retreat and made his way over to the breakfast table. Destry was already seated.

"Cafay?" Destry asked, pouring out a mug without waiting for a reply.

Allenson sipped the hot, dark, bitter drink, welcoming the caffeine rush. Cafay was made from a variety of sterile hybrid plant whose origins supposedly reached back to Old Earth. It tasted not unlike aromatic coffee. He selected an oatmeal biscuit and broke it into eatable chunks. The sweet, spicy flavor perfectly complemented the cafay.

Hawthorn joined the table, covering a slice of toasted bread with fruit spread. Allenson found rather to his surprise that he was desperately hungry, so he joined Hawthorn in taking the more substantial dish and also added some cheese and ham slices to his plate. Destry toyed with the oatmeal.

The friends had reached the stage where they were drinking a second cafay and finishing up the sweetmeats when Rimmer joined them. Destry pushed the biscuits in his direction.

"Thank you, no." Rimmer said, wistfully. "Well, perhaps just a cafay and a small snack. I have a favor to ask of you, sars."

"Indeed," Allenson said.

"We have been plagued by Rider raids over the last few years."

"We saw the bounty notice," Hawthorn said. "I am surprised that Riders are a problem this close to the Cutter Stream."

Rimmer shrugged. "We rarely catch any Riders. The bounty is mostly unclaimed. It serves more of a political than a practical purpose. One must be seen to be doing something, however useless. I lack the budget to recruit decent lictors and so have to rely on watchmen, who are little more than the town drunks, and volunteers."

"You mentioned a favor," said Allenson, dragging Rimmer back to the issue.

"Ah, yes. I have just had a report of another raid on an outlying island. Some of Master Taproot's men are organizing an armed band to pursue the Riders. I wondered if you gentlemen might spare the time to accompany them?" asked Rimmer.

"Of course we will," Destry replied. "What an excellent way to repay your hospitality. I haven't been on a decent hunt for months. It will be an adventure."

Allenson could have cursed him. A wild goose chase back into the Hinterlands was about as welcome as a slipped disc at this stage of their expedition. He arranged his features into a polite smile.

"It will be our pleasure," Allenson said.

Hawthorn poured himself another cup of cafay.

Rimmer escorted the survey team to where the armed band was assembling in the compound. They divided quite noticeably into two groups—the Watch, older, unfit men in cheap town clothing, and Taproot's men, younger, leaner, hungrier, and dressed in Hinterlands gear.

The watchmen were equipped with three-man tricycle frames and cheaply stamped out shotguns with thick metal barrels that would act as a significant drag in the Continuum. Their uniforms consisted solely of a yellow armband bearing the Cutter Stream logo of five stars in a cross. One had an additional yellow sash, marking him as the sergeant in charge.

Taproot's men had personal frames similar to those used by the team and were armed with an assortment of rugged pellet guns made largely of imported ceramic components. The only significant mass of metal in them would be the pellets and magnetic coils.

"These gentlemen will be accompanying you," Rimmer said to the Watch sergeant, gesturing at the survey team.

"I don't know about that. Master Taproot said nothing about no gentlemen," said a surly individual who Allenson recognized from the night before as one of Taproot's minders.

The sergeant stepped back, looking nervously from Rimmer to the minder.

"Sar Rimmer was giving you an instruction, not asking your opinion," said Hawthorn.

The minder stood his ground, glaring at Hawthorn.

"Mind your manners, Williamson," Taproot said, from the open rear window of a luxury Ramanda ground effect car parked to one side of the compound. "The gentlemen are welcome, of course."

Allenson had noticed the vehicle earlier but had assumed that it was the official car of the Agent. Transporting such a machine to a Hinterlands colony would be ruinously expensive.

Taproot's minder shrugged and turned away to adjust his frame. The Ramanda's tinted window slid up; the car rose thirty centimeters above the ground with barely a whine from its ground effect rotors. It slid out of the compound, bottoming with a clang on the uneven surface between the gate and the road.

The car raised a cloud of dust when it hit the road, manoeuvring slowly and with difficulty along the narrow streets. The dust settled to reveal a new bright silver scar where the car had grounded.

"He would be far more comfortable in a Rover," Hawthorn said with a grin.

"I suspect comfort is not the issue," Allenson said, thoughtfully. "The Ramanda is a statement of wealth and status. It speaks volumes about Taproot's personality and ambitions." He raised his voice, "Williamson!"

"Sar," the minder replied.

The minder had completely lost his truculence. Clearly, Taproot ran a tight ship.

"Brief us, if you please," Allenson said.

"We got a phone call. Smoke is rising from Greenfey. It's a small island in the 'pelago. The Svenson family farm it."

"Very well, Williamson. Lead and we shall follow," said Allenson.

Nobody asked the watch sergeant's opinion, an omission for which he seemed grateful.

They made poor time through the Continuum—the tricycles were slow and their occupants unfit—but it was barely a hop to Greenfey. The armed band materialized directly at the farmhouse. A thin curl of smoke still lifted from the burnt-out building. There was no sign of life.

"Spread out and see what you can find," said Williamson. Men rushed in all directions, seemingly at random. Allenson doubted they would find much. The raiders must be long gone.

The plasticized farmhouse walls were noncombustible but their blackened surface indicated the ferocity of the fire. The roof had burned and fallen in. Two charcoal human-sized objects were presumably the Svensons. A smaller body in the corner might have been a child or an animal. It was too burnt to be certain. Allenson moved the body with his foot and discovered the remains of a small shoe. Charcoal flaked off the remains, releasing the sweet smell of roast meat. It reminded Allenson of the Rider encampment. He forced down the urge to gag and put his handkerchief over his mouth.

Allenson methodically examined the remains in and around the building. The men drifted back in twos and threes, Destry and Hawthorn among them. Destry was white-faced and seemed to be in shock. Hawthorn was deceptively calm, but Allenson knew him well enough to sense the fury pent within him.

"The family is inside," Allenson said. "Two adults and a child."

"There was a teenage girl as well," Hawthorn said. "They took her away from the fire."

"Did they kill her?" Allenson asked, knowing in his heart the answer, but clinging to a faint hope.

"Eventually," Hawthorn replied.

"Right, men; let's go," Williamson shouted. "We will follow the current into the Hinterlands. Let's see if we can find the trail of the murdering bastards."

The men ran for their frames, mounted, and disappeared one by one. Allenson watched them go without making any effort to follow. His friends looked at him curiously.

"It occurs to me," Allenson said, "that there is a distinct lack of any sign of high-value portable property among the debris."

"They were only poor farmers," Hawthorn said.

"True, but over there is the remains of a solar tracking dish. Someone has taken the capacitor."

"Maybe it had been removed before the raid—for maintenance or somesuch," said Destry.

"Maybe," Allenson agreed, "but what's left of the steam generator is in that wooden annex." Allenson pointed. "I can find no trace of the control module. There surely would have been something ceramic that would have survived the fire. Why would Riders want to steal a control module?"

"No reason at all," Hawthorn said, his voice cold and hard. "Renegades did this."

"It explains why the armed bands never catch anything," Allenson said. "Renegades are hardly likely to flee deeper into the Hinterlands. They will need to fence their loot, which means someone is laundering it for them."

"And the best place to do that would be here on Laywant." Destry finished the argument for him.

"Right," Allenson said. "If we carry out a spiral search over the world surface from this point, we may yet pick up their track."

It was Hawthorn who found the trail, of course. He had an instinctive insight into human behavior that Allenson envied. Allenson thought in complex ways and often made the mistake of projecting that world view onto other people's behavior. Sometimes that meant one missed the obvious. By unspoken agreement, Destry and Allenson let Hawthorn lead. They followed his frame at a good distance to minimize the chance of the Renegades spotting they were being followed.

Hawthorn paused at intervals to match phase with realspace. After a longer stop than usual, he dropped back into the Continuum and pedaled back to where his friends waited. He signaled them to follow him closely. Hawthorn veered off to the left, circumnavigating the faint shimmering ball of silver left by a group of frames dephasing from the Continuum.

They emerged onto a narrow ribbon of fine sand that separated the sea from the trees. The sun was low on the horizon. Something in the atmosphere tinted the light, illuminating the sea so that pink froth rode on top of violet water.

Allenson jumped out of his frame and looked around to get his bearings. Their frames stood on the shore of a small bay. Trees blocked his view of what lay beyond. A low, tree-covered island was separated from the end of the nearest promontory by a sliver of water.

"The renegades debussed on the far side of that island," Hawthorn said, rifle in hand. "I kept my distance, so I did not set off any alarms. I suggest we cross the creek on this side and move in on them through the trees."

Allenson realized that Hawthorn's plan put the sun at their backs. He would not have thought of that tactic. He made a mental note for future reference. The sun's position gave them only a small edge, but no advantage was to be spurned. He estimated that there could be up to a dozen renegades, going by the size of the track they left in the Continuum.

Allenson unclipped his lasercarbine from his frame. He switched it on and ran the test diagnostic. The holographic sights flashed green, showing complete functionality. A side bar indicated a full charge.

Hawthorn took point, covering the ground at a brisk walk. He carried his laserifle. It was a more powerful weapon than the carbines used by Destry and

Allenson, with a longer range, greater accuracy, and harder punch, but it suffered from a slow rate of fire.

Allenson and Destry moved out to either flank such that the team was far enough apart to prevent a single burst taking them all out. The instinct to huddle together for safety had served mankind well for most of the species' evolution, but the invention of rapid-fire weapons made such behavior suicidal.

The creek appeared shallow, barely boot deep. Allenson splashed through but stumbled into a pothole. The water reached up to his waist, soaking his clothes. The sudden chill on his fundamentals made him inhale sharply.

A curse and splash announced that Destry had also found a pothole. He had gone in up to his neck. Destry raised his carbine above his head. The guns were guaranteed waterproof, but a firefight would be a bad time to find that the manufacturer had lied.

Allenson could not help chuckling as a response to the release of tension. Destry glared at him before also seeing the funny side.

"I expect dinner at a restaurant of my choice as an apology for that smirk, Allenson," Destry said in mock anger.

Allenson waved a hand to indicate acquiescence.

"Gentlemen, if you have quite finished," Hawthorn said, standing on the island. He managed to cross the creek without incident. Allenson sighed. He did not, of course, wish his friend any harm, but, just occasionally, it would be nice to see Hawthorn fall into a bog.

The island was covered in trees in copses, as if they had been coppiced by someone in the past. Line of site varied enormously. The low sun cast long shadows that further confused the brain's pattern recognition system.

The three friends advanced slowly through the trees in line abreast, staying within sight of each other. Hawthorn gave instructions by hand gesture. Allenson heard voices and then Hawthorn held one hand palm out, indicating that they should halt. Allenson slid into the cover of a copse and stared hard, but could see nothing.

People were arguing about something. One voice raised in indignation until silenced by a snarled curse. Three men appeared suddenly in a sunlit avenue between copses. Allenson slid off the safety catch of his carbine and set the gun to fire short bursts. He laid his holographic sight on the targets and waited.

The renegades got closer and closer, until it seemed certain that they must see the ambushers. The leading renegade held a shotgun casually in one hand.

Allenson shifted position slightly to keep his carbine aligned. He momentarily lost balance, catching a branch and causing it to shake. The lead renegade reacted with lightning speed, raising his gun.

There was a flash of light on the renegade's jaw. His head was hidden by an explosion of red steam. A piece of skull spun lazily out of the cloud, trailing hair. The renegade's hand tightened on the trigger in a muscle spasm, causing it to discharge heavy shot into the branches over Allenson's head.

Allenson fired a burst at the second renegade who danced sideways toward cover. The shots fell behind the man, igniting ground litter. Allenson cursed his lack of skill with a gun. His carbine whined as it transferred energy from storage up into the quick-discharge capacitor.

Destry fired a three shot burst at the diving man. Destry came from a class whose primary recreations were gambling and hunting. He had shot much smaller prey on the wing. He tracked the target through the burst. Two flashes lit up the man's torso. He crashed heavily onto the ground and lay still, legs sprawled out at uncomfortable angles.

The third renegade favored a strategy of discretion rather than valor. He dropped his gun and fled. Allenson tried to lay his sight on the running figure, but kept losing contact as the man weaved between the trees. He fired a burst but missed.

The renegade dodged sideways and for a split second was clearly illuminated. His back flashed and exploded, throwing him to the ground. This time Allenson heard the deep hum of Hawthorn's rifle recharging.

They checked the bodies. All were very, very dead and none carried identification.

Allenson smelled the renegade encampment before he saw it. A rather delicious smell of burning charcoal and roast meat filtered between the trees making him salivate. He was suddenly felt hungry. A great deal had happened since breakfast.

The three friends filtered quietly through the thinning cover. The renegades had built their encampment just upshore from a narrow beach in an area cleared of vegetation. A long, narrow, one-story wooden barracks ran at right angles to the shoreline. It was raised up about a meter on wooden posts, presumably to avoid tidal floods or the local wildlife.

Wooden steps led up to a single door. Wooden shutters protected glassless windows. Many were thrown open. Some had fallen off and not been replaced. The group of renegades stood and sat around a long pit of burning charcoal, passing bottles of tonk from hand to hand. A cook turned over strips of meat barbecuing on metal griddles over the fire.

Two men worked on a multipedal transport frame. One unloaded while another carried items into the barracks.

Hawthorn signaled a halt. Allenson counted at least eight renegades. The friends were horribly outnumbered and there would be no cover once they left the trees. He expected Hawthorn to back off and lead them around the camp to make an approach behind the barracks. Instead, Hawthorn stepped out of cover and ambled nonchalantly toward the barbecue, making no attempt at concealment. Allenson followed, feeling like a man heading for his own funeral.

Renegades noticed their arrival but otherwise paid them no heed. Allenson felt stupid as he grasped what Hawthorn had already realized. Three men had left the encampment and three men returned, three men who were mere silhouettes against the light.

A burly man in an orange waistcoat finally noticed them. "I thought I told you to check the fish traps," he said. "What are you doing back so quick?"

Hawthorn ignored him and continued to close the range.

Orange waistcoat put his hand up to shade his eyes and studied the friends. "You're not..." he said, reaching for a weapon in a chest holster.

Hawthorn swung his rifle up to the shoulder and fired. The renegade went down in a burst of steam, his orange waistcoat on fire.

Destry fired a single shot from his carbine, dropping a renegade. He fired a second time, catching a man in the shoulder and spinning him around. A third shot took the man between the shoulderblades and he fell.

Allenson fired a single shot at a renegade aiming a weapon. He missed, but the man ducked, triggering his shotgun into the sky. Hawthorn's next shot punched a hole in the man's skull.

Allenson cursed his poor marksmanship. This was hopeless. He was never going to hit anyone at this range. He ran at a diagonal, closing down the range but moving out to a flank to draw fire away from his friends. He pushed the selector on his carbine through the gate to continuous.

Slowing to a walk and locking the carbine in to his hip, he held the trigger down, walking laser bursts across the encampment. Several shots hit the fire, adding to the mayhem by tossing burning embers into the sky. Few, if any, renegades took a hit, but they ducked and fired back wildly. A detached part of Allenson's mind noted the "whap" of passing shot and something plucked at his jacket.

The recharger on Allenson's carbine howled in protest at the energy demand. Red lights winked on his hologram display. He ignored them, triggering another sustained burst. Hawthorn and Destry fired coolly and steadily, dropping renegades as if they were shooting targets on a practice range.

Allenson's gun shut down with a click, refusing to tolerate more punishment. He gave up on it and charged toward the renegades, yelling and swinging the carbine around his head.

He was the only man standing when he reached the fire. He lowered his weapon, feeling rather foolish.

The long gray shape of a gun barrel poked through an open window. Blue-electric light flickered from badly adjusted magnetic rails, followed by the sharp snap of a pellet gun. Allenson raised his carbine, but pressing the trigger merely caused a cascade of error symbols in the holographic sights. However, the threat caused the gunman to duck down.

Hawthorn fired his rifle at the wood below the window ledge. Wood exploded in a shower of splinters. The gunman screamed and reared up, pawing at his face. A burst from Destry's carbine lit up the renegade's chest, chopping off his scream like it had been cut by a knife. The man dropped back into the barracks.

"Got you," Destry said with satisfaction.

Allenson turned to thank his friends. He flushed, unsure what to say, when he saw the strange expression on their faces.

"Hawthorn, should I ever chance to risk being called out by our friend here, pray do not hesitate to remind me of this day," Destry said.

"You can be sure of it," Hawthorn replied. He cocked his head. "I suppose we should bind up our hero's wounds before he bleeds to death."

Allenson looked down. Blood ran down his arm, soaking into his jacket.

"I thought that last renegade had missed me," Allenson said.

"Oh, he did," Hawthorn said. "It was the one in the green overalls that winged you. Destry put him down before he could correct his aim. Rather a pretty shot."

Destry gave an "it-was-nothing" shrug. "I had all

the time in the world. Our friend here had their full attention. You took one hell of a risk, Allenson." He shook his head, as if he could not decide whether to scold or praise. He decided on the latter. "Bravest thing I have ever seen."

Allenson felt embarrassed. He was not brave at all. He had simply felt humiliated by the way his poor marksmanship had let down his friends. It was vain pride that had spurred him on, not courage.

Allenson examined where a pellet had ripped along his forearm. A centimeter deeper and it would have caught the bone, ripping his arm off.

"It doesn't hurt," he said in surprise.

"It will," Hawthorn said. He ripped open Allenson's sleeve and stretched a patch along the wound. The material reacted with flesh, sealing the injury and releasing bacteriophages, analgesics, and other epigenetic virions that promoted cell-growth.

"One of them is still alive over here," Destry said.

The renegade lay still on his front. A round had exploded on his side, cooking the flesh just above the hip. It was a nasty wound but treatable, should someone take him to an infirmary.

Destry looked at the renegade doubtfully. "I was sure I saw him move. Perhaps I was mistaken?"

"Perhaps," Hawthorn replied. "Or maybe he's faking."

He kicked the renegade's wounded hip. The man groaned and clutched his side.

"Bastard," the renegade said.

Hawthorn kicked him again.

"Mind your manners, scum," Hawthorn said, without heat.

"These people are just hired thugs, easily replaceable,"

Allenson said. "We need to know the name of the principal."

"You heard Sar Allenson, scum. Who paid you? Who gave the orders?" Hawthorn asked.

The renegade replied by suggesting an imaginative unnatural sexual act that Sar Allenson might like ·to try. Hawthorn laughed with genuine humor and kicked the man again. The renegade whimpered.

"Please, no," he said. "You don't know what he will do to me if I grass."

"True," Hawthorn replied, "but I know what I will do to you right now if you don't."

"Mercy, sars," the man pleaded.

"Mercy will be granted if you give me the name," Hawthorn said, remorselessly. He drew back his foot.

"Taproot!" the renegade screamed. "Taproot gives the orders."

"So our local entrepreneur has a lucrative little sideline to his stores," said Hawthorn with a sigh. "He sells the customers goods, and then steals them back. Sweet." He looked at Allenson. "You don't seem surprised?"

"No," Allenson replied, "I was half expecting something of the sort. It would appear that nothing happens on Laywant without Taproot's influence."

"Sar Rimmer knew?" Destry asked.

"Knew? Perhaps suspected," Allenson replied, "but suspicion is not proof."

"You promised me mercy," the renegade said, drawing their attention. "You don't know what Taproot does to those who cross him."

"Mercy?" Hawthorn mused. "Why yes, I will grant you mercy. More than you showed the Svenson family."

He put his foot on the renegade's neck and pulled

back the man's head, twisting it sharply. The renegade's neck gave way with a crack and his eyes whited over. Hawthorn let the head fall with a thud that the renegade was past feeling.

"There goes our only witness," said Destry.

"Can you imagine bringing Taproot to justice in a Laywant courthouse stuffed with his hired goons?" Hawthorn asked, impatiently.

"I suppose we can file a report with the Governor's Office back in the Cutter Stream," Destry said. "But I doubt much will come of it."

"I have had enough of Laywant for this lifetime," Allenson said. "Let's torch the buildings and go home."

"Then the Hinterlands Survey is officially over," Hawthorn said. "In which case, I think I will stay on Laywant for a while. I find I have some business here."

Allenson could not meet his friend's eye. He had a strong suspicion as to the nature of Hawthorn's business, but he did not want to know for certain. If he knew, then he might feel morally obliged to protest, even though the business was necessary.

Allenson was self-aware enough to curse himself as a hypocrite. He thought back to the hands that the Rider had taken as trophies. He was disturbed to find that they did not bother him as much as they should. Is this what the Hinterlands did to men, turn them into savages?

Well, maybe—but the Hinterlands belonged to the colonists, not Brasilia, and certainly not Terra. The colonies *needed* the space to grow and develop into self-sufficient communities. Todd was right and so was Linsye. Todd could no longer oversee his dream, but Allen Allenson could—he could and he would.

Rough Justice

Taproot turned off his account book with a slap of his hand on the screen and poured himself a generous glass of Terran gin. He favored a London dry brand that was triple distilled with juniper berries and lemon spice. It was named after some Old Earth Imperial city. He went through the ritual of adding tonic water from a separate bottle. He sipped the mixture, savoring the bitter taste of the drink.

His mind was on the figures. Takings were down from one of the knocking shops that serviced agricultural servants. He could think of no acceptable reason for the decline. Maybe the whores just weren't putting their backs into the work. Another possibility was that the pimp was creaming profits off the top. Taproot's lips tightened. He could not believe that anyone would be stupid enough to cheat him. Either way, it might be time to send a couple of boys around to administer a kicking.

It never hurt to put the frighteners on a victim, even if he wasn't guilty. It kept everyone else in line and taught them some respect. He took another long sip, welcoming the warm glow of alcohol and spice deep in his guts.

Respect! That was a laugh. Here he sat, the ruler of Laywant, undisputed king of a dungheap, worrying about the loss of a handful of crowns where once he had dealt in tens of thousands of Terran marks.

He tossed the rest of the drink down his throat and poured himself another, slopping gin on the polished desk. Rage and hate were never far from the surface of Taproot's mind. It simmered like a charcoal fire, hotter than the gin.

Bloody aristocrats, what would they be without their inherited wealth and family influence? He had worked for every pfennig. Nobody had ever given him anything. Then the damned aristos had taken it all away.

He had been a big man when he ran the Dockers Union at Terra's Firenze Freeport. Nothing moved in or out of the sheds without his approval. His power bought him a villa on The Hill, starlets on his arm, and politicians in his pocket.

Then he crossed the Fraterni clan, who were the heredity owners of the land on which the port was built. Where were his tame politicians then? They had been keen to take his money, to attend his parties, to drink his vintage wines and screw the girls he provided, but where were they when he needed them? Unobtainable, that's where.

Taproot sipped the gin, his rage boiling over into his conscious mind. It was sheer chance that he escaped when the Fraterni buccelari came. He got away with not much more than the clothes on his back and the marks in his pocket. He had run as far as he could, but safety lay in keeping a low profile. The Fraterni had a long reach.

He had learned that respectable society was completely unprincipled and dangerous. That was why he tolerated that idiot Rimmer. The Agent was useful camouflage. Except that recent events made him wonder whether Rimmer was quite the fool he looked.

The visit by the Cutter Stream gentlemen was unnerving. Why did such men come here? What was Rimmer up to? What did he know? Taproot mulled over his options. It was not in his nature to await events. The authorities would come down hard if Rimmer was murdered, but suppose he had an unfortunate accident? Shit happened in the Hinterlands.

Taproot calmed himself. He had a new girl waiting for him at home, a real beauty of about fifteen years. He liked to break the young ones in himself before passing them on to one of his cathouses. He triggered the intercom on his screen.

"Brown, Rattis, get in here, now."

The enforcers came into his office at the run. He ignored them, letting them wait while he finished his drink, savoring the spices—and the power. He touched his screen and a curtain slid aside, revealing a door at the back of his office. Another touch and the door unlocked.

"Go out and start my car."

"Yes, boss."

The pair swung the heavy steel door open and disappeared into the darkness. The door was Taproot's private exit onto a street where his armored Ramanda was always parked. He doubted that any of the Laywant yokels would have the skill, let alone the balls, to wire a bomb to the engine, but it never hurt to take precautions. The Fraterni had a long reach.

Taproot closed down his screen and put his overcoat on. He went to put the gin away, but had second thoughts and slipped the bottle into an inside pocket. Where the hell were his men? Brown should have come back to escort him to the car. Couldn't the stupid bastards do anything right? His anger flared and he stormed out of the door.

"Brown, where the hell are you?" Taproot asked.

There was no answer.

The lights were out, leaving the street in darkness. Nothing worked right at Laywant. Taproot's eyes were adjusted to the bright illumination of his office, and he strained to make out details. A dark bulk indicated where his car was parked a few meters up the road. He could just hear the hum of its engine on idle.

As Taproot's night vision returned, he could see the silhouette of someone in the driver's seat. That would be his chauffeur.

"Rattis, where's Brown?"

Rattis didn't answer. He seemed to be inspecting something on the dashboard. Where the hell was. Brown?

Taproot stormed toward the car, cursing as he trod in some ripe refuse.

"You useless Laywant bastards are gonna wish—"

His foot struck an obstacle. Glancing down, he could just make out the outline of a body. He grabbed for his pistol but found only the gin bottle.

Something hard slammed into his back with such force that it paralyzed his legs. Taproot dropped to his knees. He tried to call out, but an arm circled his throat, crushing the windpipe.

His attacker punched him in the right kidney. He didn't realize that he had been stabbed until he felt hot, sticky blood run down his side. The pain started then. A voice whispered in his ear.

"The Svenson family sends their regards."

The knife twisted in his side, causing intolerable agony. He tried to scream but couldn't breathe. He welcomed the nothingness that washed away pain.

· CHAPTER 8 ·

Destry Demesne

The Destry Demesne was the largest estate on Wagener, one of the Five Worlds of the Cutter Stream. The original fortified settlement had been pulled down by Royman Destry's grandfather and replaced by a magnificent mansion built to resemble a Brasilian country house. It boasted three stories and a crenelated tower on the east wing. The tower actually came in useful as a communication center.

The family and selected guests used a private beacon that landed frames on a front drive that ran through ornamental gardens. Other beacons for employees and tradesmen guided frames into commercial areas.

Allen phased in with Destry. For the first time it struck him how utterly defenseless was the mansion, with its large glass bay windows and spacious balustraded balconies. A magnificent, wide stairway gave access to the main entrance on the middle floor. The ground floor was pierced by many doors, so that servants had easy access to the working areas, kitchens, storerooms, and suchlike.

There had not been an attack on a Wagener demesne in living memory. The idea was so unthinkable the mansion lacked even a point defense system. The security guards standing smartly at the base of the stairs may have had lasercarbines slung over the shoulders, but the men were probably chosen more for their panache in bright yellow uniforms than for any martial skills.

Small villas dotted the gardens for the use of family guests and visitors of similar rank. Servants were housed in less comfort in utility barracks that were out of sight at the back of the mansion.

Allenson climbed off his frame and stretched. Servants hurried to take care of the frames. Royman led the way up the stairs, ignoring the guards who stared straight ahead. It began to rain gently as the two friends entered the mansion. Water drops ran off the water-resistant yellow cloth.

Inside the reception room, a footman in blue and gold greeted Royman.

"Welcome home, sir. Mistress Sarai awaits you in the Extempore Hall," said the footman.

"Very good, Jackson. And the Master and Mistress?" asked Royman.

"The Master is out, sir, and the Mistress is taking tea in the Olive Garden."

"Thank you, Jackson," said Royman, having ascertained the location of his father and mother. He stripped off his jacket and dropped it on the floor. A maid materialized to help him on with a housecoat. The maid approached Allenson with a second housecoat, but he waved her away. He had no intention of staying for more than a polite exchange of greetings. The maid snatched up Royman's discarded jacket and vanished.

✧   ✧   ✧

The Extempore Hall was on the main floor, as were all the public rooms, the upper floor being reserved for the family's private apartments. They found Sarai reclining on a couch, reading something from a holographic stick, her legs tucked under her. Her hair was tinted violet today, to match her sleeveless day dress. Her hairstyle involved complex spirals, falling onto her bare right shoulder. Ever changing patterns of light and dark flowed up and down the spiral. Her eyes were outlined in a pigment that shimmered metallic blue when she turned her head. In short, she followed the current casual dress code for a lady of her rank and status.

She glanced up only briefly when Destry entered the room, concentrating primarily on her reading.

"Good morning, Sarai," Destry said.

She shut down the stick and carefully placed it on a side table before replying. "Good morning, Destry—Allen."

She inclined her head in Allenson's direction. He gave the short bow from the neck that was appropriate for greeting an in-law's wife. Destry went to kiss Sarai, who turned her head to offer her cheek. He seemed satisfied with such minimal intimacy. Perhaps he had little choice.

"Refreshment, Allenson?" Destry asked.

"Well, perhaps just one," Allenson replied.

"My dear?" Destry asked.

"Yes, why not?" she replied. "A Rekki fizz, I think."

Rekki fizz was the currently fashionable party drink—an expensive dry white wine diluted by natural sparkling spring water infused with herbs and blueberry juice. By chance or design, Allenson suspected the latter, the color of the drink complemented Sarai's dress and make-up.

"Fizz, capital idea," Destry said. "Service—three fizzes."

An off-white cube, about half a meter across, lifted from where it sat inconspicuously in a corner. The automaton moved silently across the room about a meter off the floor. Dust motes swirled in the air, whipped up by its drive fields. It stopped in front of a drinks cabinet. There was a pause while it downloaded instructions and waited for the cabinet to act upon them.

"I trust your enterprise was successful?" Sarai asked.

"Most certainly, my dear. I believe I have data for a new paper on the evolution of the Rider-beast relationship," Destry said.

"Indeed," Sarai said, without enthusiasm. "That's nice. And your survey, Allen, did it bear fruit?" she asked.

"I believe it will, Sarai. We acquired some valuable data on the Hinterlands and now have a map of the Continuum."

"The Hinterlands must be useful for something, although I confess that I can't imagine what that might be," Sarai said. "I suppose one needs somewhere to send undesirables."

Allenson smiled politely.

"You did not bring that friend of yours back with you?" she asked. "The one with the striking eyes."

Allenson felt a twinge of jealousy.

"No, Hawthorn had business elsewhere," Allenson answered.

The drinks cabinet opened and placed three fluted

glasses on the automaton, which extended its top surface to act as a tray. The machine moved back to Destry, who took two glasses, handing one to Sarai and the other to Allenson. Destry picked up his own drink and flipped a hand. The automaton drifted back to the corner of the room.

Allenson always found service automatons vaguely irritating. It would have been faster to pour one's own drinks. Standing around waiting for a machine to slowly complete such a simple task seemed a sinful waste of time. That was the point, he supposed. Possession of service automatons demonstrated not just that one could afford them, but that one was also wealthy enough for leisure.

He sipped his fizz, which was rather good. The bubbling air and alcohol had a refreshing zing. The wine caressed the palette with flavor following upon flavor, and the herbs left a spicy aftertaste. He sipped again, hoping that this fashion would last longer than most.

Sarai uncoiled, swinging long legs out from under her bottom and stretching them in a single fluid motion. Her gown opened along the length of her thigh. She stretched, pushing her arms back, outlining her breasts under the thin material of her dress. A gentleman would have averted his gaze, but Allenson was fixated.

He could not breathe. His stomach froze. Saliva filled his mouth, but he could not swallow. Why did she have to do that? He had been holding it all together, treating her with the cool politeness appropriate for a friend's wife. So why did she have to do that?

It was not her fault; it was his. She was younger than Destry, only two years older than Allenson, and she was elegant and beautiful. Why shouldn't she relax in her own home? She was hardly responsible for his base instincts—he was. Allenson's mind went around in a frantic loop. What a fraud he was. He had the exterior polish of a gentleman, but he secretly lusted after his friend's wife. Hawthorn was more honorable in that he was at least honest about his intentions. Hang on—what intentions—he had no intentions toward Sarai. Did he?

He was aware that he was holding his glass so tightly that his hand was shaking. He forced himself to relax, letting his breath out slowly. He flashed a guilty glance at Royman. Fortunately, his friend was looking out of the window at the gardens and so had noticed nothing. What had Sarai noticed? Had he insulted her?

Sarai was not looking at him. Thank God, she was oblivious to his social gaffe. The whisper of a smile played on her lips. A daemon whispered in his ear. Was she aware of his reaction? Did she enjoy it? Was she provoking him deliberately? He pushed the thought down, despising himself for even considering it. That was just another attempt to blame her for his weakness. He finished his drink with a gulp, taking no further pleasure in it.

"Thank you for your hospitality, Destry, Sarai, but I really should be taking my leave." Allenson bowed.

"Leave?" Sarai asked. "But you have only just got here. What have you done, husband, to offend Allenson so? Can you not prevail on him to stay longer?"

"Indeed, Allen, you are very welcome to stay," Destry replied.

"I thank you bu—"

Sarai interrupted him. "Then it must be me? Fie,

what have I done to insult you so grievously that you must rush away?"

She turned the full wattage of her gaze on him. Her irises were tinted lemon yellow to contrast against the blue shadow. He swallowed and began to babble.

"I, uh, really should get home. Long time away, things to do."

She lowered her head modestly, but he could almost imagine that he saw that faint smile again.

"After all, Allen, it's not as if anyone in the Allenson Demesne has the slightest interest in you. Your stepmother could not care less where you are. Her attention is exclusively focused on her own desires. Why not stay with more congenial company?" Sarai asked, patting the sofa cushion beside her to illustrate her point.

"Well, if you put it like that," Allenson said.

"Excellent, then the matter is settled," said Destry.

"Service—prepare the Yellow Room for a guest," Sarai said to the automaton.

The cube drifted out of the room through a door that opened automatically.

"Come now, Allen," Sarai said. "Sit beside me and regale me with stories about your adventures among the mudgrubbers."

"Well, I, ah," Allenson replied, not moving.

"Or, if you preferred, you could take a turn around the demesne with me," Destry said. "I have a new toy to show you."

The manufactorum ran on a positive air pressure intended to keep dust out, so was entered through a double door airlock. Inside, it was gleaming white.

"Impressive, don't you think?" Destry asked, pointing

at a convoluted silver machine—a two-meter cuboid; most automatons were cubic lately. The designers changed shapes every so often to stimulate sales.

"Is it working yet, Master Cruss?" Destry asked the technician who stood respectfully to one side. As a skilled employee, rather than an indentured servant, Cruss merited the title "master." Cruss's "skills" would be considered slight by the standards of the Home Worlds, but this was the Cutter Stream, where one had to take what one could get.

"Pretty much, sar," the technician replied. "We had a little problem matching the manufactorum's power fields to its inputs, but I just kept fiddling with the frequencies until all the green lights came on."

"Can we give Sar Allenson a demonstration?" Destry asked.

"Yes, sar," the technician replied. He keyed a remote control and the faint hum of energy fields filled the manufactorum. Allenson's hair stirred despite the still air and the metallic tang of ozone filled the air. He wrinkled his nose.

"There is still a bit of a mismatch between the power supply and the automaton," the technician said defensively, noticing Allenson's expression. "But enough power is getting through to make it work."

The automaton lifted off the ground and drifted toward the storage racks. It pulled modules off the racks and fitted them together in midair, rotating the composite structure as necessary. The machine paused for minutes at a time, apparently inactive. However, a green flashing hologram of a turning wheel showed that it was busy establishing connections and links within the structure. Mechanically bolting the modular components together was a trivial problem—even the technician could probably do it if he had the necessary tools—but matching the modules' sensory, control, and power systems was tricky.

After thirty minutes the automaton lowered the finished construct to the ground. The new machine was an agricultural tractor, a field automaton. It had four large solid wheels with scoops to get traction in mud. The elongate tubular body slung between them at axle height contained the drive and power systems. Sensory systems were contained on a rotating cylinder on the front. Mechanical arms at the rear deployed agricultural tools, such as ploughs and cutters.

The technician switched the tractor on with his remote. An orange hologram divided into squares appeared over the top. The technician pushed his finger through a large button, which began to flash. One by one, the orange squares flashed and turned green. When the whole hologram was green, it blinked and disappeared.

The technician bowed to Destry. "As you see, sar, I can make an automaton every forty-five minutes or so, provided we have the modules in stock."

"How many of these modules can you make here, Destry?" Allenson asked.

Destry nodded at the technician to indicate that he should answer.

"It varies from tool to tool. We have sufficient manufacturing automatons in house to make about half the modules used in this tractor, things like universal power plants, fuel cells, and drive motors, but we have to import the more complicated control and sensory modules from Brasilia," the technician replied.

"And some of the control components in the modules built here are also imported from the Home Worlds?" Destry asked.

"Yes," the technician replied.

"How long does a tractor like this last?" Allenson said.

"Not long enough," Destry replied ruefully. "There is no theoretical reason why we should not get four of five years out of them, but something critical always seems to malfunction."

"Could this construction automaton repair the field equipment?" Allenson asked, walking around it. "The machine seems sophisticated enough."

"It could be upgraded, I suppose," Destry replied. "But the intellectual property license charge on each repair would be prohibitive. It's cheaper to make new tractors."

"And we remain a reliable income stream for the Brasilian producer," Allenson said, softly. "What happened to your old construction automaton?"

"It broke," Destry shrugged. "We couldn't repair it, and it's cheaper to order a new one from Brasilia than pay shipping costs on the old one both ways across the Bight and the cost of repairs at Brasilian rates."

Allenson knew the answers to his questions before he asked them, but he was curious to hear Destry's answers or, to be more precise, to observe Destry's reaction. But there was no reaction at all. As far as his friend was concerned, the system was as it was and Destry saw no reason why it should or could be changed.

"Thank you, Master Cruss, carry on," Destry said.

Destry took out a packet and lit a cigarette, tapping

the end to initiate a thermal reaction. He inhaled deeply.

"Sorry Allenson, forgot my manners," he offered the packet to his friend.

Allenson politely declined.

"I am glad you decided to stay, Allenson," Destry said. "Sarai enjoys your company."

"Indeed," Allenson said, noncommittaly. He wondered where this conversation was going.

"Her family is at the center of society in Manzanita, and I fear she gets terribly bored here on Wagener. I take her back as often as circumstances permit but..." Destry's voice trailed off.

Sarai was a Tymbro, a wealthy merchant family with influence in the Cutter Stream legislature on Manzanita. Destry and Sarai's marriage was an arrangement between old status and new money to mutual advantage. The Destry Demesne would have faced financial ruin without Sarai's marriage settlement. Allenson often wondered if Sarai regretted the alliance. Her personal wishes would have been of little import, of course. House Tymbro would have expected her to do her duty.

There were personal advantages for her. Her social status as Lady Destry was considerably greater than Lady Tymbo, however wealthy the latter. Marriage status also gave her certain liberties denied an unwed girl from an ambitious family. But Allenson had never seen Sarai show Destry much affection, let alone passion—and she was a passionate person.

"Was there anything else you specifically wanted to see?" Allenson asked, changing the subject.

"Indeed, the jaffa fruit harvest should be well

underway. I may as well check their progress," Destry replied. He examined his cigarette. "My genesurgeon says he will insist on another cancer flush if I keep smoking so heavily." He took another long drag before dropping the cigarette and extinguishing it with his boot.

The friends climbed back onto Destry's quad-bike and continued their run through the demesne. Allenson rode pillion; at least the seat was more comfortable than that on a one-man frame. The bike had soft balloon tires, and an independent suspension and drive system designed more for traction than speed.

He enjoyed the ride. The rain had stopped and the Wagener air smelled fresh and new. Gusts of air carried traces of agricultural odors that hinted at the rich productivity of the farmland. Jaffa fruit had a distinctive clean sharp smell that became overwhelming as they neared the plantings. The crop required shelter from spring winds for early pollination, so it was grown in "rooms" surrounded by high bushes.

Early pollination meant early fruiting, and the first fruits commanded the highest prices on the Home Worlds. You could quadruple your profit margin if you could get in before the bulk of Wagener's jaffa crop ripened. Some would be shipped home as fruit but most would be dried and reconstituted as jaffa juice.

Destry parked the quad on the edge of the fields and the friends walked into one of the rooms at random. The jaffa scent was so strong that it almost made Allenson gag. The smell was almost clinical, like disinfectant, recalling unwelcome memories.

"What in bloody Hell's bloody name?" Destry asked.

The reason for such an overpowering smell was obvious. Jaffa fruits were scattered all over the ground.

Some were sliced, others crushed into the ground. Destry tore up the aisle between the bushes. At the end, a field automaton methodically stripped the bushes of fruit with ultrasonic cutters, catching the fruit in fields and dropping them into a cargo hopper.

The beam focusing was inadequate to the task, and many of the fruits fell beyond the reach of the fields. Barely half made it into the hopper unscathed. Destry hopped from foot to foot in anger.

"I gave firm instructions to use fleeks for the harvest. I even bought in extra fleeks all the way from Camphor. Our automatons are too bloody crude for this. Where the Hell is the bloody fleekmaster?"

They drove to the entrance to the next field. Inside, they discovered fleeks at work. Fleeks were chimp-sized, but more birdlike than mammalian. They had long, sturdy legs with a backward "knee" joint—but only vestigial wings. A long neck and heavy pointed beak allowed them to probe the ground for the buried eggs that were their staple diet. They were covered in thin feathers colored in bright patterns of red and green.

Fleeks were no more intelligent than chimps, but they had excellent vision and manipulatory skills. Their birdlike brains could learn complex patterns of behavior so they could be trained in agricultural work, such as picking jaffa fruit. A fleek cocked its head, selected a fruit, picked it delicately, and dropped in a hopper.

"The fleeks are making a better job of it," said Allenson.

"But there aren't enough of them," Destry said. "The fruit will rot on the bush before they can harvest it all."

The next field they tried was empty of both fleeks

and automatons. They were about to move on when the friends heard a laugh from deeper into the crop. When they investigated, they discovered a group of a half dozen servants lolling around eating the crop. One of the men was squeezing a jaffa into the open mouth of a woman lying on her back. Jaffa juice worth about five florins in a Brasilian cafe ran down her face onto the ground, and she laughed again.

"Bloody Hell," Destry said.

Allenson reflected that stress was severely reducing his friend's vocabulary, understandable considering the circumstances.

"Who's in charge here?" Destry asked. He had pink spots high on his cheeks and his voice shook.

The group rose to their feet and huddled together for protection.

"Well?" Destry asked, almost screaming the word, such was his anger.

"Please, sar, that would be the gangmaster," a servant replied.

"Where is he?" Destry asked.

The group looked at each other for support. Eventually, a woman pointed toward a thick patch of bushes. The gangmaster staggered into view, attracted by the yelling. He attempted to slip a bottle into his pocket but missed, dropping it on the ground. He was followed by a woman servant who was still in the process of adjusting her clothing to cover a substantial bosom. The gangmaster stopped dead when he saw Destry, and his face whitened. He sobered up faster than if he had taken a detox pill.

"You have ten minutes to get off this demesne," Destry said through clenched teeth.

"But I don't work for you. I am employed by the hire company to oversee their servant teams. I can't just leave," the gangmaster said, pleadingly.

"Ten minutes," Destry said, "and then my guards will have orders to shoot on sight."

The man ran, pausing only to pick up his bottle.

"Get back to work," Destry said to the servants. "I expect to see progress in this field, or I will take a whip to the lot of you."

Allenson hid a smile. His friend was a kind-hearted soul who had never whipped a servant in his life. He did not even own a whip. But the servants were apparently convinced and attended to their task with vigor.

"I go away for one miserable trip and the entire demesne falls apart," Destry said. "My father is getting old. He is Master of this estate in name only."

"We all have our cross to bear," said Allenson.

"You are thinking of your stepmother," Destry said, giving Allenson a sharp glance. "I don't know why you put up with her. You are well past maturity. By rights, control of your father's estate should pass to you."

"To Todd," Allenson said, correcting his friend. "Todd is the elder."

"Ah, yes, Todd," Destry said.

Neither spoke. The sudden appearance of a quad, driven hard, spared them further embarrassment. Destry shaded his eyes.

"The fleekmaster, good. Now we'll get some answers," Destry said.

The master was middle-aged with graying hair and beard. Life had given him a stoop. He had grown to resemble the ornithoids he trained. He jumped off the quad and hurried to Destry, bowing low.

"I'm sorry, sar, it really was not my fault. I took every precaution," the fleekmaster said. He wrung his hands together as if he were washing them. Allenson noticed that the man's knuckles were arthritic.

"What wasn't your fault?" Destry asked.

"The fleeks, Master Royston, the fleeks died. The new flock from Camphor had some disease. They passed it to our own birds before showing any symptoms," the fleekmaster said.

"Didn't you try quarantining the sick birds and dosing the rest with protective tonic?" Destry asked. "Yes, of course you did. Calm yourself, fleekmaster."

The man looked greatly relieved, as well he might. Many a master would have thrown him off the estate. At his age, it would not have been easy to find a new home and employment.

Destry took out a handkerchief and wiped his forehead.

"Bloody flies," Destry said.

Allenson knew his friend was playing for time so he could gather his thoughts.

"How many fleeks have we left?" Destry asked.

"Perhaps fifty, sar," replied the fleekmaster.

Destry sighed. "Not nearly enough."

"There is no use trying to borrow fleeks from other demesnes. They will all be at full stretch. We will have to hire in more servant labor. Round up all employees to oversee them. I won't have any more useless drunks for gangmasters in my fields," Destry said.

"Including the technicians, clerks, and social managers, sar?" the fleekmaster asked.

"I said everybody," Destry said, with a flash of temper. "I will be out in the fields myself. Anyone who thinks field work beneath them can come and discuss it with me."

The fleekmaster rushed away. From the grin on his face, he was looking forward to his task. No doubt he would take the opportunity to pay off a few old scores.

"I am sorry, Allenson, would you mind making your own way back to the house? You see how things are."

"Not at all, Destry, I am at your disposal. I will help any way I can."

Allenson liked the yellow room. Its walls were painted light yellow ocher and the roof, cream. The furniture was made from a Manzanita soft wood that came up bright lemon yellow when polished. The window caught the yellow-orange light from Wagener's setting sun, flooding the room in pastel shades. Normally the ambiance raised his spirits but not today.

He stared moodily into the full-length mirror, his shirt undone. He was supposed to be dressing for dinner, but the man in the reflection was a stranger. Oh, the image superficially resembled Allenson, but something had changed. His eyes, the windows to his soul, had hardened. They looked warily back, as if challenging him.

"You can't play the hero-worshipping little brother any longer." Those words still stabbed at him.

There was a quiet knock on his door. It opened immediately and Sarai entered, closing the door quietly behind her. She was still dressed in casual daywear. She walked slowly across the room in small steps, putting one foot directly in front of the other so that her hips swung rhythmically. The hard-eyed man in the mirror watched her, and Allenson watched him.

Sarai stopped a meter away and tilted her head. "Fie Allen, I clearly *have* offended you. You lurk up here rather than entertaining me, and now you won't even face me. What coldness! Has the Hinterlands frozen your affections?"

He turned. "Sorry. I have been resting, Sarai, and I did not wish to compromise your honor by seeing you without your husband."

She laughed and slid her right foot forward, causing her dress to fall away from her leg. Allenson could not help but notice.

"But you are family, Allen. Are you not Royman's brother-in-law? He doesn't care. If you carry on like this, I shall wonder about your motives," she said, mimicking a look of exaggerated shock.

"Sarai..." He paused, unsure what to say.

She took a step forward, moving within his personal space, and placed her hand on his chest. It burned his bare skin like frozen nitrogen.

"Sarai..." he said, trying again.

"Shush," she replied, moving her finger to his lips.

She cupped his chin, stroked his neck, and ran her fingers lightly down his chest. He trembled.

"So, not so frigid after all," she said, throatily.

He moved closer, until they touched, and put his hands around her slender waist. She tilted her head back and gazed up at him with electric blue eyes. How could he not kiss her? Allenson ceased to care that his behavior was way beyond the socially acceptable.

Sarai still had her hand on his chest. She pushed him away. He grabbed her shoulders, pulling her back. Allenson was a strong man and easily overcame her token resistance. As he bent to kiss her again, he caught a flash of something in her eyes—triumph.

He had a flash of self-awareness. This was exactly what she wanted, a way that gave her power without responsibility. He would be the aggressor who would bear the blame. She would have that hold over him forevermore, a chain around his neck to be yanked at will—her will. He stopped, passion chilled, and pushed her away.

"What in Hell do you want from me, Sarai?" he asked, trying to make her say it, to involve her in the guilt.

"How would I know?" she shouted. "You're supposed to be the man."

He flushed, and almost reached out for her in temper. Checking himself, he replied, wearily, "Get out, Sarai."

She ran from the room, slamming the door so hard that the sound must have echoed through the mansion.

CHAPTER 9

Mowzelle

Allenson left early the next morning. Mowzelle, the Allenson compound, was ten minutes hard pedaling away, but he was in the mood for exercise; anything to burn away his frustration. Such passion frightened him. He suspected that Sarai was equally scared, hence her manipulative behavior.

He was a gentleman and Sarai was a lady. They both knew what society considered proper behavior. A carefully conducted affair between social equals was one thing, but the strength of feeling between the two of them threatened to overcome all discretion. An open love affair would force Destry to call him out or be publically humiliated as a cuckold. How could he do that to his friend? How could he do that to Sarai? It would be an utter social disaster.

Destry probably hoped that Allenson and his wife would have a quiet affair and get it out of their system. Fidelity was not particularly prized in the arranged marriages of Destry's class, but social propriety was quite another matter. Could he and Sarai have an

affair by the rules? He shut the thought down. It was
too dangerous, too tempting, and he knew it would
not work. He knew that he would never get enough
of Sarai. He was not the sort of man to have affairs.
There could be no happy ending down that road, just
misery and shame.

He locked on to the Allenson compound beacon
and let the machine guide him in. He knew Wagener
like he knew his own bedroom layout, but he felt like
letting something else make some decisions.

The frame dropped with mechanical competence
onto stabilized soil inside the high fence surrounding
the compound. The fence was topped with razor-wire
to discourage petty thieves and keep out Wagener's
wildlife, although there was precious little in the
way of large indigenous animals left in the area. The
main house stood in the center of a cluster of sheds
and servant sleeping accommodations, like a flagship
in the midst of its flotilla. Only one of the servant
barracks was currently used, so the rest doubled as
storage rooms.

The Allenson family property was not quite grand
enough to be classed as a demesne. The house was a
comfortable two-story brick cottage with six bedrooms
upstairs and family and social rooms below. At some
point an owner had added a small portico made of
stabilized sand plastered to look like marble. It jarred
horribly with the style of the rest of the cottage. His
father had wanted to knock it down, but Bella, his
stepmother, considered the monstrosity classy.

He unpacked his frame and stacked it in the portico. Petersen, the steward, insisted on helping him.
This was not particularly helpful, as the steward was

stooped by advanced years. He had been in the employ of the Allensons for many years. Todd had paid for basic rejuvenation therapy for Petersen, but only so much could be achieved.

"Good trip, sar?" Petersen asked.

"Productive, if exhausting. I trust all is well at Mowzelle?" Allenson asked.

"Yes, sar, I have been testing and charging up the automatons for the next ploughing," Petersen replied.

"How are they holding up?" Allenson asked.

"Tolerably well, sar. One refused to take a charge, so I have had it dumped. Another keeps losing direction, but the reset button seems to cure the problem," Petersen replied.

Allenson sighed. "Try to keep it going. My stepmother will be reluctant to purchase a new one."

He paused to look around the compound. Many of the sheds were in poor condition and showed signs of patching. He noticed that the barn roof had lost part of its waterproofing.

Petersen noticed his interest. "We had a twister while you were away, sar. It was only a small one, but the roof was already in a bad way."

Allenson's stepmother could never grasp that money saved on maintenance was no saving at all but simply a greater cost delayed.

"I had the servants fix the sheds, but my knee has been playing up and I did not trust myself on a ladder," Petersen said, apologetically.

"What do you mean?" Allenson asked, astonished. "I do not expect you to be climbing ladders at your age. Send a servant."

Petersen hung his head and did not reply. This

was an old problem. In the absence of authority, indentured servants saw no reason to do anything but the bare minimum. The steward lacked the necessary respect to command obedience, and Bella would not back him up. Allenson spotted one of the servants, a young man, ambling across the compound as if he were on holiday.

"You!" Allenson yelled, gesturing at him.

The servant took his time. He appeared to be chewing something.

"What are you doing?" Allenson asked.

"I'm helping Sylvia feed the chickens," he replied, not bothering to remove his hands from his pockets.

"Stand up straight when I address you," Allenson said.

The servant stared at him blankly, mouth open in astonishment, before he hurried to comply.

"Sylvia will have to manage the chickens on her own. You will fix that barn under Master Petersen's supervision and you will do it right. I will be out to inspect the results in one hour and I will sell your contract to a logging company if the job has not been done to Master Petersen's satisfaction. Do you understand me?" Allenson asked.

The servant gawped.

"Well?" Allenson asked.

"Yes, sar."

"Then you had better get on with it. The clock is ticking."

The servant shot off in the direction of an equipment store.

Allenson raised his voice so that his words carried across the compound. "Things are way too lax, Master

Petersen. Let me know if you see signs of slackness, any at all, and I will deal with the culprits personally."

"Yes, sar," Petersen replied.

Allenson winked at him.

"Where have you been?" asked Bella.

Welcome home, Allenson thought.

"Don't bother to lie about it. I know where you have been. You have been gadding around with your snooty friends again instead of coming straight home, without a thought for my feelings," she said in a whining voice that grated on his nerves.

What had his father ever seen in the wretched woman? That was a rhetorical question not worth wasting time over. It was not the first time it had occurred to him.

"I had business at Destry," he said, adopting a reasonable tone.

After all, the woman was his stepmother and her rank deserved respect, whatever he thought of her as an individual.

"You!" he said to a female servant hovering nearby. "Make us some tea and serve it in the drawing room, please."

"You have no right to order my servants around," Bella said. "I heard you yelling outside."

The servant hesitated. Allenson gave her a look, and she scuttled off. News traveled fast in the servants' quarters. Allenson walked to the drawing room, forcing Bella to follow if she wished to continue the conversation. She talked at him, raising old grievances and slights. Allenson waited until she ran down, which took some time.

"Have you news of Todd?" she eventually asked.

"I saw him on Paragon. Todd is desperately ill and the prognosis is poor," Allenson replied.

"You mean he's going to die," she said.

"Yes," Allenson replied.

"Oh, my poor Todd," she said, beating her forehead with her fist in the traditional display of grief. "He was the best of you, as true and decent a man that ever lived. He married well and made something of himself."

Unlike you, Allenson thought, predicting her next accusation from experience.

"Unlike you, who just waste your time gallivanting around with your rich friends and that horrible Hawthorn fellow. He was always a bad 'un."

The wailing abruptly halted. You could almost see a new idea entering her mind and being digested.

"You are Todd's executor?" she asked.

He confirmed the truth of the matter with a nod.

"Has he left me a property or a pension in his will?" she asked.

"No," Allenson replied. "It is left in trust for his children."

"And where does that leave me?" she wailed. "Todd was the only one who cared for me. He let me keep Mowzelle and its income. Now I suppose you will want Mowzelle, and I shall be thrown out into the street to starve."

"Calm yourself, stepmother," Allenson said with an evenness that he did not feel. "I have no intention of seeing you impoverished."

Right now, Allenson wished he had the moral courage to do just that.

Bella gave him a crafty look. "You say fair words now in the hope that I will sign over Mowzelle to you, but once you have it you will get rid of me like a sick fleek."

"That's not true," Allenson said.

"Well, I won't sign," she said, defiantly. "I will appeal to the Governor if necessary. I will instruct a solicitor to drag the case out for years; you see if I don't."

Allenson found the whole conversation distasteful. He changed the subject.

"I will be leaving early in the morning for Manzanita. I have business there with the Governor's Office."

Bella's face twisted in fury. "You see! You've just got back and you're off again already. You're a wastrel. You have no sense of filial duty. I'm entitled to your support."

"You know what, Bella?" Allenson asked, patience finally cracking. "I think I'll leave right now."

He stormed to the door, where he collided with a servant coming in with a tray. Teapot, crockery, and finger cakes were thrown across the floor.

"Tea," Allenson said, "is canceled!"

Outside, Allenson stopped and took a few deep breaths to allow his temper to dissipate. Once calm, he considered his options. He was tempted to return to the Destry Demesne where he could get a hot meal and a comfortable room, but that meant dealing with Sarai, and that he could not face. He would have to bed down in one of the unused bunkhouses.

He selected the only one with an intact roof and pushed open the door. The smell caused him to gag. There was an explosion of motion. Multi-legged skinks ran in all directions to escape the light, fleeing from the rotting corpse of a fleek. A cloud of flying bugs lifted off the rotting meat in a shrill whine of beating wing membranes. One of the skinks ran between his legs in blind panic, stubby legs churning as it fled around the corner of the barracks. Allenson backed out, pulling the door shut.

"Can I help you, sar?" Petersen asked.

"Good grief, man, don't sneak up on me like that," Allenson said, startled by the man's sudden appearance. "I have had enough shocks for one afternoon."

"Sorry, sar," Petersen said.

"I thought that there were no fleeks at Mowzelle?" Allenson asked.

"That's right, sar," Petersen said.

"Then how..." Allenson began before biting his tongue. There were some mysteries best left unsolved. "I need to sleep in one of the equipment sheds tonight. Which one do you recommend?"

"None of them," Petersen said, succinctly. "I heard that there had been some..." Petersen paused, choosing his next word carefully, "discussion in the House."

Discussion was a suitably neutral word. Allenson had long since stopped marveling at how fast word sped from the House out to the servants' quarters.

"You might say that," Allenson replied, wondering where the conversation was heading.

"My wife and I would be pleased to offer you the spare room in our cabin tonight," Petersen said.

The next day, Allenson checked his datapad. It pinpointed the last known location of Hawthorn's frame at Farnen, Wagener's commercial center. Cargo tramps landed there, shuttling goods in and out along the local trade routes. He attempted to ping Hawthorn without success. It was probably too early in the morning for his friend, despite Farnen being to the east of Mowzelle and hence down-sun. Allenson assembled his frame. If Mohammad would not go to the mountain, then the mountain had to go to Farnen.

Allenson landed in the compound of the Wayfarer Inn, which was part of Farnen Town, a residential district that stood a little apart from the port. The town boasted only one paved road, unimaginatively named The Street. Along its length stood terraces of high syncrete buildings, with shops and commercial offices on the ground floor and living accommodation above. Alleys between the terraces gave access to villas that served as townhouses for Wagener's elite, and the mercantile and government agents. The Wayfarer compound occupied an entire block along The Street. It rented rooms to minor nobility, like Allenson, who could not afford the upkeep of a townhouse, and also served as a restaurant and lounge for respectable women who wished to avoid the more exciting entertainment to be found in the Port.

It was late afternoon in Farnen Town when Allenson arrived and checked in. Regular frame users learned to be flexible about such things as meals and sleeping times. Even so, Allenson was starting to feel the effects of too many time zones in too short a time. He decided to take tea and relax. He had much to mull over and much to plan.

In the lounge, a group of ladies were entertained by a slim girl who sang soft songs about love and dying of a broken heart and consumption. Few of her audience looked likely to be stricken by such a fate.

"Sar?" a waitress materialized at his elbow. -

She was middle-aged. Her uniform of dark blue dress indicated that she was an employee rather than a servant. Servants would only be used in backroom positions where they would not be seen by the guests. That was one reason the Wayfarer's prices were so high; employees were expensive. Another reason was to keep out the riff-raff.

"I think a cafay-chocolat," Allenson said, perusing the menu. He left the final "t" silent, to demonstrate that he was a gentleman. "A carafe, please. Book it to room seven."

"Room seven, one carafe of cafay-chocolat," the waitress repeated. "At once, sar."

The waitress took a long time over such a simple order. Allenson reflected that the more expensive the house, the greater the expected gratuity, and the slower the service. Presumably, in a really top-hole establishment on a Home World, one ordered a drink three weeks in advance or camped out on the porch.

While he waited, he perused the latest financial figures for Mowzelle that the steward had downloaded for him. They made grim reading. The estate was barely holding its own. To be fair to his stepmother, it was only Bella's frugal life style that balanced the books. The trouble was that she applied the same frugality to everything. Mowzelle had not enough workers, not enough automatons, and no fleeks.

He agreed with Bella about the fleeks, but for different reasons. His stepmother disliked fleeks as naughty smelly things and she had often remarked that their cawing gave her the shivers. Allenson disliked them because they were expensive and inefficient. They could be decent workers if properly trained. But you needed a decent fleekmaster and those were in short supply. And, as like as not, a devastating plague would sweep through the trained flock and one would have to start all over again.

Mowzelle should be prosperous, situated as it was on good agricultural land within easy reach of Farnen Port, but the system in the Cutter Stream Worlds was so wasteful and inefficient. The indentured servant system meant that the colonies were awash with the unwanted underclass of the Home Worlds. Such people had few skills and even less motivation.

Skilled employees were in short supply. One had to pay ridiculous wages to attract capable young people on short-term contracts. Most employees were drawn from people who had already failed to make a living in the Home Worlds, or had some pressing reason to emigrate.

One demesne manager had recommended that Allenson hire drunks on the grounds that at least you knew what their problem was, and you could get some decent work out of them if you kept them off the sauce. That particular manager had fled Brasilia after a scandal concerning underage girls, one of which had turned out to belong to a gens powerful enough to demand retribution.

Mowzelle was trapped in an economic swamp. It could not afford to hire a more dynamic assistant to support the steward as two salaries were beyond its means. Allenson could not stomach replacing the steward, who was a loyal and long standing retainer. Therefore, the indentured servants barely did enough work to cover their food and clothing expenses. The smallholding relied heavily on automatons, which had to be replaced from an outside supplier when they broke—something that happened with monotonous regularity. It was not just Mowzelle. The Cutter Stream socioeconomic system stank. Mowzelle was just a rather worse example than most.

For many reasons, Allenson shrank from forcing Bella to sign over the property so he could sort the place out. Not least was that he dreaded the life of a smallholder. He classed the problem as one for another day and put down his datapad. His immediate problem was how to persuade the Governor to confirm him in Todd's place as Inspector General of Militia. He needed to think this through carefully.

The entertainer had moved on to a song about unrequited love and was pondering whether to cast herself into the Continuum or to wander the streets as a beggar, a permanent admonishment to the man who had done her wrong. Looking around the room, Allenson was struck by how little interest most of the ladies showed in the song. Surely the entertainment was the whole point of the exercise? What other reason could they have to climb into uncomfortable finery and sit exchanging polite chit-chat while drinking endless cups of overpriced tea?

Allenson had a sudden flash of insight. The singer was the excuse, not the reason. The purpose of a lady attending such a function was to be seen in the right company. In that way she cemented her social status. That was why the ladies were wearing the most fashionable and expensive clothes that they could afford. The display was all.

He almost laughed out loud. Now he had a plan.

❖   ❖   ❖

"Oy, watch your back!"

Allenson leapt to one side of the unpaved road just in time to avoid a tractor towing a container trolley. It splashed mud onto his trousers.

"Tosser!" yelled the brawny woman driving the tractor.

Allenson raised a hand in acknowledgment. He had been standing in the middle of the road, checking his datapad with his back to the traffic. Farnen Port bred an independent class of self employed workers who were notorious for their lack of deference to their betters. The woman probably owned her own vehicle and worked under contract rather than being an employee or a servant.

He picked up his datapad and wiped the mud off. It proved once more what a tough piece of kit it was by flashing green. Hawthorn was still not answering messages, but his datapad was switched on, so Allenson could easily track him down.

His trail led to a one-story wooden tavern on the edge of the main strip. From the noise level, a party of some intensity was in process. Allenson sighed and stowed his pad safely away in a sealed pocket. He took a deep breath and entered. A seething mass of individuals swayed backward and forward in an attempt to assault each other with fists or blunt instruments.

Allenson picked his way clockwise around the edge of the room, stepping over casualties as necessary. An elderly drunk circled toward him in an anticlockwise direction, on the lookout for untended drinks. A bottle tempted the drunk to venture too far into the fray, and he disappeared beneath the battling throng.

The barman was engaged in leaning over the bar waving a blackjack. He struck out indiscriminately at any customer within range. A man in a checkered shirt pinned an opponent against the bar. He proceeded to throttle his victim until the latter's face turned purple. The barman took checked shirt down with a single forehand strike to the temple. Purple face turned to express his thanks, but the barman got him on the backswing.

Allenson searched the struggling bodies for his friend. Occasionally he caught sight of a flash of blond hair. Hawthorn suddenly flew through out of the scrum and landed almost at Allenson's feet.

"I need to talk to you," Allenson said, lifting his friend up.

"Did you see that big bugger in the red bandana?" Hawthorn asked. "He got in a lucky blow when I wasn't looking. But I'll have him, see if I don't."

Hawthorn threw himself back into the fray. Allenson sighed. A drunk in a boiler suit reeled toward him and swung a roundhouse blow. The punch was so slow that Allenson could have read a good book before dealing with it. He leaned back so the punch missed. Momentum swung the drunk around. Allenson took a firm grip on the neck and seat of the boiler suit and hurled the drunk headfirst into the confused mass. Several fighters broke his fall, the whole lot going down like dominoes. Hawthorn crawled out from underneath.

"I had him. I had the swine cold when someone dropped a drunk on my head," Hawthorn said, indignantly.

Allenson took a firm grip on his friend's arm and

hauled him upright. He maintained the grip this time and steered for the exit.

"Where are we going?" Hawthorn asked.

"Outside. I need your help," Allenson replied.

"Tell me that you're pulling my leg, please?" Hawthorn pleaded. "I look like the doorman from a Terran brothel."

"You look fine," Allenson replied. "I need an aide when I go to Manzanita, and my aide must look the part with an appropriate uniform."

Hawthorn re-examined himself in the tailor's full-length mirror. The basic color of the suit was navy blue, but that was where sobriety ended. It sported silver buttons decorated in starbursts, silver epaulettes with silver tassels and additional silver starburst decorations on the breast. Matching silver buckles and laces on the shoes served to reinforce the theme, just in case a casual observer had missed it. The jacket sleeves were fashionably slashed to show a plush scarlet lining. Stripes in the same color ran down the trouser seams. There was even a blue hat with a scarlet band and a spray of silver feathers.

"If I may say so, sar carries off the suit awfully well," said the tailor. "Sar cuts a dashing figure in navy blue."

"Do you think so?" Hawthorn asked, doubtfully.

"Indeed, I am sure the ladies will be similarly impressed," the tailor replied, confidently.

"Hmm." Hawthorn turned sideways to examine his profile. "I suppose it does have certain flamboyant elegance."

Allenson hid a smile. The tailor was a shrewd

judge of character and knew just how to pitch his wares to a client.

"Well, I suppose if *you* are going dressed as an ice cream cone..." Hawthorn said.

Allenson winced. His own outfit was primarily yellow ocher topped off with a white jacket and feathered hat. He did look like an ad for frozen confectionary, but he could hardly help that. Nothing ever seemed to suit him, no matter how expensive the tailoring. That was why Hawthorn's support was so important to his enterprise. Hawthorn would have looked good in a field servant smock.

"Excellent. Then it's agreed," Allenson said, turning to the tailor. "Please charge the invoice to the Allenson account."

The tailor made no move to comply. He wrung his hands and would not meet Allenson's eye.

"Would that be the Allensons of Mowzelle account, sar?" the tailor asked.

Allenson grasped the problem. He wondered how much debt his stepmother had accrued among Farnen's tradesmen.

"Ah, no, charge it to the Allensons of Pentire account," Allenson replied.

Pentire was Todd and Linsye's demesne.

"Of course, sar," the tailor said, brightening up.

"And we hope to enjoy your patronage again, Sar Allenson," the tailor said unctuously, bowing and showing them to the door.

"Linsye will approve," Allenson said, defensively. He was conscious of blushing.

"You don't have to explain yourself to me," Hawthorn said.

"No, well, I would not wish you to think I was taking advantage of my position as Todd's executor," Allenson said.

Hawthorn laughed. "Of course you are taking advantage. What is the use of a position if you don't take advantage of it? I do not think you are taking *improper* advantage, Allenson. You're the least improper person I know."

They took the bus back to Farnen Town to avoid walking along the muddy track in their finery. The bus was a trailer with bench seats, towed behind one of the ubiquitous tractors. The other passengers eyed the friends with astonishment. People in expensive clothes normally used private carriages.

An oaf sniggered at them. Hawthorn quelled him with a glance. The girl traveling with him examined Hawthorn with a bold eye and tossed her hair. Hawthorn rewarded her with a broad smile. The oaf simmered but was wise enough to let it go. Allenson hoped that he would not take it out on the girl later, but she did look as if she could take care of herself.

They debussed in The Street. The tractor driver parked where his passengers could step straight onto the pavement.

"What now?" Hawthorn asked.

"Now we arrange our transport to Manzanita," Allenson replied.

He pointed to a shop that advertised chauffeur-driven "Continuum carriages" for hire. An illustration depicted one of their conveyances. It was a large frame with two seats at the rear, on which lounged a gentleman and his lady, drinking from ornate glasses. The center was packed with flywheel motors. These were spun to maximum revs before entering the Continuum to supply power on the journey. The chauffeur sat at the front. He had pedals, but they would do little more than maintain the reality field if the motors failed.

An experienced single-seat frame pilot acquired a feel for the transient local eddies in the Continuum and positioned his agile craft accordingly to take maximum advantage, something that was just not possible in the underpowered carriage.

"What?" Hawthorn asked, aghast. "Those things are slow and so limited in range. Why don't we use our personal frames? They took us through the Hinterlands."

"The carriage has enough stored power to worldhop around the Cutter Stream," Allenson replied. "We don't need to travel efficiently; we need to travel like gentlemen. We must be seen to be men of substance. The display is all."

· CHAPTER 10 ·

Manzanita

It was not a pleasant trip through the Continuum. The carriage was too large to ride easily over the energy waves and too small to shove through them, so it tended to pitch and toss. The centrally located chauffeur was least disturbed, as the hull tended to rotate around him, but the passenger seats at the back got the full pendulum effect.

"Are you feeling all right, Allenson? You've gone a rather peculiar color," Hawthorn said.

"Of course," Allenson replied. His stomach lurches in counter corkscrew to their conveyance gave him the lie.

"Hmmm," Hawthorn, said, fiddling around in the complimentary drinks and snacks cabinet, which was positioned on his side of the carriage, so a gentleman could serve his lady, or an aide his superior.

"Perhaps food would settle your stomach," Hawthorn said sympathetically.

He thrust something in Allenson's face. The rich aroma of greasy sausage and spiced tomato oil invaded Allenson's nasal passages. It was the final straw.

Allenson managed to keep his stomach contents down, but it was touch and go. An iron will alone would not have sufficed, but in this case will was buttressed by sheer horror at the humiliation of arriving at Manzanita in a vomit-stained dress uniform. Nevertheless, acid seared the back of his throat.

Allenson glared at Hawthorn, who shrugged and dropped the offending hot dog into the waste tube.

"Sorry, only trying to help," Hawthorn said, holding a hand up in a conciliatory gesture.

"I suppose you don't have any problems with motion sickness?" Allenson asked through gritted teeth.

"Ah no, I have a robust constitution," Hawthorn replied.

The chauffeur coughed before Allenson could formulate a reply, which was probably fortunate, as several possibilities had sprung to mind and none were gentlemanly.

"The sar might find the Traveler's Companion refreshing," the chauffeur said, diplomatically. "You will find it with the drinks."

Hawthorn located the dispenser and poured a generous measure into a fluted wine glass. Allenson eyed the blue fluid suspiciously. He had no wish to arrive sedated. At that moment his stomach attempted a backward roll as his seat lurched sideways and up, before dropping like a sick fleek. He gulped the drink down. The effect was instantaneous, almost magical. It smoothed away the pain of the acid burn and his nausea disappeared.

"You know," Allenson said. "I believe I am a little peckish after all. Perhaps I might trouble you for another sausage and some berry soda."

Hawthorn grinned and did the honors. "I will also keep a glass of the Traveler's Companion handy. In case you need further, um, refreshing."

As Hawthorn predicted, it was a slow trip.

Hawthorn had a marvelous ability to shut down when he was bored, to withdraw inside himself. He almost seemed to need this time. Allenson often wondered what was going on in his friend's mind at such moments.

Allenson bored easily and needed diversion. The carriage trip would normally have been a severe trial, but not this time. He spent the journey picking over the political arguments he would deploy to the governor. The prospect of the meeting filled him with dread. Given the choice, he would rather face an entire clan of Riders armed only with his fluted wine glass than negotiate with a Brasilian functionary.

Todd had been the head of the Allenson family, the outgoing brother who could talk with servants and senators and treat them—well, not the same— but appropriately. Nothing worried Todd, unlike his younger brother who was racked by insecurity, but Todd was probably already dead. The mantle now fell on Allenson's shoulders. Linsye was right. He had to grow up.

Slowly, grindingly slowly, the carriage reached Manzanita. The shadow of the world darkened the Continuum ahead when the carriage was hit by an energy pulse. It keeled over and the frame field flickered. Allenson had the impression of a leviathan moving silently past.

"Sorry, sars, that must have been an interworld ship," the chauffeur said.

He engaged the autopilot and the carriage steadied back on course to the world. It slowed and partially phased on reaching Manzanita so that its passengers could enjoy a scenic view, and the chauffeur could watch out for other frames. There was too much traffic in and out of Manzanita City to allow frames to phase directly onto the urban area.

Allenson could see the land below was broken into compounds and demesnes similar to those on Wagener. Perhaps they were more intensively farmed, but that was a difference of degree rather than kind.

The five hundred square kloms of Lake Manzanita was the dominating regional feature. The carriage circled around the port of Clearwater on the shore of the lake. A large interworld cargo ship sat on a concrete landing apron, looking like a gray rectangular brick covered in pins. Hatches opened on the upper surface and the air shimmered above the ship. Superheated steam blasted upward before coalescing into a mushroom cloud of white vapor that shadowed the ground underneath as it spread out.

"That's the ship that must have caused the bow wave that hit us," said the chauffeur. "They've only started to vent heat so they must have just landed."

"Quick work," Allenson said. "I would not have thought it possible to connect the water hoses in that short time."

"They don't hang around. Time is money to those interworld guys," said the chauffeur.

Container ships crossing the Bight used fusion motors that supplied an infinite stream of energy. The problem was heat buildup. The ships had iron heat sinks that were chilled to near absolute zero before sailing. Heat sink capacity limited a ship's range and speed. The further, or faster, a ship traveled, the more heat had to be stored. This required larger heat sinks. The extra iron in the larger sinks created greater drag so the ship used more energy to move, creating more heat, requiring more iron for the heat sinks, and so on. It all ate into cargo capacity, raising the cost of transport per ton. The Cutter Stream current across the Bight gave just enough help to make the shipping lane economically viable. A current flowing down a similar chasm in the Continuum from the Brasilian Colonies around the interworld port at Perseverance boosted ships back to the home worlds.

On landing, freshwater was forced into the ship and superheated steam vented. It would take two or three days to flush the heat out of the ship and then chill the sinks using onboard systems. By that time, rain would be falling all across the region. The vast military and civilian ports on the home worlds used closed systems to extract waste ship heat, preventing climate instability and supplying useful energy. Such expensive technology was beyond the reach of the Cutter Stream Colonies and not really required, given the limited interworld traffic.

Colonial ports required a large supply of cheaply available freshwater. Salt water would not do as it clogged ships' heat exchangers. Lake Manzanita offered an unending supply of free freshwater. And so Manzanita City had grown into the largest city and administrative capital of the five worlds of the Cutter Stream.

There were two empty aprons large enough to dock interworld ships. Loaded interworld ships were heavy and surprisingly fragile. They required hard stands that were perfectly flat to within a millimeter, and that stayed flat under great weight. Otherwise the stresses on a loaded hull would exceed tolerances. So the aprons were reinforced with ten meters of layered syncrete.

Military transports and pleasure yachts had reinforced hulls and self-leveling landing struts capable of withstanding the stresses of soft landing sites, but this raised operating costs and severely limited cargo capacity. Even with these modifications, disasters occurred, such as when a landing strut on the cruise liner *Morning Gold* broke through the roof of an underground stream, cracking open the hull. Casualties were few, but the wreckage had served as a useful source of luxury items for the colonists.

Worse catastrophes had occurred. An entrepreneur had tried to set up an interworld port on Wagener, but had cut costs by using substandard local syncrete on the landing apron. Subsidence caused the apron to crack under the first loaded interworld ship to dock.

The entrepreneur escaped prosecution only because he was vaporized when the ship broke its back and its heat sinks failed. The builder was sued by vengeful investors who doubted his explanation for the catastrophe—a freak meteor strike. He fled Wagener the day before the court case, disappearing into the Hinterlands never to be seen again.

The crater became something of a ghoulish tourist attraction. An enterprising hotelier had done quite well out of a romantic vacation lodge there, until one of his competitors started a rumor that residual radiation in the crater caused impotence and acne.

Half a dozen small tramp-ships squatted on less impressive hard stands strung along the shore of Lake Manzanita. These were short-range vessels that moved goods in and around the various colonies, including Farnen Port on Wagener. One tramp had been cannibalized; the pylons were gone and a cargo door was missing.

The carriage left Clearwater and moved out over the lake, paralleling the causeway that ran to the island on which stood Manzanita City. Manzanita government buildings clustered around a plaza at the end of the causeway. The commercial district in the center of the island boasted a cluster of high rise structures, some up to five stories. Villas were dotted among gardens along the shore. and townhouses crowded together anywhere there was a space. At least ten thousand people lived on the island, making Manzanita City the greatest center of population in The Stream. Allenson had always found the place immensely disturbing.

The social structure on Wagener was reassuringly simple. There were only three classes: the gentry who owned the land; the middle classes who were small-holders, tradesman, and employees; and the indentured servants. Allenson knew exactly where he stood in the social pecking order. But Manzanita City society had many more layers and parallel vertical structures. The agents of the shipping houses and mercantile combines were not gentry but they were wealthy and powerful, possessing a greater sophistication than any of the Wagener families save the Destrys. Then there were the technocrats who ran the bureaucracy, who were appointed from the clients of the senior gens of Brasilia. They spoke with the authority of both the

Republic and of their aristocratic masters. Allenson found it difficult to navigate his way through this social minefield.

On Wagener, Allenson was a big fish in a small pond. Manzanita City was an ocean by comparison, an ocean filled with sharks and barracuda.

The friends' carriage headed for the VIP drop-off point in the plaza, right outside the Council House. They had to wait some little time in line for their turn to land. Allenson found the short delay interminable and he fidgeted, unnecessarily adjusting the hang of his jacket. It was tempting to tell the chauffeur to head for a less busy location, but that would have sabotaged his entire purpose.

Hawthorn alighted first and deferentially held open the carriage door for Allenson to step onto the red-carpeted platform. Only Allenson saw Hawthorn's smirk. He had an urge to giggle nervously, but instead fixed his face into a bored expression, as if he had not opened a door since he came of age.

Hawthorn slammed the door shut and spun a half-crown to the chauffeur. The man plucked it expertly from the air before phasing out the carriage. A *maître d'affaires* stood at the end of the platform, watching Allenson with disinterest. Seen one colonial gentleman, seen them all, his demeanor implied.

The *maître* was splendidly attired in the purple and gray colors of the Manzanita bureaucracy. Of course, he made no attempt to speak to Allenson personally. Hawthorn marched across the carpet and whispered something into the *maître's* ear. The man had to remove his gold-brimmed cap and tilt his head as Hawthorn overtopped him by nearly half a meter.

Indigo flashed as a half-crown changed hands. Allenson reflected that politics was proving to be an expensive business. Hawthorn retreated to stand by Allenson.

The *maître* touched his lapel to activate a microphone. "Sar Allen Allenson of Pentire, Acting Inspector General for Military Forces of the Cutter Stream to see Sar Stane Fontenoy, Vice-Governor of the Cutter Stream."

His voice boomed out of hidden speakers all around the Plaza, carefully orchestrated with delays so that the words arrived like a series of diminishing echoes. Allenson's name and picture would already be logged with Fontenoy's appointment secretary and such other officials as might need the information. The *maître* unclicked the catch fastening the twisted golden strands that roped of the back of the platform. Allenson walked off the platform, followed by Hawthorn.

Officials, merchants and gentlemen stopped their conversations to examine Allenson. Sharp glances assessed the new player. Some did not seem overly impressed; others looked thoughtful, obviously assessing how this interloper might impinge on their own interests.

Allenson had an urge to break into a jog, to clear the focus of interest as fast as possible. He forced himself to ignore the gawpers and use slow measured steps. The display was all.

Hawthorn wrinkled his nose. "The air pollution over Manzanita isn't getting any better." He looked around. "Impressive architecture though."

The dome of the Council House sparkled silver in Manzanita's harsh blue-tinted sunlight, making Allenson squint. The Cutter Stream Legislature met in the theater beneath the structure. The dome sat atop a blockish rectangular building that was faced with a dark gray stone laced with purple marbling. It looked like a novelty cake.

"Something was lost when they resized the plans from the original," Allenson said, shading his eyes.

"The Palace of the Council on Brasilia is more impressive, then?" Hawthorn asked.

"I have never seen it in the flesh," Allenson replied, carefully, "but the original design looks more balanced in pictures."

"Ah, pictures." Hawthorn snorted cynically. "Girls always look prettier in their portraits—and men taller."

He paused and gave Allenson a quizzical look. "Are we going in or what?"

"Yes, ah, yes definitely," Allenson replied.

He took a deep breath and marched across the plaza.

They passed through a static field inside the portico of the Council House that cleaned and conditioned the air. It lifted their hair and rustled their clothes.

A cough sounded.

"Perhaps the gentlemen would care to refresh themselves from the rigors of travel." An attendant in a purple and gray worksuit indicated that they should enter an atrium.

An entire team of flunkies fussed over them with brushes, polishing cloths, and refresher sprays. When the attendants had finished, they walked around the friends with two full-length mirrors so they could observe themselves in the round. Actually, their appearance was much improved. Hawthorn doled out more coins, threepences this time. A strict class hierarchy governed gratuities.

Spiralled gray columns decorated by purple mineral veins supported the hypostyle's high roof. Purple and gray square flags paved the floor, reinforcing the corporate color scheme. The walls were decorated with mythical scenes from Old Earth. Cavemen armed with muskets and pikes hunted fabulous creatures such as dragons, blue whales, unicorns and kangaroos.

The hypostyle's sound dampers were either switched off or reversed. Footsteps could be heard clearly from all over the hall, echoing of the walls. Young women, in gray employee dresses and purple hair, manned reception podia that were scattered at random throughout the hall like a handful of pebbles thrown across the floor. Allenson picked the nearest free podium. The sounds of the hall cut the instant he entered the podium's damper field. The girl glanced down at her screen.

"Sars Allenson and Hawthorn, to see the Vice-Governor," the girl said, before Allenson could open his mouth.

She waited patiently, her eyes lingering momentarily on Hawthorn. Allenson hesitated before deciding that her statement was actually a question and that she wanted confirmation. He hesitated; pretty young employees tended to unnerve him.

"Yes, Inspector General Allenson of Pentire and his aide to see Vice-Governor Fontenoy on a matter of some urgency," Hawthorn said, cutting in.

The girl touched her screen and frowned. "You don't have an appointment. The Governor is extremely busy. Perhaps if you could come back tomorrow?"

Allenson flushed. This was precisely the sort of run-around that he had feared. His status would fall immediately if he was publically rebuffed and forced to join the end of the line.

Hawthorn turned the full mega-wattage of his smile on the girl.

"This matter is urgent and important," said Hawthorn. "I'm sure that slots are reserved in the Governor's schedule for unexpected events. By the way, has anyone ever told you that you have the most intriguing eyes?"

The girl blushed. "Well, if it's important."

"Oh it is," said Hawthorn leaning in toward her. "And if you're free while I am in town please give me a call. Perhaps you could show me the sights."

"I can only pass you on to the Governor's private office," the girl said, weakly.

"That will be fine," Hawthorn said.

The girl's fingers danced across her screen. A tray slid out of the podium containing brooches depicting the Cutter Stream logo. She affixed one to each of their jackets, smoothing Hawthorn's down to make sure it was properly aligned.

"The brooches will guide you. Just follow the arrows," the girl said.

"Thank you," said Allenson.

Hawthorn winked at the girl. She blushed again and quickly looked down at her screen.

The hubbub of the hall returned as soon as they left the dampened area around the podium. A purple arrow appeared in the air in front of Allenson, curving to the right. He could not see one in front of Hawthorn, or anyone else for that matter, which probably meant that the brooch hologram was tightly focused so as to only be visible from the perspective of the wearer.

The brooches guided the friends down the hall to a set of high narrow wooden doors decorated in gold curlicues sculpted over the inevitable purple and gray panels. They were guarded by an attendant in a uniform that had seen better days. The purple had faded to the point where it clashed horribly with the surroundings.

"Inspector General Allenson to see the Vice-Governor," Hawthorn said, playing his role of aide to the full. The man checked his podium before ceremonially pulling open each of the doors. He was a somewhat weedy fellow and had to throw his full weight into the act. One of the upper hinges on the right door needed oiling. It grated in a way that Allenson found highly irritating. Couldn't anyone in the Manzanita bureaucracy use a lubricant spray?

The friends mounted a long narrow staircase that ended in a waiting room, the central feature of which was a podium manned by a slim woman of perhaps thirty or forty years. She wore a blue business suit, a discreet purple and gray silk scarf indicating her allegiance to the Manzanita bureaucracy.

Wooden benches covered in gray leather lined the walls. A half dozen men and women sat on them. A number looked the new arrivals up and down, no doubt trying to gauge their political importance. One man had wedged himself into a corner and was clearly asleep. Another chewed his nails compulsively, inspecting them every so often. Hawthorn went back into aide mode.

"Sar Allen Allenson of Pentire, Acting Inspector General for Military Forces of the Cutter Stream to see Sar Stane Fontenoy, Vice-Governor of the Cutter Stream," he said to the woman.

"If you would like to wait," said the secretary motioning toward an empty bench.

"The matter is of some importance," Hawthorn said, not moving.

He displayed his most dazzling smile, but unfortunately the secretary was made of sterner stuff than the girl downstairs.

"Of course it is important," she said sweetly, "or you would not have gotten this far."

"It is also urgent," Hawthorn said.

"It's always urgent."

"And Sar Allen has but little time to devote to this matter," Hawthorn said, doggedly.

The woman gave a sardonic smile that all but invited them to leave if they wished. Allenson's heart sank. They might wait for days on those benches, getting progressively bumped down the list as more important supplicants appeared.

"On a different note, has anyone ever told you that you have the most intriguing eyes?" Hawthorn said, sincerely.

"My eyes have been much remarked on by certain persons wishing to see the Governor, also my mouth and hair," said the secretary, cynically.

But Allenson noted that she nevertheless smiled back at Hawthorn. Women found it difficult not to.

"The Governor no doubt relies on you totally, but he must let you escape from the office eventually," said Hawthorn.

"Oh, I sometimes sneak out of a side door," the secretary said.

"I was so hoping to immerse myself in some of Manzanita's cultural life," Hawthorn said. "But one needs a discerning guide to derive the most appreciation from sophisticated pleasures."

"No doubt," said the secretary, clearly enjoying the flirtation. "Did you have anyone in mind?"

"I hadn't really thought about it," Hawthorn replied, furrowing his brow. "But wait, how silly of me not to think of it sooner? You, yourself, would be the perfect companion."

The secretary tilted her head to one side and lifted her chin, showing her profile to best advantage.

"And would my husband be invited to come?" she asked.

"I see no reason to bother him on my account. Two, in my experience, is the perfect number for a cultural diversion."

The woman smiled and shook her head. Hawthorn pressed on.

"Sar Allenson really is short of time. He has just returned from leading the Harbinger Survey Expedition into the Hinterlands..."

"Has he?" the secretary asked, interrupting Hawthorn.

The woman slipped out of flirtation mode and morphed into the perfect, efficient PA. She took a silver stylet out of a top pocket and wrote something on her screen without waiting for Hawthorn to answer. She made a series of notes, writing with her right hand and keying the screen with her left.

This was a somewhat tedious way of conveying information, but it meant that she could discourse privately without impolitely excluding the Governor's supplicants by a damper field. Thus the Governor's privacy and the visitors' status were both protected.

She waited a few moments until an icon formed on the screen. "Vice-Governor Fontenoy will see you now," she said formally.

"Hang on, I was next," said a florid-faced man, rising from his bench.

"You *were* next," said the secretary, coldly. "Now you're not."

"Thank you," Allenson said, smiling an apology at the bumped supplicant. The latter sank back with an exasperated snort but didn't comment further. If he annoyed the secretary too much, he could find himself in the waiting room until he died of old age.

"I really would be honored to escort you to dinner," Hawthorn said to the secretary. "Call me if you change your mind."

The woman did not reply, but put the silver stylet in her mouth. Allenson got the impression she was seriously considering the offer.

"Inspector General Allenson," Fontenoy rose from his chair and offered his hand.

Allenson shook hands with a degree of relief. Fontenoy greeted him in the manner adopted by one gentleman to another of equal rank. That simplified matters hugely for Allenson as it defined the social niceties.

"Please be seated." The Vice-Governor ushered Allenson toward a chair.

Fontenoy was technically an employee, which on Wagener made him of inferior rank. There were conventions appropriate for that situation. Indeed, it would be patronizing to an employee to treat him as an equal.

However, Fontenoy was also the senior Brasilian

official in the Cutter Stream, which made him one of
the four or five most powerful men this side of the
Bight. By that count, he should be given all courtesies
due to a gentleman of senior rank, such as one would
offer to Trance Destry.

"Sar Hawthorn," Fontenoy nodded politely in Hawthorn's direction.

It occurred to Allenson that Fontenoy was far more
used to dealing with complicated social conventions
than any Wagener gentleman, and so had taken the
initiative to put his guests at ease. Fontenoy was both
intelligent and sophisticated, but that was hardly a
surprise.

Fontenoy wore a casual business suit cut in the latest
Brasilian style. You had to look very carefully at his lapel
to find an unobtrusive gray pin denoting his allegiance.
Allenson might not have noticed the pin at all were it
not decorated with a purple jewel that caught the light.

The Vice-Governor was a featureless bureaucrat
with light brown skin and dark brown eyes and hair. It
was impossible to guess his age. He looked biologically
about forty, but his chronological age must be double
that. He was a little on the thin side, with a sharp face
and alert eyes that gave him a hawk-like appearance.

A quote from an old play looped through Allenson's
head. *Yon Cassius has a lean and hungry look. He
thinks too much; such men are dangerous.* He told
himself to get a grip. This was no time for distractions.

"It is good of you to see us at such short notice,
Vice-Governor," Allenson said.

Fontenoy waved a hand dismissively, like an uncle
who has just been thanked for a generous gift to a
favorite niece.

"I trust that your journey from Wagener was not too tedious?" Fontenoy asked.

"It had moments of interest," Allenson replied, adopting the suitably blasé tone of one who regularly travels by carriage.

"And your enterprises on Wagener are prospering?" Fontenoy asked.

"Tolerably so," Allenson replied.

He thought it was time that he reciprocated in asking a polite question but he knew so little about Fontenoy's personal life that it was difficult to frame something suitably anodyne. He would normally have asked after the Vice-Governor's family, but he did not know whether Fontenoy was married, let alone whether he had children. Allenson realized that he had missed a trick. He should have researched some suitably trivial details about the man for purposes of small talk. He marked the error down as something not to be repeated.

Fontenoy's title of Vice-Governor made him the most senior official responsible for overseeing Brasilian interests in the Cutter Stream. The official Governor was a member of the powerful Gens Tegalliano. He had never visited the Stream and it was not expected that he ever would. The title was honorary and brought certain political and financial advantages, such as a monopoly on tea imports. About the only active duty required of the Governor was the requirement to appoint a Vice-Governor to do the actual work.

Allenson considered asking after the fortunes of the Tegallianos, as it was likely that Fontenoy was a Tegalliano client—likely, but not certain. In the end, he settled for the most banal of polite inquiries.

"I trust your duties do not weigh too heavily?" Allenson asked. "The responsibility must occasionally be wearisome."

"Indeed," Fontenoy replied. "I often yearn to return home to Brasilia to catalogue my collection of Old Earth buttons. One does not seek high office, but if called upon to serve..." Fontenoy spread his hands in supplication and adopted a pious expression.

"Quite," Allenson said, not daring to look at Hawthorn for fear of loosing a giggle.

Fontenoy would have schemed and maneuvered for such a plum position as Vice-Governor of the Stream, and it would probably take nothing short of a plasma bomb to unseat him before he had made his fortune. The screen on his chair arm flashed, attracting Fontenoy's attention. He glanced at it briefly before shutting it down with a single tap.

Interesting, thought Allenson. *Fontenoy must want to talk to me. He has something on his mind.* Maybe Allenson had found a lever.

"I was a little confused," Fontenoy said, breaking across Allenson's train of thought. "I thought Sar Todd Allenson was Inspector General of the Militia, but I see that you are Acting Inspector General?" Fontenoy raised an eyebrow.

"My brother is unwell and unable to perform his duties," Allenson replied. "I did not seek the office, but if called upon to serve..."

There was a pause, filled only by Hawthorn turning a snort into a cough.

"Your brother is likely to be indisposed for some considerable time?" Fontenoy asked.

Allenson nodded.

"And so you wish me to ratify your appointment?" Fontenoy asked.

"I believe it is within your gift." Allenson replied.

"Yes," Fontenoy said, "and no."

He rested his elbows on the arms of his chair touching his fingertips together to form an inverted V.

"While it is true that I have the authority to make such appointments unilaterally, I would normally allow the legislature to recommend a candidate. Politicians, in the lower house in particular, are prone to demagoguery. There would be accusations of cronyism and so on if I just appoint you," said Fontenoy.

The lower house represented the smallholders and mercantile classes. Their interests lay primarily in matters such as local taxation—they were against it—and public works paid for by taxation—they were for them, especially when they won the contracts. Normally, they would simply ratify official appointments recommended by the upper house, since it was of little consequence to them how the gentry divvied up political appointments among themselves.

"Many in the upper house are associates of Destry Wayfaring and investors in the Harbinger Project. I believe they would appreciate the need for continuity in the post of Inspector General with a candidate close to both the previous incumbent and the Destry family," said Allenson, drawing attention to his political connections.

"Ye-es," Fontenoy said, without conviction. "I am also an investor in the Harbinger Project, but of course I cannot let that influence my decisions, which must always be in the best interests of Brasilia."

"And the Cutter Stream," Allenson said.

Fontenoy made a dismissive gesture. "What is good for Brasilia is good for the Stream."

Allenson was nonplussed. He did not understand why Fontenoy was being so unhelpful. The Vice-Governor's position and personal chance of enrichment depended on the good offices of the Stream's leading families for support. Fontenoy must want something, but he would never come straight out and ask for a favor.

"It seems we are at an impasse." Allenson said.

"Not entirely," said Fontenoy. "I will put a bill before the upper house in your favor when the opportunity arises. Unfortunately, at the moment I have a tricky problem that is taking up all my time and until it's solved…" Fontenoy spread his hands, indicating the heavy burden that he carried.

"Indeed, perhaps I can help?" Allenson asked, with foreboding. Of course, he had no choice. Fontenoy had him over a barrel.

"Possibly," said Fontenoy. "You are aware that we have an alliance with some Riders." He consulted his screen. "The Chieftain of the Stone People Overclan, to restrict exploitation of much of the Hinterlands to Brasilia, excluding Terra."

"No, I was not aware," Allenson said.

"Well, we do, at least in theory," said Fontenoy. "However, it has so far not been entirely productive. I have to find an emissary who can travel into the Hinterlands to contact the Stone People and win their trust. We want to determine the extent of Terran penetration, if any, into the Hinterlands. We suspect that they are moving along chasms from their colonies in Foundworlds."

Foundworlds were a cluster of Terran colonies on

the Cutter Stream side of the Bight. Chasms were fast-moving, permanent currents within the Continuum. The Cutter Stream was a large chasm.

"I see," Allenson said, with resignation.

"The emissary will need to be an individual in possession of a rare mix of qualities," Fontenoy said. He ticked them off on his fingers. "The emissary will have to have a proven ability in team leadership, experience of the Hinterlands, skill in dealing with Riders, and great personal fortitude and determination."

"And where would one look for such a paragon?" asked Hawthorn, softly.

Fontenoy pretended not to have heard him. "The emissary will also have to be a person of suitable social status and official rank, as they will be representing Brasilia," Fontenoy said. "But I cannot send an ordinary diplomat for obvious reasons. You can see my difficulty?"

"Indeed," Allenson said, dryly.

Fontenoy's eyes widened. "But of course, why did I not think of it before?"

"I think he's got it," said Hawthorn, to no one in particular.

"You, yourself, are perfect for the position of emissary, Sar Allenson. You are a gentleman who has recently led a successful survey of the Hinterlands. You lack official rank, of course, but that is easily fixed. I can ratify your appointment as Acting Inspector General of Militia immediately and, if I can regard this issue as solved, find the time to put a bill before the upper house to make the rank permanent on your return. There could be no suggestion of cronyism or influence peddling in such circumstances." Fontenoy sat back in his chair, which rocked slightly. "It seems we can help each other."

Hawthorn cut in. "And you would guarantee in writing to veto any attempt to pass a bill that back-dated the appointment of any other individual to Inspector General, in any way that might supersede Sar Allenson's claim."

Allenson found the comment embarrassing, as it implied that Fontenoy's word could not be trusted.

"Of course. I will have a Memorandum of Understanding prepared immediately and placed on record. What say you, Sar Allenson?" asked Fontenoy, who did not seem insulted at all.

"As you said, Vice-Governor, it seems we can help each other."

They shook hands.

"Excellent." Fontenoy rose to his feet and ushered them to the door. "If you will excuse me, gentlemen, my next appointment is here."

Allenson held the door open for a striking lady who swept regally past him into the office. It appeared that the florid faced man had been bumped again.

The friends walked across the plaza.

"You realize that we will have to penetrate deeper into the Hinterlands than we have ever gone before?" Hawthorn asked.

"Yes, but we will be in friendly territory. After all, we do have an alliance with the chieftain of the regional Rider overclan," said Allenson.

"I wonder whether anyone has told them?" Hawthorn asked, sourly.

CHAPTER 11

Redfern Villa

"Am I tying this right?" Allenson asked, tugging at the intractable knot in the ribbon looped around his neck.

Hawthorn rose from where he sat in an armchair in Allenson's room.

"I feel like a man preparing his own noose," Allenson said, gloomily.

Hawthorn cocked his head and examined the offending article. "If you loosened the knot slightly and put it beneath your chin rather than under your ear, then it might make you look a little less like a condemned man."

Allenson made the suggested adjustments and had to admit that he did look better. That did not lift his mood.

"Are you sure that you do not want to come to the party with me?" Allenson asked, hoping he did not sound too desperate.

"The invitation was for you only," Hawthorn said.

"A formality," Allenson said. "As my aide, you would be automatically included in any invitation."

Hawthorn picked up his jacket and slung it over one shoulder.

"You know how I hate these well-bred dos," Hawthorn said. "Besides, I have already accepted another invitation for tonight."

Allenson stopped adjusting his evening wear. "Not the young receptionist. Don't tell me she contacted you?" Allenson said.

"No. Well, yes," Hawthorn replied. "That is, the receptionist did get in touch, but I'm seeing her tomorrow. I'm dining with Fontenoy's secretary tonight."

"I see," Allenson said, examining himself in the full-length mirror and wondering whether it was too late to order a different suit.

"You'll be fine," Hawthorn said, sauntering to the door. "You look very fashionable."

Hawthorn paused to say, "Don't wait up," and then he was gone.

Allenson checked his reflection again. "Fine, hmph. I look like a fleek done up in harvest festival finery," he said gloomily.

He considered retying the ribbon but doubted if that would improve matters. He considered taking it off and being fashionably opened-necked, but discarded the notion as madness. You had to be sartorially confident to break the rules of formal dress. Hawthorn could pull it off because, well, just because.

Allenson picked up the invitation card that had been delivered by hand within an hour of his checking in to the hotel. The card was lavender in both color and scent. Embossed gold letters invited Inspector General of Militia Allenson of Pentire to attend a soiree at the villa of Sar Redfern of Redfern Dealing. The invitation was from Lady Redfern, indicating a social event rather than a business meeting. That puzzled Allenson, because he knew no one on Manzanita socially other than a few of Sarai's relatives. Word had clearly got around fast. That was the whole point of his ostentatious behavior, of course.

He checked the location of the Redfern property on his datapad and was not surprised to find that it was one of the lakeside villas. Nowhere was very far from anywhere else in Manzanita City so he intended to walk. The cool air would be welcome to clear his head, and he intended to rehearse some small talk on the way. It was a device that he had adopted as a psychological crutch for social events. He was hopeless at unprompted repartee.

Unfortunately, it was still raining when he left the hotel so he was obliged to hire a cab. This involved giving his destination to the hotel doorman, who took one step forward and raised his right forefinger, alerting a waiting taxicab. The doorman had so much silver braid on his uniform that he rattled when he moved.

Manzanita taxicabs had twin seats slung between the front wheels, while the driver sat behind over a single rear wheel, to which the pedal drive was also attached. This wheel was also used for steering. It was possibly the most ungainly and inefficient transport device ever devised, with the possible exception of the jet airliner. The vehicle did at least have a waterproof canopy, colored in rather bonny orange and white stripes.

A cab pulled up outside the door and the doorman ceremonially raised an umbrella to escort Allenson the four paces to his seat. He also passed the address on to the cab driver so Allenson was spared that onerous task.

Allenson sat back in his seat but the cab remained stationary.

There was a polite cough.

The doorman waited patiently.

"Ah, um, yes," Allenson said, clawing through his pockets in embarrassment. His money was in the last possible pocket and he could not quite get any out. His face burned as he struggled with his garments. He held out the first coin he managed to extract, cursing the malevolence of inanimate objects.

"Thank you, sir." The doorman smiled and touched the brim of his hat.

The so-in-so should look pleased, Allenson thought. That coin was a silver shilling rather than the threepenny piece that would have sufficed.

The cab started with a jerk, soon leaving the central business district where his hotel was located. It wound through the narrow winding suburban streets. Allenson soon lost all sense of direction. The terraces consisted of commercial premises on the ground floor—shops, bars, and cafes—with living accommodations above. They all looked alike, except for the advertising signs. A neon sign on a bar advertising a drink called Jago caught his eye, as it plumbed the depths of tastelessness. The letters were lit by revolting pink light while the drink was depicted in bright fluorescent green. The letter "o" was damaged, spluttering and fizzing.

It was still malfunctioning several minutes later when the taxicab passed it for the second time.

"Right, you've given me the scenic tour, now could

we just get on," Allenson said, craning his neck around to glare at the cabby, who did not reply.

The cab dived down an alley, emerging onto the ring road right by the Redfern villa.

"Two shillings, squire," said the cabby, twisting the meter around so that Allenson could check the fare.

Allenson counted out the exact value in coins and passed them to the cabby.

"Oy, service isn't included you know," the cabby said in a surly voice.

"I noticed," Allenson said.

The man opened his mouth, but Allenson cut in first.

"Is there a problem?" Allenson asked, coldly, fixing the man with a gimlet gaze.

The cabby looked at Allenson carefully, possibly noting for the first time his height, and the breadth of his shoulders.

"No, governor," he replied.

"Good," Allenson said, "I will give you a tip."

The cabby brightened.

"The next time I hire a cab, I expect it to take the direct route, or I'll take a crop to the driver. Pass the word."

"Yes, governor," the cabby said.

The little confrontation had quite cheered Allenson up. It felt good to be in control of a situation. The shyster had given him an excuse for some morale-boosting intimidation.

The villa's *maître de porte* stood under an umbrella. The man was suitably solemn, but a twinkle in his eye suggested that he had noted and enjoyed the exchange.

"Sar Allen Allenson, I believe I am expected."

The *maître* consulted his datapad.

"Yes, Sar Allenson, if you would be good enough to come with me."

The *maître* escorted Allenson up the drive, holding the umbrella to keep the rain off Allenson's clothes. A footman opened the front door and the *maître* whispered something in his ear.

"If you will follow me, Sar Allenson," the footman said.

He led the way down a corridor into a central garden illuminated from concealed lighting in the surrounding peristyle. The area was paved, plants being restricted to pots laid out in geometric patterns. Fish swam slowly in a long rectangular pool in the center. They fluoresced yellow, blue, and orange as they moved up and down the pool.

"Sar Allen Allenson of Pentire, Inspector General of the Cutter Stream Militia."

The footman announced Allenson through his lapel microphone. A plump, short lady in a green gown that made her look like a brightly colored waste bin, rushed over and kissed him on both cheeks. He had started to bow, which was fortunate, as it lowered his head sufficiently for her to complete the gesture without having to jump up and down.

"Sar Allenson, how delightful you could attend my little soiree at such short notice," she said. "You must be terribly busy with official business."

"I am honored, Lady Redfern," Allenson said, aware that he was stiff.

"Let me introduce you to the other guests," she said.

Lady Redfern bustled off with extraordinary energy. She towed Allenson in her perfumed wake like a battleship behind a tug. The next few minutes were a whirl of faces and names that blended into a montage. He bowed to men and air-kissed women. On the way he managed to acquire a glass of wine and a canapé, which made the expected social gestures all the more difficult to perform.

And then another guest was announced and Lady Redfern was off. He tasted the wine. It was actually rather good; not that he was a connoisseur but he had attended enough parties at Destry's to enable him to distinguish quality from plonk.

He took a bite of the canapé. It had a sour taste, like rotting fish. He glanced around, hoping to find somewhere to dispose of the thing. A man caught his eye and sauntered over. He was slim and rather short. Something he tried to hide with high-heeled boots and a tall conical hat.

"These suburban parties are a bit of a bore, are they not?" the man asked.

He did not wait for an answer. "I see you made the mistake of trying one of our hostesses' canapés," he said. "She has them prepared specially. Ghastly, aren't they? Edwina claims that they are made to an ancient Old Earth recipe. It's no wonder the third civilization fell if that was the best they could do. Do you want me to get rid of it for you?"

"I was looking for, ah, somewhere . . ." Allenson's voice trailed off.

The man took the canapé from his unresisting hand. With a practiced flick of the wrist, he chucked it behind him across the floor, winking at Allenson as he did. A huge fat man in a yellow suit laughed uproariously at some comment from a woman whose breasts were as prominently displayed as her teeth. He stepped back, grinding the sweetmeat under his heel.

"My name's Lekhurst," the man said, holding out his hand. Allenson attempted to shake it, but discovered he was being handed a card. It read, "Lekhurst Stores, purveyors of fine uniforms, in association with Redfern Dealing."

"I'm afraid that I forgot to bring my cards," Allenson said, patting his pockets as if an incompetent dresser had inadvertently left the offending items behind. He was, he thought, getting the hang of this.

"No matter," Lekhurst said. "I know who you are, Sar Allenson, the new Inspector General of Militia. Have you seen the militia on parade?"

"No," Allenson replied.

"Disgraceful," Lekhurst said, tutting and shaking his head. "All they have is an armband, no ceremonial uniform at all. I have a fine selection of cloths and designs."

They made small talk for a while before Lekhurst excused himself and disappeared.

"I noticed your glass was empty, so I took the liberty of bringing you a replacement." The speaker was a lady of mature years in a severe black business suit. In one hand she held two glasses and, in the other, a lit cigar.

Allenson noticed that his own glass was indeed void of refreshment, so he took one of the glasses from the lady, depositing the empty one on a passing canapé tray. The canapés were not going well. The lady drew a deep inhalation of her cigar. She blew the smoke upward. It rolled lazily up to the level of the villa's roof in blue spirals. There it exploded outward in ripples. It was like looking at water poured into an upside-down pond. Now that he came to think about it, no rain fell. There must be a static field above the garden.

"My card, Sar Allenson," the lady said. "I'm Lady Ranko."

Allenson dutifully took and read it: "Ranko Security and Armorers, in association with Redfern Dealing."

"Have you seen the arms used by the militia?" the lady asked.

"Ah no," Allenson replied.

"Total junk," the lady said. "Many of them were donations, with half a dozen different calibers and a dozen different power supplies."

"Sounds a logistic nightmare," Allenson said.

"Damn right," said the lady, puffing on her cigar. She coughed, looked at it, and frowned. "My gene-surgeons forced me to give up for a while during my last desenescence. I have not yet properly reacquired the habit. You have to work at a vice."

"I guess so," Allenson said, wondering why anyone would want to.

"Come to me when you need new weapons. Those crooks at Salo Arms will offer you a cheap deal but they sell reconditioned crap from the Home Worlds. The stuff is jigged up to just about survive a few test fires."

"Thank you for your advice," Allenson said. "I shall certainly keep it in mind."

There was a pause in the conversation. Allenson had no idea what to say. Then an idea occurred. "I say," he said. "I believe that man is trying to catch your eye." Allenson pointed at random.

"Oh, him," she said, her lip curling. "I suppose he wants to whine again about the alarm system we installed on his warehouse. It's hardly my fault he hires incompetent staff. Still, I had better sort him out. Excuse me."

"Of course," Allenson said, to her retreating back.

Somehow his glass had emptied once more so he acquired a full one. He took the precaution of slipping a detox tab into his mouth with the first sip of wine. He wandered along the length of the pool, watching the ornamental fish change color. He had the impression that the garden was a larger pool, one filled with barracuda. A fish rose to the surface and blew a bubble. He leaned over for a better look. Rings of bubble-gum pink passed down the fish's otherwise yellow body.

"That is truly hideous," Allenson said, to himself.

An amused feminine chuckle sounded from under his elbow. He jerked upright, spilling his wine into the water where it fluoresced deep blue. The fish flipped its tail and the wine dissipated like an ink drop in a stream. The woman laughed again, covering her mouth with one hand.

"They are rather hideous," she said, "but it is a little unkind of you to try to poison them."

Allenson winced. "I believe you, ah, may have misheard me."

"Really?" the lady asked, raising an eyebrow. "What word did you use then—horrendous, horrible, horrific?"

Allenson tried desperately to think up a word that sounded like hideous but meant the opposite. The best he could come up with was "humorous," which was not much of an improvement. To cover his confusion, he bowed.

"Allen Allenson," he said, introducing himself.

"I know," she said. "Our new Inspector of Militia, the guest of honor at our little soiree."

Allenson held out his hand to receive the inevitable business card. The lady looked at it quizzically. Time stretched out, tenths of seconds lasting hours, and he flushed with embarrassment.

"How gallant of you," she said, pressing her glass into his hand. "Something sparkling, if you please?"

"Yes, indeed, a drink," he said. "Sparkling, right."

It took a little time to track down suitable drinks and make his way back to her. He was accosted twice by men who extolled their products and pressed business cards into his hand. The lady stood where he had left her, gazing into the pool. He studied her as he returned. She was petite and a little plump, homely even. However, her gown was expensive, and it suited her perfectly. He was impressed by the way she had disguised his social gaffe. He guessed her age as little more than his own, making her the youngest woman at the party.

"I'm sorry about mistaking you for . . ." Allenson's voice trailed off.

She laughed again with genuine mirth, her eyes sparkling.

"I am not sure that I have forgiven you yet. Has childbirth aged me so much that I look like a hard-nosed businesswoman in the arms trade?"

"Indeed not," he said, sheepishly. He scraped around for something suitable to say. "You are here with your husband?"

"There is no husband," she replied, the mischievous smile back on her lips.

"Ah, I, ah, see," he said, cursing his social clumsiness.

"He died," she added.

"Oh, I'm sorry," Allenson said, wondering how he could extract himself from this topic.

"No need," the lady replied. "He was much older than me and he drank himself to death."

"I did not think that was possible for a gentleman in this day and age."

"It depends how hard you try," she replied. "The genesurgeons can only do so much. I am Trina Blaisdel, by the way." She held out her hand.

He took it in his own and bowed over to air kiss it.

"Forward of me to effect an introduction, I know, but I suspected you might never get around to asking me for my name."

"I am happy to meet you, Lady Blaisdel."

"You shall call me Trina and I shall call you Allen. See, there is no limit to my boldness tonight."

A woman wearing what looked like a purple chicken on her head approached. Trina slipped her arm determinedly through Allenson's.

"You will have to excuse us, Lady Jignal, but my cousin, Sar Allenson, was just about to show me Sar Redfern's collection of neoprimitive art."

"Hmm! Nobody told me you were related to the Inspector General, Lady Blaisdel." Lady Jignal said.

"A distant link, through marriage," Trina said, steering Allenson away.

"Are we related?" Allenson asked, when they were out of earshot.

"No idea," Trina replied. "But I won't tell if you don't."

"I thought this was a social not a business occasion," Allenson said.

"Naive boy," Trina replied. "Everything is a business occasion in Manzanita City. The neoprimitive art is in an alcove over there."

She nodded slightly to indicate the direction.

"I don't actually know anything about neoprimitive art," Allenson said.

"Who does?" Trina replied. "It's just fashionable junk."

Allenson laughed. He was astonished at how at ease he had become in Trina's company. He normally felt clumsy and ill-at-ease around young women.

"I hate social occasions. I never know how to hold myself or what to say," Allenson confided to her.

"Maybe you should just try relaxing and being yourself," Trina said. "I doubt that you know enough of the world to invent a convincing construct. I know I don't. Besides, I rather like the real Allen Allenson."

She squeezed his arm.

· CHAPTER 12 ·

The Daemon Drink

"Good afternoon," Hawthorn said sarcastically, when Allenson joined him at the interview table.

Allenson automatically checked the time on his datapad. "Oh come on, spare me the hyperbole. It's true I'm a little late..."

"Over an hour late," Hawthorn said, with a degree of relish.

Allenson was usually obsessively punctual, unlike Hawthorn. He was also prone to reprove Hawthorn for this fault, so he could hardly object to the man enjoying the moment.

"Sorry, I was late getting to bed," Allenson said, holding up a hand as a gesture of contrition and sitting down.

"Yes, I know," Hawthorn said. "You woke me when you knocked over the vase stand in the corridor."

"Sorry," Allenson said again.

"You're in a surprisingly good mood for someone who's had only four hours' sleep. Why were you so late anyway?" Hawthorn asked.

Allenson shrugged.

Hawthorn looked at him suspiciously.

"You pulled at the party, didn't you?" Hawthorn asked.

"It's true that I met a lady," Allenson conceded.

"You little beauty, you only went and pulled."

"An unattractive expression," Allenson said.

"I suppose you went back to her place?" Hawthorn asked, resting his chin on one hand.

"She had no escort so, as a gentlemen, I was obliged to see her safely home," Allenson replied, stiffly.

"Of course you were," Hawthorn said with a grin. "And no doubt she expressed her appreciation by inviting you in for refreshment."

"Well, yes," Allenson replied.

"And?" Hawthorn asked, raising an eyebrow.

"We discussed the incarnate poets of the Early Galactic Period," Allenson replied. "We discovered that we both admired the work of Suggersun."

There was a silence before Hawthorn sighed.

"The awful thing is that I believe you," Hawthorn said.

"Who have we got lined up to interview?" Allenson asked, changing the subject.

"Only three people have responded so far to our call for a guide," Hawthorn said.

"The ad was a long shot," Allenson said. "I suppose we might as well get on with it. Who's the first candidate?"

"I haven't been able to find out much about him," Hawthorn replied. "He's young and well connected and that's about it."

"Doesn't sound inviting," Allenson said. "Nevertheless, wheel him in."

Hawthorn went to the door and called in the first interviewee. Allenson studied the candidate while Hawthorn made the introductions and explained the duties. He was a young man dressed in expensive, fashionable clothes. He flopped down in the interview chair without waiting for an invitation. Allenson asked a few routine questions to put the candidate at ease, although this candidate would be comatose if he was any more at ease.

"So what makes you suitable for the position of Hinterlands guide?" Allenson finally asked, getting to the nub of the issue.

"Well, I think that a short spell as a guide would be very beneficial for my personal development," the young man replied.

"I see," Allenson said, somewhat nonplussed by the answer.

"Have you had experience as a guide?" Hawthorn asked.

"Oh yes," the young man replied. "When my club— I'm a member of the Roosters, you know. Anyway, when my club got lost in the backcountry, I took charge and got us out."

Hawthorn looked at Allenson and raised an eyebrow as if to say "Roosters"? Allenson shook his head slightly. He had never heard of it.

"The Roosters is a social club?" Allenson asked.

"Oh yes," the interviewee replied. "For young people of an adventurous disposition. It's very exclusive, don't you know, difficult to get into."

"What are the entry qualifications?" Hawthorn asked.

"One has to come from a decent family, the right sort, you know," the young man replied.

"How did you find your way out of the backcountry?" Hawthorn asked.

"I buzzed my father's butler and he picked us up

in our aircar," the young man said proudly. "I have a lot of initiative, you see."

"Yes, I can see that," Allenson said dryly. "Didn't you have maps on your datapads?"

"Well, yes, but they can be so confusing," the young man replied.

"Have you been into the Hinterlands?" Hawthorn asked.

"No, that's why I am so keen to go," the young man replied brightly.

"Is there anything you want to ask us?" Allenson asked, bringing the interview to a close.

"Ah, yes, the Roosters are playing the Old Rotting-hamians at footy on the twenty-ninth of the next. We will be back on time, won't we, as I wouldn't want to miss the match? It's an important annual fixture."

"I am sure that won't be a problem," Hawthorn said solemnly.

Hawthorn rose and showed the interviewee to the door. He was still burbling about exciting opportunities when Hawthorn firmly shut it. Allenson put his head in his hands.

"Shall I show the next one in?" Hawthorn asked.

"Why not? It can't get any worse." Allenson said. "Who is he?"

"She," Hawthorn replied. "A Mistress Goodbar, who is an experienced guide to hunting parties."

"That sounds promising," said Allenson, perking up.

Mistress Goodbar was a tough-looking woman in no-nonsense clothes, with short cropped red hair. She sat down, folded her arms, and glared at Allenson.

"Um, you have some experience of the Hinterlands, I believe?" Allenson asked.

"No," the woman replied. "I have *extensive* experience of the Hinterlands. I have led more groups into the Hinterlands than you have had girlies, laddy."

Which, Allenson reflected, was probably true but he did not quite see how pointing that out would be useful to her quest to be hired.

"So you have successfully guided a number of expeditions," Allenson said.

"No, I said *led*, as in commanded, not guided," Goodbar insisted.

"Have you any experience of the Nengue region?" Allenson asked.

"Why Nengue?" asked the woman, answering his question with a question. "No one goes to Nengue. The hunting is piss poor and the place is crawling with savages."

"Nengue it has to be," Allenson said, remorselessly. "So tell me about Nengue."

The woman shrugged. "Not much to tell. There's a Rider settlement there and a rundown trading fort. Not sure what they trade. The place has been hunted out."

"But you know the Continuum around Nengue?" Allenson asked.

"Sure." She shrugged again.

Interviewing the woman was like pulling teeth with bare hands. Allenson struggled on but elicited nothing more of interest.

"Is there anything you would like to ask me?" Allenson finally said.

"No," Mistress Goodbar replied, "but I will tell you something. I am prepared to lead you to Nengue, but I run a tight ship. I expect you to follow my instructions without argument, and I decide when we go on and when we call it a day. Those are my terms." She got up. "Let me know if you agree."

Mistress Goodbar headed for the door without further ceremony and let herself out. There was a long pause, and then Allenson said, tentatively, "She has got the necessary background knowledge and skills."

"Quite," Hawthorn said.

There was another pause.

"You were very quiet during her interview." Allenson said.

"Allenson?"

"Yes?"

"If you hire that bloody woman I may be forced to shoot her—or you," Hawthorn said, looking him straight in the face.

"She was somewhat overbearing," Allenson said.

"Overbearing? She's a cast-iron ball-breaker. I will not be ordered around like some chinless Brasilian wonder by an oik with attitude."

"Well, we have one more to go before we make any decisions," Allenson said diplomatically.

The third candidate was a bald, stooping fellow with poor muscle tone. There were broken blood vessels on his nose, and his teeth were in poor condition. His clothes had once been of a decent quality but showed signs of wear and staining. They fitted, so had probably been bought new but never cleaned. This, Allenson thought, was a man who had fallen on hard times.

Payne nodded deferentially to Allenson.

"Master Payne?" Allenson asked.

"Yes, sar," Payne replied.

His voice had a timid quality, as if he expected to be kicked if he spoke out of turn. Allenson had the impression that Payne would agree if he insisted that the man's name was actually Smith.

"Please sit down."

Payne hurried to the chair. There was a distinct clink from his jacket pocket.

Allenson asked a few routine questions to put the man at ease, without much success. Hawthorn took over the questioning.

"I see that you have experience as a trader in the Hinterlands, Master Payne. Ever been to Nengue?"

"Many times," Payne replied.

"What were you trading?" Hawthorn asked.

"Oh the usual," Payne replied. "Tonk, cheap plastic and ceramic decorations, some basic tools, mostly knives. Whatever the Riders wanted that didn't cost too much." He became more animated as he talked.

"Weapons?" Allenson asked.

"That would be illegal." Payne shrank back into himself, as if he were being interrogated by Lictors. Allenson noticed that Payne's hands were shaking. He clasped them together in his lap.

"Don't look so frightened, man. I was not accusing you of anything. I was just curious."

"Yes, sar," Payne said. "It would also be very stupid to sell Riders anything too dangerous. They would probably test it out on you first—you being conveniently to hand, like."

"What did you get in return?" Hawthorn asked. "We have been told that the hunting is poor there."

"Natural gems, sar." Payne looked surprised, as if everyone knew that.

Synthetic gems of any composition could be manufactured, but they lacked the random imperfections that made each natural gem unique—and difficult to cut. Uniqueness dictated value in a society that could make almost anything. No Brasilian lady would be seen dead wearing synthetic jewelry.

"Gems, well, well," Allenson said. "That explains everything."

"The Riders aren't stupid enough to tell us where they get them. They can be cunning devils, for savages. I bribed one with a crate of tonk once to show me the gemfields," Payne said.

"What happened?" Allenson asked, curious.

"Not sure, but we found his head on a pole outside the trading post." Payne shrugged. "I never got the tonk back either."

"You negotiated with the Riders in Kant?" Hawthorn asked.

"Yes, and I also speak the local lingo a bit," Payne replied.

"What do you know of the Rider political structure at Nengue?" Allenson asked.

"Not really my concern. Human politics are bad enough without getting mixed up with the affairs of Riders. Their political disagreements lead to spilled guts."

"But you must have picked up some idea," Allenson said, persisting.

"S'pose, so," Payne replied, rubbing his head. "Nengue is a sort of neutral place where the usual clan warfare is taboo. That's why the Trading Post is there. It doesn't stop fights between individual Riders, you follow. It just means that only personal grudges are fought out."

"So, do they have an enforcement body?" Allenson asked.

Payne stared blankly at him.

Allenson rephrased the question. "Are there Rider lictors, enforcing discipline?"

"Good heavens, no sar," said Payne, showing surprise at the naiveté of the question. "It's not like that. The taboos are more like religious custom, you see. If a clan broke the custom they might be massacred by all the other clans—or they might not. You never can tell with Riders. They're contrary beasts," Payne said. "You keep your gun in hand at all times, sars." He looked concerned, as if his potential employers were about to do something stupid.

"Just so," Hawthorn said, dryly.

"But there must some sort of authority at Nengue, man," Allenson said. "Brasilia has a treaty with the overclan leader."

"Has it?" Payne asked.

"Yes," Allenson replied.

"You must mean the Viceroy, sar," Payne said. "He's the chief of all the clans in the region," said Payne.

"Viceroy?" asked Allenson.

"That's what the traders call him. It's as good a word as any. He's appointed you see, by some sort of Rider council."

"Really?" Hawthorn asked. "I have never heard of such a thing. Where is this council based? What is it?"

Payne shrugged. "No one knows. It is deep into the Hinterlands. I was trading, you see, so I had to deal with the Viceroy but the council was too far away to matter."

Allenson pondered what the "council" might mean for his negotiations and wondered what else officialdom had not grasped about Rider social structures.

"But you are not trading now?" Hawthorn asked.

"I had some bad luck," Payne replied, not meeting Hawthorn's gaze. "I need this job to get a stake, so I can start again."

"Is there anything you wish to ask us?" Allenson asked, concluding the interview.

"Well, yes, sars." Payne hesitated.

"Spit it out, man," Hawthorn said.

"Well, sar, as I said, I have had some bad luck and need a sub. Could you advance me some pay to equip myself?"

"Don't worry about that. Something could be arranged," Allenson said.

Hawthorn showed Payne out.

"What a pity," Hawthorn said. "He would be a perfect choice..."

"If he wasn't a drunk." Allenson finished the sentence for Hawthorn.

"Yah, you should have smelled him up close. I reckon he had at least half a bottle to fortify himself before the interview," Hawthorn said.

"I heard the bottle clink when he sat down," Allenson replied.

"I suppose it has to be the ballbreaker, then," Hawthorn said gloomily.

"Or maybe not," Allenson said. "Look, we know what Payne's problem is. If we stop him drinking, then we should have a useful employee."

"Have you ever tried to keep a lush off the sauce?" Hawthorn asked rhetorically.

"Normally I would agree with you, but he is out of cash. I keep him starved of cash until we leave, then we run a dry expedition," Allenson said.

"A trip through the Hinterlands without booze."

Hawthorn shuddered theatrically. "The things I do for you, Allenson."

The door to the cheap apartment was locked. Allenson hammered on it again and called Payne's name. Silence.

"Are you sure he's in there?" Hawthorn asked.

"I am sure his datapad is in there, and he does not appear to be anywhere else." Allenson replied, anger coloring his voice. "I have had enough of waiting for him to surface."

Allenson kicked the wooden door under the lock. The lock held but the door frame splintered. Allenson put his shoulder to the wood and pushed the entire structure in with a crash.

"Payne!" he yelled into the unlit interior.

There was no answer so he went further in. The apartment was one room with curtain-partitioned alcoves for the bathroom and kitchen. The atmosphere was rancid with the stink of stale vomit and urine.

Payne lay on his back on a bed, fully dressed, snoring like a buffalo. Allenson crossed the room in two steps and shook him. Payne moaned but remained unconscious. A thin line of vomit rolled from the corner of his mouth. Empty bottles of tonk littered the floor.

"Don't say I didn't warn you," Hawthorn said.

Allenson kicked a bottle so hard that it shattered against the wall.

"I don't understand where he got the money!" Allenson raged.

Hawthorn picked a strip of paper off the floor and examined it.

"I have an idea," Hawthorn said, handing Allenson the paper. "Don't some of these prices seem a little steep?"

Allenson read the paper. It was a receipt for a series of goods from the supplier where he had opened a line of credit for Payne. The idea was that Payne could order supplies without touching actual cash. Some of the prices were high. Allenson looked at it uncomprehendingly until the other shoe dropped. He finally saw what Hawthorn had grasped immediately.

He stormed out of the apartment, receipt in hand. The supplier's shop was some little distance away, but Allenson covered the ground quickly in long strides, his anger building with each step. Hawthorn had to jog trot every few steps to keep up.

"Maybe you should have a drink and calm down before deciding what to do?" Hawthorn asked.

He did not get a reply. Allenson strode on as if he had not spoken. He barged into the shop, pushing aside the solitary customer. The supplier stood behind a counter wearing the apron that served as a uniform for his trade. He was a big man with beefy forearms.

Allenson threw the receipt on the counter.

"You cheated me," Allenson said quietly.

"I don't know what you mean," the supplier said, blustering.

"You padded the bill with Payne's connivance and paid him off in booze. You exploited his weakness to cheat me," Allenson said.

The other customer sidled toward the door but bumped into Hawthorn, who shook his head. The customer sensibly discovered an urgent need to examine the tools on sale at the far end of the shop.

"You can't talk to me like that!" the supplier said.

"Oh, you had to say it," Hawthorn said quietly to the ceiling. "You couldn't just apologize and offer restitution."

"Can I not? Can I not?" Allenson asked rhetorically. "And who will stop me?"

He reached behind the counter and grasped the supplier by the lapels. Allenson slammed him face down on the counter, holding him down with one hand on the back of his neck. The man struggled and attempted to push himself up. For all the good it did him, he may as well have pushed against an interworld ship. He could not have been held more securely if a granite pillar had phased out of the Continuum clamped to his head.

In desperation, the supplier tried to punch Allenson but his position was hardly conducive to fisticuffs. Allenson caught the fist easily with his free hand and slammed it down on the counter. There was a crack of something breaking and the supplier cried out.

Hawthorn winced.

"I estimate that you have cheated me by twenty percent," Allenson said.

"It was only ten percent," the supplier said, whimpering.

"I estimate that you have cheated me by twenty percent," Allenson said, as if the man had not spoken. "You will advance that amount immediately to my account. I will continue to deal with you, but you will not pad the bill, and you will not give Payne booze. Do we understand each other?"

The supplier did not reply.

Allenson still held the man's fist. He closed his

fingers on the damaged hand and squeezed. The supplier squealed.

"Do we understand each other?" Allenson asked again, his voice quiet and cold as if he were addressing a recalcitrant child.

"Yes, yes, sar, let me go. It shall be as you say," said the supplier.

"Good," Allenson said. "Payne will be round to order the next batch of goods, when he has recovered. I will take it as a personal insult to my honor as a gentleman if anyone gives Payne access to alcohol. Pass the word."

"Yes, sar," the supplier said.

Allenson turned to the customer in the corner, bowing slightly.

"Please accept my apology, master, for interrupting your business and manhandling you. I regret I let my temper get the better of my manners."

"Ah, no problem, sar," the customer finally said.

Allenson considered himself a gentleman, and a gentleman is obliged to maintain certain standards even when dealing with the lower orders. The man had offered no offense, so deserved an apology for such cavalier treatment.

"Everything alright, sar?" asked the waitress, topping off their mugs of cafay.

"Fine, most tasty," Allenson replied.

"Good," she said, before retreating behind her counter.

Allenson speared a chunk of ham with his fork and rubbed it in his egg yolk before putting it in his mouth. Actually the meal was rather good. He had a taste for simple nutritious food. Sarai always called it "nursery food." He smiled at the thought of her, but then frowned at his presumption in thinking fondly of another man's wife. Smiles and frowns, excitement and guilt—there was always an emotional rollercoaster ride with Sarai.

He had chosen this place to eat because it specialized in home cooking, but was upmarket enough to deter crowds. It was patronized by prosperous tradespeople and their dependents. The Manzanita wealthy ate in more fashionable restaurants, where they paid handsomely to eat Cutter Stream copies of Home World dishes.

Hawthorn had announced his attention of lunching at a bar where a bare-knuckle bout was scheduled between the local champion and a contender from Clearwater Port. This was not an entertainment that appealed to Allenson, so he left his friend to it.

Allenson finished his meal and caught the waitress's eye. She filled his mug with fresh cafay and removed his empty plate.

"Is the manager available?" Allenson asked.

"Mistress Cantona is the proprietor, sar," the waitress replied. "She also is the chef."

"Pleased give her my respects, and ask her if I might have a word," Allenson said.

"Of course, sar."

He sipped the cafay, which was satisfactorily strong and hot, while watching local news on a screen in the corner. A sensibly dressed matron appeared from the swing doors to the kitchen, carrying a steaming dish of fruit pie and englaze. He half rose when she approached his table, but she waved for him to sit down.

"I am—"

"Sar Allenson, I know," the lady said. "You have been on the news. I believe you wish to speak to me?"

Allenson indicated that she should sit down. "Indeed, mistress. Can I get you any refreshment?"

She raised a hand in polite refusal.

"I have engaged an employee, but he has been ill and needs good food. Could I open an account here for him?"

"Of course," the lady replied.

"Please serve him anything on the menu for which he has a fancy except—"

"Except strong liquor," the lady interrupted him, again. It was a habit that he might find irritating with longer acquaintance.

"I see you are familiar with Master Payne's illness," Allenson said, dryly.

The woman frowned. "It is such a shame. Clement, that is, Master Payne, was not always like he is now. Once, he was a fine man."

Mistress Cantona sounded almost wistful.

"People took advantage of his—weakness," she said, choosing the word carefully.

"So I discovered," Allenson said. "I was required to intervene."

"I heard about that." Mistress Cantona smiled broadly. "Not before time, in my opinion. The word has gone around that serving Clement alcohol is inadvisable."

Allenson laughed. "It would appear there is some value in gossip."

"I suggest you eat your pudding, sar, before the englaze congeals." Mistress Cantona got up from the table so Allenson also rose. "Leave Clement Payne to me, sar. I'll feed him up."

Later that day, Allenson met Hawthorn at a frame hire, whose advertising spoke most highly about their vehicles. The ads showed a plush showroom featuring attractive young ladies swooning over highly polished conveyances. The reality was a dirt floor yard with canvas screens overhead to ward off the endless Manzanita rain. No attractive young ladies were in evidence, swooning or otherwise, but there was a salesman in a checkered jacket, the fur of some unidentifiable animal decorating the collar.

"Yes, gents, what can I do you for?" He laughed. "Just my little joke, you understand."

"We are looking for a functional four-man luggage frame in good condition. We will need crew as well," Allenson said.

"Of course gents, of course, come over here."

The salesman showed them to a large object covered in a plastic sheet, which he pulled off to reveal a baroque carriage decorated with silver and gold cherubs blowing horns.

"Only the best, for gents like you. I can see that you are men of quality," the salesman said.

"I believe I used the word functional," Allenson said patiently. This was clearly going to be a long haul.

"Right, nothing gaudy then. I have just the thing," said the salesman.

They wound through the yard to another plastic mound. The salesman removed the sheet with a flourish.

"A Saxo Speeder," he said with pride. "She's a beauty, isn't she?"

The Speeder was a low-slung frame equipped with completely unnecessary fins on a streamlined blue and white body. Painted fireballs rolled down the hull. It probably was fairly fast in the Continuum because it boasted a four-man power system and large batteries on a vehicle that had barely the luggage capacity of a lady's handbag.

"What part of the phrase 'functional luggage frame' are you having trouble grasping?" Allenson asked.

"All right, all right, keep your hair on, squire. If you want to go downmarket—how about the Lardu, there."

He pointed to a frame that was upended against the yard wall. At first sight it certainly looked like just the sort of light transport frame that would suit their needs. Hawthorn pulled it down and examined it closely, checking connections and motors. He rejoined the others, wiping his hands on his trousers.

"That frame would be a perfect choice, if I wanted to commit an insurance fraud," Hawthorn said. "When Sar Allenson asked for a functional vehicle, he meant one that might have a sporting chance of surviving a trip through the Continuum. My patience is exhausted. Do you have such a frame for hire or not?"

"This way, squire," said the salesman.

He showed them to a Rover, which survived Hawthorn's examination. They dickered for some time over the fee, until Allenson had got it down to something almost reasonable.

"At that price, I expect you to throw in four crewmen," said Allenson.

"No problem, squire, I will get you four servants," said the salesman.

"I prefer employees," Allenson said. "They have more incentive to return."

The salesman's smile didn't slip. "That can be arranged. Shall we say a ten percent surcharge?" he asked.

"We shall not," Allenson replied firmly. "Take it or leave it."

"Done," said the salesman, shaking his hand.

"Tell the employees that I will give them a bonus on successful completion of the journey."

"You can pay it all to me and I will pass it on," said the salesman.

"I think not," Allenson replied.

"Can't blame a man for trying, govnor," said the salesman with a grin.

Allenson could not help grinning back. "Govnor" was obviously a step up from "gent" or "squire" in the salesman's vernacular.

As they left the yard Allenson said to Hawthorn, "You know, I think I am getting the hang of dealing with Manzanita people."

"Let's hope it works with Riders," Hawthorn replied, puncturing his smugness.

CHAPTER 13

Nengue

Allenson watched Payne personally checking that the porters properly secured the luggage vehicle once their camping gear had been offloaded, and that its motion detectors were functioning. Once they were well on the way into the Hinterlands, Payne had not disappointed him. Payne then dispatched the porters to fetch wood for the campfire, but he first insisted that they reload every item not immediately needed back onto the luggage frame.

The porters were willing enough workers, once Allenson had explained his bonus system, but were a sorry crew. Various inadequately treated injuries and infections had severely damaged their health. None could write, so he had been obliged to use DNA prints on their terms of employment rather than signatures.

"You were right; he really is quite competent when sober," Hawthorn said, sipping his mug of cafay and watching Payne.

Payne joined them after checking the tension on

a retaining strap with a final tug. Allenson handed him a cafay.

"The vehicle will have to be repacked in the morning, before we move on," Allenson said.

"Yes, sar," Payne replied, "but it never hurts to be prepared for a quick getaway. The more gear we have loaded, the less we will leave behind if we have to run for it."

"You think we might be attacked?" Allenson asked.

Payne shrugged. "No idea, but this area is thick with Riders."

"These Riders are supposed to be on our side," Allenson said.

Hawthorn snorted but kept his counsel.

"In my experience, sar, Riders are only ever on their own side," Payne said politely.

Payne drank his boiling hot cafay in gulps, seemingly oblivious to burns. His hand was steady and his eyes had lost the worst of their yellow tinge.

"You look well, Master Payne," Allenson said.

"Yes, sar, I often do when I dry out," Payne said with brutal honesty. "I suppose one day I won't—dry out, I mean. There's only so much deotox pills can do."

"Dammit, I like a drink and a party as much as the next man, but why does someone like you, with useful skills, debase themselves in that way?" Hawthorn asked. "You could be respected instead of the town drunk."

Allenson winced.

"No, it's alright, sar," Payne said to Allenson. "It's a fair question seeing as how you are paying me."

Payne stared into his cafay. "I'm not much one for thinking about things. Everyone drinks, where I come from. I used to drink plum brandy to help me sleep. Not much to do going backward and forward through the Hinterlands. When I ran out of brandy there was always plenty of tonk on the frame, for trading, see. It sorta creeps up on you. Then the detox pills don't work so well in the morning and you need a sip o' tonk to pick you up. I think that's where you cross the line. When you first find out that a nip of the hard stuff in the morning gets you going. You think you've gotten on top of it, found a magic solution, like."

He paused and stared into the fire. Allenson and Hawthorn didn't interrupt. After a while, Payne looked up.

"But it's a trap, innit? You need a bigger nip every morning until you can't work at all without a ton of booze aboard," Payne said. There was another pause. "Then you can't work even with it," Payne said, softly.

Allenson emptied out the rest of his cafay. "We might as well turn in and get an early start. I want to make the trading post on Nengue before local nightfall."

Allenson checked the receivers on his frame and cursed under his breath. There was no sign of a locator beacon on Nengue. Finding the trading post would be like locating a single leaf in a jungle. He glanced over to Hawthorn in the hope that he had a signal, but Hawthorn gave the universal wash out sign.

The two friends pedaled one-man frames. Payne rode in the luggage frame with the four porters; Allenson had been pleased to see that the guide had taken his turn on the pedals. The porters were not the strongest of men, and rotating them allowed the small convoy to maintain a decent pace. Fortunately, Payne showed every sign of knowing where he was going.

Payne moved to the front of the luggage frame to see what the holdup was. His image shimmered and pixellated. The frame's field was badly balanced, distorting light passing through. It took much hand waving before he grasped the problem.

Payne phased the luggage vehicle partly into real-space above the planet, handling the unwieldy machine with great skill. The contrast with the reeling drunk of a few weeks before was startling. They materialized over a continent obscured by turbulent smoke. It was brightly lit from below. As Allenson watched, something exploded in the atmosphere with a flash. Sparks burst out from the explosion like an opening flower before falling and being lost in the haze. Allenson had seen simulations of strategic plasma bombardment in plays. The effect was disturbingly similar.

Payne steered the luggage vehicle down toward the planet, maintaining partial phase. They headed for the coast, descending gently. Glowing lava ran into the sea, setting off explosions of steam and spray. The sea spat and boiled but the heat-plasticized plastic rock pressed on relentlessly.

Allenson wished they could loiter to watch, but Payne pressed on out to sea. Nengue was in the grip of a continental-scale tectonic event. No wonder there was so little to hunt here. It had nothing to do with the Rider presence and everything to do with volcanism. Nengue must be experiencing a mass extinction of animal and plant life like the Permian disaster on Old Earth, when the Siberian Traps covered a million square miles in lava.

The geological catastrophe offered a likely explanation for the trade in gems: unusual minerals brought to the surface under conditions of great heat, massive pressures, and sudden cooling was ideal for gemstone formation. The Riders probably did no more than comb through the debris along shorelines on the edge of lava-flow regions. This planet was ripe for industrial exploitation. The traders were just pecking at the edges of its commercial possibilities. Allenson was also willing to bet there were large, minable reserves of rare earth metals and other elements.

For the first time, Allenson could visualize Todd's dream. Nengue would never be a clean environment for human beings, but it was a treasure trove, a veritable dragon's hoard. This could be the economic powerhouse to open up this whole region for colonization. Somewhere close by would be better worlds for human life. Nengue would need food supplies and logistic support. Colonization would start with farms, but then rapidly proceed to industrialization. An administrative and economic center could develop in the Hinterlands to rival the Home Worlds.

A nagging thought crossed his mind. There were many vested interests in Brasilia that might not smile at such a development. That, though, was a problem for another day. The immediate issue was to keep Terra away from Nengue.

He was dropping behind the others. He turned his attention back to pedaling, but visions of a new home world kept dancing through his imagination.

Payne found the Rider camp by following a series of landmarks using point to point navigation. The man had not lied when he had claimed familiarity with the world. The Viceroy agreed to see Allenson immediately, no doubt impressed by the novelty of the visit.

"You big man, box people," said the Rider. He hit his chest with his fist. "Me Viceroy, big man, Stone People."

"Sar Allenson," Allenson said, hitting his own chest.

The Viceroy's body bore multiple scars and he looked about thirty, a great age for a Rider. He was dressed like all the other savages except for a fluorescent orange waistcoat. When the Viceroy hit his chest, the waistcoat projected a purple hologram asserting that he was a friend and ally of Brasilia.

They met under the chief's shelter, a hut open on three sides with a sloped roof so that the rain drained off. It was made from cut-down local saplings, twisted together to form a continuous structure supported by branches resting on the ground. It would not withstand much of a wind. The Rider encampment consisted of similar temporary shelters; only the trading post was a permanent structure.

The Nengue climate was ghastly. It was hot, the air so humid you could chew it. The high carbon dioxide concentration forced the party to take a geneadjustor to prevent tachycardia and respiratory disruption. Every breath stank of sulfur compounds, the foul smell of rotten eggs cut by the sharp tang of dioxide.

The Viceroy's beast shifted, moving its crystal spears with a grating noise, like a knife against a whetstone. The Viceroy made a low crooning sound and the beast twisted and settled down like a labrador finding a sleeping place. It had never occurred to Allenson that beasts could hear, but he supposed that there was no reason why crystals could not detect vibrations.

The meeting started with an exchange of gifts. Allenson presented the chief with a ceramic chopper, colored bright yellow. The Viceroy's return gift was a withered hand that had belonged to a clan chief who had transgressed in some way. Allenson received the revolting item with a great show of pleasure.

A Rider woman appeared with two plastic storage boxes. The Viceroy sat on one and indicated that Allenson should sit on the other. Everyone else was expected to squat on the floor. The woman left without speaking or being spoken to. Everyone in and around the shelter was male.

The Viceroy launched into a long list of his ancestors and their more notable deeds, using a mixture of Kant, his local clan dialect, and human speech. Riders arrived and left during the Viceroy's speech. If this was a court, it was a very informal example. The list of names ended with the Viceroy himself. Apparently his deeds of valor and cunning surpassed even those of his noble ancestors. He completed his account and looked expectantly at Allenson.

"You should recite the deeds of your forefathers, sar," Payne said.

Allenson took a deep breath and started with his family's key role in the subjugation and colonization of Brasilia. He stopped at the end of each paragraph, so that Payne could translate. The break gave him a chance to think up the next outrageous lie. Hawthorn watched with admiration, clapping when Allenson recounted how his ancestor, Long John Allenson, had slain the jabberwocky in single combat while crossing the Bight. Allenson recanted his own deeds and the trail of corpses he had left. He finished with an account of how he had charged an entire clan of heavily armed men single-handed with a useless gun, putting them to flight.

"I was there. I witnessed that," Hawthorn said, repeating the statement in Kant.

Allenson was perturbed to be reminded that the last story was actually true. What did that indicate about his character? He prided himself on being a rational, enlightened man, not some sort of savage or berserker. He suppressed the thought. This was no time for introspection.

The Viceroy stood up, indicating that the interview was over.

"We have not yet discussed anything useful. I need to know about Terran activity," Allenson said quietly, to Payne.

"There will be time tomorrow, sar," Payne said. "You cannot appear too eager when dealing with Riders or it will be taken as disrespect or, worse still, desperation and weakness."

Allenson bit back his frustration. There was no point in hiring an expert advisor and then ignoring his counsel. The diplomatic party returned on foot to the trading post. They wore sashes of purple and gray. Allenson had been assured on Manzanita that this would grant them immunity from attack at Nengue. However, he and Hawthorn placed far more faith in Payne's additional suggestion that they be very visibly armed at all times. Hawthorn carried his rifle and Allenson a carbine. They also wore shoulder belts with spare batteries and ionization pistols. Payne had a short barrelled combat shotgun. It would be useless at more than ten meters but utterly lethal at short range.

The trading post was in far better condition than Allenson anticipated. It was surrounded by a stockade that showed signs of recent repair. Firing loopholes were positioned above head height, so that an attacker on foot could not use them. Ceramic razor wire was twisted in loops along the top of the stockade. The traders might let items like the signal beacon fail through lack of maintenance, but they were far more assiduous about the post's defenses.

Payne tapped a code into a keypad by a small double door in the stockade wall. There was the thump of solenoids engaging and an alarm went off. The doorway was so low that the friends had to stoop to enter. Payne shut the doors and wooden bars dropped down, automatically blockading the doors, and the alarm went off.

"The system also bolts the doors if the power goes off," Payne said, noting Allenson's interest.

Dirt was piled up against the stockade walls under the loopholes to make firing platforms. The single building inside was strongly built of logs. It also had firing loopholes, but no windows. Someone opened a loophole to examine the arrivals. They stood perfectly still. After what was probably a few moments, but felt subjectively longer, the loophole closed.

The expedition's luggage vehicle was parked between the stockade wall and the blockhouse. The porters sat cross-legged beside it, playing a dice game. A smaller two-man frame was parked nearby. Iron-tipped posts were spaced at intervals, mounted on stands so they could be moved to provide additional parking space.

"What's to stop Rider beasts landing on the roof?" Allenson asked.

"We have more spikes up there," Payne replied. "There is also a trapdoor that leads up to a fortified firing point."

"You don't place much faith in the Rider's truce, then," Hawthorn said.

Payne looked at him uncertainly.

Hawthorn grinned. "I am joking, of course."

"Yes, sar," Payne said, smiling dutifully at the boss's quip.

"What's to stop Riders overflying the post and lobbing in rocks and torches?" Allenson asked.

"Nothing really," Payne replied, "except that they would make great targets." He raised his gun to illustrate.

"The post could not hold off a serious assault for long," Allenson said.

Payne replied, "But it doesn't have to, you see, sar. The defenses are more to stop a handful of Riders from trying their luck, or to give us time to get the frames and run for it."

Allenson privately thought that the average trader frame had no chance of outrunning Rider beasts and, from the expression on his face, Hawthorn concurred. Nevertheless, the stockade and blockhouse were not useless. They deterred thieving and so reduced the risk of an incident escalating out of control. Walls also supplied a psychological barrier between the traders and Riders.

The blockhouse was divided into a communal area for domestic activities and a series of tiny private rooms with beds. The team had gotten into the habit of Payne eating with Allenson and Hawthorn, leaving the porters to enjoy their meal in peace, so they had supper inside, while the porters ate *al fresco*. The only other occupants were a surly trader and his assistant, with whom they barely exchanged ten words. Allenson was not unhappy to keep it that way.

The next morning the three went back to the Viceroy's shelter. He held court, enthroned on his plastic box. The only other box had been set to one side for Allenson to observe the proceedings. Plaintiffs and defendants, escorted by fellow clansmen, came before the Viceroy to have cases judged or arbitrated. Each case started with a ceremony that involved plaintiff and defendant making a cut on their hands and allowing a drop of blood to drip into water held within a human skull. They took turns to drink.

"It's like taking an oath, you see, sar," Payne said in response to Allenson's inquiry. "They are supposed to tell only truth and abide by the Viceroy's decision on pain of spilled blood."

Allenson found the first case interesting, in an anthropological sense, but that soon paled. Evidence went on indefinitely with much histrionics and arm waving, until the Viceroy had decided he had heard enough and pronounced a decision. Most of the cases involved arguments over compensation for theft or insults.

One case involved deep and genuine passion, going by the looks exchanged. The plaintiff opened with a charge against the defendant. The Viceroy indicated he could speak by handing him a token made from bone.

"What is this about?" Allenson asked Payne, curious at the hatred displayed.

"The Rider on the right claims that the one on

the left has stolen his woman." Payne replied. "It has escalated into all out clan warfare so the, ah, principals have been pushed into going before the Viceroy for a decision."

"Oh, it's over a woman," Hawthorn said.

The Viceroy stopped the plaintiff after some moments, signaling that the token should be given to the defendant. He seized it and launched an impassioned defense, gesturing at the plaintiff with his thumb. The plaintiff screamed in rage and a fast exchange of abuse followed. The defendant threw the token at the plaintiff.

The Viceroy stood up and yelled a single word. There was immediate silence.

"What was that about?" Allenson asked.

"The woman-stealer claimed that the woman had gone willingly with him as the other man is impotent with a tiny, ah, organ, sar. He was boasting about his own sexual prowess in comparison," Payne replied.

"I told you Riders weren't so different from people," Hawthorn said, a cynical smile playing across his lips.

The Viceroy sat and gave his decision, waving at the plaintiff with the back of his hand, as if flicking away a mosquito. The defendant smiled broadly and flashed a look of triumph at his accuser. Allenson gathered that the Viceroy had rejected the suit and found in favor of the defendant. It seemed that possession was nine-tenths of Rider law when it came to ownership.

The rejected Rider screamed with rage. Pulling a knife, he hurled himself at the Viceroy. The Rider's trajectory took him past Hawthorn, who stuck out a leg, bringing the man down. The Viceroy kicked the plaintiff in the stomach. Other Riders grabbed the would-be assassin and forced him to his knees.

The Viceroy giggled. He seemed to be in a surprisingly good mood for a man who had just survived an assassination attempt. Presumably it was not a novel experience. He retrieved the yellow chopper from the back of the shelter. He sauntered back to where the Rider was restrained, and smiled down at him. The Rider looked up in hatred but did not struggle. If anything, he seemed resigned. The Viceroy raised the hand ax and, taking careful aim, smashed it down on the Rider's head, splitting the skull and splattering blood and brains.

Allenson tried to look bored when the Viceroy glanced over to see how he had taken the execution. Hawthorn sighed and flicked a piece of bloodied bone off Allenson's jacket.

"I do wish that chap would be more careful with his chopper. The nearest tailor is back in the Stream," Hawthorn said, in his role of aide.

The Viceroy looked inquiringly at Payne, who translated Hawthorn's words, in so far as they could be translated. The Viceroy looked blankly at Hawthorn before bursting out laughing. He gestured for the corpse to be dragged away.

"Me big man, you big man," the Viceroy said. "We talk now."

It was possibly the strangest conversation in which Allenson had ever participated. It was conducted in three languages, only one of which he spoke. Riders dropped in to observe the proceedings and, just as readily, drifted away when bored. Allenson kept his eyes fixed on the Viceroy, despite communicating through Payne.

"I want to know whether he has reports of Terran

explorers or traders operating within the region. Ask him in the appropriate manner," Allenson said.

"Yes, sar," Payne said, launching into a long exchange with the Viceroy.

"Well?" Allenson asked, interrupting.

"He says box people—that's humans, sar—come and go, but he wants to know why you don't know what your clans are up to," Payne replied.

Allenson was aware that the Viceroy was observing his reactions, so he made a point of maintaining a neutral expression.

"He doesn't know that humans across the Bight are divided between two nations?" Allenson asked.

"I suppose not, sar," Payne replied. "I could ask if you like?"

"Wait, let me think," Allenson replied.

"Do we want to give him that information?" Hawthorn asked, his words mirroring Allenson's own thought processes.

"No, I can think of several reasons why we might regret that," Allenson replied, "but I can't think of any way to get the information I need without revealing our own political situation. Very well, Payne, explain that the Terrans are an irritating, but inferior, human clan who are our enemies. Stress that the Viceroy is fortunate to have a treaty with the stronger clan."

Payne launched into an explanation. Hawthorn chipped in the odd remark in Kant. The Viceroy watched Allenson with shrewd eyes. He seemed to be digesting the implications that humans acknowledged no single authority, however tenuously. Allenson wondered what the shadowy Rider's Council would make of this information, assuming the Viceroy passed it on.

Would the Rider Chief see some personal advantage in keeping things to himself? Allenson pushed the thoughts aside. This was a problem for another day. Stay focused, Allen, he told himself.

"Tell the Viceroy that we are concerned that the Terrans have plans to establish forts and colonies deep into the Hinterlands, intruding on this area."

The Viceroy cleared his nose while Payne explained, blowing each nasal passage noisily onto the ground. He waved a hand airily and replied to Payne.

"He says that there are no permanent Terran settlements in his lands," Payne said.

"Ask him if he will guarantee to keep the Terrans out," Allenson said. "We need to be sure that he will discourage Terran penetration by whatever means necessary."

Payne did as he was bid. "The Viceroy agrees. He says that all humans are barred from settlement in Rider Lands."

"I thought Fontenoy told us that Brasilia had a treaty with the Riders to exploit the Hinterlands?" Hawthorn asked.

"He did," Allenson replied grimly. "Clearly Brasilia's understanding of the treaty differs substantially from the Riders'."

He was disturbed by this revelation. Exploitation implied settlement, at least to Brasilia. How could such a critical negotiating point be completely confused between the two principals? This did not bode well for the future. Ah, well, yet another problem for another day. Nothing would be gained from opening this particular pit of vipers. There was still the matter of establishing the degree of Terran activity.

"Ask the Viceroy whether his Riders have seen Terrans in the Hinterlands," Allenson said.

"He says—yes," Payne replied.

"Is there any chance of pinning down where?" Allenson asked.

There was a long exchange between Payne and the Viceroy. Hawthorn and various Riders joined in. Hawthorn called up a map on his datapad and tried to show it to the Viceroy. He gazed at it in incomprehension. He turned it over, apparently fascinated by the stitching on the hand-tooled leather case.

The discussion wound down.

"Well?" Allenson asked. "Will someone enlighten me?"

"I'm sorry, sar, but I can't," Payne replied.

"I suspect I know the reason, but tell me anyway," Allenson said.

"The Riders know, but they can't explain it," Payne said, struggling with his own explanation.

"I was afraid of that. We lack a sufficiently shared cultural frame of reference with Riders," Allenson said.

Payne acquired a hunted look.

"Sar Allenson means that Riders can't read our maps," Hawthorn said.

"Ah," Payne said, his face brightening.

"Well, that leaves us no choice," Allenson said, "We will have to go and look for ourselves."

· CHAPTER 14 ·

Larissa

Allenson thought he was going mad. The talks and negotiations were interminable. The Viceroy made speeches, pleaded and cajoled, but his subjects, if that was the right word, were sulky and uncooperative.

"What is going on?" he asked Payne, patience quite exhausted. "All I want is for the Viceroy to give us a guide to the Terran post and a small escort of fifty Riders or so, as per the treaty with Brasilia. Why is that so difficult? Is he deliberately stalling?"

"No, sar, the Viceroy is doing his best, but he can't get any volunteers."

"Volunteers!" Allenson exploded. "Why doesn't he just pick some volunteers and give them their marching orders? Is he in charge or not?"

"Well, yes and no," Payne replied, not entirely helpfully. "The ordinary Riders didn't agree to any treaty, you see?"

Allenson gave him a poisonous look.

Payne hurried to explain. "The Viceroy is the Rider overchief, but that is more a matter of status and custom than being in charge in a human sense. He can only try to persuade."

"But large Rider warbands do exist," Allenson said. "All I want is fifty men."

"Warbands are a matter of individual Riders joining a chief in expectation of loot or glory. It depends on the chief's *shrek* as well."

"Shrek?" Allenson asked.

"Reputation or gravitas," Hawthorn said. "It doesn't translate very well. The word implies potency or even luck. It's an important concept to Riders."

"I see," Allenson said. He did not really understand but he accepted that this was an issue. He didn't understand the Continuum either but used it all the time.

"The Viceroy has a difficult job," Payne said. "He lacks the shrek of a great warchief since the treaty, and escorting us is likely to provide little in the way of either glory or loot. It must seem a piddling task to most Riders, so they are not interested. Another problem is that there are only a few warriors here at the moment. Riders don't really live at Nengue, sar. They sort of drop in when passing."

"Drop in?" Allenson asked.

Payne shrank back at Allenson's expression. Allenson forced himself to compose his features. It was hardly Payne's fault and nothing would be gained by frightening the man, especially just when he had just got his confidence back.

"Never mind, Master Payne, I am sure you are doing your best," Allenson said.

"Yes, sar."

"Fontenoy and the Assembly are in a fool's paradise

with that treaty," Allenson said to Hawthorn. "Their assumptions about Rider society and organization bear no relation to reality."

"Politicians making decisions in a fantasy land of optimistic expectations?" Hawthorn grinned. "Like that never happened before?"

Riders drifted away from the discussion until only three were left.

"Three men," Allenson said. "We have an escort of three men."

He tried to keep a poker face but the Viceroy picked up something because there was an exchange with Payne.

"The Viceroy has announced his intention of guiding us himself, sar," Payne said. "I think he is a bit embarrassed at having so little shrek."

"So, four men," Allenson said. "Who are the other three?"

"Two are clan chiefs who owe the Viceroy a favor and I don't know the third, the one with the gammy leg. He probably has nothing else to do and is bored."

"Terrific," Allenson said. He thought quickly. "I am not risking taking that damn baggage frame along with such a small escort," Allenson said. "You and I will go, Hawthorn.

"Master Payne," Allenson said, looking the man straight in the eyes. "I cannot in good conscience order you to accompany us as it is beyond our agreement, but I would ask you to come. Your skills will be useful but, more importantly, Sar Hawthorn and I will feel safer knowing we have a good man watching our backs."

Payne straightened his back, returning Allenson's

gaze. "Very good, sar, I will unpack a spare single seat frame. There is a fourth frame in the baggage. Would you like me to get it out and ask one of the porters to come with us?" Payne asked.

"Would any of them be of any use?" Allenson asked, in reply.

Payne considered. "Not much."

"Then just the three of us," Allenson said crisply, and stood up. "Let's go before any of our escort change their minds."

Allenson watched the beasts with fascination. He had never been this close to a Rider in the Continuum. The Viceroy and chiefs rode their own beasts but Gammy Leg rode pillion. The beasts were surrounded by translucent orange bubbles that shimmered through the spectrum from lemon yellow to scarlet. Their crystals splayed out, maximizing the energy field around them. Power bled off continually in a spiral, leaving the wake of orange coils that he associated with Riders.

A soft chime drew Allenson's attention back to his frame's screen. The navigational icon was flashing. The frame had an inertial navigation system that predicted its position while traveling through the Continuum. The system could not cope with the random flows and eddies that forced the frame off track but, provided the currents were random, and they usually were, it gave an approximate position.

Allenson had instructed the navigation to continually test the Continuum topography around them with any records, no matter how sketchy. The chime indicated that it had found a match within the permitted ten percent of error—he had tried a more accurate five percent limit without success. He touched the icon, activating the report. It suggested they were intersecting the path of the ill-fated Stenson-Rowland expedition at Larissa.

He zoomed in. Larissa had rated a name, rather than just a survey number, because it was an inhabitable world close to a permanent Continuum feature marked as Three Chasms. A base at Larissa would dominate a number of chasm currents, giving control over a large area. Allenson instructed the navigator to extrapolate the likely course taken by the Viceroy based ·on their route so far. It ended in nothingness, empty space. He keyed the navigator to ripple outward from that point to locate anything of interest. It did not take long to find a match—a world named Stikelstad.

He examined the Stenson-Rowland navigational map. There were chasms crossing both to and from Larissa to Stikelstad, and then more chasms reaching out from both into unmapped zones. The Terran Post must be on Stikelstad.

Allenson thought hard, turning over the options. They should have a look at Larissa before alerting the Terrans to their presence at Stikelstad. He pedaled harder to overtake the Viceroy, who was leading, and turned the expedition toward the world.

Allenson phased in and out, jumping around Larissa in short hops to reconnoiter. There was nothing remarkable about the world. It was like a hundred others in the Hinterlands, about fifty percent ocean with extensive ice caps covering the poles and reaching down onto the single continent. Rivers bled the melted water away from the ice sheets, passing over barren tundra on their way to the world-ocean. Once, he saw a herd of some slow-moving large animals. Equatorially, the tundra turned into thick forest.

A line of ice-capped mountains bisected the continent. Their height and steepness suggested that they were geologically new, perhaps indicating where north and south land masses had collided to make the supercontinent.

He chose the southern land mass, because it was somewhat larger, and dropped down to take a closer look. Rolling hills stood clear of the forest offering open land so he concentrated on these, but saw no signs of human colonization. He was about to give it up as a bad job when an icon lit up on his frame. It was not a beacon, but something on Larissa was using energy. The signal was small, but it stood out against the uninhabited wilderness. He identified the source, homed in, and landed.

Allenson jumped off his frame and looked around. There was nothing visible but grass interspersed with a few trees. A small furry quadruped with large ears reared up on its hind legs to watch him. He pointed his datapad at it to get a reading and it bolted, fleeing into a burrow. *Interesting,* Allenson thought, *it is scared of humans. I wonder why that is?*

The rest of the expedition landed around him. Allenson ignored them and adjusted his datapad until it picked up the energy discharge. He followed the signal and, under a tree, he found a cheap entertainment unit playing a pornographic movie purporting to show a third civilization orgy. It was a well known fact that the third civilization was licentious; its fall being attributed to immorality by those who worried over such things, so the subject matter was commonplace to this type of entertainment. Allenson checked the unit over. A shadow fell across him, and he looked up to see Hawthorn.

"If you are into that sort of thing, I know where you can obtain a higher quality product," Hawthorn said, dryly.

Allenson blushed, provoking a wicked grin from Hawthorn.

"I was checking the battery," Allenson said defensively. "It's nearly exhausted. Another twelve hours and it would have died."

Hawthorn squatted down beside him. "I doubt if it is good for more than a week's continuous use."

"Yes, someone was here recently, and they were probably Terran." Allenson pointed to the manufacturer's logo on the unit. "Let's have a look around."

"Good idea, but first go back to your frame and fetch your carbine," Hawthorn said.

Allenson's first instinct was to argue. After all, what could happen to him in this empty spot? A moment's reflection raised several possibilities, none of them pleasant.

"Righto." He trotted meekly back to his frame.

It did not take long to find a filled-in waste pit, containing empty supply packs of the type issued to Terran soldiers. The sod had been carefully replaced over the top, but the vegetation had died. Perhaps something in the waste was poisonous to the native flora.

"Someone, presumably Terran surveyors, has gone to a great deal of trouble to conceal this campsite," Allenson said. "So why leave a player running? They might as well have put a neon sign up. That's just damned careless."

Hawthorn grinned. "I would imagine the scenario ran something like this. Private Pratt bunked off to give himself a treat when Sergeant Scary came to find him. Pratt clocked Scary coming and quickly stashed the player behind a tree, intending to come back for it later, but never did. Scary probably kept an eye on him from then on to make sure he was pulling his weight. What's Pratt going to do? Complain to an officer over Scary's head?"

"Put like that, no," said Allenson.

"It's the little things and the little people that trip up the plans of the great and the good," Hawthorn said. "The Pratts of this life do not share the goals of their masters."

"I must remember that," Allenson replied. "We may as well camp here for the night and get some rest. Tomorrow, we can go on to the Terran post when we are fresh."

"At Stikelstad," Hawthorn added.

"Very good, sar," Payne said.

Allenson smiled. He had been hoping that Hawthorn had failed to analyze their path so he could casually drop the real name of their destination and be one up on his friend. He should have known better.

"What are we going to do with them?" Hawthorn nodded casually in the direction of the Riders.

"We don't need a guide anymore, and four Riders are a fat lot of use for an escort against the Terran military—not that I anticipate any problems. Terra and Brasilia are currently at peace, even here across the Line."

It was not unknown for skirmishes between Brasilian and Terran forces to occur over the Line, as the Bight was sometimes called, even when relations between their home worlds were cordial.

"I am tempted to send the Riders home. I can think of several reasons why we should not encourage Riders to have dealings with the Terrans," Allenson said.

"It certainly is not in our interests for them to become pally," Hawthorn agreed.

Payne cleared his throat.

"You wish to make a point, Master Payne?" Allenson asked.

"Well sar, it occurs to me that the Riders might still be useful as an escort on the way back. Maybe we could leave them here?"

"What a good idea," Allenson replied. "Explain it to them, if you please, Master Payne."

Allenson picked up a Terran beacon and rode it down to the Terran post on Stikelstad. He briefly considered trying to sneak up for a quiet reconnaissance but rejected the idea. The beacon was Government issue and he led a diplomatic mission, not a raid. It would send all the wrong messages if he was caught. Such an open signal also implied that the Terrans were confident they could defend themselves, which told him all a concealed reconnoitre would anyway, so he locked onto the beacon and let the automatics guide him in.

His frame semi-phased into realspace four or five hundred meters out from the post, and perhaps a hundred meters up. Except that it wasn't a post; it was a fort.

The compound consisted of four large two-story buildings arranged around an open square courtyard.

Diamond-shaped bastions projected out from the corners, making a continuous fortified structure. A field gun in the center of the nearest bastion tracked his frame as he approached.

The automatics landed the party in the middle of the yard. A young officer, resplendent in the scarlet uniform of the Terran Regular Army, sauntered over to greet them.

"Brasilians?" the officer said. "We don't usually get Brasilian visitors in this part of New Terra."

"New Terra?" Allenson asked. "Surely this part of the Hinterlands has been claimed by Brasilia."

The officer gave an expressive shrug and pointed to the Terran flag hanging from a horizontal pole over the entrance to what Allenson assumed was the headquarters building. Possession, the officer seemed to imply, was nine-tenths of the law.

"And you are?" the officer asked.

"Sar Allenson of Pentire, Inspector General of the Cutter Stream Militia," Allenson said. "Here to confer with your commanding officer."

"I see," the officer said. It was obvious that he didn't. He also appeared to have problems coping with unexpected events outside his training.

"If you would wait here . . ." the officer began.

Allenson interrupted him. "Lieutenant, my aide and I have had a long and tedious journey and we need to tidy up before meeting the Commandant. You will show us to rooms appropriate for gentlemen."

"Yes, sir," the young officer said.

"And my civilian guide, Master Payne, will also require appropriate hospitality," Allenson continued remorselessly.

"Yes, sir," the officer said, looking miserable. Allenson guessed that someone was about to lose their space, probably the most junior officers.

"You will also want to arrange for our luggage to be unpacked from our frames and brought to our rooms."

"Yes, sir, if you will follow me, sir." The lieutenant turned.

"Lieutenant!"

"Yes, sir?" He turned back.

"Have you stopped saluting senior officers in the Terran Army?"

"No, sir." The lieutenant's hand shot up in a parade ground salute.

After a brief pause, Allenson casually raised his own hand to his forehead. "Lead on."

The young man trotted off, and they followed.

Hawthorn caught Allenson's eye and winked.

"I thought I'd start as I mean to go on," Allenson said somewhat defensively to Hawthorn in a low voice.

"Oh, I'm not complaining," Hawthorn said. "Mind you, I am not sure you are properly dressed to meet a Terran commandant."

"I will be. I have my uniform in my luggage," Allenson said.

Hawthorn grinned. "Unfortunately, I forgot to pack mine. I'll leave you to it, then."

"On the contrary, you will be coming with me," Allenson said. "I was concerned that your memory might fail you, so I had Master Payne pack your uniform."

Allenson felt a smidgeon of guilt at Hawthorn's discomfort, but only a smidgeon.

❖   ❖   ❖

"Inspector General Allenson of the Cutter Stream Militia, and his aide, to see Commandant Bolingbroke."

"Thank you, Lieutenant, that will be all," Bolingbroke said.

At first glance, Commandant Bolingbroke looked like the presenter on a children's entertainment show. He was bald with elaborate waxed moustaches that projected well beyond his cheeks. The moustaches were a startling black, contrasting with an entirely bald head. A portly figure, in his scarlet uniform, he resembled a roly-poly man, a children's toy that always rolled upright no matter how hard it was struck.

Allenson marched across the room to the Commandant's desk, saluted, and removed his hat, tucking it under his arm. The downside of having a large white feather in his cap became apparent when he nearly poked himself in the eye.

"My credentials, sir," Allenson said, slipping his data pad out of his pocket.

Bolingbroke waved the pad away. "I am sure your credentials are in order, Inspector General. You can download them to my clerk later. A tiresome necessity, I am afraid, but it gives the administration something to do. I always find it pays to keep them busy or they start poking their noses into other people's business."

"Yes, sir," Allenson replied.

Bolingbroke conveyed the attitude of a gentleman who would not dream of questioning another gentleman's word and so was mildly embarrassed at having to require him to jump through hoops for a load of tiresome bureaucrats. Allenson found himself warming to the man almost immediately.

"Pull up a chair and relax, young man. We don't

stand much on ceremony here in the wilderness."

Allenson did as he was bid. Taking the Commandant at his word, Hawthorn did likewise without waiting for an invitation.

"Is this merely a courtesy call, or are you here on some specific mission?" Bolingbroke asked.

"I am afraid I have a demand from my government," Allenson replied.

"A demand, eh? That sounds serious," Bolingbroke said. His smile and easy manner implied that he did not take it seriously at all.

Allenson proffered his datapad again and, just as before, Bolingbroke waved it away.

"Something else for my clerk to file, I fancy. Why don't you summarize the main points for me?"

"Well, sir, it's very simple. This fort has been built on territory claimed by Brasilia, and my government requires you to leave immediately," Allenson said.

Bolingbroke looked at him and chuckled. Allenson felt his face reddening.

"Sir, this is not a laughing matter."

Bolingbroke shook his head. "I admire your pluck, Allenson. I have a fortified barracks that could not be taken by any force this side of the Bight. It is defended by one hundred armed men and four guns. You march in with one aide and a civilian guide and announce that you are evicting me. I am afraid that I take my orders from Geneva, not from some pleasant youths from a Brasilian colony. I mean no insult to you or your uniform, but it is a laughing matter."

"I must protest, sir," Allenson said.

"Of course you must and your protest is duly noted, but neither you nor I are responsible for

our nation's strategic policies. You may go back to
your superiors in Manzanita and tell them that their
request is denied. Or, better still; refer the matter
back to Brasilia."

"Some might consider this an act of aggression little
short of a declaration of war, sir," Allenson said hotly.

"Really? I fear you are showing your inexperience,
young man. Your superiors say this is Brasilian territory: mine consider it part of New Terra. I see no
reason why you or I should argue. This is a matter
that we can safely leave to our principals in the Home
Worlds to thrash out."

Allenson found himself at a loss. He had not considered what he would do if the Terrans were courteously
obdurate. He had already pushed his instructions to
their limit. He had no authority to threaten Bolingbroke and, to be realistic, had nothing with which
to threaten him. Bolingbroke obviously grasped this
point quite clearly.

"Come, come, Inspector-General, do not look so
glum. You have carried out your duty admirably.
Now enjoy our hospitality for a few days before you
start the arduous journey back to the Stream. You
may look around Fort Rivere to your heart's content.
You can convey to your superiors how much effort
it has taken to build such an extensive base and
how unlikely Terra will be to give it up lightly. That
might prevent any unfortunate misunderstandings."
Bolingbroke stood up, indicating that the interview
was at an end. "My officers are keen to host a
dinner in your honor in their mess. May I pass on
your acceptance?"

"Of course, sir." Allenson stood and bowed. What

else could he do? It would be ungentlemanly to refuse hospitality. He would not have the Terrans think Cutter Stream colonists were uncouth.

Later that night, he and Hawthorn made their way somewhat unsteadily out of the mess.

"I would be surprised if a gentleman like Bolingbroke would bug our rooms, but there may be others less scrupulous," Allenson said. "So why don't we take a turn around the courtyard while we talk."

"If that is the Terran idea of an informal gathering, then I doubt I would survive one of their formal dinners," Hawthorn said. "The only thing longer than the list of courses was the speeches. I did admire your address on Terran-Brasilian relations, by the way."

Allenson winced. "Fortunately, the Terrans were drunk by the time I was called on to talk so I doubt they will remember any of it. At least I hope not. We may as well take the opportunity to look around the fort tomorrow. We will be dancing to Bolingbroke's tune but the chance to examine their defenses is too good to miss."

"So what are those holes in the walls for, Bombardier?" Allenson asked, with as much wide-eyed innocence as he could muster. "Couldn't an enemy fire through them into the bastion?"

"Bless you, sir," the Terran NCO replied indulgently. "We call them embrasures. The gun can be taken off point defense and retargeted to fire through them. Matilda here will make any enemy standing in line of sight of those there embrasures all carboneezy." The Bombardier patted the gun affectionately and chuckled at his own wit.

The gun was disturbing and impressive close up. It was a quadruple laser that rotated, firing each barrel in turn. That allowed a high rate of fire for a weapon with low grade components and a limited power supply. Each barrel had time to cool and recharge before rotating back into the firing position. It would still be a useful weapon even if a barrel or two overheated and malfunctioned.

A set of power-driven gimbals gave the gun an all-around traverse and variable elevation right up to vertical so all sectors of the sky could be targeted. Handles and sights showed that the gun could still be manually operated if the power drive or automatics failed. It was a robust and practical heavy weapon, entirely suitable for a colonial fort.

"Indeed, how jolly ingenious," Allenson said, in his persona of naive young gentleman.

He wandered over to the embrasure, bending down to look out. The embrasure splayed outward from a narrow throat on the inside wall, optimizing the trade-off between giving the gun the maximum sweep and presenting an enemy with the minimum target to shoot back through.

"I notice that the gun can only fire to the right or left. What do you do if an opponent attacks the bastion head on?" Allenson asked.

"They would be swept by fire from the bastions to each side of us, sir, all carboneezy, no worries. It's better to fire down the flank of an attacking line rather than head on," the bombardier said. "You get more of them in a single burst that way, you see."

Allenson could see only too well. Every direction was covered by intersecting cross fire from two guns.

A handful of men could hold this fort against a much greater number of attackers.

Earth was piled up between the embrasures to reinforce the protection offered by the log wall and to give a banquette, a platform, for troops to fire over the top. The bastions were theoretically vulnerable to artillery shells dropping inside but you would need a high rate of fire to get a shell intact through the point defense system. That was a lot of mortars and ammunition to haul through the Hinterlands.

"I know what you are thinking, sir," said the bombardier. "They're only wooden walls and one good shot from a heavy cannon would smash them to splinters."

Actually, Allenson was thinking no such thing. How the hell would you get a siege artillery piece as far as Stikelstad?

"But we're throwing up an earthen embankment one hundred meters out to block direct fire and give us a killing ground. Engineer-General Vorbon himself recommended this design for the colonies of New Terra."

Vorbon was considered the greatest expert in fortifications of his generation. Allenson thought it unlikely that he would have overlooked anything. Fort Rivere could only be taken by a regular military force with heavy weapons.

Allenson's data pad beeped. A message from Hawthorn asked him to come to the front gate.

"I have been on a little tour of the grounds," Hawthorn said. "There's something I think you should see."

He led the way, following a well trodden path. They went past a convict group manually digging out a ditch. The earth was grainy yellow ocher, almost like sand. The convicts were dressed in loose-fitting grimy orange boiler suits, presumably so they would be easy to spot from the air if they tried to flee. They dug with little energy and less enthusiasm.

A Terran soldier in scarlet uniform guarded the group. His gun lay on the ground, and he sat with his back against a tree stump, smoking. He jumped up when he saw Allenson and Hawthorn, dropping the cigarette and scooping up his rifle with a practised movement.

"Private Pratt, I presume?" Allenson asked rhetorically, under his breath.

"Oh, there will be many Private Pratts in an army," Hawthorn replied. "At least he didn't give his weapon to a prisoner to hold while he had a nap."

Allenson glanced at his friend, unsure if he was joking. He decided not. The soldier saluted, Allenson and Hawthorn returning the compliment by touching their hats. The convicts stopped work and gawped at the friends, obviously impressed by their gaudy uniforms. The soldier ordered them back to work but seemed not to care whether they obeyed him or not. The last sight Allenson had of the man was of him searching in the grass for his dropped cigarette.

"That is a staggeringly incompetent way of constructing anything," Allenson said.

"The ditch will get dug eventually," Hawthorn said casually. "And what else would the convicts, or Private Pratt, be doing?"

"At one level, I am glad to see that the Terran colonial system is at least as inefficient as ours. On another, I despair. This is no way to build a civilization."

Allenson became aware of a rhythmic chugging.

"What on earth is that noise?" He asked.

"Steam generator," Hawthorn replied. "They have a manufactorum complex, over there." He pointed further down to where the path wound into some trees.

The wood was only a few meters deep and beyond it was a set of one-story wooden buildings, thrown up roughly from local timber. Steam drifted from a chimney. Under a lean-to, three men sliced up timber into building planks using a power saw. An artisan controlled the machine and two convicts pushed wood through manually.

"Good grief, there are no guards on that machine. The accident rate must be awful," Allenson said.

"Plenty more convicts where they came from," Hawthorn said, cynically. "Especially after that revolt on Unteranglia."

Unteranglia was a Terran province on the Home Worlds side of the Bight. It had an eccentric orbit and was barely capable of supporting human life but was an important mining center. The workers had formed a guild and stopped production to demand better food and living standards. The resulting riots had been ferociously put down by the Terran security Lictors and the guild members sentenced to an indefinite term of hard labor at the state's convenience—which usually meant life.

Allenson opened his mouth but shut it again without commenting. It was not so different from Brasilia's system of indentured servitude, and he would not play the hypocrite.

Hawthorn pointed at the largest building, which was the size of a warehouse.

"You need to see what's in there," Hawthorn said.

Allenson wondered why his friend was being so mysterious. He soon found out. The warehouse was filled with assembled and part-assembled transport frames, large enough to be useful but small enough to navigate the chasms around Stikelstad. Allenson wandered among them, noting troop transports, baggage transports, and load carriers.

"Larissa," he said to Hawthorn. "They are going to fortify Larissa. That must be what this is all for."

"If they control Stikelstad and Larissa..." Hawthorn's voice trailed off.

"Then they control the Hinterlands all the way to Nengue," Allenson said, flatly. "We can't let that happen."

· CHAPTER 15 ·

The Short Way Home

"Sar, sar." Payne was waiting for them at the fort gate, hopping from foot to foot in agitation.

"Calm yourself, Master Payne. Take a deep breath and tell me the worst," Allenson said.

"This morning, after you left, I saw someone sneaking out of the fort. I know him, sar," Payne said.

"Yes," Allenson said encouragingly.

Payne took a deep breath. "His name is Lars Costeen, sar. He's a Terran, or at least he says he's a Terran. No one knows, really. Don't suppose he knows either. I 'spect he made up the name."

Payne paused again. Allenson resisted the urge to snap at the man. Showing irritation would only unsettle Master Payne further, which wouldn't help.

"Costeen was raised by Riders, you see. He was the only survivor from a village."

"What!" Hawthorn said. "You must be bloody joking. Riders don't adopt human children. I never heard of such a thing."

Payne shrugged. "Well, they did. Costeen was old

247

enough to speak human when he was taken, so he sort of became a half and half, Rider and human, a foot in each camp, you see."

"This Costeen isn't left-handed, is he?" Hawthorn asked.

"Left-handed? No, I dunno." Payne considered, looking at his hands and turning around to work out the mirror image of a left-handed person. "Yes, he is."

"That might explain it," Hawthorn said.

"You saw this Costeen sneaking out of the fort," Allenson said, in an effort to get Payne to the point.

"Yes, sar, and I wondered what he was up to so I followed him. He had a frame hidden out where the shanty town is."

"What shanty...?" Hawthorn asked.

Allenson stopped him with a glare. They would be here all night if he kept asking Payne questions.

"I couldn't follow him, because my frame was back at the fort, but he must have gone to Larissa."

"What makes you think that?" Allenson asked sharply.

"Because he's come back, and he's brought our Rider escort with him," Payne replied.

The party for Allenson's escort was in full swing when he went down into the Courtyard. There were at least a dozen Riders present. Presumably, others had come in from the shanty town to add to the gaiety of the throng.

The Terran captain in charge, Bateman, had insisted the Riders leave their beasts and weapons outside the fort walls, but otherwise allowed them to camp in the corner of the courtyard. He had even piled up some wood for them to have a fire. The courtyard was lit by spotlights on the inner walls of the buildings. Allenson looked carefully, shielding his eyes from the glare. He could just make out the silhouette of armed guards at open windows behind the lights.

Bateman looked like the sort of aristocratic young fop that does a stint in the Regular Army before taking his rightful place in politics. However, looks could be deceptive. Bateman was fluent in Kant and exchanged shouts with the Riders. Each Rider had a bottle of tonk and, judging by their behavior, had already imbibed liberally.

"Good evening, sir," Bateman saluted. "Glad to see you came down to join us. Our Rider friends have already entered into the spirit of the thing."

"So I see," Allenson said tonelessly, casually touching his hat.

"Would you care for a drink?" Bateman asked.

"Tonk isn't really a favorite of mine," Allenson replied.

"You jest of course, sir," Bateman said. "I have reserved plum gin for the gentleman."

Bateman raised his hand in the air and clicked his fingers. All the time he kept his eyes on Allenson. A Terran private soldier hurried over with a glass for Allenson. He slipped on something unsavory and spilled the drink.

"Sorry, sir, sorry sir," the soldier said. He looked as if he was about to burst into tears.

For just a moment, Bateman forgot he was a fop and silenced the soldier with a reptilian glare. "Get another one, now."

While Allenson made small talk with Bateman, he remembered Trina's advice and was just himself, a minor

Brasilian colonial gentleman. It was useful camouflage when Bateman tried to pump him about the Cutter Stream's military capabilities. He even started to enjoy the game as he tried to pump Bateman in turn.

"Big men, all big men," The Viceroy said, putting his arms around Bateman's shoulders and breathing tonk fumes. Bateman winced but managed to keep the smile pasted on his face.

"Terra box men boil my father, eat him," the Viceroy said. He laughed until he doubled over in tears.

Allenson could not help but notice that the Viceroy seemed more familiar with Terra as a political concept than he had let on during their negotiations at Nengue. The Viceroy was either a very fast learner or he was playing a deeper game.

The interruption gave Allenson the chance to disengage from Bateman. He discovered Payne on the edge of the party, staring morosely at a fizzy drink that looked gray-green in the dim light.

"I'm sorry, sar, if I hadn't suggested that we ask the Riders to wait for us at Larissa this would never have happened."

"Not at all, Master Payne, you advised—I decided—and I take responsibility for my decisions. I am not even sure it was a bad decision, just an unlucky one. We could not have foreseen that this Costeen fellow would be here. Speaking of which, is he here? Could you point him out to me?"

Payne indicated a shriveled up runt of a man. Allenson moved determinedly in his direction. "Costeen, I believe," Allenson said. Costeen shied away but Allenson would have none of it.

Costeen grunted, not looking at Allenson. Allenson

gripped him by the left arm and turned him around, so the man had to face him. Costeen had rough scar tissue on his face, passing right through the right eye socket. The remains of the eye looked as if cauterization by fire had been used as treatment. Allenson was unmoved. He had seen worse inflicted as the result of agricultural accidents and knife fights.

"I understand that you lived with Riders, Costeen," Allenson said.

Costeen grunted again. Allenson stared at him eye to eye until Costeen looked away.

"Yes, sar."

"That's better, Costeen. I dislike communication by grunt," Allenson said. "Have you ever ridden a Rider beast?"

"Yes, sar," Costeen replied.

"Have you controlled one?" Allenson asked.

This was the big question. Human attempts to tame and ride beasts had not been entirely successful; the beasts inevitably crushed any human who climbed inside their crystal arrays. Beasts would be so useful if tamed. They could carry up to four riders, and without all that exhausting pedaling. The first people to control beasts would own the Hinterlands and beyond.

"No, sar. A Rider did the controling. I just went along as a passenger."

"I see," Allenson said. "How does a Rider give instructions to a beast?"

Costeen looked directly at Allenson, meeting him eye to eye for the first time.

"I don't know. I wish I did. Sometimes the Rider talks to his beast, sometimes he prods it and sometimes he just ignores it—it all works, just the same."

Allenson accepted Costeen's ignorance. Indeed, he had anticipated it. Why would the man use a frame if he could control a beast? But he had to ask. He tightened his grip on Costeen's arm until the man grimaced in pain.

"One last thing, Costeen. You interfered in my business today to my disadvantage. I will overlook it this time, but I will not be so tolerant if it happens again. Do we understand each other?"

Payne said nothing, so Allenson squeezed a little.

"Yes, yes, let go of me."

Allenson released him and he scuttled off rubbing his arm. A drunken Rider reeled past screaming, clawing at Allenson for support. He pushed the Rider away. The man fell over and vomited, rolling in his own spew. Sickened, Allenson walked away. Bateman intercepted him.

"Leaving, Inspector General Allenson? The night is yet young," Bateman said.

"I have not yet developed a taste for partying with Riders," Allenson replied, trying not to sound provincial.

He handed Bateman his empty glass and went to bed.

In the morning, the Rider party had restarted. Perhaps it had never stopped. Allenson found the Viceroy sitting back against a wall clutching an unconscious Rider woman in one hand, and a bottle of tonk in the other.

"We go now," Allenson said, pointing to the sky.

"Go, now?" The Viceroy looked blearily at him, trying to focus.

"We go—now," Allenson repeated, gesturing with greater exaggeration.

"Plenty tonk," the Viceroy waved the bottle. "Plenty food, plenty women."

He squeezed the woman's breast for emphasis. She stirred and moved against him but did not open her eyes.

Allenson knew a losing proposition when he saw one. He went in search of Hawthorn, bumping into him at the courtyard door leading to the officers' mess.

"The Viceroy won't budge," Allenson said.

"Yah, the Riders will stay there until the booze runs out," Hawthorn said. "Which I suspect will be not until it suits the Terrans' purpose."

"They want to strip us of our Rider protection, you think?" Allenson asked.

"I don't think it would unduly upset that weasel Bateman if we pedaled off and were never seen again." Hawthorn replied.

"The Commandant wants us to get back to the Cutter Stream. He is relying on us to report that the Terrans are unassailable," Allenson said.

"The Commandant is a gentleman; Bateman is, I suspect, something else. Look at it this way; heads we survive and the Terrans win, tails we don't, so we lose."

"Whatever, we go anyway. Where's Payne?" Allenson asked.

"He's, ah, getting ready," Hawthorn replied.

Something in Hawthorn's manner alerted Allenson. "What are you keeping from me?"

"Payne took it so hard that he let us down, at least in his own mind, by the Costeen business that he had a little slip," Hawthorn said, making a rocking motion with his hand to imitate a man drinking from a glass.

"How bad is he?" Allenson asked.

Hawthorn considered. "He's stuffing himself with antitoxins and stimulants. I guess he's okay."

"I had better have a word with him and see if he is fit to travel," Allenson said.

"I wouldn't," Hawthorn said, catching Allenson's arm. "He's beating himself up already for his weakness. He does not want *you* to know. For some reason, he thinks a great deal of you and wants your good opinion. Can't see why myself." Hawthorn grinned to show he was joking.

"That's why you are just an aide and not a leader of men," Allenson said, striking a pose.

Hawthorn slapped him on the back. "Let's have a leisurely breakfast, O leader of men, if you can bring yourself to eat with a mere aide, and give Payne a chance to get his act together."

"Lead on, my man," Allenson said. Actually he was glad of the diversion. He needed to think.

Payne looked awful. His eyes were yellow and shone with feverish intensity.

"The situation, gentlemen, is as follows," Allenson said. "Our baggage and porters are back at Nengue. Someone has to go and pick them up. I am prepared to lose the baggage, but I cannot leave our porters to the mercy of the Riders. At the same time, we have a duty to inform Fontenoy of our findings as fast as possible. Nengue is not on the direct route home, so we will have to split up."

"Back up a minute," Hawthorn said. "I don't like the sound of that. I don't understand why a few days one way or the other matter overmuch? Why don't we all go back via Nengue?"

"You saw that flotilla of frames. The Terrans are almost ready for the next strategic advance. My guess is that they intend to fortify a base on Larissa. Once they do, we will have the devil's own job winkling them out. We need to get in first. I think a few days could make all the difference. Or is there something I have overlooked?"

He waited, but neither Payne nor Hawthorn spoke.

"Very well, Hawthorn, you and Master Payne will go home via Nengue while I take the direct route."

"Out of the question, Allenson," said Hawthorn firmly. "I will go with you. Master Payne will be quite all right alone."

Allenson looked at Hawthorn and then looked at Payne. The man's hands were shaking.

"I will be alright, sar," Payne protested, thrusting his hands in his pockets.

Allenson and Hawthorn ignored him.

"You don't know the route or its hazards," Hawthorn said. "The frame's navigation won't be able to cope."

"I won't be entirely running blind," Allenson said defensively. "There is some useful navigational data from the Rowland expedition."

"Yah, and look what happened to them," Hawthorn said, snorting.

Actually, no one knew exactly what had happened to the Stenson-Rowland expedition, but pointing this out might not entirely help Allenson's argument.

"Anything could happen," Hawthorn said. "Just one little accident in the wilderness, like a twisted ankle, and you would be as good as dead on your own."

Payne coughed.

"Yes, Master Payne," Allenson said.

"Sar Hawthorn is right, and he hardly needs me to hold his hand," Payne said. "Why don't *I* go with you?"

Allenson paused. Why not, indeed? Payne might not have firsthand knowledge of the Continuum zone they would be traversing, but he was an experienced Hinterlands hand.

"Very well," Allenson said. "That's decided then."

By the third day of travel, Allenson was feeling the strain. He was even more concerned about Payne's effectiveness. The binge at Fort Rivere had done the man no good. Nevertheless, he kept up and never complained.

They repeatedly were forced to detour around unfavorable energy gradients and once had to retrace their path completely, to avoid a chasm that would have swept them away. He looked at his inertial navigator and cursed quietly under his breath. Their progress in a straight line toward the Cutter Stream was painfully slow. An unmapped world lay close by and the minimal information on his chart indicated that it might be habitable. He decided to make their third stopover early. They needed to rest and forage for food. Their food packs were disappearing at an alarming rate and additional calories would be useful.

Once in the world's atmosphere he triggered the frame's biocheck. It came up clean, so he went down to land where a stream ran across a grass plain. It seemed a likely place for animals to come to drink.

They spent eighteen hours on the world, mostly eating and sleeping. Allenson located a herd of six-legged herbivores and Payne brought one down, after Allenson missed. Its flesh tasted rather like goat.

They had barely started to break camp when a beast phased in nearby. The Rider guided it to their camp and landed. He jumped off the beast, which closed its crystals and settled down, twisting like a bolt pushed into a socket. Allenson noticed that the Rider limped.

"Is that Gammy Leg?" he asked Payne.

"Not sure," Payne replied. "I'll try to find out."

Payne and the Rider had a long conversation in Kant.

"It's Gammy Leg," Payne said. "He claims the Viceroy sent him after us as a guide. He says we are drifting off course."

"I suppose he would know," Allenson said. "Very well, Master Payne, ask him to take point, if you please."

They had only been pedaling a few hours when Allenson became concerned. While it was true that the Rider found convenient energy gradients, Allenson's inertial navigation implied that they were turning slowly in a giant circle. He dropped back a little and rendezvoused with Payne, being careful not to touch energy bubbles. Allenson made a circular motion with his hand and gave the sign for a question. Payne nodded vigorously and gave an exaggerated shrug.

The Rider dropped back also and came close to Allenson, as if he wanted to communicate. Allenson could see the man clearly inside the energy field around the beast. Only the Rider's head projected over the scissoring crystal rods. The Rider heaved himself up to his feet, grasping a crystal for support with his right hand. His left came up to point to Allenson. The Rider was holding something.

Allenson had but a moment to register that it was a spring gun before the Rider fired. The solid bolt barrelled through the Continuum leaving a blue wake, penetrating his frame's energy field with a white flash. It clipped the control panel in front of him before exiting his reality bubble with another flash. He automatically jerked the control stick away from the Rider. His frame's energy bubble slid alongside Payne's in an iridescent cascade of colors. The shield vibrated like a giant bell, deafening him.

He reached for his own spring gun but found his laser carbine still clipped to the frame from when he had gone hunting. It would be utter suicide to fire that inside a frame. Very little energy would escape through the field. Most would be reflected straight back. He scrabbled inside a pannier for his spring gun. The Rider was intent on re-cocking his weapon for a second shot.

Payne swung his frame over the top of Allenson's and discharged his own spring gun. The Rider dropped down behind a crystal. Payne's bolt hit it square on. Allenson distinctly saw a flash of light. The beast shied like an animal prodded with a pike. It lurched and the Rider half fell out, having to grab with both hands to stay on. His spring gun pitched over the side and fell away into the Continuum.

The Rider tried to escape but Payne and Allenson pursued him ruthlessly, firing bolts to force the beast down. The beast landed and the Rider jumped off as it touched the ground, just before its crystals closed with a snap. The Rider would have been crushed had he not reacted so promptly.

Gammy Leg made a run for it without looking back. Allenson had had enough. He was damned if he would break into a sprint after all that pedaling, and he was sick of unreliable Riders. He unclipped his carbine and loosed a long burst in the general direction of the Rider. He missed of course. He always missed. This did nothing for his temper. . . .

The burst went over Gammy Leg's head, setting light to the vegetation in an arc in front of him.

"Oh, good shot, sar, and with a carbine too." Payne said.

"Hmm," Allenson replied. "Lucky shot."

Payne regarded him with respect, clearly his leader was modest as well as a crack marksman.

Gammy Leg threw himself on his knees and bowed his head. He was singing in a minor key when they reached him. Allenson looked at Payne and raised an eyebrow.

"It's a dirge, sar. He expects us to kill him so he is singing a final lament."

"I see," Allenson said. He prodded Gammy Leg with his carbine, making the Rider look up. "Ask him why he tried to kill me, if you please, Master Payne."

There was an exchange in Kant.

"He denies trying to kill you, sar. He claims the shot was a mistake."

"Twaddle," Allenson said. "That was as deliberate an act as I have ever seen. What's a Rider doing with a spring gun anyway? Push him harder, Master Payne. Threaten him."

Payne hesitated.

"Well?" Allenson asked. "What are you waiting for?"

"It won't work, sar," Payne replied. "He expects us to torture him to death whatever he says or does."

"Should we try bribery?"

"We could, sar, but he will likely take the bribe and tell you what he thinks you want to hear."

Allenson sighed. "Then I suppose we are finished here. We had better get rid of him."

Payne raised his shotgun high, intending to brain Gammy Leg with the stock.

Allenson grabbed the gun, stopping the move. "That's not what I meant, Master Payne. Tell him that we accept his explanation, that we are abandoning the journey and intend to return to Fort Rivere, and that we want him to go on ahead and inform the Viceroy to be ready for us. Also say that I do not trust him and that we shall travel alone. Make it clear that I will kill him if I see him in the Continuum. We don't want him to assume that I am completely half witted."

"No sar," Payne replied, dutifully. He clearly did not understand, but he carried out his instructions.

They watched the Rider depart. "We'll give him an hour or so to get clear so we may as well have some cafay," Allenson said.

"Who was behind him, sar, do you think?" Payne asked.

"You don't think he was acting on his own initiative?" Allenson replied, answering a question with a question.

"He might have been, sar. Or he might have been put up to it, by the Terrans, or the Viceroy."

"Exactly," Allenson replied. "We have no way of knowing, and the Rider would hardly tell us."

"Are we going back to the Terrans, sar?" Payne said in a carefully neutral tone.

"Good grief, no! We are going to the Cutter Stream, Master Payne. Never hurts to sow a little confusion among the ungodly. That's why I let the Rider live."

Allenson would not have killed Gammy Leg even if

he had no use for the man. What would be the point of a cold-blooded execution? He suspected his conscience would be burdened enough before this business was over without adding unnecessarily to the load.

Payne was in a bad way. Allenson shot a rabbit, or something that looked like a rabbit, and fed him a hot stew before knocking him out with a sleeper. They had fought opposing energy gradients from a rising Continuum storm, before Allenson finally gave in and suggested a layover. With hindsight, he regretted his stubbornness. Refusing to bow to the inevitable had cost them time by pushing Payne further than his health could stand. Allenson checked the Continuum's condition each day before hunting for fresh food. After five days, Payne had recovered to the extent that he could walk.

"Surely, the storm has blown itself out by now, sar," Payne said while turning a rabbit on a stick over their campfire.

"Pretty much, Master Payne." Allenson reclined against a tree, eyes shut, carbine in his lap. Something sporting long claws also hunted the rabbits. Allenson had no reason to think that it would attack fully grown humans, but then, he had no reason to think that it would not.

"You should be on your way then, sar," Payne said.

Allenson opened his eyes, genuinely surprised.

"You feel up to travel, then, Master Payne?" Allenson asked, doubtfully.

"No, sar, I would only slow you down. I meant that you should go on ahead and I will follow when I can." Payne said, looking carefully at the fire.

Allenson gazed at the man, assessing the probability of Payne surviving alone. Not high, he fancied. It was tempting to accept the man's offer at face value. No one would criticize him for following his duty to Brasilia and letting Payne take his chances. No one except Allenson himself, and in the final analysis, his was the only opinion that counted. He would become someone he did not want to know if he started abandoning dependants, dressing up expediency as duty.

"I think not, Master Payne. We started this journey together, so we will finish together," Allenson said, in a tone that shut off further discussion.

"Yes, sar," he said, unable to keep the relief out of his voice.

Allenson considered the options. There was a way out, one that did not require him to abandon Payne or his obligations to the state. It did increase his own chance of dying, but that wasn't a problem. If he died, the Terran Threat was SEP—someone else's problem. Allenson felt almost cheerful.

"There is a compromise solution," Allenson said. "We will abandon your frame and all but essential supplies—food and one gun. You will ride pillion with me."

"Yes, sar," Payne said, eyes widening. People rode pillion on frames for short hops, but it was unheard of for long journeys through the wilderness.

"That rabbit looks about done to me. We will leave directly after lunch."

"Do you require assistance, sar?" asked Destry's footman.

He arrived at the run, still pulling on his blue and gold jacket.

"Yes, Jackson. Unstrap my passenger and get him some treatment."

"Yes, sar. I have informed Sar Destry of your arrival. He will be with you shortly," said the imperturbable Jackson, as he struggled with the buckles.

Allenson stretched his aching joints and muscles. A couple of servants arrived to assist. They carried Payne away. Allenson had had to tie Payne to the frame for the last leg of the trip after the man had lapsed into unconsciousness. Wagener was closer than Manzanita, so Allenson had diverted to get medical attention for Payne. He was not sorry to rest. The Destry demesne had the best medical facilities on Wagener so it was an obvious choice.

A frame materialized dangerously low and bumped off the ground. Destry sprang out the instant its field collapsed.

"Good God, Allenson, we feared you were dead. Where's Hawthorn?" Destry asked.

The inquiry meant that Hawthorn was still out there, somewhere, coaxing back the baggage frame. Somehow it would have been frustrating if Hawthorn had got back first, making Allenson's own exertions pointless. Of course, it did not matter provided the Stream got news of the Terran incursion as soon as possible.

"He will be along with the rest of the expedition later. I have to get to Manzanita, Destry. Look after my man please."

Allenson went to climb back on his frame. Destry moved to intercept him.

"Have you lost your wits? Your clothes are hanging off; you must have lost four or five kilos. Your frame looks almost as knackered. I can't let you go."

"It's important," Allenson said.

"Why are all my friends insane?" Destry asked rhetorically, holding up his hands as if appealing to a higher power. "Very well, but rest for a moment. Take some tea and food. For God's sake, bathe. I will get pater's carriage ready to take you, and a chauffeur."

Allenson held up his hands in mock surrender. "If you insist."

"That's settled then," Destry said with satisfaction.

Various flunkies materialized around Destry. He gave instructions for Allenson to be taken to a guest room to refresh himself. When Allenson was alone, he stripped off his shirt and examined himself in the mirror. He had a shock. He looked leaner, stripped down, like a wild animal. The analogy was heightened by the wary look in his eyes. His reflection looked guardedly back. Did it see an earlier, tamer self?

There was a soft knock and the door opened. Sarai slid inside, shutting the door with one hand behind her back.

"Well, well, the dashing hero returns," Sarai said, in mock awe. She put her hand lightly on his bare shoulder. "And with such manly sweat upon his body, it is enough to turn a maiden's head."

Allenson eyed her reflection in the mirror. She was blond this time, with saffron eyes, and wore an orange silk, wispy thing, that wound loosely around her body. Allenson had a feeling of déjà vu. He and Sarai were looping around the same scene. She would tease him but retreat when he responded; then he would throw her out.

"Do you want me to help you wash anything?" she asked innocently.

Allenson lost his temper. He didn't say anything but he felt his mouth twist. Sarai backed away a step with an alarmed expression. She really looked at him for the first time instead of posing.

"Is something wrong, Allen?"

He covered the ground in one step, seizing her wrists tightly and pushing her arms above her head.

"Yes, Sarai, something is wrong. I have been lied to, betrayed, patronized, shot at, gone hungry and pedaled my ass off. And it's not yet over, so I don't need you playing cocktease right now."

He pushed her backward with each step. They reached the bed and she fell backward with him on top. They looked at each other without speaking.

"Get out, Sarai," he finally said. "Or I will do something we will both regret."

He let go of her wrists and was not proud to see that he had left marks. He did not feel especially guilty either.

"Cocktease, am I?" she asked, throatily. "What makes you think I am teasing?"

The orange material was as thin as it looked and ripped easily when he pulled it from her breasts downward. She wore nothing underneath and she opened her legs in blatant invitation. And he was lost.

· CHAPTER 16 ·

The Councillors

The crowd surged forward when Allenson and Fontenoy stepped into the plaza. The majority screamed their hatred of Terrans, waving banners proclaiming "Deff To Tera," "Kill The Basturds," and so on. A hardy little group raised a "No War, No More" banner, provoking a howl of outrage from the patriotic mob. Allenson noted wryly that the peace mongers were better educated than the patriots, or at least better spellers. A fight broke out and rapidly spread, although it was not clear who was on what side.

The Lictors surged forward, ramming the various protestors back with their shields. A Lictor staggered as a banner pole struck him in the side of his helmet, end first, like a hoplite's spear.

"Batons," ordered the officer just behind the line of purple uniforms, his voice booming out from the amplifier built into his helmet.

Black clubs rose and fell in unison, beating back the crowd. Yellow sparks showered whenever a baton hit metal and over-discharged. Protestors dropped silently, limbs twitching.

The people in front turned to flee but were blocked by those behind pushing forward. Batons crashed into shoulders and legs, eliciting screams. The crowd swayed and then broke, pouring backward in streams like water from a broken damn. Small knots of protestors huddled together for protection, standing like sand islands in a torrent, eroding body by body until they were swept away.

The mob disappeared out of the plaza and down the alleys between the state buildings. The Lictors pursued them for a short distance until recalled to form an honor guard. The officer turned and saluted.

"It is safe to proceed now, Governor."

"The Upper House has confirmed your appointment as Inspector General, Allenson," Fontenoy said, continuing their conversation as if nothing had happened. "Your news of the Terran incursion has raised serious alarm."

"No doubt—especially among those who have an interest in the Harbinger Project," said Allenson cynically.

"Which is most of them, one way or another," Fontenoy replied. "No, the problem is in the Lower House, particularly with a faction led by Rubicon."

"Why is he objecting?" Allenson asked.

"You can ask him yourself," Fontenoy replied. "We have an appointment to meet a delegation of the heads of the more important factions."

Allenson was conflicted at having this dropped on him without warning. He had half a mind to protest to Fontenoy that he had not been given time to prepare, but he had no idea what preparation would be required and he knew that a delay would simply give him more time to fret. After all, this was what he planned, an entry into the political arena. That did not mean that he was going to enjoy the process.

"So, to sum up, the Upper House and the mob see the need for action to block further Terran expansion, but the Lower House doesn't and is blocking my appointment as a way of negating the policy."

"Quite so," Fontenoy said. "You will have to change their collective mind."

The Lictors stopped at the door to the Council House. Fontenoy was legally permitted to take a bodyguard into the House but it could be seen as a provocative act, one that might harden opposition.

Outside the door to the meeting room, Allenson took a deep breath before entering. He could never understand how some people seemed to relish these sessions. The room had office chairs for around thirty people, of which perhaps a dozen were occupied. They faced five chairs on a raised stage. The occupants of the room stood politely when Fontenoy and Allenson entered, except for a stout, bald man who remained seated, arms crossed and legs spread wide. He eyed Allenson pugnaciously.

"That's Rubicon," Fontenoy said, nudging Allenson.

Allenson climbed the stage and lowered himself into a chair, like an ancient king taking his throne.

"Councillors," Fontenoy said, "Please be seated. May I introduce Acting Inspector General Allenson, who has just returned from leading the expedition in the Hinterlands charting Terran expansion. Sar Allenson has kindly agreed to answer such questions as you might like to put to him."

Actually, Allenson could not remember agreeing to

any such thing. Gentlemen did not normally give expla-
nations to their social inferiors, but he supposed that
it was expected in political matters. After a pause, the
questions came. Mostly they were of a technical nature,
involving calling up maps and videos on the chair's
screens to elucidate or expand some point. Finally, a
lady of substantial girth and shocking pink hair asked
a blunt question that got to the heart of the matter.

"Why should a young, inexperienced man like you
hold such an important position as Inspector General?
We give too many jobs to the boys around here."

A number of Councillors muttered their agreement.
Allenson had been warned to expect something of the
sort from Fontenoy. He held up a hand for silence.

"Councillor?" he asked.

"Councillor Roofer," she replied.

"Inspector General is an important position, Councillor Roofer," Allenson said. "And I can well understand
your concern that the right candidate be appointed,
especially since we face a military crisis. I suggest I
am that man. I am the brother of the current Inspector General."

There was a murmur from the Councillors. Allenson
held up his hand again.

"That in itself is not a qualification, but it does have
the advantage of continuity of authority. No, my real
qualification is that I have led expeditions deep into
the Hinterlands. I have negotiated face to face with
the chiefs of our Rider allies and won their confidence.
I have seen the Terran military machine with my own
eyes and spoken to their commanders. I think I can
confidently state that there is no other person in the
Cutter Stream who can match my experience."

Allenson meant that no other *gentleman* could match his experience. It went without saying that the position was only open to a gentleman. One could not expect soldiers, let alone their officers, to take orders from just anybody, no matter what their abilities.

"I also suggest that my youth is a positive advantage, given that the new Inspector General is likely to involve physically taxing duties," Allenson said.

Councillor Roofer looked at him thoughtfully before nodding her head.

"You'll do for me, sonny."

Allenson was pleased to see that a number of the other Councillors seemed willing to follow her lead.

"Well, if there are no more questions..." Fontenoy said.

Councillor Rubicon climbed to his feet and began to clap, a slow sneering handclap. Some of his supporters took up the rhythm. Fontenoy stopped speaking, looking flustered.

"You have a question, Councillor Rubicon," Allenson said, politely.

"I sure do, sonny," Rubicon said, sticking out his jaw.

One or two of his cronies sniggered. Other Councillors looked embarrassed.

"You are friendly with the Destrys, right?" Rubicon asked.

"I have that honor," Allenson replied.

"And the Destrys own a chunk of the Harbinger Project. In fact, they made you their surveyor, so you are on their payroll."

"That is hardly a secret," Allenson said.

"So you can be relied upon to do their bidding like a good little boy. This whole Terran story is just a scam put about by the Destrys to get support for their business interests in the Hinterlands. They want to expand their landholding at our expense using taxes raised from us. I say they already own too much around here."

Allenson found that he was also on his feet, which was odd, as he did not remember getting up from his chair.

"Good grief, man. You have seen the evidence with your own eyes."

"And what evidence do we have that these so-called records aren't just a colossal fraud?" Rubicon asked.

"You have my word," Allenson said, quietly, expecting that to end the matter.

"And what worth should we put on your *word*," Rubicon sneered. "With you, hand in glove with the Destrys."

Allenson was incandescent with rage. "By God, master, I am not used to being called a liar to my face. I would call you out but..."

"But you won't dirty your hands by dueling with oiks like us," Rubicon finished the sentence for him. The man spread his hands to encompass his fellow councillors.

That was true, but Allenson perceived that he had allowed Rubicon to goad him into a political trap.

"I was about to say that I believe dueling to be a stupid way of settling disagreements," Allenson said, biting back his anger. "Ask around; everyone knows my views on the matter." Allenson spoke directly to the other councillors in the room.

"That's true, his dad was the same," an elderly councillor remarked.

Allenson could have kissed him. He made a note

to get the man's name and see what he could do to return the favor.

Rubicon must have felt the moment slipping away, because he pushed just a little too hard.

"You 'gentlemen,'" Rubicon managed to turn the word into an insult, "don't duel with commoners because you haven't got the balls to face a real man."

"You think not?" Allenson asked.

He launched himself off the platform. The Councillor swung a roundhouse punch that was so slow Allenson could have brewed a cup of tea while considering his options. He ducked under the blow and, putting his hand on Rubicon's elbow, gave him a push, adding momentum to spin him around.

Allenson took a grip on the back of Rubicon's collar with one hand and grasped his belt in the small of his back with the other. He hauled Rubicon up by his trousers, until the man danced on the tips of his toes. Then he pushed forward, faster and faster, until they were both running. When they reached the end of the room, Allenson gave one last heave and threw Rubicon through the window with a thunderous crash of breaking glass.

There was dead silence in the room. Someone outside screamed.

"If no one has any further questions, I declare the meeting adjourned," Fontenoy said, as if nothing had happened. "Please consult with your factions, Councillors, and be ready to vote in one hour."

"Sar Allenson."

He turned to face Councillor Roofer.

"Possibly you forgot we are on the third level?"

"Oh dear," Allenson said. "I hope I have not killed him."

"We should be so lucky," Councillor Roofer said, with a broad smile. "No doubt Rubicon will bounce back like a bad penny. He usually does. Still, we can but hope that his injuries are not too trivial, eh?"

Allenson had no idea how best to answer that, so he restricted himself to a short bow and hurried after Fontenoy, catching him up in the corridor.

"Will the vote go our way?" Allenson asked.

"I think you've crossed the Rubicon," Fontenoy replied.

This is the Stream Militia," Allenson said to himself, appalled.

He walked down the lines of wheezing old men and concave-chested boys in ill-fitting uniforms, many of which still showed evidence of previous owners. At least half of them were unfit for duty. They shouldered a variety of weapons, from ancient laser carbines to single-shot bird hunters.

"Is this all?" Allenson asked the embarrassed captain who was senior officer on parade.

"Well, there should be another fifty or so we could muster but the roll call has not been updated for a while, so some of the troops may have moved away or died."

They passed an old man with white hair and a stoop. The trooper next to him appeared fitter until Allenson noticed that one of his feet was a cheap prosthetic.

"Where are the other officers?" Allenson asked. Only the captain and a cadet had attended the parade.

"Some are back on their estates and I couldn't get word to them in time. We don't normally have parades at short notice, sir. Others may be here in Manzanita.

I have sent runners around the clubs and societies," the captain replied.

"Very well, captain...?" Allenson looked inquiringly at the young officer.

"Rutchett, sir, of Tynsdale Mountain."

"Very well, Captain Rutchett, you may dismiss the men. I think I have seen enough."

"Yes, sir."

Rutchett saluted, which Allenson acknowledged by touching his hat, and gave the necessary orders to the NCOs. The Cutter Stream Militia shuffled off in small groups, most heading for a conveniently sited row of bars.

An elderly man hurried across the parade ground. He was dressed in a uniform that was half a size too small around the midriff despite having been let out. On reaching Allenson, he saluted.

"Colonel Avery, sir. Sorry I'm late, but I was lunching at my club when the muster was called and had to go home to change. You gave us no warning, sir."

"Indeed not, but this is supposed to be a rapid reaction force, is it not?" Allenson asked.

"That is true. We are a mobile force in theory, sir," Avery replied.

"In theory?" Allenson asked, raising an eyebrow.

"We are short of transport. We only have a lift capability of thirty men at a time," Avery replied.

"I see," Allenson said.

Clearly there was nothing to be gained by pursuing that line of inquiry. Allenson had taken the trouble to look up Avery's background, learning from the experience of his first meeting with Fontenoy. Eos Avery had once been an officer in the professional Brasilian

Army, but for many years he had been headmaster of a military-style school for the sons of the aristocracy.

"I am not familiar with soldiers, colonel, but I have to say that I am disappointed in the quality of the men," Allenson said, with masterly understatement.

"Yes, sir," Avery agreed gloomily.

"I have already inspected some of the local reserve regiments. I have to say that all of them gave a better impression of a fighting force than this," Allenson said.

"Yes, sir, but they don't have our disadvantages," Avery replied, somewhat defensively.

"What disadvantages?" Allenson asked. "They have to attract volunteers but these men are drafted. I had expected better."

"Yes, sir, but the draft has so many exceptions," Avery replied.

He began to tick them off on his fingers. "Men who own their own land are exempted, men who own their own businesses are exempted, men in full time employment are exempted if their employers confirm that they are too valuable to be drafted, men in reserve regiments are exempted, men in full time education are exempted, and men who pay a fine are exempted. The payment per day for mustered men is intended for expenses only. Frankly, sir, it is miserable."

"So, broadly speaking, the draft consists of the poor, the unemployable and the disabled," Allenson said.

"Exactly, sir. There are one or two who sign up for adventure but they tend not to last long when faced with the reality."

"So the Militia consists of the dregs of our society. I can tolerate that if they can fight. Can they fight, Colonel, in your opinion?"

Colonel Avery would not meet Allenson's eye.

"I thought not," Allenson said. "What about the officers?"

"Good men, sir. They just need something to work with." This time Avery met Allenson eye to eye.

"Very well, Colonel, you have had longer to think about this than me. What do you recommend? How do we fix the draft?"

"Well, sir, I have tried to get the draft exemptions stopped, or at least curtailed, but the Lower House won't wear it, so we have to find a new way of recruiting."

"From the reserves?" Allenson asked.

Avery shook his head.

"Won't work sir. They can only be mustered for use by special order of the Legislature, which could take months. They will only operate in their own regions in defense of their own communities. They are typically made up of smallholders or trade guilds and see themselves as guarantors of the rights of common people. They are so egalitarian that they elect their own officers, who are often members of the Lower House. Frankly, sir, you may as well try to draft the great land-owners' bucellarii."

Bucellarii were the security forces of the great demesnes, like the Destrys. Some were the size of small private armies.

"So the draft is unfixable," Allenson said.

"Yes, sir. We need an all volunteer force as a professional mobile army. That means better pay, so we can choose from better quality applicants, and we need better equipment so we can fight. The recruits will still probably be the dregs, but they will be fighting dregs." Colonel Avery shrugged. "I know what needs to be done, sir, but I lack political clout."

"Write a report for me detailing your plans. I will worry about the politics."

Avery coughed. "As it happens, sir, I have something already prepared, just in case our conversation took this turn. I will drop it on to your data pad."

"I think we are going to get along famously, Colonel," Allenson said.

"It has always puzzled me how intelligent educated human beings are capable of ignoring a logical train, if they find the conclusion unattractive. Indeed some seem it easier to hold two mutually exclusive ideas held simultaneously. Fontenoy wants the Terrans dislodged, but he is reluctant to expend political capital by taking unpopular decisions, like raising money to produce a decent fighting force," Allenson said.

"So how did you wear Fontenoy down?" Trina asked.

Allenson laughed. "I am naturally stubborn. Apparently in politics, as in most things, persistence is the secret to success. Eventually, he gave me the money to make me go away."

Trina's maid put the tray down and gave the pot one last stir before pouring a cup for her mistress and Allenson. He took a sip.

"How do you find the tea?" Trina asked.

"The tea?" Allenson looked down at his cup. "Oh, it's, um, nice, thank you."

"Nice," Trina chuckled, hiding her mouth behind her hand. "Now you've upset my maid."

The maid gave Allenson a look that would have boiled water.

"Thank you, Sasha, That will be all," Trina said.

The maid curtseyed and left them alone.

"The tea is Twyning Special Blend and Sasha considers herself something of an expert in its preparation," Trina said in explanation.

"Oh, I'm sorry," Allenson said, cheeks burning.

Trina held up a hand. "Don't be. I like your indifference to social pretensions. It's part of your charm."

Allenson was astonished that this sophisticated woman should consider him charming. He wondered whether she was making fun of him and looked at her sharply, but she met his gaze guilelessly. He decided to change the subject.

"My next problem will be purchasing suitable equipment," Allenson said.

He had found himself using Trina more and more as a sounding board. Hawthorn, despite his other sterling qualities, was useless in that role. Trina was intelligent with no personal ax to grind. Her observations inevitably clarified his thinking.

"I received a number of business cards at the Redfern party, if you remember?" Allenson asked.

"Of course I remember; that's where we met," Trina replied. She tasted her tea and added a smidgeon more whitener.

"I suppose I could buy from them," Allenson said doubtfully.

"That would certainly be a most satisfactory solution for the Redferns and their clients," Trina said. "On the other hand, you could meet a friend of mine."

Trina and Allenson took a hop in a light carriage frame to Clearwater. They parked in the industrial district and she took his arm when they walked to a large lock-up that displayed no advertising sign.

Trina pressed an intercom by a small door.

"Yes?" a voice said.

"Lady Blaisdel, with a visitor, to see Master Mansingh."

The door clicked open and they went inside.

The interior was a large open-plan warehouse filled with rows of container racks that reached up to the roof of the two-story building. The whine of a container truck drifted from the innards of the building. Trina followed a green holographic track of arrows that meandered sinuously around the racks. She climbed steel stairs up to a second-level building within a building that had windows of blank glass.

She knocked on the door and went in without waiting for a reply. A man in a motorized wheelchair moved to greet them.

"Lady Blaisdel."

"Master Mansingh, may I introduce Inspector General Allenson?"

"A pleasure," Mansingh said.

"Master Mansingh was in business with my father," Trina said.

"I had that honor," Mansingh confirmed.

"What business would that be?" Allenson asked.

"The security equipment business," Mansingh replied.

They followed Mansingh down a corridor into a large office. One-way windows looked out into the warehouse.

"Sar Allenson has to equip an expeditionary force of about three hundred men for an expedition into the Hinterlands," Trina said. "I wonder if he could benefit from your advice."

"Redfern Dealing and their associates have suggested shotguns to me as the primary infantry weapon," Allenson said. "They have a Brasilian supplier."

"Shotguns have their uses," Mansingh said, pursing his lips. "Clearing buildings or shooting grouse, for example, but I would hardly recommend them as a general purpose weapon in the wilderness. Their range is far too short, for one thing."

"Obviously laser weapons would be my first choice, but my budget will not run to military specification Home World weapons. And I am not sure troops could be trained to use them effectively in the time I have available," Allenson said.

Mansingh swung his chair around, controlling it with a small joystick. He touched an icon. "Bring up an FN rifle please."

Allenson could not place Mansingh's accent. It was clipped, suggesting he originated from a Home World, but not Brasilia or Terra.

"Where do you come from, Master Mansingh?" Allenson asked, for the sake of making conversation as much as curiosity.

"Beelzebub," Mansingh answered.

Things began to make sense. Beelzebub was one of the Old Colonies. It supported a much smaller population than Terra or Brasilia so was not usually ranked among the major Home Worlds, but it was of equal wealth and sophistication. It had a lucrative arms trade, specializing in inexpensive but reliable medium technology weapons made to a high quality standard. A Beelzebub military weapon might not have the complexity of a Terran or Brasilian gun, but it was said you could park a ship on one and it would still work afterward.

"You were in the security business there?" Allenson asked, wondering what the man was doing in the Cutter Stream.

"You could say that. I was an officer in the Paras until a suspensor failed," Mansingh said.

He gave a tight little smile and gestured toward his legs, which were missing below the knees.

Allenson winced. Paras in the Home Worlds were drop regiments, the drop in question being from a transport frame at a higher altitude than could be reached by point defense weapons. Drop infantry were slowed to a landing by suspensors, wire spools that used similar technologies to frames. They had just enough power for the drop, so it was very easy for the technicians to get it ever so slightly wrong.

Paras were elite assault infantry. They expected to suffer fifty percent casualties in a drop onto hostile ground, but that was better odds than for an infantry assault in frames. Once down, paras were tasked with suppressing the defenses so reinforcements could debus from transports.

Fortunately, a servant arrived with the rifle so Allenson did not have to think of a reply.

"This is an FN2 assault rifle," Mansingh said. He expertly stripped it down in front of them.

"It's a ceramic coil gun firing rigid-carbon pellets with a samarium-cobalt or neodymium core to give the gauss field something to work on," Mansing said.

"As you know, sar, neodymium has a stronger magnetic field, and so neodymium pellets have a theoretically

higher velocity than samarium-cobalt, but I nevertheless recommend the latter for your needs. Neodymium
contains iron, which adds to Continuum drag. Also,
samarium has a higher temperature stability, which
means the ammunition is cheaper to manufacture. The
pellet cartridge fits in here and is good for fifty shots.
The battery goes here and should power two hundred
shots, more if you don't use the rock and roll setting.
The gun can be set to full auto, but I recommend
presetting it to single shot or three round bursts. The
trouble with rock and roll is that it gets through a lot
of ammo and power cells. In my experience, sir, only
veterans can be trusted to use full auto productively."

"Like your Paras?" Allenson asked.

"Yes, sir," Mansingh replied. His eyes flickered and
his mouth twisted. The thought of his old regiment
still drew strong emotions.

Allenson noticed that somewhere in the conversation he had gone from the civilian "sar" to the
military "sir," which probably indicated an upgrade
in Mansingh's opinion.

Allenson took the rifle and examined it, unloading
and trying the trigger mechanism. The gun felt solid
and well machined. It was the sort of weapon to give
a man confidence.

"How much are these rifles?" Allenson asked.

Mansingh named a figure. It was only twenty percent more than Redfern's shotguns.

"I think we have a deal, Master Mansingh," Allenson
said, shaking his hand.

"One thing, sir. I would like to be a member of
the expeditionary force," Mansingh said.

Allenson's eyes went hard.

"Is that a condition of the sale?" he said.

"No, sir," Mansingh replied stiffly. "It is a request, sir. Let me join the militia. They have always refused me."

Allenson's eyes softened. "The force is mobile, Master Mansingh." He looked down at Mansingh's legs, which were missing above the knee.

"I have legs, sir. Top quality prosthetics granted to me on discharge. As good as the real thing, sir."

"Then why?" Allenson gestured at the wheelchair.

"I only use my legs when I have good reason, sir. They have to go back to a Home World for servicing after so many hours use. No one in the Stream has the skills."

Allenson intended to refuse. The Hinterlands was no place for cripples, even with synthetic limbs, but something in Mansingh's eyes stopped him. He told himself that Mansingh was the first honest man he had met in Manzanita and he was an experienced soldier, but the real reason he changed his mind was the desperation in those eyes.

"I believe we have need of a weapons officer. Welcome aboard, Mister Mansingh. We have an army to raise and equip."

· CHAPTER 17 ·

On Campaign

"I don't know what effect they'll have on the Terrans, but they frighten the hell out of me," Hawthorn said, surveying the paraded ranks of the New Model Militia.

Avery huffed but made no comment; Allenson made a note that the man had no sense of humor. Allenson wore the dress uniform of a Lieutenant Colonel of the Cutter Stream Militia. That technically made Colonel Avery his military superior in the Militia, but Inspector General Allenson was Avery's political superior. It made for an interesting arrangement. As Allenson's aide, Hawthorn had been commissioned with the rank of captain.

"Half of them are drunk and the other half are sobering up," Hawthorn said.

"Yes," Allenson said. "But they will dry out and harden on the march."

Paying the Militia a campaigning salary had attracted somewhat better recruits, but they were still a collection of life's misfits.

"Are you sure it's wise to split our force, Inspector

284

General?" Avery asked. "Is there not a possibility of defeat in detail?"

"I don't think that's likely, Colonel," Allenson replied, making a mental note to look up what "defeat in detail" meant when he was alone. "No, we will stick to the plan. I will take an Advance Force of eighty men, Rutchett, and three lieutenants to Nengue to negotiate the addition of Rider auxiliaries to our strength. It's best that I talk to the Viceroy, as he knows me, and it's best to negotiate with Riders from a position of strength. You follow, leading the main body."

"Very well," Avery said, but he didn't look happy about it. "If you will excuse me then, I have matters to attend to," Avery said stiffly, ignoring the salutes he received.

"Have you received written confirmation of our orders from Fontenoy?" Allenson asked.

"Actually no," Hawthorn replied. "I'll follow up."

"Don't bother," Allenson said. "Fontenoy gave me clear verbal instructions—fortify and garrison Larissa, if necessary, dislodging any Terrans squatting there by whatever means necessary. He probably does not want to tie us down by second guessing the situation. Having freedom of action suits me fine."

"The Advance Force could overnight on Wagener, if you wished to visit Destry," Hawthorn said.

Allenson looked at his friend sharply, wondering what Hawthorn knew, or guessed, but Hawthorn kept a neutral expression.

"I think not," Allenson said. "The sooner the men get used to camping out, the better."

"Or you could divert on your own for a day or two," Hawthorn said, persisting. "I can look after

the column for a couple of days and, given the lack
of fitness of our troops, you will soon catch us up."

Allenson was tempted, oh so tempted, to see Sarai,
but he shook his head.

"It sets a bad example to the men to see their
commander deserting his duty for personal reasons.
I intend to lead from the front."

The expeditionary force was a purposeful bustle.
Perhaps not quite the smoothly organized military
machine that Allenson would have liked, but not an
ineffectual shambles, either. He remembered their
first overnight camp with a shudder. Some of the men
never did get their tents up that night.

He walked around the camp, making sure that
the men saw him. Each section was responsible for
erecting their own tent and throwing up their section
of a low berm for defense. The berm was to prevent
outsiders having a clear line of sight to shoot into the
camp but, with the accompanying ditch, it also made
an obstacle to impede an assault. Allenson had no
expectation that the berm would be needed, but it
was good practice to always put one around a camp.
At least, that is what it said in the Brasilian Tactica
that had become his Bible. The men were looking
sharper and fitter. Four days of exercise and no tonk
had worked wonders.

The force was still too slow through the Continuum.
The problem was the baggage train of two transporters,
which were already showing signs of mechanical faults.
He headed over to where they were parked in the
center of the camp. Lieutenant Frapes was in charge
of the train. Allenson found him standing on top of

a transport frame looking down and whistling a tune. Frapes threw a hurried salute when he saw his CO.

"Do you think this frame will make it as far as Nengue, Mister Frapes?" Allenson asked.

"Oh yes, sir, Marks has found the problem and is fixing it. He used to service the ones in the docks before he lost his job."

"Really," Allenson said, wondering who Marks was. He could not remember hiring a mechanic. Something else he would have to put right next time. God knows how much he would have to pay a competent mechanic to get him to accompany the militia into the Hinterlands. It had been difficult enough getting anybody with even a modicum of medical experience.

A head popped up and gave him a gap-toothed smile. He remembered Marks now. The man had been so drunk that a corporal had to hold him up when he signed The Articles.

"He's a pretty fair hand with a tool kit when sober, aren't you, Marks?" Frapes asked.

"That I am, sir," Marks replied, disappearing back under the machine.

Frapes seemed to have the matter in hand, so Allenson decided to leave him to it. "Very well, carry on, Mister Frapes," Allenson said touching his hat.

Most of the frames were two-man machines. The officers had servants to do the pedaling. At the moment that was satisfactory, as the most of the enlisted men were appallingly unfit, but they were drying out and hardening so there would come a time when the officers would have to pedal as well, so their frames could keep up. Allenson and Hawthorn preferred to use their personal single-seat rides.

Allenson sought out Captain Rutchett. "Have you carried out a roll call, Captain?"

"Yes, sir, all present and correct."

"Really?" Allenson asked, astonished. There had been a trickle of desertions on the first couple of days, although fewer than he had expected. It was so very easy for a two-man section to slip away into the Continuum.

"The men's morale is quite good, sir. No tonk was a bit of a shock, but they have gotten used to the idea now. Many of them are better fed and clothed than they have been in years."

"Good," Allenson said. "I want every single man's feet checked by an officer before we eat, no exceptions. I expect blisters to be forming about now. I have bought some antiseptic and regrowth patches. You will find them in my personal baggage. I have also brought spare socks. Give them out as necessary."

"Yes, sir," Rutchett said, saluting.

Allenson had read that units on campaign in the wilderness could lose more men to injury and disease than enemy action. He was determined that this would not happen to his men. The officers had been a bit mulish when they discovered that he would not allow them to eat the food prepared by their servants until their men had eaten first, but he had forced the point. Obviously, he did not try to insist the officers to eat with their men, or even the same food. He had no wish to ignite a well-bred mutiny.

Generally, it had turned out easier to persuade the officers to care for their men's well being than he had feared. Recruited from the landed gentry, they were used to being responsible for the condition of their estate workers and livestock. They came to regard their responsibility to their men in the same light. They were not required to consider the troopers to be equals, that would have been ridiculous, but they were required to conserve them as a valuable asset.

One anomaly was that Payne ate with Allenson. As a civilian guide he was out of the line of command, and Allenson had grown used to relying on the man's advice. The other person to regularly dine with Allenson was Hawthorn, in his role as the CO's aide. Protocol meant that Allenson could only dine with the other officers when they chose to issue an invitation.

Allenson was jolted out of his thoughts by the hovering person of a young lieutenant. He invited the man to speak with a nod.

"Sir, my sergeant reports that one of my men is not pulling his weight on the pedals. He is slowing down the whole platoon. He wonders whether to discipline the man."

"Is he lazy, or is he just not trying?" Allenson asked.

"I don't think he's lazy, sir. The sergeant said that he pedals until he throws up with exhaustion."

"I doubt if punishment will improve him then," Allenson said dryly. "Swap him with a man on the baggage train."

Allenson secretly hoped that the officers and NCOs would stop coming to him with trivial issues as they gained experience but, for the moment, he would rather they sought his guidance than do something stupid.

"I sent word ahead that I was coming to Nengue, so where is he?" Allenson said, anger showing.

"The chiefs say that the Viceroy is away on important matters but will be back soon," Payne translated.

"How soon is soon?" Allenson asked.

"I could ask, sar, but I don't think you'll get a reply. 'Soon' to a Rider generally just means in the future, maybe."

The rest of the Advance Force had landed by the Nengue Trading Post. Allenson was pleased to see that they maintained a combat-ready march order, with a rearguard protecting the baggage train.

"Right. We need to keep the men occupied doing something useful, Captain Rutchett."

"Yes, sir."

"Extend and refortify the trading post so that it is a useful asset and throw up a berm beside it for a military camp. I want the men restricted to camp. No one is to leave without my personal approval."

"The Viceroy may not take to us building new stuff," Payne said diffidently.

"Too bad," Allenson said. "If he doesn't like it he will have to lump it."

As it happened, the Viceroy reappeared the next day with some dispiriting news. The conversation that followed was difficult, as Payne found translating hard going. However, it seemed that the Riders had been on a scouting mission to Larissa and found the Terrans present in force. The Viceroy's garbled description suggested that they had built some sort of fortification.

"Are you completely mad?" Hawthorn asked, rhetorically.

"I am open to suggestions," Allenson replied, "but I can see no alternative to scouting Larisa personally."

"I could go in your place," Hawthorn said.

Allenson shook his head. "*I* need to reconnoiter their

defenses," he said. "I cannot decide whether to commit the advance force or wait for reinforcements before attacking until I can assess what we are up against. If the defenses are incomplete, or weakly defended, there they may well be an advantage in an immediate assault but I need to see with my own eyes."

"Okay, why not go as a diplomatic mission? There is less likelihood of them gunning you down as soon as you materialize."

"And then attack them? That would be dishonorable."

"Oh, honor," Hawthorn said. "And where will your honor be when you are dead and the entire Cutter Stream Expeditionary Force is stranded on Nengue without orders or leadership?"

"Avery will be in charge," Allenson replied defensively.

Hawthorn simply raised an eyebrow.

This was a new experience for Allenson. Generally, he considered that getting killed while doing one's duty absolved one of further responsibility. To act without regard for the outcome to oneself was almost a definition of honorable. The idea that he had a greater obligation to survive was disconcerting, but Hawthorn had a point.

He glanced around the camp, searching for a way out of the impasse. The Viceroy was still present, arguing with Payne. He found it difficult to grasp that the humans had brought no tonk. The Rider overlord had an escort of chiefs who seemed to act as courtiers. Allenson recognized one who had accompanied them to Stikelstad. An idea germinated in his mind.

"The Riders reconnoitered Larissa without any problems," Allenson said.

"Yes, but you will be on a frame, not a beast. Any automatic defenses at Larissa are probably set to ignore the odd Rider beast or two, but they may be set to blast any unauthorized frame upon materialization. Even if you escape, you will have alerted the Terrans to our presence," Hawthorn said, sarcastically.

Allenson grinned at him, "Why shouldn't I ride pillion in a beast?"

"You are mad—completely barking, bloody mad," Hawthorn said, restating his original opinion.

Any other time, Allenson would have been fascinated by the ride in the beast, but today he had another fish to fry. The Rider took a degree of persuasion to semi-phase close enough to the Terran base for observation. Allenson resorted to threatening him with a spring gun. The beast veered in a loop, making a pass a klom or so above the base, Allenson recording the scene with his datapad.

Allenson was shocked at what he saw. This was no temporary camp, or even an armed fort, but a fully functional firebase that could easily hold a thousand combat troops or more. The Terrans were making Larissa their primary stronghold in the Brasilian Hinterlands.

The main camp was a leveled circle of yellow ocher soil, a greasy sheen showing that it was artificially stabilized. A high berm topped with razor wire surrounded the area. The single entrance through the berm was guarded by sandbagged emplacements around crew served weapons. The outer berm slope was studded with pillboxes, from which projected the barrels of more crew-served guns. The interior of the firebase seemed largely devoid of buildings, although Allenson saw tents, transport frames, and equipment.

A moving shadow in the center of the firebase caught his eye. He keyed his data pad to magnify and used the screen as a telescope. What he saw made his mouth go dry. The firebase was protected by a three-gun automatic defense battery. One of the guns tracked the Rider beast, the shadow from its barrels flickering as the gun traversed. Allenson had no idea how vulnerable a semi-phased beast was to a point defense lascannon and had no intention of finding out the hard way.

He thumped the Rider on his shoulder and ges-ticulated that they should flee. The Rider needed little encouragement and the beast dephased into the Continuum, swinging onto a course away from Larissa. Allenson released the breath that he had not realized he was holding. There was no particular reason for the Terran air defense controller to fire on a Rider beast, other than to test the equipment or for the simple pleasure of killing something.

It occurred to Allenson that the Terrans might send a fast frame in pursuit of the beast. He wondered how he could convey such a complicated concept to the Rider, when they lacked a common language. Fortu-nately, he did not have to. The Rider obviously had the same concerns and he urged the beast to its best speed, veering off the direct route and deliberately seeking out turbulence to break their trail.

The Rider seemed to know what he was doing, so Allenson stopped backseat driving. He occupied his time by going over the recordings on his pad, concentrating mostly on the visual and near spectrum. The video was badly blurred by heat haze and the energy field around the beast. He used enhancement software to tweak the images and extract a three-dimensional holographic rotational image with artificial contrast and color.

The Rider watched with a mixture of fascination and horror. He shrank from Allenson and made a series of gestures, presumably to ward off evil spirits. Allenson blew up sections of the hologram and lit it by a setting sun, rotating the light direction through three-sixty degrees, causing shadows to rotate around structures, making them easier to see.

He was wrong about there being no buildings. The firebase was full of bunkers. Hard emplacements surrounded larger equipment. The design of the firebase suggested that it was intended to house artillery, so he was not surprised to identify a battery of eighty mil mortars. Modest weapons by the standards of the Home Worlds, and probably with a limited supply of rounds, but more than powerful enough to slaughter any likely attacker from the Hinterlands.

For the sake of completeness, he ran a full spectrum check. The firebase had a military beacon with Identification Friend or Foe interrogation codes. He also found signs of electromagnetic leakage in various parts of the radio and microwave spectrum from automatics and other devices, indicating inadequate screening and poor tuning of components.

The technical sloppiness would no doubt have made a Brasilian Quarter Master Sergeant puce with rage, but all it did was depress Allenson, because it meant that the Terrans had a wide range of functional equipment. He thought long and hard on the journey back to Nengue.

❖ ❖ ❖

"Well, gentlemen, you have had time to go over my findings at Larissa. Comments please, starting with the spokesman for the platoon leaders," Allenson said. "And remember, I want you to be candid."

Allenson had read that it was best to invite comments in reverse order of seniority; otherwise there was a reluctance to contradict a senior in the chain of command. One of the lieutenants, Dontey, leapt to his feet.

"Well, sir, we think we should go straight over there and give the Terrans a damn good thrashing. That'll teach them to invade Brasilian land, what?"

Dontey looked to his peers for reassurance before speaking. Frapes gave him a surreptitious thumbs up. Allenson chose not to notice.

"The Terrans are in a strong position and they may even outnumber us. That doesn't bother you at all?" Allenson asked.

"No, *sir*," Dontey replied. "A Cutter Stream gentleman is worth a dozen damn Terrans."

"I see," Allenson said. "Do you share that view, Captain Rutchett?"

"While I commend the young gentlemen for their patriotism and applaud their spirit, I regret I cannot support their plan," Rutchett said, dryly. "The Advance Force has no possible chance of successfully assaulting the Larissa Firebase. We would have to debus from our frames at some distance, or be shot out of the sky by their point defenses. They will detect us dephasing, unless we land a week's march away. They will probably still detect us, as the Terran commander will have patrols out, unless he is a complete fool."

"I think it would be unwise to rely on that," Allenson said.

"Yes, sir," Rutchett said, "which means that they will be waiting for us. They will pin us down with their heavy weapons from those bunkers," Rutchett gestured at the hologram around which the meeting sat, "and then they will massacre us with their mortars."

"Go on," Allenson said.

"We could attempt to invest the base but I doubt we have the numbers," Rutchett continued. "Unless we simply want to just make a heroic demonstration for political reasons, I believe our only chance will be to wait for the main force. Even then, our losses will be steep and a favorable outcome is far from certain. I am sorry to be so negative, Colonel Allenson, but you did ask me to candid."

"So I did," Allenson said. "And I find your assessment largely agrees with my own."

The lieutenants looked disappointed.

"Patience, gentleman. Your chance to fight will come," Allenson said. "Do you have any thoughts, Captain Hawthorn?"

Hawthorn sighed. "We either sit tight on Nengue and wait for the Main Force, or we accept reality and retreat. I don't see any other choice."

"Surely, we are not just going to run away like cowards," Dontey said, half rising. He flushed and sat down again, quelled by the look directed at him from Rutchett.

"When the Colonel wants to receive your pearls of wisdom, no doubt he will inform you," Rutchett said. "Until such time, remember your place, mister."

"Yes, sir," Dontey said, crestfallen.

"No, we are not going to run away, Mister Dontey," Allenson said. "That would be strategically and politically disastrous for the Stream. The first thing that would be likely to happen is that our loyal Rider allies would defect to the winning side."

Payne coughed.

"You have something you wish to suggest, Master Payne?" Allenson asked.

Payne was not an officer, not a soldier even, but Allenson had asked him to be present in case the meeting needed his specialist knowledge.

"If we stay on Nengue, sar, it occurs to me that the Terrans are bound to hear of it. Riders like to gossip, you see."

"So we should anticipate an attack," Allenson said thoughtfully.

"In that case, I suggest we immediately upgrade our camp to a full blown fort," Rutchett said.

Payne looked anxious.

"Master Payne?" Allenson asked.

"The Viceroy might take that as a sign that we intend to take over Nengue, sar," said Payne.

"Quite," Allenson said. "So let me sum up your views, gentlemen." He counted them off on his fingers. "We can't retreat, we need to fortify a base in expectation of an attack by superior numbers, and, finally, we can't fortify Nengue." He looked around, but no one had anything to add.

Allenson put up a hologram of the Continuum around the Three Chasms. "My solution is to fortify a base blocking the main chasm from Larissa to Nengue. I suggest here." He circled an unnamed world. "Any comments?"

There were none.

"In that case, gentlemen, we move out after breakfast.

You should get some sleep. Tomorrow is going to be a long day."

The officers filed out. Rutchett hung behind to have a quiet word with Allenson.

"You had that plan in mind before the meeting, did you not, sir," Rutchett said stiffly. "You did not have to persuade us, you know; we would have obeyed orders."

"I know, Captain, but I need enthusiastic support. I need the younger officers to buy in to the plan, so that they can lead their men with conviction."

Rutchett smiled. "I see, sir. If you will excuse me, I have some preparations to make." He saluted and left the tent.

"Good man, that," Hawthorn said.

"Yes, he is," Allenson replied.

Allenson, Hawthorn, and Payne went on ahead on single-seat frames to select a location for the new fort, traveling up the chasm that ran from Larissa to Nengue. They were running against the main stream but could get a boost from the backwash by traveling at the sides. That made for a fast, if bumpy, ride.

The world was eighty percent water with a single patch of land large enough to just qualify as a continent. It was shaped like an isosceles triangle with the base running north-south and the point toward the west. The east coast was mountainous with active volcanoes.

Rivers arose in the mountains and flowed east, ending in a single large, marshy, tropical delta that formed the eastern point of the triangle. Most lowland areas were covered in dense jungles of high, slim trees.

Allenson ruled the tropical delta out as a suitable base without investigating further. Such places were hellholes in his experience. Similarly, he had no intention of playing roulette by basing his troops on a volcanically active mountain range. He took a close look at the dry-land jungles. The trees were tightly packed into a tangled knot of branches covered with sharp-edged leaves that glittered in the sunlight. They might have been designed to fend off landing frames, and he lacked the heavy equipment to clear a defensible area.

A small herd of large armored lizards fed on the trees. One heaved itself up to flatten a section and then slowly chomped on the wreckage. Smaller lizards, which may have been juveniles or separate species for all Allenson knew, followed the giants, feeding on their leavings. Arboreal animals scuttled from the felled trees in packs.

The trail of destruction behind the herd closed up in a remarkably short distance. The trees must have a phenomenal growth rate; yet another reason to dismiss the idea of clearing an area for a base.

He discovered clear meadowland in upland areas besides the major rivers. He selected a site and landed on a flat section alongside a tributary that flowed into a river channel. Allenson debussed and examined his surroundings, going through a mental checklist: protected on three sides by water, a flat area of easily worked soil to build bunkers, copses of thickset trees close by on the surrounding low hills to provide timber for building and fueling steam generators, and a convenient supply of freshwater. He activated the beacon on his frame to guide in the Advance Force.

When they arrived, he gave the order to dig in the vehicles and prepare defensive bunkers linked by

trenches. The bunkers were created by digging out a
pit to about waist high and covering it with low timber
walls and a timber roof. Earth was thrown over the
timber to both disguise and reinforce the structure.
The trees turned out to be easy to cut down and
shape. Their leaves were spongy, unlike the dominant
foliage found away from the rivers.

Allenson went around checking progress until he
bumped into Hawthorn.

"Will you take a platoon up the chasm toward
Larissa for a reconnoiter? I don't suppose that the
Terrans will move in force against us for a while, but
I would rather not surprised by a raiding party while
the men are still digging in," Allenson said.

"Sure," Hawthorn replied. "What are you going to
do? Like to come with me?"

Allenson looked around at the anthill of activity.
The NCOs and junior officers seemed to have matters
well in hand, but he was uneasy about moving out of
communication with the camp.

"No, I do feel a bit superfluous to requirements,
but I want to be on hand in case anything breaks. I
think I may take a transport and do some hunting.
The men will no doubt welcome some fresh meat
after all this work."

"Good idea. Between ourselves, Rutchett pleaded
with me to think of a way of getting you out of the
way so he could get on with his job without the CO
looking over his shoulder," Hawthorn said.

Allenson laughed ruefully. "It's difficult to resist the
urge to micromanage."

He sought Payne out and borrowed a transport.
Lieutenant Frapes insisted that he take a couple of

soldiers to help with the pedaling and loading. Allenson acquiesced to put Frapes's mind at rest. One of them was Marks; clearly Frapes was taking no chances of leaving his CO stranded by a broken down frame.

They found the signs of a lizard trail and turned to follow until they caught up with the herd. Payne landed thirty meters or so from the giant lizards for the sake of safety. You never could tell with herbivores. Some could be more aggressive than predators when defending territory or calves. While he didn't want to be so close that the frame would spook the beasts, equally, he wanted it close by if they had to leave quickly. Thirty meters seemed a reasonable compromise.

If the lizards were impressive from the air, then they were awe-inspiring up close at ground level.

"You stay here with the frame and wait for us," Allenson said to the troopers.

He jumped down then assisted Payne, who had not completely recovered from their previous adventures. The crushed vegetation crunched beneath his boots like a shell beach. He wondered what it was made of.

The soldiers looked unhappy. Marks screwed up his face.

"What?" Allenson asked, distracted from the flattened plants.

"Begging your pardon, sir, we can't stay on the frame. Lieutenant Frapes, he gave us orders, sir."

Allenson sighed. "Mister Frapes told you to stick to me like glue, I suppose?"

"Yes, sir," Marks replied. "Very firm, he was."

"Then you had better obey Mister Frapes's orders, Marks," Allenson said.

This was ridiculous. Here he was, the CO and Lord of all he surveyed, being pushed around by a mere lieutenant. And he had to acquiesce or he would erode Frapes's authority. It seemed the higher he rose, the less freedom he had. He looked suspiciously at Payne. Had the man sniggered? Payne kept a straight face under his examination.

"What big buggers," Payne said, pointing at the lizards.

"They must grow their whole lives," Allenson said, irritation at being nursemaided forgotten. "There seem to be fixed cohorts of sizes. They must reproduce in synchronicity. I wonder what the timing mechanism is?"

They walked slowly toward the lizards, which ignored them. Humans must look very insignificant to something twenty meters long. The animals were covered with thick scale armor of strong iridescent colors that changed as the animals moved and altered their angle to the sun's rays. Possibly they had layers of air sandwiched between reflective materials—like a butterfly's wing. What was that called, constructive interference? Allenson dredged the term up from the deeper swamps of his memory. Why would a giant lizard have butterfly scales? His friend Destry would probably know. Thoughts of Destry naturally turned to Sarai. Guilt and passion: why were they so intertwined?

"You were not thinking of killing one of those monsters, were you, sar?" Payne asked.

Allenson gave a genuine chuckle. "Not unless you have a plasma cannon about your person, Master Payne. No, I noticed earlier that they disturb smaller beasts from the trees. Let's have a pot at those. We'll wait until one of these leviathans smashes a new section of jungle." He checked his carbine and was pleased to see that Marks and his comrade did likewise with their rifles. Payne carried his combat shotgun. Allenson had pointed out that it was useless for hunting, but Payne was uneasy without the short-barrelled gun.

A lizard stiffened its bulky tail, slowly lifting it into the air. The redistribution of weight raised the lizard's head until its front legs dangled free. It was astonishing to see the vast beast rear up until its head was ten meters above the ground. It took a slow step forward on its hind legs, then another, until it overbalanced and fell forward like a swimmer entering a pool in slow motion. The monster hit the foliage with a crash like a wrecking ball going through plate glass. The trees disintegrated in scintillating shimmers, branches falling like spears to shatter on the ground.

"They're glass; the trees are glass," Marks said in wonder.

"Silicon in the trunks, certainly," Allenson said, so glad that he had not tried to clear a base in the jungle.

Spray of mineral shards covered the lizard, sticking into its armor, explaining the iridescent quality of the lizard's cuticle. Butterfly wings, indeed! Allenson laughed inwardly at himself.

"Get ready, the tree-dwellers will flee now," Allenson said.

A herd of sand-colored animals that looked vaguely like apes shot out of the trees all around the lizard. They ran awkwardly on grasping hands designed for climbing. Allenson fired a three round burst from his carbine, knocking one of the apes over.

"Good shot, sir," Marks said.

Allenson didn't reply. He was loath to admit that

he had been aiming at a quite different ape, but it would be intolerable to lie, even to a social inferior, so he said nothing.

The soldiers opened fire with their rifles and apes began to drop. Purple blood splashed across the ground. The apes kept on coming in an endless rain. They did not appear to connect the humans with their dead comrades. Presumably they had no experience of guns.

Other animals were in among the herd, sinusoidal, fast moving, short-legged, weasellike things, with claws that ripped when they caught an ape. The apes redoubled their efforts to escape, running straight for the humans. The weasels followed, slashing at anything that moved, even each other.

The danger came out of nowhere. Allenson cursed his lack of anticipation. Of course native predators would exploit the situation, just like the humans. It was obvious, if he had bothered to think things through.

"Get to the frame," Allenson said, backing away and firing short burst from his carbine to try to turn the herd.

Payne opened up with his shotgun, blowing holes in the column. For a moment, it looked as if he had succeeded. The surviving apes recoiled, probably scared by the noise. They ran around in circles, while the weasels worked themselves into a killing frenzy. Then Payne's shotgun exhausted its magazine and the column burst out, resuming its flight toward the hunting party.

"Run!" Allenson said.

He stayed with Payne, pulling the older man with him. When they reached the frame, he pushed Payne on board before jumping on himself. Marks had got there before them. He looked past Allenson with a face frozen in horror, his gun forgotten.

Two weasels had the other soldier on the ground, slashing at his legs. The man rolled and screamed. Allenson swore. He started to raise his gun but realized that he was as likely to hit the soldier as the weasels. Hawthorn or Destry might have taken the shot, but they could shoot.

Allenson jumped down, and ran to for the soldier. He fired a burst one-handed into one of the weasels at point-blank range, almost pushing the muzzle into its hide so he couldn't miss. A backwash of heat seared his hand and face. The weasel exploded, body fluids converting instantly to steam.

He grabbed the soldier by his jacket and started to pull him back toward the frame. The second weasel reared up. He had an image of a head with lateral cutting mandibles like an insect. What caught his attention were the mineralized scimitar-shaped claws on the forelegs. Raised high to strike at his head, they caught the sun, refracting the light like prisms.

He aimed his carbine and squeezed the trigger. The gun refused to fire; a red hologram flashed above the sight, indicating that it had overheated and shut down. It was not designed to be fired so close to a target, but he had ignored that in the heat of the moment. Unfortunately, the laws of physics don't have an out clause.

The claws slashed down, probably quickly, but it seemed to take forever. Years later, he would still see those claws in his nightmares, waking sweating in the middle of the night.

The boom of Payne's shotgun deafened him, and

the weasel disappeared in a purple mist of blood and torn flesh. He threw the soldier onto the frame and leapt up himself. Hands reached out to pull him to safety. Payne had the transport in the air before Allenson caught his breath.

"Marks, do what you can to stop the bleeding until the medic at the camp can see to him properly. What are you gawping at? Move, man!"

Payne and Marks looked at him with strange expressions. What the hell was wrong with them? Just them the phone on the frame's instrument channel chimed. Allenson reached over and tapped the screen. He noticed his hand was burnt, and at that point it began to hurt. Rutchett's face appeared on the screen.

"What?" Allenson said, grumpily.

"I think you had better get back here, sir. Rider scouts have come in. A Terran attack is on the way."

· CHAPTER 18 ·

Contact

Allenson crouched behind a stunted bush. The warmth of his knee melted the hoar frost lying thickly across the stony ground. An uncomfortable wet patch seeped through his supposedly waterproof uniform. The air was crystal clear. Stars blazing in the night sky illuminated the ground in soft light.

He counted a dozen tents. Assuming five or six men per tent, they could be facing a Terran force of seventy men or so. He used the night sight on his carbine to search the camp again, but still could see no sentries. According to the Riders, the Terran force had avoided Hawthorn's platoon by approaching along minor routes, avoiding the main chasm. The only explanation Allenson could think of for them taking the more arduous route was that they wanted to approach unseen. That meant they were a scouting or raiding force. Were they really so confident or incompetent that they couldn't be bothered posting lookouts?

Decision made, he signaled for the Riders to circle around and envelop the Terran camp on each flank.

They disappeared silently into the darkness. Allenson waited, watching a five minute countdown on his datapad. He had no idea whether the Riders would be ready in five minutes. The problem was, neither did they. A minute was a meaningless concept to a Rider. The datapad gave a subdued flash.

"Give the order to advance," Allenson said to Padget, rising and moving forward.

The lieutenant signaled to his men. Shadows detached themselves from the vegetation, and the whole platoon followed Allenson.

"It's very quiet, sir," Padget said.

"Yes," Allenson replied curtly, wishing Padget would shut up.

It was too quiet. Allenson worried that he was leading his men into an ambush. That was why he had sent Rider scouts out, but nothing disturbed the night. He felt like a ghost moving across a monochrome underworld.

The sudden rasp of a proximity alarm jerked him back to reality. The Terrans had taken the minimal precaution of setting motion detectors. There was no further advantage to be gained by creeping around.

"Fire," Allenson said.

He triggered a long burst from his lasercarbine. It went clean over the camp. He had told the Riders to stay out of the direct line of fire but was not sure if they had understood. They seemed to regard firearms as magical devices rather than projectile weapons. Oh well, it was too late to worry about that now. He lowered his aim and triggered another burst. A tent exploded in flames. The outline of a man danced in the flames: danced and screamed. The agonized shrieks went on and on. He triggered another burst at the tent but missed.

His soldiers fired their rifles. The high velocity pellets made whiplike cracks and the guns' barrels glowed blue from ionic discharge around the magnetized coils. The tents jerked, as if plucked by invisible fingers. A figure shot out from a tent, raising a rifle to his shoulder. Allenson looked down the barrel. Padget fired and the man fell backward, discharging his laserifle at the sky. It left a shimmering track of ionized air over Allenson's head, like a meteor in reverse. He recalled that Padget was a member of the hunting, shooting, and fishing aristocracy, like Destry. The one skill you could be certain such people would possess was accuracy with a gun.

Other men rolled and fell among the tents. The Terrans fired few shots in return, and none even came close to the Stream soldiers. Whooping Riders charged into the Terran camp from each flank to cut the throats of the Terran wounded.

"Cease fire," Allenson yelled, cursing the Riders for getting in the way. He doubted that they had killed more than a handful of Terrans.

A few more shots sounded.

"The colonel said cease fire, that bleeding means you as well, Caswell," a sergeant said.

"Sorry, sir," said an excited voice.

"Sergeant, you call me sergeant."

"Yes, sir."

It didn't take long before the surviving Terrans ran away from the Riders toward the platoon, yelling for mercy and throwing down their weapons. One sobbed loudly.

"Steady, hold your fire," Padget said, his cut-glass accent demanding compliance.

"Take them prisoner," Allenson ordered.

The Terrans reached the sanctuary of the Cutter Stream platoon, holding their hands out in supplication. The Streamers pushed them roughly to the ground, searching them for weapons—and probably anything worth stealing. Allenson didn't want to know. He would have to punish his men if he saw looting, so he didn't look.

Riders ran after the Terrans, whooping and waving knives. Allenson fired a burst over their heads to turn them back. A Terran officer, judging by his uniform, ran to Allenson.

"Bastards, filthy bastards," the Terran said. He seemed more sad than angry, and it was not clear who he thought were bastards. A pistol hung in his right hand.

"Your gun, if you please, mister," Allenson said, pointing his carbine at the man.

"What?" the man looked at the pistol in his hand, as if seeing it for the first time.

Allenson took it from the officer's unresisting hand. The pistol still had a full charge; it hadn't been fired. Allenson switched it off and ejected the battery before handing it back to the officer, who put it back in his belt holster.

"Lieutenant Padget."

"Sir?"

"Leave some men to guard the prisoners, and then go through the camp before the Riders rip everything apart. Let them have a few knives and clothes, but they are not to take weapons or personal items. Look for datapads."

"Sir," Padget saluted and hurried off, rounding up some men.

"Why did you attack us?" the officer asked, strangely calm, as if discussing whether the correct card had been played at a bridge match. Allenson noted that his hands shook.

"You were an armed invasion force in Brasilian territory," Allenson replied gently. "What sort of reception did you expect?"

"We were an embassy," the Terran officer replied.

He fumbled in a pocket. Allenson resisted the urge to point his carbine again. The man was an officer and he had accepted his surrender. Certain protocols applied. The officer pulled out a datapad and showed Allenson identification protocols of a high ranking diplomat in the Terran Foreign Office.

"Where are the rest of your men?" Allenson asked. He counted nineteen prisoners and there could not be more than a dozen bodies in the camp.

"There was only the ambassador and a small escort," the officer replied.

"Where is the ambassador?" Allenson asked.

The Terran officer turned and looked back at the destroyed camp. The Riders were occupied lopping off hands.

His officers stood and clapped when Allenson entered the dugout that served as an officers' mess and conference room. The lieutenants cheered and began a hurrah in his honor. Rutchett's initial response was to glower at them, but he relented and joined in.

Allenson held up his hand for silence. "Thank you,

gentlemen but Lieutenant Padget and his men did all the work. I was merely there as an observer."

"Rubbish." Padget's voice could clearly be heard. "We had no casualties, except for Atkins. Rontel fell over and shot him through the buttocks."

"Thank you, Mister Padget," Allenson said. It was so embarrassing. Now everyone thought he was being modest and hurrahed all the louder. Allenson actually meant what he had said. He was useless as a soldier. He never hit anything he aimed at.

A shadowy outline writhed and danced in fire on the wall of the bunker. Allenson suppressed the image, pushing it down into the depths of his subconscious.

"If we could get down to business, gentlemen, no doubt word is already spreading from Rider to Rider of our victory. It can only be a matter of time before it reaches Larissa. Now, what will be their reaction, I wonder?" Allenson asked.

"They might sit back and wait for instructions from the Terran governor in the First Tier Colonies, or even Terra itself," Rutchett replied. "But we would be foolish to count on it. We must expect an attack or, at the very least, a reconnaissance in force."

"Agreed," Allenson said. "That means we stay on high alert and dig in deeper. The men will complain, but remind them that sweat now will save blood later."

He paused and looked around the bunker, examining each face before him to see if they had grasped the situation, and was reassured.

"The Terran prisoners will have to be sent back to Manzanita. It was clever of them to dress their force up as an embassy," Allenson said, ruefully. "I have no doubt that it was phony, but, used properly, it could look bad." A small but voracious worm of doubt gnawed at his vitals. He rejected it; what was done was done.

"Protocol demands that an officer command the escort. I will need an advocate back at Manzanita who can refute any misconceptions about our attack on the Terran patrol. Lastly, the rest of the Expeditionary Force must be brought here before the Terrans have time to launch a counterattack. The officer I send will have to be someone who is authoritative and persuasive."

"If I may interrupt, sir," Rutchett said.

He probably suspected that Allenson was about to nominate him, and wanted to cut in before his CO gave the order. Rutchett was right, of course.

"Lieutenant Padget's family has a great deal of pull in the Assembly. Mister Padget has already had the opportunity to win his spurs, so it would seem unfair to send one of the other lieutenants before they have their chance."

Allenson grinned at Rutchett, who managed to keep a straight face. Rutchett meant that it would be unfair to send himself. Allenson considered. Padget had shown himself to be a reliable officer and it was true that his family was well connected. Also, he would need Rutchett should the Terrans assault the base.

"Very good, Captain, make the arrangements if you please."

Padget and the prisoners left, and they continued to dig in. Day by day the field defenses were turned into something more permanent and much larger, to accommodate the rest of the Expeditionary Force. They set up a sawmill, cutting planks to line the walls of the trenches and bunkers. The squat trees along the river valley had flexible fibrous trunks that cut easily, which was convenient, as the silicon-filled wood of the primary forest splintered dangerously when sawed. Inevitably, somebody did try.

Allenson considered putting a berm around the base but decided that he would never have the manpower to garrison it, so it would simply block defensive fire from the bunkers and trenches.

The men toughened up under the exercise. Other than a single saw and steam generators, they had not been able to bring heavy power tools, so most of the work was done by hand. He organized a three-shift system whereby one shift rested, one built and a third learned basic military skills. One drawback of deploying the new force right after it was raised was that they did not know how to operate as an army rather than an armed mob.

They practised trench defense, firing by the numbers so that a continuous suppression fire was laid down on an attacker. They practised with live ammunition, and took their first casualties when some genius waiting his turn triggered a burst into the men in front of him.

Allenson deemed it necessary to use up some of his precious ammunition on the grounds that healthy ammunition stores would be of little value if his men could not defend themselves. He was appalled at how fast mock combat used up resources. Ammunition reserves were something else he would have to look at afresh in the future. The combat training slowed down the building work, but Allenson thought the trade-off essential.

✦   ✦   ✦

They were still not ready when the Continuum alarms went off. There was pandemonium. Men ran around in circles looking for their guns and trying to link up with the rest of their units. Allenson heard an agonized cry when a soldier threw himself into an already occupied fire pit. He was taking more casualties without a shot being fired at the enemy. Allenson connected his datapad to the command circuit so he could issue orders over the loudspeakers. He had a receiver behind one ear and a microphone attached behind a tooth.

"Do not fire. No one is to fire until I give the word." He scanned the sky waiting for frames to phase in.

The alarms cut out and were replaced by the friendly cheep that indicated that IFF had established that the incomers were friendly.

"Unload your weapons and put on the safety catches," Allenson ordered over the speakers. There was the flat crack of a short burst of rifle fire as some fool pressed the wrong control in his excitement. Allenson winced.

Frames materialized well above the base, out over the river. Allenson's datapad indicated a contact so he triggered verbal communication.

"Sir, don't fire, it's us," Lieutenant Padget said. His message was not entirely couched in military terms, but it sufficed.

"Very good, Mister Padget. Come in on the marked landing ground. There are anti-invasion stakes elsewhere."

He watched the frames land, counting them in. A quick calculation suggested that they carried some two hundred men, fewer than he had hoped, but more than he had expected. He had at least sixty so he could count on around two hundred and fifty "runners" at any one time. With Rider auxiliary support, he now had the core of a useful light infantry battalion.

Padget hurried over to him, accompanied by a man that he had never seen before, who wore astonishingly bushy facial hair and a captain's uniform with the orange and yellow flashes of the Isfahan militia, another Brasilian colony. Like the Stream, it was a First Tier colony perched on the edge of the Bight where it was in direct communication with the Home Worlds.

The lieutenant saluted, but he noticed the strange captain merely nodded a greeting.

"Where is Colonel Avery?" Allenson asked.

"Perhaps we could talk in private, sir," Padget replied.

Allenson showed them into the command bunker that also served as his office and sleeping accommodation.

"I have dispatches for you, sir," Padget said, handing Allenson a bundle.

"And Colonel Avery?" Allenson asked, taking the papers and flipping through them.

"He has resigned his commission, sir, on grounds of health." Padget said, his face carefully expressionless.

Allenson stopped, astonished. "So who is to replace him?"

"You are, sir. The legislature passed an emergency act. It is in the dispatches."

Allenson found the right document confirming his appointment as commander of the Expeditionary Force. His orders instructed him to act at his discretion in carrying out his objectives as previously laid down from Brasilia. Presumably that meant Fontenoy's verbal instruction to displace the Terrans by force if necessary, as he had no written orders from Brasilia. Effectively, he still had a free hand as the document gave him a great deal of latitude.

Allenson nodded toward the Isfahan officer and turned an inquiring eye on Padget.

"This is Captain Broch, sir," Padget said, somewhat belatedly. "He commands a company of the Isfahan Militia."

"You are all the more welcome, captain," Allenson said.

"My pleasure, Colonel Allenson." Broch said, casually holding out his hand.

Allenson shook it automatically, although this was surely hardly military etiquette for an officer meeting his new CO. Perhaps this lack of formality was just the Isfahan style.

"Perhaps you would confer with Captain Rutchett about where to place your men in the work rota when they debus, Mister Broch."

"Work rota?" Broch asked.

"Yes, the fortifications are not finished, and the Terrans must know that we are here. We must be ready to withstand a major attack."

"I see," Broch said. He stroked the beard on his chin. "I am afraid that won't be possible."

"What? Why not?" Allenson asked, taken aback.

"The Isfahan Militia are gazetted as Regulars in the Brasilian Army," Broch said.

"So?" Allenson asked sharply, fast losing patience.

"Regulars don't do construction work."

Broch explained. "My men would dig in, if in contact with the enemy, but I cannot possibly order them to work as skivvies. They would be within their rights to refuse, and I don't blame them."

Allenson had heard enough. "I am not asking you, captain. I am giving you an order."

"You can't," Broch said.

Padget sucked in his breath.

"Regular Brasilian Army officers outrank all colonial militia officers," Broch said, smugly. "So I am your superior officer, Allenson. By rights, I should be in charge of this force."

"You come here with thirty men and a captain's commission in the Isfahan Militia and think you outrank a Cutter Stream Colonel with two hundred soldiers under his command? You make too much of yourself, sar. Either you put yourself under my command, or you get the hell out of here and take your chances on your own," Allenson said.

Broch stroked his beard again. Allenson already found the habit irritating and he had only known the man five minutes. Broch looked carefully at Allenson and clearly decided that this was not an idle threat, so he was not entirely stupid.

"I take your point, Colonel Allenson. Perhaps it would be better if I put myself under your command— for tactical purposes. But my men will only take orders from me and won't work as laborers," Broch said, stubbornly.

"Very well, Captain Broch, but your company will be responsible for your own accommodation. My men have better things to do than build them bunkers. Lieutenant Padget will introduce you to the other officers."

Allenson turned his back on the man and began to

read his correspondence. Much of it was from contractors querying payments, future orders, and similar matters. Allenson leafed through them briefly to see if there was anything there that actually mattered. A letter from the wife of his business agent assured him that her husband was on top of things and that he should ignore any direct communications from contractors. He was happy to take that advice and tossed the pile into the stove that powered the bunker's steam generator, keeping only a letter from Trina Blaisdel.

The papers at the bottom of the bundle lit up with yellow flames that caught his eye. Flames had always held a fascination when he was a little boy. He remembered them as friendly and warm, a symbol of good times on camp with Todd. Now he saw a dancing shadow that screamed.

He was about to look away when he noticed the end of a lavender envelope attached under the flap of the report from his business agent. He flicked it quickly out of the fire. The envelope was intact except for some slight charring. On it was written simply "Allen," in a writing style that he recognized: Sarai's hand. That explained why his agent's wife had written rather than the man himself. Sarai would have cajoled her.

The letter started by calling him her true love. It was written with an intensity that was chilling. She used the words that she had whispered into his ear when they made love. She begged him to be careful and let the common soldiers take the risks. She insisted that he held her heart in his keeping and he must, therefore, hold himself safe, lest he slay both of them through recklessness. Finally, she demanded he write soon reassuring her of his affection. She had arranged for the wife of the agent to act as go between, and he should conceal his response in a reply to the wife. She explained that the wife was entirely trustworthy.

Allenson sat looking at the letter for a long time, then he very deliberately dropped it in the fire, watching it burn until not a scrap remained. It was too dangerous to be allowed to exist. Digital media could be denied, as it was easy to fake, but a handwritten note was difficult to explain away. Sarai was insane to take the risk of writing, but she would feel that only a note in her own hand could properly convey her feelings.

Allenson would not reply. Suppose the wife, or one of her employees, betrayed them? Sarai would not destroy his letter after reading, even if he told her to. The danger would add to the romance. She would want to keep it close, to hide it somewhere idiotic where a servant might find it. He would not reply; he could not reply. It would be like priming a bomb and sitting on it. No, much worse, now he thought of the matter. At least the bomb would be quick.

He opened Trina's letter and read it. Although cordial, she referred to him as Inspector General Allenson throughout. She hoped he was well and that the expedition prospered. After these preliminary niceties, she mentioned that he would be pleased to hear that Councillor Rubicon had recovered from his unfortunate accident, as she knew that he had been concerned for the Councillor's health.

Allenson laughed out loud at that. He had not told Trina that he had tossed Rubicon out of a window, but no doubt she had heard.

She continued that he would no doubt also be pleased

to hear that the good Councillor had resumed his service to the Stream in the legislature. He had been proposed for the budgetary committee that oversaw security spending, including the militia. The chairman of the committee was a cousin of hers, so she had taken the liberty of inviting said cousin to tea, where they could discuss Councillor Rubicon's application. She was sure the Inspector General would wish her to convey his concern that the Honorable Councillor should not overtax himself so soon after leaving hospital care.

"You clever, clever girl," Allenson said, admiringly.

There was nothing in this letter that would sound untoward if it were to be leaked, but it told him quite clearly that Rubicon had tried to work himself into a position to harm Allenson, and that she had used her family connections to block him. The rest of the letter was filled with social gossip, really useful social gossip about whose star was falling or, more importantly, rising in Manzanita's political and commercial arenas. She repeated what she had heard about the public response to his victory; it was favorable.

She informed him that the Terran prisoners were soon to be repatriated. That brought Allenson up with a jerk. He could not quite decide what that meant, politically speaking. Were the Terrans not prisoners of war? Trina's letter finished with conventional wishes for his well being. She signed herself "Lady Blaisdel." Allenson put her letter carefully away. He would read it again later, to make sure he had grasped all the subtexts. Meanwhile he penned a report back to Manzanita, requesting reinforcements, and a letter to Trina, which underneath the formality said, "Thanks, keep up the good work."

The next day, he half wished he had kept Sarai's note as well as Trina's, but her words were burned into his memory. He would not, could not, forget them.

Payne set up a meeting with the Viceroy. As a matter of protocol, Allenson agreed to visit the Clan Chief's shelter on Nengue, rather than insist that the Viceroy came to him. It probably gave the man points in some complicated Rider social status, but Allenson was the supplicant, and the ride to Nengue would be useful exercise. Pedaling through the Continuum cleared his head and allowed him to think. On Payne's advice he took a platoon with him as an honor guard.

The Viceroy sat on his plastic box in his lean-to. He failed to rise to greet Allenson; in fact, he ignored him. Allenson halted a few paces away and tapped the barrel of his carbine against the top of his boot. Other than that he said, and did, nothing. The Viceroy blinked first and spoke. Payne translated.

"The Viceroy says that you built defenses on Nengue and extended the Trading Post without his permission," Payne said.

"Tell the Viceroy that it was a temporary arrangement and that he was not here to ask. Add that I knew he would not mind given the close alliance between the Stream and him," Allenson said.

There was an exchange between the Viceroy and Payne.

"He says that he has decided to give you permission now," Payne said.

"Thank him for his courtesy," Allenson replied.

Rider politics was not so different from human. Claiming ownership of any successful *fait accompli* was not unknown in the Council, usually as a last resort to save face.

"Ask the Viceroy how many Riders he can bring in support, should the Terrans attack," Allenson said.

The Viceroy gestured at Allenson's platoon during the conversation with Payne.

"He says you have plenty of men and don't need his warriors," Payne said.

"Remind him of the treaty and alliance," Allenson replied, tight lipped.

There was a brief conversation, and then the Viceroy got up from his box and walked out, ignoring Allenson.

"It's no good, sar, he has orders from his bosses. This is to be a human fight only. The Riders will not get involved."

"His bosses?" Allenson asked.

Payne shrugged. "The Rider council, sar. You remember I mentioned them when I was interviewed."

The remaining Riders showed no hostility, but they simply ignored the Streamers, as if they were not there. There was nothing he could do but go.

"Well, gentlemen, it seems we have problems." said Allenson to the council of war. "Let me summarize. We have fewer men than I had hoped, our Riders allies have suddenly decided they are neutrals and will offer us no support, and, to cap it all, Captain Hawthorn's scout platoon has detected a large Terran force advancing on us down the chasm. The good news is that our fortifications are about as good as they will ever be, given the limitations of our equipment. Comments please?"

"How many Terrans do we face?" Rutchett asked.

Hawthorn shrugged. "At least five hundred, maybe

more. They are using those transports we saw at Stikelstad, Allenson."

Hawthorn must be keyed up. He was normally punctilious about using Allenson's rank in public.

"I couldn't get close enough to get a clear count. The transports are slow and in convoy, moving in close order. They have good discipline. I considered trying an ambush in the Continuum, as I reckon we had a mobility advantage with our two-man frames, but it was impossible."

"Why?" Allenson asked. Hawthorn was not known for his reluctance for a fight.

"They had Rider auxiliaries as escorts. We would have gotten embroiled in skirmishes with the Riders and been sitting ducks for concentrated fire from the transports if they brought them up in support. I reckoned it was more important to get back with the news than take out a few expendable savages."

"Quite right," Allenson said.

That was what had been bothering Hawthorn. He worried that his friend might think him cowardly for taking the pragmatic decision. Actually, Allenson thought the contrary. Any fool could blindly attack. It took balls to think clearly in the face of a superior enemy force and withdraw without loss.

"I thought the Riders had decided on neutrality," Broch said.

"Yes, so did I," Allenson said sourly.

"They will be able to seal us in, cutting our communication," Hawthorn said. "I am beginning to feel like a rat in a trap. I suggest that we retreat and conduct a fighting mobile defense."

Allenson shook his head. "We can't retreat without

triggering a political crisis. The Rider clans around Nengue will defect, probably harassing us as we withdraw. And we have unblooded troops. I can't take the risk that they might panic and rout in a running battle. If there is a risk of losing the whole expeditionary force, then I would rather do it here, defending Brasilian territory. We have the advantage of position and so should inflict losses on the enemy even in defeat, and at least some political good would come from the sacrifice."

Broch stroked his beard, a sign that he was about to interject. Allenson braced himself but was pleasantly surprised.

"I agree with you, Colonel," said Broch. He still refused to refer to Allenson as "sir," but that was hardly of importance. "We have a strong position here and I think we could hold it indefinitely."

"We don't have to hold indefinitely, only until reinforcements arrive," Allenson said. "I have already requested more men, and we should send another messenger to Manzanita immediately, apprising Fontenoy of developments."

"In that case, I think we should stay and fight, sir," Rutchett said. "I would not like to have spent my whole military career doing nothing but training."

"You're all bloody mad," Hawthorn said, with a grin, "but I never intended to live forever. Count me in."

At that point the Continuum alarms went off with a wail. Allenson waited for the IFF chirp indicating friends. It never came.

"It seems that events now out of our hands, gentlemen," Allenson said, rising. "The enemy is upon us."

· CHAPTER 19 ·

Siege

"So if it wasn't a Terran invasion force, what the Hell did trigger the alarms?" Allenson asked. He searched the skies again, but they remained just as empty. "Any movement on the perimeter?" he spoke into his data pad on the command group.

There was a pause while the Rutchett checked with his subordinates. "Nothing, colonel."

"Nothing moving overhead," Broch reported.

Broch's men had laserifles, which had a longer range and harder punch than his men's coil guns, so he had delegated air defense to the Isfahan contingent. This also neatly solved the political problem of their semi-independent status.

"Maybe, a Terran scouting force came too close," Hawthorn suggested.

"Um, colonel?" Rutchett asked.

"Yes, captain," Allenson replied.

"A couple of frames are missing. I anticipate that a roll call will uncover some missing names," Rutchett said.

"Deserters?" Allenson asked.

"I'm afraid so," Rutchett replied.

"Desertion in the face of the enemy. I could take out a platoon and bring them back," Hawthorn said angrily.

Allenson considered. It was very tempting to authorize retribution, but what would he do with the deserters if Hawthorn caught them? A trial and execution would tie up too much time and he had more important matters to attend. He could not bring himself to order Hawthorn to shoot them on sight. He could just arrest them and hand them over to a civil court on Manzanita, but he was loath to waste men as prison guards. He triggered the command group to talk to his officers.

"Explain to the men that a couple of cowards have run for it. Say I am glad to see the back of the gutless scum and that they will never be able to show their face in the Stream or anywhere else in Brasilian territory—assuming that the Riders don't get them. Stress the last point as highly likely."

Allenson took a walk along the river with Hawthorn. Only with his friend could he speak openly, sharing his fears and doubts. For the first time he properly understood the cliché "loneliness of command."

"The river is remarkably swollen," Hawthorn said, stopping to look along the length of the bank. He pointed, "Look, the roots of those shrubs are submerged. I'm sure that they were clear of the water yesterday." Hawthorn turned and scanned the western horizon. "Does it seem to you that there are storm clouds over the mountains?"

Allenson shaded his eyes. The western mountain range was a purplish smudge on the horizon. He used his datapad to take a closer look. The resolution was awful, but the pad cleaned it up to show peaks obscured by cloud and rain.

"So there are," Allenson replied.

"That explains why we've been having communication problems with scout and hunting parties," Hawthorn said. "That must be one hell of an electrical storm."

"Yes," Allenson said, dismissing the matter from his mind.

The next day a front passed over the base, dropping a quick burst of rain. It left the air fresh and clean, taking down the dust created by the Expedition Force's activities. Hawthorn had the men rig up catchers to refill their freshwater stores. Sterilized river water was perfectly safe but it had a high mineral content, giving drinks a tart taste that could not be entirely overcome by flavoring.

The fronts continued to pass over day by day, turning the base into a muddy skating rink. The stream overflowed, fortunately, on the bank opposite the base, meandering across the meadow in riverlets.

Then Allenson received a report of flooding in the trenches. A huddle of soldiers stood around their trench. It didn't look too bad to Allenson. The bottom was muddy—hell, everywhere was muddy—but the duck board was still visible. He jumped down for a closer look.

"No, sir." A soldier tried to grab his arm, succeeding only in throwing him off balance.

His feet hit the duck board, which turned out to be floating. It submerged and shot out from under him like a badly-ridden water ski. Allenson fell back, arms windmilling, into the filthy water. When he sat up it reached almost to his waist. He wiped his eyes. A cluster of horrified faces looked down at him.

"You appear to have fallen in the water, colonel," Hawthorn said.

Allenson began to chuckle. He laughed at the sheer foolishness of the situation. The alternatives would be to lose his temper and blame someone else, or pretend he wasn't sitting in a mud bath. The first was intolerable and the other undignified. Laughter at his misfortune was by far the best response. Besides, it was genuinely funny.

"There's no fooling you, Captain Hawthorn, is there?"

The soldiers began to laugh as well, albeit somewhat nervously. Hands hauled him out.

"Joking aside, we may have serious flooding if it carries on raining," Allenson said to Hawthorn when they were alone.

"Could we put in drainage?" Hawthorn asked doubtfully.

"I don't see how," Allenson replied. "The problem is a rising water table."

"Well, it's too late to relocate," Hawthorn said. "We would be slaughtered if the Terrans caught us out in the open."

"Yes," Allenson replied. "We shall just have to put up with it. It shouldn't be for long. If the Terrans come at all, it will be soon."

"I've been thinking. I could move a platoon out of the base, as a mobile unit to harass Terran supply lines if they try to besiege the base," Hawthorn suggested.

"I can see the tactical advantage. Indeed, it also occurred to me," Allenson replied. "I discussed it with Broch this morning. He gave his opinion that a

Stream unit would desert to a man if separated from the main body."

"Cheeky sod," Hawthorn said.

"Yes, but is he right?" Allenson asked.

Hawthorn sighed. "Probably. He's still a cheeky sod, though."

Allenson picked his way across the mud from his morning perimeter inspection. The morning mist had not entirely dissipated, so the air was cold and clammy. Mansingh, in his role as weapons officer, occupied an ammunition store and bunker in the center of the base, which doubled as their workshop. He sat on the edge of the roof smoking a pipe, his synthetic legs dangling. When Allenson passed, he jumped down, throwing an immaculate salute. It was not the salute used by the Stream militia but it was perfectly executed.

Marks's head popped out of the bunker, greeting Allenson with a friendly wave. The man had attached himself to Mansingh as his technical assistant. The two were the next best thing to an engineering squad that Allenson possessed.

Then the sirens wailed.

Allenson dropped to one knee, where he was arming his lasercarbine. His conscious mind noticeably lagged behind his subconscious in registering and reacting to the stimulus. A large dark shape phased into appearance in the mist overhead. Allenson triggered three bursts from his carbine in the general direction of the shape, the laser pulses punching visible trails through the wet air. He had no expectation of hits, but the tracer would point out the enemy.

"Streamer platoons with even numbers support the

Isfahans with air defense, odd numbers watch the perimeter. Repeat, odd numbered platoons to watch the perimeter. Do not get sucked into the battle," Allenson said, using the loudspeakers and the command group communication.

"Copy that, Colonel," Rutchett replied on the command group.

The flat crack of coil rifles complemented the zip of laserifles. Both were drowned out by the shriek of high-energy laser bursts fired upward in quick succession. The pulses carved tunnels of exploding steam through the mist.

"What the hell." Allenson followed the bursts back to their source. The roof of Mansingh's bunker lay to one side on the ground. It was just a thin veneer of wood. The long barrel of a lasercannon on a high anti-air mount projected out of the resulting fire pit. Mansingh swung the gun, blasting the phasing Terran transport with laser bolts until its fields sparkled and flared. The power overload earthed to ground as a lightning bolt. The transport dropped back into the Continuum. Allenson hoped it was crippled.

Without warning, the world grew bright and exploded. Allenson felt a deep *whump* in his chest. The explosion tumbled him across the ground. Something slapped him hard between the shoulderblades. Mansingh's gun stopped firing.

A second transport turned and dropped, fully phased into realspace. Its field was low, flaring with just enough power to hold it in the air. That meant the troops inside could fire out. The nose-mounted cannon discharged a second time. It targeted something well behind Allenson. Another flash was punctuated by the whoomph of displaced air. Men leaned out of the transport, firing laserifles at the militia on the ground.

The Streamers returned fire. Their shots penetrated the frame's weak field, striking little splashes of blue light. Laser bolt explosions and sparklies from coil gun strikes sprinkled along the transport's hull. A wounded Terran dropped his rifle and slid out, falling head first to the ground. High above, two more dark shapes dropped through the mist, like whales coming up for air.

Mansingh's cannon reopened fire. The Terran heavy gunners had failed to ensure it was permanently out of action, a novice's error for which they would pay a heavy price. Mansingh walked the bolts down the transport frame. Its hull exploded in fire, shooting out sprays of red-brown debris. The transport's field flared up and it swung violently sideways, causing Mansingh's next burst to miss. Not that it mattered. The transport rolled slowly over, shedding burning debris. Some of the debris thrashed as it fell.

The burning transport dropped like a brick, crashing somewhere outside the base. Black smoke rolled upward, twisting in convection loops. Mansingh fired again into the mist. Allenson was not sure what he was firing at, as the other transports had disappeared.

"Attackers on the perimeter," Rutchett informed Allenson through the datapad. "Repeat, we are being attacked at the perimeter."

"All Stream troops move to perimeter to repel attackers. Keep your men on sky watch, if you please, Captain Broch, but stand by as a reserve," Allenson said.

The flat crack of coil guns sounded again. An incoming laserifle shot reflected off the top of a bunker. Allenson sprinted for the perimeter trench line. Laser shots carved streaks through the wet air around him. He jumped into a trench held by second platoon. "Where's Mr. Padget?"

"That way, sir," a soldier pointed.

Men squeezed back to allow him through. He located Padget, who tried to stand to attention and salute. Allenson dragged him back down.

"I would rather you did not involve me if you wish to set yourself up as a target, Mr. Padget," Allenson said.

"Sorry, sir."

Allenson stuck his head out to see what was going on. The Terran troops were shockingly close to the base, emerging like shadows out of the mist. They hesitated when they came under fire, halting to fire back. A few crouched down, but most stayed on their feet. Officers urged them on and the advance restarted.

Allenson had no hope that his men would withstand close combat with a superior force. There was nowhere to run, but that would not stop them routing in panic. His only hope was to break the morale of the attackers by inflicting more casualties than they were prepared to accept. He doubted if the Terran colonial force were elite shock troops. If they were, Allenson and his whole command were dead whatever he did, so there was no point planning for that eventuality.

Some of the Streamers were firing but not nearly enough. Too many of his men were frozen in combat shock, not running, but not fighting either. He had to change that. He only knew one way. He vaulted onto an ammunition box that served as an observation point and scrambled to the top of the trench in full view. He needed his men to see him. That meant that the enemy could see him, of course, but he was dead anyway if his ploy failed.

"Pour it into the bastards! They couldn't hit a barn let alone a man in a trench," Allenson ordered, underlining the point by firing long bursts from his carbine.

His men cheered and the flat crack of coil guns merged into a continuous crackle. Most of it was probably unaimed, but Terrans fell anyway. Laser bolts hissed around Allenson. He gave the Terrans one more burst before jumping back into cover. A one-eyed soldier in the trench caught him when he stumbled.

The Terrans wouldn't advance into the storm of pellets. Some dropped to one knee to fire aimed shots, but the Streamers in trenches presented a difficult target. Others backed away slowly, firing more or less randomly from the hip. One turned and ran. He made only a few steps before a shot from an ion pistol took him between the shoulderblades. The victim dived forward into the mist, dropping his rifle.

A Terran captain screamed exhortations, waving his discharged pistol. Terrans stopped retreating and began to reform a skirmishing line. The Streamers weren't safe yet.

A single laserifle shot from behind Allenson blew out the back of the captain's head. At that the Terrans ran, a trickle at first, then a torrent like water from a collapsing dam, until the enemy were in full rout. Streamers continued to spray fire into the mist even when there were no visible targets left.

"Cease fire, cease fire, stop wasting ammunition!" Allenson said over the datapad to the command group.

He doubted anyone would hear the loudspeakers. The firing died away raggedly as the order was passed down the command chain.

Allenson looked for the one-eyed soldier to thank him, but he was on the bottom of the trench. He had no eyes, now.

A low moan sounded beyond the camp. It rose and fell like a distant lament, as if a squadron of giant bees were moving from bloom to bloom.

"What is that noise?" Padget asked. The young man looked unnerved.

"It's the Terran wounded," Allenson replied.

The information did not make Padget look any happier.

Allenson called Hawthorn on their private circuit. "Was it you who took out the Terran captain?"

"You know of someone else here with a hunting rifle?" Hawthorn asked rhetorically.

"Well done, you may have just saved the camp."

"Naw, it was the idiot cavorting around on top of the trench who did that," Hawthorn said.

Allenson decided to ignore that particular remark.

"Could you lead some volunteers out beyond the camp while it is still misty?" Allenson asked.

"Sure, I'll select some men to volunteer," Hawthorn replied.

"Pick up anything useful to bring back; especially search the leaders for datapads. It would help if we knew what we were up against. The next priority for recovery are laserifles."

"What about the Terran wounded?" Hawthorn asked.

Allenson hesitated, until decency trumped common sense.

"Bring back for treatment those that have any hope at all of survival."

"And the others?" Hawthorn asked.

"Give them an overdose of painkiller, to ease them on their way," Allenson said.

"We may need that painkiller," Hawthorn said. "Why not just cut their throats? It has the same effect."

"No," Allenson replied. "We can't do that. Don't ask me to explain because I can't, but an overdose is treatment; a cut throat is a war crime. Logic doesn't come into it."

By the time the mist lifted, it revealed a battlefield empty of all but the dead. Allenson walked back across the camp, carbine over his shoulder. He stopped off at the weapon bunker. A deep rut surrounded by glass fragments and frozen splashes of liquidized soil showed how close the cannon hit had come. Mansingh and Marks fussed over the lasercannon like female relatives preparing the bride.

"You know, I really do not remember ordering that weapon, Mister Mansingh," Allenson said.

"Indeed, not, you couldn't possibly have afforded it, colonel," Mansingh said, wiping the barrel lovingly with a soft cloth. "It belongs to my company. It's a display sample. Never have been able to make a sale; nobody can afford it. I thought I would bring it along and test it out."

"Glad you did, Mister Mansingh. Glad you did," Allenson said.

"I think we owe a vote of thanks to Mr Mansingh," Allenson said, nodding toward the weapons consultant. "His little toy probably made the difference."

A chorus of "Hear, hear!" sounded around the command bunker.

"Unfortunately, I opened fire too soon, sir," Mansingh said, shaking his head at what he considered as his own incompetence. "I should have waited until that first transport fully phased. I would have gotten it then."

"No doubt as a para, you were more used to being on the receiving end," Allenson said.

"I think you underrate your own contribution, sir," Rutchett said. "Your example stiffened the men's morale at the critical moment."

Murmurs of agreement sounded until Rutchett held up a hand for silence.

"However, correct as your decision was at the time, I must counsel you not to repeat such a dangerous gesture. You are neither laserproof nor expendable," Rutchett said.

Allenson flushed and searched for some reply. Hawthorn came to his aid by changing the subject. "The Terrans have only pulled back to the hills on the edge of the crystal tree line. They intend to besiege us, and we may suffer more attacks."

"I doubt that they will try another assault any time soon," Allenson said. "That surprise attack was their best shot and it failed. Mister Mansingh will confirm is that it is very difficult to coordinate simultaneous attacks from the Continuum and realspace. Their commander was too overconfident."

Mansingh nodded.

"The delay between the air and land assault permitted us to destroy them in detail." Allenson had looked up the expression "destroy in detail," after Avery had used it. It described a smaller army destroying a larger but disconnected force by attacking each of its components in 'turn, establishing local numerical superiority in each encounter.

"However, it is clear from the intelligence that Captain Hawthorn acquired from the dead officer that the Terrans still heavily outnumber us despite their casualties," Allenson said. "I expect them to try to starve us out. They won't succeed, gentlemen. We can easily hang on until reinforced. Any other business?"

He looked from face to face.

"In that case, the council is over." Allenson walked the men to the sheeting that doubled as a door to the bunker. The exit faced a wall of sandbags for blast protection. When he pulled aside the sheet, the wind pushed stale air into the room.

"What is that bloody awful stench?" Allenson asked.

"The river has risen higher in the night and the 'bogs' are overflowing back into the camp," Hawthorn said.

Allenson was about to ask what idiot had ordered the latrines sited down by the river when he remembered that he was the fool in question. It had seemed logical at the time. "Get new ones dug, if you please, Mister Rutchett," Allenson said.

"I intend to," Rutchett replied, "but it seemed sensible to wait until the river stopped rising, so I know how high up the meadow they need to be."

Allenson nodded, annoyed at himself for interfering. Rutchett was perfectly competent and would only resent micromanagement.

He went outside and looked up the meadow toward the treeline. He had not given much thought as to why the regions along the rivers were free of silicon forest. Unpleasant possibilities presented themselves, but he dismissed them. He had plenty of real problems without inventing things to worry about.

The crisis came the next day. Allenson walked briskly from his bunker to a forward trench. Sniper fire struck inside the base, raising puffs of steam that exploded in the mud with a curious hiss. Allenson could see the flash when a Terran laser pulsed. They occupied positions among the spongy trees in the low hills a few miles away at the edge of the meadowland. Allenson had not realized what a tactical advantage height would give a besieger.

A man ran past, zigzagging to throw off the Terrans' aim. Allenson could see little point in adopting that course. The Terrans could not possibly target individuals at such ranges. The Terrans had night sights so the dark brought no respite. Their intention was to harass the defenders with area fire. You were no more likely to get hit walking than running. Of course, every so often the Terrans got lucky. Thank the Lord they hadn't any heavy weapons or it would all be over by now.

He slid into a perimeter trench knee deep in fetid water. Allenson barely noticed the stink; he was so used to it. The men were disinclined to move far from their trenches for all but essential purposes. For many of them, visiting the new latrines did not come under that category. Inevitably, the floodwater in the defenses was contaminated, with the inevitable result of food poisoning and diarrhea, causing a vicious spiral of deterioration.

The mud sucked at his feet, slowing him down. He had not slept properly since the siege started, and he was tiring. Hawthorn was in the trench, sniping on the Terran position. He had his long hunting rifle on the lip of the trench and was squinting down the site. Hawthorn adjusted his aim fractionally and fired.

"Did you get him?" Allenson asked.

"Who knows?" Hawthorn replied. "Probably not. They fire a few quick shots and then change position. I am shooting blind."

"Can't we suppress the Terran fire somehow?" Allenson asked. "The men are tired, dirty and hungry. They haven't had a hot meal since this harassment started."

"No." Hawthorn replied succinctly.

"How about using Mansingh's cannon?" Allenson asked.

"Daren't risk it," Hawthorn replied. "It's the only weapon that keeps the Terran transports grounded. We're finished if they get into the air. They'd shoot us to pieces with their bow cannon. Fortunately, they don't seem able to dismount them. Mansingh's cannon is doing its job just by continuing to exist."

"Surely the risk to the cannon from laserrifle fire is minimal?" Allenson asked, unsure why Hawthorn was so uncharacteristically timid.

"Our lasercannon is a big fat target. We'd have to mount it right out in the open to hit the Terrans. One lucky shot is all it would take," Hawthorn said. "You want to take the risk?"

The question was rhetorical and did not require an answer.

"The Terrans have a new tactic," Hawthorn said, cryptically. He checked a time counter. "That should be long enough. Give us a hand, trooper," Hawthorn said. "And keep your bloody head down."

"Yes, sir."

Hawthorn reached down into the mud and pulled a body up by the scruff of the neck. A soldier helped him shove the corpse upward, until it projected out of the trench almost to the waist.

"Come one, little fishy, take the bait," Hawthorn said.

The corpse exploded with a large orange flash. Its upper chest disappeared in a spray of burnt flesh. The head dropped down into the trench. Allenson automatically caught it. The eyes looked surprised. Allenson threw the head away into no man's land.

Hawthorn popped up and shot five times, aiming at the source of the flash.

"What the hell was that?" Allenson asked. "I thought they didn't have any heavy weapons."

He remembered his insouciant walk across the open ground, and felt like throwing up.

"They don't exactly," Hawthorn replied. "The weapon has an incredibly slow rate of fire. I suspect they have to service and recharge it after every shot. Rutchett thinks it is an armor-piercing rifle, a light infantry weapon with long range sights."

"I've never heard of it," Allenson said.

"I'm not surprised. Apparently they're obsolete in the Home Worlds and hardly of much value out here. It's a single-shot weapon used to take out light armor. Apparently, it also makes a decent long range sniper rifle."

"So we are stuffed," Allenson said.

"Maybe not," Hawthorn replied, with a shark-like grin. "Two can play at snipers."

Marks had dug a pipe into the side of Mansingh's gun-pit and carefully excavated the end. Looking through it, Allenson could see a Terran position in the hills, a small clump of trees by some orange bushes. Mansingh had the cannon lowered so it could be pointed down the pipe. The narrow pipe allowed the gun just two or three degrees of traverse.

"Very useful, if you can persuade the Terrans to form a narrow column and march toward us exactly on the right bearing," Allenson said, sarcastically. He was short tempered. A random laserifle round had come depressingly close on his trip from the command bunker. He'd automatically thrown himself down on the mud, an utterly pointless thing to do. So now he was wet, cold, and stinking, as well as tired, and wondering whether he was losing his bottle. If Hawthorn had dragged him out to see a pipe then their friendship was about to undergo a degree of strain.

"I noticed something about matey with the sniper rifle," Hawthorn said. "He's not very bright. He's been taught to move after every shot so he does, but he moves to a set sequence along the same fire points, as regular as taxes."

"And I take it that pipe is pointing at one of his regular fire points," Allenson said.

"Promotion to colonel hasn't entirely dulled your wits yet, then?" Hawthorn asked with a grin.

"No, as it was a field promotion, I have not yet had the necessary lobotomy required for commanders," Allenson replied, recovering his sense of humor.

The friends suddenly remembered that they were not alone. Mansingh and Marks had their heads down making a fine adjustment to the cannon, something that apparently caused a transient deafness.

"In a few minutes time, matey will be looking for a new target," Hawthorn said.

At that point, two men dragged in a corpse. Hawthorn inspected it.

"There's no head," Hawthorn said.

"You didn't say it had to have a head," one of the troopers replied.

"You don't think that a sniper with long range sights might not notice that his target is missing a head?" Hawthorn asked.

Neither trooper replied, which was sensible of them. Hawthorn did not raise his voice, but his tone had acquired a dangerous edge.

"We'll only get one chance at this. I think we will have to wait until we can get more convincing bait." Hawthorn shook his head.

"And in the meantime, the sniper will kill more of my men," Allenson said.

He was really pissed off. Nothing was going right and there seemed to be damn all he could do about it.

"Are you ready to fire, Mister Mansingh?" Allenson asked.

"Yes, sir," Mansingh replied.

"Then let's do it," Allenson said.

Allenson scrambled up onto the pit wall and shook his fist in the general direction of the Terrans. He drew his ion pistol and discharged a series of shots at the distant hills. The pistol had an effective range of twenty meters, assuming you were a crack shot, which he wasn't, but it did fire spectacularly noticeable rounds.

The hills lit up with sparkles as the Terrans took pot shots at the madman with their laserifles. He noticed a blue flash from the orange bushes, like he was looking down the beam from a surveyor's theodolite. Before his fore brain identified it as range-finder, his reptile hind brain threw his body backward into the pit. He had the impression of a bright orange flash and the crack of ionized air. Then his world was filled with the shriek and pulsing strobe of heavy laser fire. He hit the ground hard on his back, knocking the wind from his chest. A sharp knock on the back of his head heralded concentric closing rings of blackness.

"Colonel, colonel," a voice said from far away. He tried to ignore it, but the voice was irritatingly persistent. He opened his eyes, quickly shutting them again. The light made the back of his head throb.

"You stupid bastard," Hawthorn said.

"I'm your superior officer," Allenson said, without opening his eyes. "Kindly treat me with respect."

"Sorry, you stupid bastard, sir," Hawthorn said.

"How long was I out?"

"Just seconds."

"So I'm not badly wounded?" Allenson asked, feeling the urge to check everything was all there.

"You fell on your head," Hawthorn replied, "so the only damage is to the duckboards."

He slapped a patch on Allenson's neck, none too gently, and the throbbing pain disappeared.

"Did we get the sod?" Allenson asked, remembering why they were there.

"Take a look for yourself, sir," Mansingh replied.

He helped Allenson to his feet. The ceramic pipe was cracked and melted from the cannon's backwash, but it was still possible to see out with a little care. Parts of the pipe still glowed orange-red.

Black smoke marked the Terran position. Orange bushes burned fiercely and the trees were stripped of foliage and blackened.

"If we didn't get him, we certainly gave him a brown-trouser scare," Mansingh said, with deep satisfaction. He patted the cannon as if it were a favorite niece.

The next day, Allenson trudged through the rain, his feet sliding on the muddy ground. The rain temporarily provided protection from the incessant laserifle barrage, but it added to the flooding that had turned trenches into ditches and bunkers into ponds. Some of the men took the opportunity to get food from the stores and carry it back to their positions. Others just stood in the rain, letting the water run down their bodies. Maybe they were trying to wash off the stink of sewage. Fat chance: the very air was contaminated. Rainwater trickled down his face and under his collar.

He had a hundred casualties, including thirty dead, caused mostly by laserifle hits and accidents. A couple of men had shot themselves, maybe by accident, maybe not. Increasingly, disease took its toll in the unsanitary conditions. They had even had cases of malnutrition where men were too scared to risk the gauntlet of laser fire to get food.

The Expeditionary Force was completely cut off. No messages got through so he had no idea when relief would arrive, or even if it would arrive. The casualty rate haunted him. You could put a trend line on them and predict fairly accurately when he would have too few men to defend the base against a renewed assault. That time was not far off.

He went into the command bunker, waded across

it, and flopped on the bed, which was propped up on old ammo boxes to be clear of the water. It was still wet, of course. Everything was wet. He lay down. Maybe a sleep would help him see his way out of this mess. He was too exhausted to think right now.

A sandbag shifted in the wall opposite and a stream of water forced its way into the bunker. While he watched, a blackened arm washed through the hole. The torso must be still attached as it blocked the hole, shutting off the flow. Allenson closed his eyes, pleased with the lucky break that meant he did not have to get up and fix the wall. He knew there was something wrong with that reaction but was too tired to work out what.

When he woke up, he knew what he had to do.

Brasilia

"What?" Marshal Ovaki asked testily.

His secretary, a pretty girl who was a perk of rank, was unconcerned. The Marshal's bark was far worse than his bite, at least for pretty girls.

"General Brine to see you, sar."

The marshal grunted, which she took as assent. She showed in a lean man dressed in the uniform of a Brasilian army general.

"Sit down, Petrov," the Marshal said, jabbing at his desk to close down a file.

"You wanted me, Sam?" the general asked.

"Yes. Some Scotch?" The marshal opened a draw and produced a bottle and two glasses.

"No thanks," the general said, shuddering slightly. "A little plum brandy will do fine, Sam," he added.

"Plum brandy—a nancy-boy's drink," Marshal Ovaki said, scornfully. Nevertheless, he drew out a second bottle and poured a glass for his guest.

"Have you been following the latest crisis on the frontier?" the marshal asked.

"Which frontier?" the general replied, frowning.

Marshal Ovaki waved a hand vaguely in the direction of one of the walls of his office. "The colonies across the Bight?"

"Oh those," the general said. "I did hear that the politicos were winding themselves up into a lather about some imagined slight from Terra."

"The Terrans are extending into the Hinterlands behind our colonies. The armchair generals in The Council have taken fright," the marshal said. "They have started babbling about strategic encirclement."

The tone of his voice made it clear what he thought of Council Delegates.

"That's ridiculous. Only the First Tier colonies across the Bight are of any value, and that's not much. Colonizing the Hinterlands is uneconomic. It will never be important to Brasilia. What has set off the latest panic?"

"Some damned fool of a colonial decided to play chocolate soldiers. The Stream Militia managed to shoot a Terran ambassador, and then fled in panic when attacked by the Terrans. We have been made to look stupid. It's now become a matter of face, d'you see?" the marshal asked.

"Yeees," said the general. He thought deeply. "The Terrans have been feeling their oats recently. It might not hurt to give them a kicking, and I suppose the Bight colonies are as good a venue as any."

"There is also a defense spending review due next year. It might not hurt to remind our masters in The Council of the army's value," the marshal said. "Two light battalions of Regulars should be enough to cow a Terran colonial militia."

He stabbed at his desk. "Battalions from the 51st and 12th are available for deployment. Who do we have available as a brigade commander?"

"Chernokovsky's patrons have been pushing for him to have a field position," the general suggested.

"Chernokovsky, yes. He's not a ball of fire but he will be a safe pair of hands. Good idea; we'll give him the commission."

The marshal discovered that his glass was empty, so he poured another scotch. "How's Regina, Petrov?"

"Cutting up a bit rough after those pictures in *The Crusader*, Sam. I had to buy her a new villa as a peace offering."

"Cheating on your wife is one thing, Petrov, everybody does that, but there's all hell to pay when you also get caught cheating on your mistress. And with her sister, too, you dog."

CHAPTER 20

Homecoming

"Not content with massacring a Terran diplomatic party without warning, not to mention killing the ambassador in the process, you get beaten by the New Terra colonial army, and then you sign this ludicrous formal surrender document. Would that correctly sum up your military career so far?" Fontenoy asked.

"I hardly think that fair comment," Allenson replied. "You completely ignored our request for reinforcements."

"Not fair? Did you actually *read* that document before you signed it?" Fontenoy asked.

"Of course, it seemed generous, considering that they had our Expeditionary Force trapped. They allowed us to withdraw unmolested, with our weapons." Allenson replied.

"Did you not notice that the preamble on this surrender document states, and I quote"—at this point Fontenoy read from his datapad—"the Terran expedition was mounted in response to the murder of their ambassador in unclaimed territory." He tossed the datapad on the desk. "Unclaimed territory—and you signed it. You effectively admitted that the Brasilian claims in the Hinterlands are void."

Allenson could not think of an answer. He had not considered the implications of that one word "unclaimed" because he was not a diplomat, and he was more interested in getting his men out of the trap that he had created for them. He was also exhausted at the time—but that was just an excuse. He would probably have signed anyway, but he should have at least understood what he was signing. Fontenoy had a point.

"Fortunately, you can be easily disowned as a colonial officer exceeding his authority. However, I have also had a most unpleasant meeting with a Representative from the Colonial Office," Fontenoy said, changing tack. "They are furious at your naiveté in handling the Riders, who were shocked at the way you threw your men's lives away in a hopeless battle. Don't you realize, man, that the Rider clans have tiny populations? They could not sustain losses like yours. The Rider clans have switched sides. Your incompetence has cost us our allies. We will face a wave of Rider raids on our outer colonies if war breaks out."

Allenson noted that Fontenoy had suddenly become an expert on Rider society—after his briefing from the Colonial Office. Pity he had not thought to explore that avenue before dispatching the Expeditionary Force. He did not voice the comment because he, himself, had made the same error.

"If you have lost confidence in my judgement, then I must offer my resignation," said Allenson, who had listened to enough complaints from someone who had never been further into the Hinterlands than the nearest hunting lodge.

"Accepted," Fontenoy snapped. "It will save me from firing you for exceeding your orders by starting a border dispute with Terra."

"I did what you ordered me to," Allenson said hotly. "You instructed me to expel the Terrans by any means necessary."

"You have that in writing?" Fontenoy asked rhetorically.

Allenson was speechless at the man's duplicity. Something unpleasant must have showed in Allenson's expression because Fontenoy stepped back in alarm.

"I am not suggesting that you are untruthful," Fontenoy said hurriedly, "but my recollection of our conversation is at variance with your own. Possibly there was a miscommunication between us."

Allenson had little choice but to leave the matter there, short of calling Fontenoy a liar, which would simply sound like sour grapes from a fired official. He scrawled a one-line resignation and left Fontenoy's office before he lost his temper.

The Plaza outside the Assembly Building was thronged with people. They surged forward as Allenson appeared, faces contorted, yelling and shouting. He grabbed the handle of his pistol under his jacket but did not draw it. What was the point of killing a few plebs? It wouldn't change anything. He looked around for a way of escape but they were all around him. The crowd called his name and laid rough hands on him. A woman with faded purple hair screamed in his face. He almost gagged on the smell of cheap booze. He thought he was about to be strung up.

A small voice at the back of his mind noted that this was an ignominious full stop to a short and less than glorious military career. He relaxed. It would be undignified to struggle. What was the point?

They hoisted him shoulder high. He could see Lictors on the edge of the crowd trying to force their way through, but they were hopelessly outnumbered. The mob paraded across the Plaza chanting "Imperator," an old Brasilian salute from the commoners for a conquering general. He finally realized that far from being strung up, he was being honored by the plebs for his failed expedition. This was almost more embarrassing than being lynched.

The crowd started on a circuit, numbers growing all the time. Most were drunk and reeling. A woman in a blue dress tilted her head back to drink from a bottle. She overbalanced and fell, setting off a domino effect. People were trampled. It was only a matter of time before there was a disaster. He yelled for them to stop, but his voice was drowned in the roar of the crowd. He looked around desperately.

A face, in the sea of faces, was familiar—what was the man's name? Jezzom, that was it, Sergeant Jezzom. Now he recognized other people. Some were still wearing uniforms. Members of the Expeditionary Force were in the crowd.

"Sergeant Jezzom, can you organize an escort and get me out of here?" Allenson asked, cupping his hands and shouting to be heard over the cries of the mob.

Jezzom gave a thumbs up and issued orders. Soldiers surrounded Allenson. They hauled him down and shoved the crowd away. Forming a phalanx, they pushed their way through to a taxiframe rank in a side alley.

"Thank you, Jezzom. Take your men for a drink on me," Allenson said, thrusting a handful of sovereigns into the sergeant's hand.

"Thank you, sir," The sergeant saluted, looking pleased, as well he might. Allenson had given him the equivalent of a month's pay.

"Where to, guv?" asked the taxi driver.

"Anywhere—up—away," Allenson said.

The taxi part-phased and rose, moving rapidly across the city. Allenson gave the driver his hotel. However, after a few moments thought he changed his mind and directed the driver to a private address. Somewhere he could get some quiet reflection and intelligent advice.

"Are you sure it was wise to resign, Allen?" Trina asked, pouring the tea. "I can see the advantage to Fontenoy. He can pass all blame onto you and avoid a black mark on his career, but what of your own reputation?"

Allenson sighed. His promise to his dying brother had taken on something of a sacred vow, and he had fallen at the first fence. He imagined Linsye's scorn at the news.

"It was not entirely done in childish pique," he replied, smiling to keep any sting out of the words. "Fontenoy would have sacked me. Resignation seemed a better course."

"Should you wish it, I believe your position is far from irrecoverable," Trina said, careful not to imply she was pushing him.

"Indeed, I don't see how." Allenson said. "But I would be most interested to hear your thoughts."

"I have taken the liberty of sounding out my family's clients in the Lower House," Trina said, a little uncomfortably. "Merely sounded them out, you understand, not indicated that you did or did not want any particular course of action."

"Please go on," Allenson said, giving her another smile as encouragement. After the disasters of the last few months, he was way past taking offense at anything Trina might do.

"You may not realize it, but you are considered something of a hero," Trina said.

"So I gather," Allenson said, dryly. "In my opinion, I was a bloody fool who allowed his army to be bottled up in an indefensible position by a superior force."

"Fool and hero are not entirely mutually exclusive," Trina said with a smile. "Indeed, I have heard it claimed by cynics that all heroes are fools."

Allenson laughed. "Maybe, but I played more the fool than the hero."

"The commoners see it differently. They think you were the only sar with the, ah, balls—I believe that is the expression," Trina said primly, "to stand up for the Stream. You also cared enough about the welfare of your soldiers to eat humble pie to get them home. Some of those soldiers have relatives who sit in the Lower House. The soldiers have also brought back stories of your gallantry. Apparently, you always reserved the most dangerous tasks for yourself. I cannot think that was sensible of you, but I can see how it plays well in the political arena."

"I don't see how that stops Fontenoy from firing me," Allenson said.

"Militia dismissals have to be ratified by the Lower

House," Trina said. "There is a core group that will vote against your dismissal and refuse to accept your resignation. A larger, non-aligned group has fastened on this popular issue as a way of curbing Fontenoy. They don't care about you, but they can be persuaded to attach a motion to the bill ratifying your resignation, one that removes many of Fontenoy's prerogatives. It is a win-win situation for this group since Fontenoy loses face whatever does. It is my belief that Fontenoy will back down rather than accept a loss of power, so your resignation will have never happened."

"Trina, you are a genius," Allenson said.

In genuine enthusiasm he leaned over and kissed her on the cheek. Trina blushed and her maid snorted in amusement.

"More tea," Trina said, to cover her confusion.

It was early evening when Allenson returned to his hotel.

"Have a good evening, sar." The porter on duty in his corridor smirked at him.

What the hell was wrong with the man? Allenson unlocked his room door and flicked the lights on. He headed for the bathroom to wash his face.

"I'm not used to being ignored."

He turned. She lay on the bed in a diaphanous slip. A bright red dress that probably cost more than a month's salary for the average Manzanitan lay in a heap on the floor. Her hair was bright yellow and her eyes flaming orange—the color of her letter burning in the fire, the color of a man dancing in the flames.

"Sarai, what are you doing here?"

"Royman is playing at farmer on the demesne and

I was bored, so I have come to Manzanita to see my family."

"How did you get into my room?"

"I bribed the porter," she said smugly.

Dear God, Allenson thought, the story would be all over the hotel by morning. The Hero Allenson has a mysterious exotic lady in his room.

"When I asked what you were doing here, I meant what are you doing in my room?"

She made a moue. "You really are the most annoying man, Allen. You don't reply to my letter, where I poured out my heart, incidentally. You leave me to go on a camping trip in the Hinterlands to play at soldiers, when you could easily have appointed a deputy. You don't even come to visit me when you get back from enjoying yourself—and then you ask what I'm doing here. Many would think themselves the most fortunate of men to find me in their bed—but if you find my presence so distasteful then I will go."

She sat up, showing every sign of storming straight out in high dudgeon—unfortunately covered by little else. That would help the rumors to no end.

"No, wait," Allenson said, holding up his hands.

She lay back down with a hint of a smile. Allenson thought she was bluffing, but lacked the resolve to put it to the test. You never knew with Sarai.

She ran a hand down her slip, smoothing out the wrinkles. "Poor, Allen, am I really so disturbing?"

"Actually, you are, Sarai," he said, wishing she wouldn't do that. "Look, I am only thinking of your reputation."

"How sweet, Allen," she said, getting off the bed and moving toward him like a leopard.

Allenson had an urge to back up.

"But, don't worry, no one knows I am here."

"Only your maid, and your cousin's servants, and the porter, and the rest of the hotel staff," Allenson said.

"No one who matters knows I am here," Sárai said. "The lower orders will keep their mouths shut, if they know what's good for them." She ran her hand down her slip again, her nail catching the seam. It opened, the slip falling from her naked body and fluttering to the floor.

He was lost. He no longer cared about repercussions. He didn't care about his career. He didn't care if he was signing his own death warrant. He had to have her, now.

The Brasilian force arrived the following week. Allenson was astonished at the enormity of the Brasilian force. He had been told to expect two Regular light infantry regiments. He had no concrete expectation of what that might look like, but he had vaguely anticipated something like the colonial militia, albeit on a larger scale. The difference was a sharp reality check of the resource differential between even the First Tier colonies of the Bight and the Home Worlds.

Allenson landed in the military base, which was under construction on the edge of Port Clearwater. He approached by a circuitous route so that he could look at the base, an anthill of activity. A protective berm and ditch had already been thrown up by earth movers. That seemed an unnecessary precaution. Manzanita was hardly enemy territory. It suggested the Brasilian commander was cautious, or maybe just thorough.

The first transport to land had included the engineering company that was building the fortifications, as well as the brigade headquarters with its attendant support platoons. The latter included mortars and air defense cannons.

Allenson was met by a young lieutenant, who looked at his dress uniform with a hint of a smirk. "You must be the colonial militia officer?" The lieutenant hazarded.

"I believe Brigadier Chernokovsky is expecting me," Allenson said stiffly.

"Oh quite," the lieutenant said. "Follow me."

Chernokovsky had his HQ in a large tent near the center of the base. Allenson was left kicking his heels in an atrium for half an hour. Eventually an aide popped his head around the door.

"Brigadier Chernokovsky will see you now."

Chernokovsky was a large stout man with a round ruddy face. He rose and greeted Allenson with a handshake. "Sar Allenson, good of you to drop by."

"Brigadier Chernokovsky." Allenson considered referring to the man by his civilian title of "sar" in retaliation for Chernokovsky not using Allenson's own rank, but decided against as it would have been petty. Chernokovsky was being friendly, and there seemed no point in making an enemy of the man by standing on dignity.

"Sorry to keep you waiting, but I have many demands on my time at the moment," Chernokovsky said.

"I quite understand," Allenson replied.

"I believe you had a rough time of it at the hands of the Terrans?" Chernokovsky asked.

"It was no pleasure trip," Allenson replied.

"Not to worry, old chap, the professionals are here now," Chernokovsky said with kindly condescension.

"I am sure we are all very pleased," Allenson replied politely, hiding his irritation.

"Is this your first experience of the Regular Army?" Chernokovsky asked.

"I am afraid so," Allenson replied.

"What do you think?" Chernokovsky asked.

"Very impressive," Allenson replied truthfully.

"I will arrange for one of my aides to show you around," Chernokovsky said. "As you have probably been told by Governor, ah..."

"Fontenoy."

"That's the chap, Fontenoy; I would like you to be my liaison with the colony. As a Light Brigade, we are not entirely self sufficient and rely on local purchase of consumables, such as food."

"I am delighted to assist," Allenson said. "But what exactly would be my rank and position in the Brigade's command structure?"

"Ah yes, that is tricky," Chernokovsky replied. "Obviously your rank as Colonel of Colonial Militia has no standing with the Regular Army. If it did, I would have to make you my second in command with rank over my battalion commanders who are lieutenant colonels, and that would be ridiculous."

"Quite," Allenson said, keeping the smile on his face.

"What I suggest is that your position in the Regular Army be that of an unpaid consultant, with the title of Colonial Liaison Officer. That way you are out of our command structure. You cannot give orders but, by the same token, cannot be given orders. Nevertheless you would be treated as an officer for all other purposes. Does that seem a reasonable compromise?"

Actually it did, so Allenson readily agreed. "Would you require me to wear civilian clothes?" he asked.

"As you wish," Chernokovsky replied. "Now if

you will excuse me, I have a line of people wanting something or other."

And with that Allenson was dismissed. He had the impression that Chernokovsky regarded a colonial militia uniform as synonymous with civilian clothing.

A young lieutenant took him on a tour of the camp. The sheer quantity and complexity of the operation was even more bewildering close up. It made his expedition look like a family picnic. He was surprised at the number of women in the Regular Army. There was nothing to stop women joining the colonial militia, but a few did.

"What do you think so far?" the lieutenant asked.

"Very impressive," Allenson replied. "My only reservation is that it will be a challenge moving all this through the Hinterlands."

"That's why we have an engineering company attached," the lieutenant said. "We are going to build a trackway."

Allenson was stunned. Trackways were roads through the Continuum used in areas where stars were clustered close together, rendering navigation by interworld ships so difficult as to be impossible or uneconomic. They involved setting up solar-powered orbiting beacons in real space, about two or three hours apart. The beacons produced a charged, smoothed path in the Continuum that gave frames greater speed and range for the same expenditure of energy.

The long-term strategic implications of the plan were stunning. It would open up the Hinterlands to exploitation and the Stream would be the gateway. For the first time in a while, Allenson was optimistic about the future.

He realized that the lieutenant had said something. "Your pardon, sar, could you repeat that?" he asked.

"I wondered whether you would like to see the men practising frame combat tactics?" the lieutenant asked.

"Very much," Allenson replied.

The army had set up a practice range outside the berm.

"Our combat sections are on a ten-man frame," said the lieutenant. "However, the minimum unit of maneuver is a company of ten to twenty sections. We rarely fight from frames, so the Brigadier thought it wise to brush up our skills. Normally we transit by interworld ship and fight as infantry, just using frames to move around."

Allenson watched a company maneuver en masse to attack a tethered blimp. The company kept a tight formation that was slow and ponderous but offered mutual support. They fired at the blimp in a single volley. The skin rippled like a child's balloon in a hail storm. The troopers used soft-nosed rounds in their spring guns for training, but Allenson could see how such tactics could bring crushing fire down on an enemy. It was very different from the whirling skirmishes for which the militia trained.

"You promised delivery within five days," Allenson said to a supplier on the other end of his datapad. The figure in the hologram spread his hands until they disappeared out of the focusing field.

"Yes, but that was dependent on my suppliers delivering on time. They haven't," the supplier said.

"What component are you missing?" Allenson asked.

The supplier told him.

"Send me the details and I will try to find an alternative vendor." Allenson shut the connection down. His datapad immediately sounded the urgent communication chime. Sighing, Allenson sipped his cafay and keyed it. One of Chernokovsky's aides appeared.

"The Brigadier requests a meeting with you at your earliest convenience, Sar Allenson," he said.

"Can't he just contact me by pad?" Allenson asked. "I have some problems to sort out."

"I believe he wants to show you something," the aide replied, somewhat apologetically.

"I'll be there in five minutes," Allenson said.

He downed the rest of his drink in a gulp. The hot liquid seared his throat, which did nothing to improve his mood.

Chernokovsky had a section of camouflage netting rolled up on the table in his office.

"Have a look at that," Chernokovsky said, gesturing toward the netting, which was made up of laminated sections, cemented together. The sections were already peeling and came apart at the slightest pull.

"The cement isn't waterproof," Chernokovsky said. "The whole bloody consignment of netting is useless. One rain shower and it falls apart. Good God, Allenson, I don't expect much from you chaps. We have brought with us anything we need that is at all sophisticated or complicated, but I assumed that you could make bloody netting even in the colonies. Is waterproof glue too much to ask for?"

"No, it isn't," Allenson said, "but us colonial chappies have to buy in even basic materials from Brasilia. That glue was probably guaranteed waterproof by the Brasilian supplier, who would have charged us three times as much as he could have gotten locally. Brasilia blocks the export of manufacturing capacity to the Stream and taxes any imports from other Home Worlds to force us to use Brasilian goods to safeguard its home industries. And Brasilian suppliers cheat us by dumping overpriced shoddy crap on the Stream that they wouldn't dare attempt to fob off on Brasilians."

Chernokovsky looked at Allenson quizzically. He seemed more amused than angry at Allenson's outburst.

"Well, do your best, there's a good chap," Chernokovsky said with kindly condescension.

Allenson stormed back to his office. He tried to work but was still seething and could not concentrate. The problem was not that Chernokovsky was unreasonable or overtly rude, but that he had a habit of talking to Allenson like he was some common employee. Chernokovsky was a gentleman, but so was Allenson. Thus, they were socially equal in Allenson's opinion, a view that Chernokovsky and his officers clearly did not share. It seemed that Allenson and his compatriots were expected to meet the obligations of Brasilian gentlemen, but without the concomitant privileges—and that was not fair.

"Hell to it, the bloody war can wait," Allenson said to no one in particular.

He slipped his datapad in his pocket and left his office in Port Clearwater, resisting the urge to slam the door. He decided to use one of the Brasilia Army officer runabouts to hop across the water into Manzanita. Given he was working for nothing, a ride was the least the Brasilian military could do.

"Villa Blaisdel, Manzanita City," Allenson said to the NCO in charge of the transport pool, while climbing into the back of a two-man frame.

The NCO hesitated, unsure whether he should be taking orders from a colonial officer.

"Is there a problem?" Allenson asked dangerously.

"Uh, no sir," the NCO coming to a decision. "Perkins, take the officer to Manzanita city."

"I am afraid these yokel towns don't have a beacon grid, so you will have to give the driver guidance, sir."

"Let's get moving," Allenson said, not taking any offense at the implied slur on the Stream capital as the opinions of an NCO were hardly of import.

On the way, his datapad bleeped with an urgent message on his private channel. He refused to take the call. Right now he just could not cope with Sarai.

Trina Blaisdel took one look at him and sat him down with a pot of tea. She refused to discuss anything other than trivial gossip until he had drunk his first cup, loosened the collar on his uniform and relaxed.

"Are the preparations for the campaign going well?" she finally asked.

"Not so you would notice," Allenson said. He brought out his datapad and showed her his latest disaster.

"But Allen," she said, horrified, "you are letting your suppliers dump their problems onto you, until you are trying to micromanage the whole supply chain."

"How else can I unblock the pipeline?" Allenson asked, genuinely confused. If one had a problem preventing one from meeting one's obligations then one dealt with it. That was how he had lived his life.

"Did you pay in advance?" she asked sharply, as if the thought had just occurred.

"No. I would have liked to, but that's against army regulations. Payment is on delivery," he answered.

"Thank God for army regulations," Trina said, dryly.

"Or thank God for cynical civil servants in the procurement office." She picked up his datapad. "May I demonstrate?" she asked.

"With all pleasure," Allenson replied.

She contacted the problematical supplier, angling the datapad focus so that only she was visible at the other end.

"Lady Blaisdel acting on behalf of Sar Allenson, my principal," she said. "Sar Allenson has asked me to inform you that he considers you in breach of contract for failing to supply within the stipulated five days. Accordingly, the contract is void and you will not be paid. Good day." She cut the connection and sipped her tea.

"What have you done?" Allenson asked, horrified.

"Trust me," she said.

After a few seconds, his datapad began to chime, indicating an urgent call on the business channel. She finished her sip before triggering it. "Lady Blaisdel."

"You can't not pay me," the supplier said, well, shouted, although the datapad adjusted the volume.

"Why not?" Trina asked, in a tone that indicated no more than polite interest.

"Because we have a contract," the supplier said.

"Which Sar Allenson considers void, due to non-performance on your part."

"There is no time stipulation in the contract," the supplier said, with ratlike cunning.

"Sar Allenson takes the view that a time stipulation was implicit as indicated by verbal agreement on your part."

"I'll sue," the supplier said.

"As you wish," Trina replied. "However, your contract is with the Brasilian Regular Army, not Sar Allenson.

I would imagine that they will demand the hearing take place in the High Court on Brasilia, but that is a matter for them."

There was dead silence on the other end. No matter how good a case the supplier thought he had, a High Court judgement on Brasilia could drag on for years and would be prohibitively expensive. Such cases tend to be won by the party with the most money, and the Brasilian Army had very deep pockets.

"Look, I am sure that there is no need for any unpleasantness," the supplier said in an oily voice. "Suppose I can deliver in the next five days?"

"I will consult with my principal," Trina said.

She paused the datapad and took her time pouring herself another cup of tea. One did not rush good quality tea. Then she switched the pad back on.

"Sar Allenson was reluctant to revisit his decision, but I argued on your behalf and he has kindly agreed to regard the contract as valid if delivery is made within three days."

"Done," the supplier said, "but I will be losing money."

"Good day." Trina cut the connection.

Allenson was aware that he had just been given a master class in project management. "What can I say," Allenson said, "but thank you. I feel a little bad about him losing money on the deal though."

Trina choked on her tea. She looked at him the way his economics teacher had looked when Allenson asked why people were reluctant to do their civic duty by paying taxes.

"I think you will find that he will squeeze a few pennies out for himself, somewhere down the line," she said dryly. "I was thinking, Allen..."

She hesitated.

"Yes," he replied, encouragingly.

"What with the marriage settlement from my family and the inheritance of my late husband's estate, I have been well provided for, and I'm frankly getting bored leading the life of a lady of leisure. It would be nice to put something back, so to speak. Would you like me to help you deal with the administration of your duties?" she asked diffidently. "I would not interfere with decision making, of course."

"You interfere all you like, Trina," he said. "I would very much like your help. Suppose we give you the title of Liaison Procurement Director, so the suppliers understand your correct status?"

"Thank you," she said.

Obviously he did not try to offer her a salary. Firstly, because he had not the authority, but mostly because a gentleman did not try to give a lady money. He went to give her a kiss on the cheek to show his appreciation but she failed to turn her head.

Trina's maid, acting as chaperone by leaning against the wall behind her mistress, grinned at him and rolled her eyes. Hell to it, he thought, and kissed Trina on the lips.

Chernokovsky arrived in Allenson's office in a state of consternation and plonked himself down in a chair. "We are short of baggage transports. I had expected to hire civilian vehicles locally to supplement our logistical train but there are almost none to be had, at least, none that are functional. Also, the price is outrageous."

"I anticipated that problem," Allenson said. He fiddled with his datapad. "Rogan Transport offered to supply thirty-five transports at standard rates. Is that enough or will you need more?"

"More are always useful but that will do," Chernokovsky replied. "By God, Allenson, how did you arrange that?"

"Mistress Rogan is on a charitable committee chaired by Lady Blaisdel, I believe," Allenson replied. "The, ah, Program for Encouraging Temperance among the Laboring Classes. The Rogan family has built up a thriving business in recent years."

"So Lady Blaisdel and Mistress Rogan are old friends?" Chernokovsky asked.

"Not exactly," Allenson replied. "They would not normally mix in the same social circles. I believe Mistress Rogan has only just been appointed to Lady Blaisdel's committee."

"I see," Chernokovsky said.

He probably did see. You did not get to be a Brigadier in the Brasilian Army without having a shrewd grasp of the currencies of social politics.

"On another note," Allenson said. "Lady Blaisdel is having a soiree at her villa tomorrow evening to raise funds for the program. She intends to extend an invitation to you."

"Well . . ." Chernokovsky replied.

Allenson had the impression that he was formulating a polite refusal, so he interrupted. "Mistress Rogan will be attending, as a committee member."

"In that case, we had better not disappoint the lady," Chernokovsky said with a smile. "It will be the last chance to relax. With those additional transports we are ready to move out. Thursday we move on Larissa."

· CHAPTER 21 ·

The Professionals

Allenson hung in the Continuum, pedaling gently, watching the two thousand soldiers of the Regular battalions file past down the trackway in a continuous column. A vanguard of the ten-man fighting frames moved first followed by the battery-powered transports. Officers stood out because of their vehicles. They were not obliged to pedal and so had to be chauffeured. The size of an officer's frame, and the concomitant number of pedalers, was proportional to rank—from one pedaler for lieutenants to ten for Chernokovsky and his three aides. The officers also carried a prodigious amount of baggage for light infantry. Allenson had been astonished to see crystal glasses and dress uniforms loaded into the transports. The 12th had even brought their regimental hunting dog pack, complete with handler.

Small gaggles of militia from the Stream and Perseverance flowed along the edges of the column, like water droplets running down a wire. The colonials were mostly in two-seater frames, but the more experienced

Hinterlands travelers, like Allenson, were in single-seaters. Allenson tasked the colonials to monitor the column and round up stragglers. Actually, there were no stragglers; the Regulars kept disciplined formations. He had also instructed his men to watch out for Riders but none were spotted.

The trackway looked like an orange tunnel in the Continuum. It dampened local energy eddies facilitating the movement of clumsy vehicles like transports and ten-man fighting frames. It was like an artificial chasm, except that there was no prevailing current to push a frame along. On the other hand, that did make trackways two-way. Turbulence at the edge acted as a barrier to seeing into the Continuum.

One problem had been solved by the arrival of an army from the Home World. Chernokovsky had squashed any attempt by the Perseverance troops to claim the status of Regulars. Reclassifying them as militia had put them firmly under Allenson's operational control.

The column was impressive, impressive but ponderous. The Regulars built a fortified camp at each stop, recharged their transport batteries with steam engines, and set up an orbiting beacon to project the next section of trackway before resuming the march. It all took time.

On a good day, the column made less than half the distance that Allenson's Expeditionary Force had achieved on their previous foray. Doctrine demanded that they keep together, so it moved at the speed of the slowest transport. This became a liability as transport batteries failed, lowering speed and shortening range. Messengers were dispatched back to the stream for replacements. Eventually, a stream of frames shuttled between Manzanita and the column.

Allenson became increasingly concerned about the complete absence of Riders, especially as they neared Nengue. It was not normal and that made him nervous. He made sure that he was at the front of the column so he could reconnoiter. Hawthorn made sure that Allenson was accompanied by a suitable, by which he meant tough, escort of Streamers that Hawthorn commanded personally.

The Rider camp on Nengue appeared empty when they made a high pass over it. On closer inspection, there were some signs of activity, individual Riders and smoke from the odd fire. The Streamers landed next to what was left of the Trading Post. Allenson squatted to examine the burnt debris. Rain had washed out charcoal flakes, and small invertebrates had already colonized the site. Weeds grew among the burnt timbers.

"This happened some time ago," Allenson said.

"There are no bodies or any signs of battle," Hawthorn said, kicking over charred wood to examine underneath. "The place was probably unoccupied when it was razed."

"Which leads us to the issue of who destroyed the post and why," Allenson said. "Let's find the Viceroy."

The Viceroy's shelter was empty. One side had collapsed, giving the structure a sad, dilapidated appearance. Allenson spotted a gleam of artificial color in the mud. He bent down and pulled out the handle of a yellow ax. The head was missing.

"That looks like the one you gave the Viceroy," Hawthorn said. "Does that mean that the Viceroy had repudiated the present as a symbolic gesture?"

Both men looked at Payne.

"The Riders are practical, sars," Payne said. "A good ax is a good ax, however you got it. I suppose it could have broke and thrown away, but the shiny yellow handle is still pretty—to a Rider."

They left the shelter and walked through the camp. Only a handful of old men and women remained in the Rider camp. They kept their distance from the Streamers, which did not surprise Allenson. Only the desperate would approach a bunch of heavily armed foreigners. They tried to talk to an old man, but he put his head down and ignored them, shuffling away as fast as he could.

"We have to find someone who will give us information," said Allenson.

"Do you want us to chase down one of the old-sters?" an NCO asked. "A few slaps and they'll talk."

"I think not," Allenson replied. "They would be terrified and would tell us whatever they thought we wanted to hear."

He did not add that he recoiled from offering even mild violence to an elderly civilian. The NCO would not understand. Hawthorn smiled—he understood Allenson all too well.

"Do you notice that there are no beasts?" Hawthorn asked. "The warriors have gone, taking their women and children with them."

They wandered through the camp. An old, emaciated woman lay under a low shelter that had seen better days. She watched the Streamers but made no move to leave when they approached. Allenson looked inquiringly at Payne.

"She's been left to die, sar," Payne said. "The Riders have no place for useless mouths."

Allenson squatted down beside her. He removed some bread from his ration pack. Tearing off a small piece he offered it to the woman. She looked at it suspiciously before snatching the food and cramming it in her mouth. She reminded Allenson of a feral animal offered a delicacy, an animal more used to receiving a kick. The woman chewed frantically, as if afraid someone were going to snatch the bread back.

"She still has her own teeth," Hawthorn said. "How old is she?"

"She ain't really old, sar, not like people get old," Payne said. "She's forty, maybe."

"So much for the life of the noble savage," Allenson said.

The woman swallowed and looked hopefully at the bread still in Allenson's hand.

"Ask her where the warriors are," Allenson said to Payne.

There was an exchange in a Rider tongue.

"She says she doesn't know, sar," Payne replied.

"Ask her where the Viceroy is?"

"He's dead, sar," Payne replied.

"How did he die? Was it accident, disease, or did someone kill him?"

"I asked that. She doesn't seem to know, sar."

"Ask her who the new overclan chief is, and whether she knows of any change in Rider policy toward the human war?"

"I'll try, sar."

There was a long exchange.

"She says she has no idea."

"I see," Allenson said. He had no idea if the woman was lying but he gave her the bread anyway.

"I am not sure if feeding her is a kindness," Hawthorn said, as they walked away. "It won't change the outcome, just delay her death."

"Possibly," Allenson replied. "But it's an unkindness that I can live with compared to the alternatives. Do you think the Viceroy's death is significant?"

Hawthorn shrugged. "Who knows? Riders do die, often violently, for reasons that make no sense to us. Maybe he just upset the wrong person."

The rest of the column eventually arrived at Nengue and busied themselves setting up a fortified camp with automated defenses capable of checking an attack by a brigade of Regulars, let alone a few Riders.

Allenson sought out Chernokovsky. He sat in his tent sipping tea, looking through various reports.

"Come in, Allenson, and sit yourself down. I must say that staff of yours in Manzanita is a wonder. They have found a supplier of high energy batteries for the transports, which should be arriving in a day or two, so we will wait for them. In the long run, it will quicker to re-equip our transports before moving on. Some of the battery arrays are down to nearly half power. Tea?"

"No, thank you, Brigadier," Allenson said politely, while taking his seat. His "staff" consisted largely of Lady Blaisdel and her servants. "I am concerned at our slow rate of progress," he said.

"Moving through hostile territory can't be rushed, dear chap. It will take as long as it takes."

"We are giving the Terrans plenty of time to react to our approach. The fact that we have seen no Riders does not mean that they have not seen us. Indeed, the fact that we have not come across any hunting groups is suspicious. I worry that the Terrans are planning something."

"They can plot all they like, old boy. It will save us a great deal of trouble if they are foolish enough to attack us on the march. That would thin their ranks a bit before we take on their base at Larissa."

"I suppose so," Allenson replied, unwilling to contradict an experienced Regular soldier, but he still didn't like the situation. All his instincts screamed to him that speed was as important as strength in any sort of conflict. "Perhaps I can suggest a compromise."

"Go on," Chernokovsky said.

"Why don't I take a vanguard of detachment of Engineers protected by, say, two hundred militia, to lay down the trackway in advance of the main column. That should speed the main force up a bit when your transports are up to spec."

"Yes, it would," Chernokovsky conceded. "But I would be concerned about an ambush crippling the beacon engineering platoon. I could not afford to use them."

Allenson noted that Chernokovsky bore the possibility of losing the colonial militia with fortitude, not so say, complete indifference. The brigadier sipped his tea; no doubt a form of displacement activity to give him time to consider his decision. Chernokovsky was not a man given to rashness.

"Tell you, what," Chernokovsky finally said. "Your idea has merit, but you must take half a battalion of Regulars to provide protection. From the 51st, I think."

Allenson groaned inside. Five hundred Regulars would slow him down considerably, but he had got

Chernokovsky to agree. Now he needed to make the plan work.

"The Regulars will need to travel light and be logistically self sufficient," Allenson said. "They must carry only light weapons. The extra space in their frames can be used for supplies."

"I don't see why not," Chernokovsky said. "They are only going as escorts. I expect you to fall back on the protection of the main column if the Terrans launch a set piece attack. Traveling light, you should easily evade a properly equipped Terran combat battalion."

"I think I will have that tea after all," Allenson said, his mood greatly improved.

"In fact, I like your idea so well that I believe I will come along," Chernokovsky said. "Nothing like leading from the front."

The tea was bitter.

The Brasilian expedition ground closer to Larissa. Preparing the trackway in advance sped up the Brasilian column marginally by shortening each layover, but they still moved at the speed of the slowest transport, and transport batteries still needed charging. Chernokovsky had joined the vanguard as threatened. Unfortunately, so had all the senior officers of the 51st. Never had so few been commanded by so many.

Two of the two-seater Stream frames stuck to Allenson like glue. He sensed the guiding hand of Hawthorn, who was back with the main body and baggage transports. No doubt they were bodyguards who had been told to make sure he came back alive, or not to bother to come back themselves.

He watched the engineers making adjustments to

the solar arrays on a beacon around an unnamed yellow-white star. The next segment of trackway was up and stable, but the captain of engineer was not entirely happy with the regularity of the power input. It took surprisingly little power to create the trackway. It was one of those technologies that used persuasion rather than brute force.

Allenson had asked the captain how it worked but had not entirely grasped the somewhat confused explanation. Essentially, the broadcast signal changed the probability of interactions between the currents in the Continuum to create a highly unlikely, but possible, high-entropic state where everything canceled out. It sounded like the efforts to create antigravity by changing the probability of the behavior of space time between two masses, except that antigravity had never worked. Of course, one did not need to understand the scientific principles behind a technology to employ it successfully, but Allenson found it fascinating. Not for the first time, he wished he could have had a better education in stochastic maths.

The engineers had a sort of workshop array that could extend its fields in part phase to allow the men to work on the beacon. The escort had already started phasing out to move down the trackway, platoon by platoon at a spaced distance to avoid both collisions and caterpillaring in the limited space. Allenson reluctantly tore himself away from the engineers. He pedaled down the column, overtaking each section of Regulars in their ten-man frames. The colonial militia moved in small groups, largely ignoring their theoretical order of battle.

The trackway stretched before him like a tunnel filled with orange mist. He pedaled toward the head of the column, overtaking trooper frames that appeared first as purple shadows, details only becoming recognizable at close range.

He spotted silver flashes ahead. They looked like sunlight reflecting off broken glass on a far hill. There was no shape or form to the irregular disturbances. This was new and, in the Hinterlands, the novel could be dangerous. He increased his speed, making his bodyguards pedal frantically to keep up. Flashes continued to light up the orange mist, metallic purple flashes as well as silver. He overtook troop-frames that, from their markings, were at the rear of the front platoon.

A half dozen Riders burst through the edge of the trackway right beside Allenson. Crystal beasts resonated as they crossed the boundary, energy bleeding away as flashes of silver light. The lead warrior was on him, hurling a spear. Allenson turned tightly. The spear crossed his front, leaving a purple trail. One of his bodyguards fired a spring gun. The Riders jinked away from the Streamers. Allenson cursed and groped for his spring gun.

The Riders rapidly regrouped and pounced on the ten-man troop frames, ignoring Allenson and his escort. The disruption to the Rider attack bought the troops time, but they panicked, squandering the brief window of opportunity. Riders flowed down the line of troop frames, bombarding them with spears, slingshots, and even one or two bolts from spring guns. There were two or three Riders per beast and all were armed. Men fell. Allenson saw a splash of blood where a trooper took a missile in the face.

The Riders turned their beasts and came back up the line, repeating their pass. Allenson found his spring gun, but it was unloaded. He dropped it in his haste. Cursing, he mounted a frontal charge on the Riders, hoping to split their formation. A silver flash marked where a bolt fired by one of his bodyguards struck the lead beast. It recoiled into its compatriots, forcing them to evade. The sounder soldiers on the troop frames shot their spring guns. The Riders broke off as soon as they came under fire, disappearing back into the Continuum.

The Brasilians attempted to close up into a defensive formation. Allenson watched where the Riders had exited the trackway, expecting them to reappear. They did, but not from there. Three Rider beasts dropped from above onto the rear frame, whose occupants had their spring guns pointed in the direction of the previous attack. Allenson gestured frantically, but the Brasilian troopers just gaped at him. The Riders closed to point blank range and unleashed a stream of projectiles. Half the men of the frame were casualties before they fired a shot. The Riders fled back into the Continuum when the troops on the next frame took them under fire.

In two attacks, the Riders inflicted nearly a dozen casualties on the platoon without losing a man. And that was just the beginning.

Allenson waited, but no new attacks materialized. The platoon slowed down to allow an understrength troop frame to keep up, reducing their advance to a crawl. Allenson pedaled hard toward the front of the column, loading his spring gun as he went. More silver and metallic purple flashes marked the head of the column.

Frames were piled up nose to tail, some broadside on. A troop frame tried to turn in the narrow tunnel, colliding with a compatriot to his rear. Their fields interacted in a bright flash of metallic purple light. Locked together, the frames disintegrated into shimmering colored fractals when their fields failed and they winked back into realspace. The frame behind braked sharply, threatening more collisions.

It never seemed to occur to the troops to leave the trackway.

Allenson and his small flotilla of bodyguards attempted to intercept Riders, but it was all too much a ratfuck for coherent action. Small groups of Riders zoomed through the tangled mess, sometimes chased by colonials on one and two-seater frames.

A young officer stood up in his frame—a lieutenant, as it was a two-seater. He waved his arms vigorously to rally his men. Three beasts englobed him. When they swept away, his frame was gone. A missile must have damaged the energy field projectors or power supply.

Three Streamer light frames attacked a beast from different directions. They got in each other's way and it escaped.

A beast flew into a coordinated salvo from a troop frame. Silver flashes marked bolt strikes. It disintegrated into crystal polygons, shedding its Riders. The polygons must have maintained a field for a few seconds because the Riders thrashed and struggled before disappearing.

The surviving troop frames managed to turn and began to make their way back down the trackway. Allenson tried to get Streamers to form on him, but the pilots were excited. He eventually organized the militia into a shield around the retreating troop frames. They tried to intercept each Rider lunge, but the initiative lay with the attackers and some inevitably got through.

Retreat turned into rout, with each troop frame fleeing at its best speed.

The Streamers stayed with the stragglers—the ones limping along at half speed after taking heavy casualties or mechanical damage. They had to abandon an immobile troop frame, with nothing but casualties left aboard. Its field flickered as the power ran down. One of the wounded on board watched Allenson pedal past. His face registered resignation, not anger nor fear, as if he accepted his fate and just wanted it over.

Suddenly the attacks stopped, as if someone had thrown a switch to bring the curtain down in a theater. There were only human frames visible. Allenson rotated his head as if it was on gimbals—but nothing. One of his bodyguard frames had disappeared. Allenson had no idea what had happened to it. The other clung on to his rear. Minutes passed, and he began to hope that the Riders had broken off.

Silver flashes ahead showed his optimism was misplaced. He accelerated, overtaking the retreating frames, taking his Streamers with him.

A huge pile-up blocked the trackway. Routing transports had crashed into those still advancing. A troop frame had hit another amidships and both rotated slowly like a giant "T." Somehow, their fields had interlaced without shorting. The crews tried to push the frames apart but the interlocked fields held the frames tight. The crews were dead; they just had not yet accepted the fact yet.

Troop frames were piled up all over the trackway like a log jam. Rider beasts weaved between them, creating chaos. Troopers firing wildly at the beasts caused havoc on other Brasilian frames in the line of fire. An officer frame raced for the shelter of a troop transport, chased by a beast. The men on board fired a salvo that drove off the beast but killed the officer's pedaler. Allenson's last sight of the officer was his frame spiraling out of control as he desperately tried to climb into the pilot's seat.

Allenson and his colonials swept into the battle, killing a few beasts and driving off the rest, but the relief was momentary. He could not control his men so many Streamers followed Riders out into the Continuum. Rider squadrons lapped around the flanks to renew their assault on the troop frames. Allenson made for the center to locate Chernokovsky. He was easy to find as the command frame was marked by banners to identify it to his men. Unfortunately, it also identified him to the Riders as a "chief." Warriors swarmed around him like wasps to a jam pot.

Chernokovsky stood high on a command deck at the back, making circular movements with his hands. He seemed to be trying to get his men to form a defensive globe. A Rider spear took him through the stomach and he sank down. One of his aides panicked and swung the command frame around. That signaled a general rout: Two more frames collided, vanishing in metallic purple fire.

A panicking trooper pointed a laserifle at attacking beasts. Allenson swerved to put distance between himself and the troop frame. The trooper fired. His frame exploded in a massive conflagration of white streamers. The trackway twisted and rocked. More troop frames collided, adding to the confusion.

Fortunately, the blast scared off the Riders and attracted back Streamers that had been decoyed away by retreating Riders. Allenson formed them into a shield behind the remaining troop frames. Riders made a few tentative passes but sheered off when intercepted by the maneuverable and fast Streamer frames. After a few more half-hearted attacks, the Riders vanished back into the Continuum and did not return.

Allenson checked his ammunition. He had only three bolts left for his spring gun. Where had the other seven gone? Had he fired them? He had no memory of shooting. He worried that his men must be running low on bolts. Normal practice was to carry just ten per man on the small frames. It occurred to him that the Riders must also be short of projectiles. They probably carried less than the militia. Maybe that was why they had backed off, or perhaps it was simply that they shied away from a battle of attrition with the militia because of their inability to replace casualties. For whatever reason, there were no more attacks.

The column retreated back into the star system where they had set up the last beacon, and made for the habitable planet. The colonials mounted top-cover until the last troop frame had landed. Allenson did not intend to try to get the exhausted troopers to fortify a camp. Riders would not challenge laserifle armed soldiers on the ground, and the Brasilians would have no choice but to surrender if attacked by Terrans in strength. They were in no condition to defend against a serious ground attack. And they could surrender to Terrans without getting their throats cut.

He found the command frame and landed alongside. Chernokovsky lay on a pallet. His aides had removed the spear and sealed the wound with an anesthetic patch. None of them would meet Allenson's eye.

"Why haven't you gotten the Brigadier proper treatment?" Allenson asked, shocked. One could not just patch up a spear stab. The internal bleeding alone would kill Chernokovsky.

"The medic frame was lost," an aide said. "We have done the best we can with first aid kits."

"Allenson, is that you?" Chernokovsky asked. He coughed up blood.

"Yes, sir," Allenson replied.

"Come closer, man, I can't see you in this gloom."

It was bright sunshine. Allenson knelt down beside the Brigadier. "I'm here, sir," Allenson said.

"I was damn glad of your colonials back there, Allenson. Without you we would have been wiped out."

"Everybody did their best, sir," Allenson said.

"Get my men home, Colonel Allenson. Promise me."

"Yes, sir," Allenson rose and saluted.

CHAPTER 22

Phony War

Chernokovsky's aides were squabbling over who was in command when Allenson sought them out the next day. They were occupied comparing notes on dates of commission and seniority. Devoting their time to who would give the orders meant that they did not have to worry about what the orders should be.

"You are wasting time, gentlemen," Allenson said. "If we just sit here, we risk attack by a Terran military unit. Brigadier Chernokovsky placed me in command. You all heard him."

"But Chernokovsky is dead. You are just a militia officer," an aide said. "Your rank has no standing in the chain of command."

"Neither does yours," Allenson replied. "So my nominal rank of colonel trumps yours of captain."

"Your orders, sir," a young lieutenant said, coming to attention and saluting Allenson.

Allenson checked the lieutenant's uniform. The flashes on his badges of rank showed that he was a combat infantry officer, albeit one without any campaign medals.

"You are?" Allenson asked.

"Lieutenant Stretter, sir," he replied. "I am the senior ranking officer in the chain of command left alive. I propose to place myself under your command in obedience to Brigadier Chernokovsky's last order."

And that was that, the issue was decided. The aides were gentlemen, chosen for their administrative and social skills. Their function was to assist the brigadier, not command troops in combat. The men would follow Stretter.

"How many officers are left?" Allenson asked.

"Two junior lieutenants and three cadets, sir."

Allenson caught his breath. The carnage among the officers was shocking. Those damned officer frames stood out like the proverbials on a dog. They were too slow to run and too weak to fight. Not that any of the officers had attempted to escape. They had fought bravely to the last. If only they had been less ineffectual.

"Very good, Mister Stretter, please get the men ready to leave within three hours. Officers are to pedal on the troop frames with the men. Dump the command frames. I want each frame fully manned so we can travel fast. Disable and abandon the rest. Dump everything except essential supplies, ammunition, and the men's personal weapons to make room for the wounded."

The aides looked scandalized but kept their mouths shut, which was just as well. Allenson was in no mood for half-witted arguments about status.

"Yes sir, what about the dead?"

"Put them in a burial pit."

"And the brigadier?"

"The same," Allenson replied.

"You can't do that," an aide said in horror. "We must take his body home to Brasilia."

The aides still shied away from grasping the desperate nature of their situation. Perhaps they clung to the norms of peaceful society to block out the horror of the reality.

"We have no embalming materials and, even if we had, we have no time. Brigadier Chernokovsky fought valiantly alongside his men. It is fitting that he should lie with them in death," Allenson said. "I want to leave in three hours' time, Mister Stretter. Anything not done by then stays undone."

"Yes, sir."

Allenson checked on the militia. The list of dead and missing, the latter undoubtedly dead, was fortunately few, barely twenty men. But around a third of his men were wounded to a greater or lesser degree. He reorganized the militia so that every wounded man was allocated to a two-seater frame crewed by an uninjured soldier. He made sure his men were instantly ready to move, and then had them eat. He was finishing his own meal when Stretter reported.

"We are ready to move out, sir," Stretter said.

"Have your men had a meal?" Allenson asked. He had forgotten to pass on that order to the Regulars.

"Yes, sir," Stretter said, unperturbed. "I had the men eat in shifts."

Allenson looked at the clock on his datapad. Barely two hours had passed. He had given Stretter a three hour deadline, hoping he would be ready in five. The young officer was proving to be gratifyingly competent. Give him an order and he carried it out without any fuss or argument. He also knew when to use his initiative.

"Then we are ready to leave," Allenson said. "I intend to retreat back on the main force in one jump. Gentlemen, we will stop for nothing, and may the Devil take the hindmost."

The survivors of the debacle made it down the trackway to the main force without further incident, casualties being restricted to some of the wounded dying and a troop frame going missing. It could have been lost to mechanical failure or the crew could have deserted. Allenson did not really care either way. His main feelings were the two he had begun to associate with military campaigns, not fear or excitement, but mind-numbing exhaustion and the constant anxiety of making the wrong decision.

A couple of frames had fled from the battle all the way down the trackway to the main force, inciting panic with wild tales of the whole vanguard being massacred.

Allenson insisted on an immediate Council of War. Looking around the assembled officers, he was shocked at the paucity of numbers. The vanguard may have been a case of too many commanding too few, but the reverse now applied.

"Where is Lieutenant Colonel Ravid?" Allenson asked.

Ravid was the commander of the 12th.

"He went hunting with the other company commanders, leaving me in charge," said Major F
"A scout found a world with interesting wild

the trackway, so they thought they would give the hound pack some exercise."

"Oh dear God," Allenson said. "Up the trackway, toward the vanguard?"

"Yes," Brown replied.

Brown was old for a company commander. He had obviously been passed over for promotion many times, a man lacking either the talent or the family influence to take him higher. The fact that he had not resigned his commission meant that he had nowhere else to go. He would be the obvious choice for an aristocratic hunting party to leave behind. No doubt he always undertook the unpopular tasks without complaint, thankful to still have a position that granted him money and status.

"When did they leave?" Allenson asked.

"Three days ago," Brown replied.

Getting information from the man was like pulling teeth. "Are they overdue?"

"Yes, I expected them back yesterday." Brown gazed over Allenson's head at the blank canvas of the command tent.

"Very well, I want the 12th to dump and destroy all unnecessary material. We will travel light. Lieutenant Stretter will oversee that. He knows what to do. Make sure your own men get some rest, Mister Stretter."

"Yes, sir."

"I expect to leave within two hours, gentlemen," Allenson said.

"Leave? Where would we go?" Brown asked.

"Back to the Stream, of course," Allenson replied, astonished at the question. "Our mission is a bust. The task now is to save the force from further casualties.

I propose to leave the trackway and plot a course through the Continuum."

"If speed is of the essence, sir, I should point out that our troop frames will move faster on the trackway," said Stretter.

"I know, Mister Stretter, but time is on the side of our enemies. They advance at the speed of their fastest units, the Riders, while we retreat at the speed of our slowest units. That's a race we cannot win. They will harry us all the way and turn retreat into a rout. We don't have sufficient officers to carry out a fighting withdrawal and I doubt the men's morale equal to the challenge. I propose to employ concealment instead. We will lose ourselves in the Hinterlands."

Brown said nothing. Indeed, he did not seem to have heard.

"Major Brown," Allenson said loudly.

Brown looked at him with blank eyes.

"No doubt you have much to do to prepare to leave in two hours," Allenson said, trying to get the man moving.

"We can't leave," Brown replied. "My orders are to wait here for Colonel Ravid."

"Face facts, man, Ravid is dead. The Riders got him."

"Why should I believe you? You're not a real soldier. You're just a jumped-up colonial peasant in fancy dress. What do you know?"

Allenson looked back at him coldly. He had just about enough of being patronized by these people.

"Lieutenant Stretter," Allenson said, never taking his eyes of Brown. "Do you still consider yourself under my command?"

"Yes, sir," Stretter said.

"Then feed and rest your men. We leave in two hours."

Stretter left the tent. Allenson turned to Chernokovsky's aides.

"Will you be joining us?"

The senior captain spoke for them all. "We will wait for Colonel Ravid. We take orders from real soldiers," he said with a sneer.

"As you wish," Allenson said, mildly, leaving the tent. There was no point arguing with the dead.

They would need to send dispatches back to Manzanita with news of the defeat and the current situation, in case no one made it home. Allenson was a lot less confident than he had sounded. Luck, plain luck, would decide their fate. He was sure that he had selected the best strategy, but there were no guarantees. All it would take was one Rider scout to stumble across the convoy. He shut the thought down and concentrated on what he could control, not waste emotional energy on what he couldn't.

He would entrust the dispatches to a Streamer patrol. They could outrun the Riders on their two-seater frames. Hawthorn would be the ideal choice to lead the patrol. Allenson checked himself and almost burst out laughing. All the books on the principles of command that he had devoured had agreed on one point. Never, never, give an order that you cannot enforce.

They left Brown's command tent. Hawthorn, who had remained silent throughout the discussion, stopped at the entrance flap to look back. "Wankers," he said, dispassionately.

❖   ❖   ❖

Allenson pushed his right foot down, and then his left. He repeated the process. A stupid little advertising jingle went round and round in his brain, the rhythm perfectly matching the rotation of the pedals. The music was so clear that it seemed to be coming from outside, as if the Continuum was singing to him. He knew that it was all in his mind but he lifted his head to look, anyway.

Todd floated past, playing a grand piano. Linsye sat upon it, swinging her legs in time to the music, tapping out the rhythm with her nails on the wood.

"Time to grow up, Allen," she said, wagging her finger at him.

"I'm trying, Linsye, really I am," Allenson replied.

She gazed at him in disappointment, lip curling. He hung his head in shame.

"I knew you would not amount to anything." Linsye had turned into his stepmother.

"Leave me alone, you raddled old witch," Allenson yelled. He fumbled for his spring gun, intent on killing her, but the piano floated away on a current and vanished before he could cock the weapon. He could still hear the jingle, and realized he was humming it.

Right foot down, left foot down, keep the pedals turning. There were worse Continuum visions than his stepmother. Sometimes, he saw a figure dancing in flames. Sometimes it was just rows of faces, of abandoned soldiers. They never spoke. They just stared without hope. There were more of them now. The convoy left a trail of corpses across the Continuum. They had buried the first few with a short ceremony, but eventually they just let them lie on alien worlds. They abandoned frames as well, as the soldiers' numbers dwindled. Allenson stopped taking a roll call. It did nothing for morale.

They existed on military emergency rations, no time to hunt for food. They stopped only to sleep. Allenson prohibited fires so they ate cold food. He wanted to be inconspicuous. The convoy never saw a Rider, but anxiety gnawed at Allenson. One Rider would be all it took to damn them.

Allenson led, while Hawthorn brought up the rear. Allenson was determined not to allow the convoy to straggle. Nevertheless, a frame disappeared between overnight halts without anyone noticing. It seemed unlikely that all of the passengers decided to desert together. Possibly there had been mechanical failure. Or maybe the men had just stopped pedaling.

Left foot down, right foot down. Hang on, did that mean he was going backward? He checked the navigation. He was on course. The analytical part of his mind noticed that Laywant was very close. That was important, he knew that was important but, for the life of him, he could not remember why. He peered forward into the Continuum. There was a shadow—Laywant?

His frame picked up the city beacon and his hands switched on the auto to guide his frame down. He watched himself do this routine task as a disinterested observer. He had something more important to do. Pedal, that was it, he had to pedal.

His frame landed in the middle of the business compound. The one a lifetime ago that he had used when surveying the Hinterlands for the Harbinger Project. Troop and two-seater frames landed all round him. Men jumped off and kissed the ground. Allenson shut down his frame and stopped pedaling. He closed his eyes, just to rest them for a while.

A hand shook his shoulder. "Allenson, answer me, are you okay?"

He wished Hawthorn would leave him alone. "Sure, I am," Allenson said, opening his eyes.

"Well, why didn't you respond when I called you?" Hawthorn said, sharply.

"Called me?" Allenson replied, confused.

Hawthorn gave a quick grin. "You were asleep, and I thought you had died or something. Want a beer?"

"I want a warm bath and a hot meal, in that order," Allenson replied. "But a beer is a good start."

Duty discharged, Allenson left the officers to shepherd their men back to Manzanita. He felt emotionally drained and needed some solitude to reflect. His confidence had been badly shaken by the second disaster, and he needed to reflect on his own part in the debacle. The only result of the two Brasilian expeditions was to tighten Terra's grip on the Hinterlands. He was too tired to think.

Protocol demanded that he make a courtesy visit to Sar Rimmer, the Brasilian Agent, who invited him to enjoy the comforts of his villa. Allenson reluctantly declined. He felt that he had to keep moving or he would collapse, so he left Hawthorn to enjoy the wilder delights of Laywant Town and returned alone to Mowzelle, the Allenson compound on Wagener. His stepmother was absent in Manzanita and had taken the steward, Petersen, with her. Mowzelle was a mess. Anything not controlled by the automatics had not been done. He arrived late in the evening to find the servants holding a drunken party in one of the outhouses. No doubt that had been their primary occupation during his stepmother's absence.

On the plus side, he did not have to put up with her whining and complaints. He was too tired to deal with the servants. He went to his room and threw himself on the bed but he couldn't sleep. The mattress was just too soft. Finally, he made a bed up on the floor and dropped off.

Allenson waded through corpses and the stink of rotting flesh. The corpses tugged at his legs, slowing him down. Something terrible chased him, but he couldn't run. He didn't dare look back, or it would have him. A corpse hung by the neck from a blackened tree. It grinned and struck a bell with a bone sticking out of the end of a rotting arm.

The *bong, bong, bong,* was his death knell. He sank into corpses with each toll. The thing behind was very close. He could feel its putrid breath. He made one last supreme effort to run and woke thrashing on the floor of his room.

But the chimes went on. He lay on his back, confused, panting for breath. The door chime sounded through the house. Where the hell were the servants? Still sleeping it off, he supposed. He was going to have to read them the riot act and make a few examples. He had slept fully dressed, so he got up and answered the front door. At first, he thought he must be still dreaming.

Sarai stood at the head of a deputation of women. She had maids and employees' wives along as chaperones. Male servants sat on carriages in the compound. Sarai was all done up in a lady's "visiting the countryside costume," which was just as impractical as other lady's outfit, but in a rustic sort of way. He noticed she held a gray parasol. Why the hell had she bothered to bring that?

"What?" Allenson asked. He knew he was gaping at the women, but they looked like aliens.

Sarai pouted. "And is that any way to greet a visitor, eh, ladies?"

The women tittered.

"You do not look your best, Sar Allenson, and I shall not comment on the quality of your toilette this morning. Suffice it to say that you should consider changing your brand of cologne. The current one is a little, shall we say, manly."

More tittering. The women sounded like a colony of fleeks.

Sarai's voice seemed to come from a long way off, and the lady's brightly colored clothes had grayed.

"I am forced to visit you because you failed to visit me, despite being back on Wagener for a whole day..."

Everything was gray. His field of vision narrowed to a small disc the exact color of Sarai's parasol.

When he woke he was in his bed. The sun shone brightly through the window, illuminating motes of dust hanging in the air. For some reason they fascinated him. He remembered watching sunlit dust as a small boy. He used to blow on them to make them dance and sparkle.

"The domestic arrangements here left something to be desired," Sarai said. "I have expressed myself firmly on the matter and I fancy things will markedly improve."

Sarai sat at his bedside. Her maid sat in the corner of the bedroom, looking out of the window and pointedly ignoring their conversation. Propriety demanded her presence, but equally insisted that she pretend not to be listening.

"You gave me quite a scare, Allen," Sarai said, softly.

The concern in her voice sobered Allenson. Sarai could be infuriating, but her emotions were genuine, for all that.

"Sorry," he replied.

Sarai touched an icon on her datapad. Within seconds there was a quiet knock on the door.

"Enter," Sarai said, raising her voice.

One of Mowzelle's servant girls shot through the door with a tray. The smell of broth and warm bread drifted across the room. The servants must have had continuous shifts cooking so hot food would be immediately ready whenever he should awaken. Sarai must have put the fear of God into them.

Allenson realized he was ravenously hungry. Sarai took the tray from the girl, who scuttled out.

"Are you going to sit up or do you want me to feed you?" Sarai asked, reverting to her flirtatious persona.

He sat up.

Allenson entered the Strangers Gallery of the Lower House as an invited guest to listen to a vote of thanks to him for saving the Cutter Stream Militia. The delegates rose and clapped when he entered. He found himself bowing and waving from the gallery, like some popular entertainer greeting his fans. Fortunately, he was not expected to smile inanely like a politician greeting voters. A military officer was permitted to maintain some gravitas by adopting a stern demeanor. War, after all, was not a light-hearted matter.

The vote was duly passed without opposition and only a handful of abstentions. Allenson stayed for the minimum time afterward that could be considered appropriately polite, listening to the delegates score points off each other while supposedly debating restaurant licensing regulations. Fontenoy intercepted him as he left and walked with him across the Plaza.

"*Laudandum adulescentem, ornandum, tollendum,*" Fontenoy said.

"Your pardon?" Allenson asked.

"It's an old quote, from Cicero—the young man should be praised, honored and immortalized—or, as we say in the administrative service, you have to be behind someone to properly stab them in the back."

Fontenoy gave a sharklike grin.

"I recall the quote, now," Allenson replied. "Cicero recommended flattering the young Octavian—to use him, and then discard him when his usefulness was at an end. But, as I recall, Octavian executed Cicero and became the first Emperor of Rome."

"So he did," Fontenoy said. "But that was then and this is now. I merely wanted to warn you that the crowd is fickle. The louder they praise you now, the louder they will call for your head later. Open war between Terra and Brasilia is now inevitable."

"Popularity is hardly the goal of a gentleman," Allenson replied. "It is merely a tool that can be used well or badly."

"You're reputation is high with the Streamers, but much less so with the Regular Army." Fontenoy held up his hand. "I know you are going to say that the remnants of the 51st are singing your praises to anyone who will listen, but the opinion of a few lieutenants holds little water among the great and the good. You can hardly expect the Army to blame one of their own for the defeat so some scapegoat must be found. You will fit the frame rather conveniently. Did you know that there have even been suggestions of treachery—that you led the Army into a trap?"

"No one has had the effrontery to suggest that to my face," Allenson said hotly.

Fontenoy looked Allenson up and down, as if measuring his height and the width of his shoulders. "No, they wouldn't. I recall you defenestrated the last man to impugn your honor. Fortunately, incompetence and naiveté is considered the more likely explanation, given your track record."

"Indeed," Allenson said coldly.

"Bolingbroke's surrender document has been widely distributed by Terra across the Home Worlds, causing Brasilia no end of embarrassment. I believe the general opinion is that you are an idiot, if not an outright poltroon." Fontenoy said.

Allenson laughed, genuinely amused at Fontenoy's astonishment. The Governor was just an employee, albeit an exalted one. No gentleman would react to gossip among the lower orders. If a gentleman accused Allenson of cowardice, then his seconds would call to arrange for a meeting to decide the matter over pistols. Idiocy, of course, was a matter of opinion.

"I fear I *was* a little naive in not reading the small print more carefully," he said. "But you know, governor, I would probably still have signed. My first duty was to ensure the safety of the men who entrusted themselves to my leadership. Their lives were more important than some minor embarrassment in the

Home Worlds. Frankly, I am indifferent to other people's opinions on the matter. Good day, governor."

He left Fontenoy standing with his mouth open. Allenson was not quite sure what the governor had been trying to accomplish, but he doubted if Fontenoy would feel satisfied by the turn taken by the conversation.

"I had no idea that I was volunteering to be an office clerk when I agreed to be your aide," Hawthorn said, staring gloomily at his datapad.

"Welcome to my world," Rutchett said, ironically. "Soldiering is nine-tenths filing."

Rutchett, Mansingh, Hawthorn, and Allenson were in conference at the Militia Headquarters. In theory, the meeting could be entirely conducted through datapads, but deep biological programming made face-to-face meetings essential for the human bonding that produced a functioning team. The Regular Army depended on Allenson's people for logistical support, whatever they said back in Brasilia.

"Come, gentlemen, it is not that bad. We tackle this like you eat an elephant—one bite at a time," Allenson said.

"Why would he imagine that I want to eat an extinct bioengineered tank?" Hawthorn said, to no one in particular.

"Delegation is also a useful device," Allenson said, glaring at Hawthorn. "Particularly when some member of the awkward squad sticks their head above the parapet. I have divided the tasks into groups, according to the solutions needed. I propose to delegate business and contractual matters to Lady Blaisdel."

Nobody disagreed.

"The military logistical chain will be managed by Major Rutchett and Captain Mansingh. I suggest you appoint deputies to take over your Militia administrative duties."

Mansingh and Rutchett treated suggestions from their commanding officer as orders.

"I will run political interference for you," Allenson said.

"So, nothing for me to do." Hawthorn said brightly, starting to rise from his chair.

"On the contrary, I have a special task for you," Allenson replied.

Hawthorn sat down with an exaggerated sigh.

"Some of the trade guildmasters have decided that government supply is a license to print money and are sabotaging delivery times unless we pay them off. They put the matter differently, of course, but that's the crux of it. They scared the wits out of the accountant Lady Blaisdel sent to negotiate. I believe they stripped the poor man and hung him from his heels from an upstairs window of the *Jolly Stoker* tavern."

"So you want me to go into low drinking dives and persuade rough men to be more reasonable?" Hawthorn asked hopefully.

"Do you think you can manage that?" Allenson asked.

Hawthorn gave a cherubic grin that had melted many a female heart. "Can a fish swim?"

Allenson was saved from answering by a chime from his datapad.

"I told Preble that I was not to be disturbed save for the direst emergency," Allenson said, in annoyance. He touched the pad and a hologram of Corporal Preble, his clerk, appeared.

"There is a lady to see you, sir. She insists that it is a matter of the utmost urgency," Preble said.

"Show Lady Blaisdel in," Allenson said. If Trina said the matter was urgent then it would be. She was not a woman given to hyperbole. It was convenient that his immediate officer cadre was present if something solid had hit the fan.

"It's not Lady Blaisdel," Preble said.

"Ah," Allenson replied, the other shoe dropping. "Show her to my office and I will join her shortly."

Preble vanished. The officers around the table showed a sudden interest in their data pads or, in one case, the ceiling.

"If that is, ah, all, I will bring the meeting to a close," Allenson said. He was probably imagining it, because they said nothing, but he felt frozen disapproval from his comrades. They *should* disapprove, by God. He would in their position.

"What the hell are you doing here, Sarai?" he asked.

She sat on the edge of his desk, swinging an elegant leg that was clothed in the proper dress for a "Lady Going Up To Town." It was a chaste style, but she made it sexy. But then, Sarai would look hot dressed in servant's overalls.

"What a greeting, Allen, and I have come all this way to see you." Sarai said playfully.

"Look, Sarai, it is wholly unsuitable for you to be here," Allenson said.

"You invite that matronly Blaisdel woman," Sarai said. "She is welcome, so why am I an embarrassment?"

Allenson saw no point in pursuing that line of conversation. Whatever he said would be wrong.

Fortunately, he did not have to answer as she was far from finished.

"You never come to see me, you don't return my calls, and you won't even attend my parties. I suppose that now you have lost interest now that you have had me," she said.

"That's not true. I care for you," Allenson said.

It was true. He really did care for her and was shocked to see genuine tears in her eyes.

"I am not rejecting you. It's just that I am very busy with work, Sarai."

He went to comfort her but she pushed him away, mistaking the gesture.

"I did not come here for that. If you want a whore to slake your lusts then hire one. Don't fob me off with excuses for avoiding me. You could hire a deputy to do the grunt work. We could entertain. That would be perfectly proper—we are family."

He realized that to Sarai, his rank was social, an honorary position that would enable him, and the lady he escorted, to shine at the top of Manzanita society, not an excuse to grub around in warehouses. He would never convince her. Trina also did not really understand why it was so important to reorganize the military, but she did grasp duty and responsibility. He touched his datapad.

"Preble, the lady is leaving now. Escort her personally to her carriage and make sure she leaves safely."

He did not look at her when she left because his datapad chimed on the urgent channel.

"The war's started. I have reports of Rider raids on our outer mudtrotter settlements," Fontenoy said. "Get over here, now."

CHAPTER 23

Hornets' Nest

"You started this war. What are you going to do to stop the raids?" Fontenoy asked him, once he had reported to his office.

"I started the raids?" Allenson asked in exaggerated surprise. "I was only obeying your orders."

"You exceeded your orders, egregiously," Fontenoy said.

"You have written evidence to prove that?" Allenson asked.

Fontenoy glowered at him, and then quite unexpectedly smiled. "You are becoming quite the politician, Colonel Allenson."

Now there was an unsettling thought. Fontenoy touched a desk icon that ran through the color spectrum before turning green with the logo of a well known security company, indicating that the room was sealed off from prying ears. This was the only sure way to have a confidential discussion.

Fontenoy could record the meeting, but Allenson doubted if he would bother. Virtual constructs were indistinguishable from honest recordings and, hence, useless for any political or criminal process. It was all too easy to produce a recording showing a political opponent taking bribes or sodomizing fleeks, according to one's taste in smear campaigns.

"Very well, *we* have a problem," Fontenoy said. "We both know that the attacks will only get worse as word spreads amongst the Rider clans that there are good pickings to be had."

"It's worse than that," Allenson said, relaxing. "Captain Mansingh was a field officer in the Beezlebub Paras on insurgent suppression duties on Carmen."

"I'm not sure I follow," Fontenoy said, confused by the shift in the conversation.

"Carmen was a colony with close ties to Beezlebub companies. A coup degenerated into gang warfare and Beezlebub sent in the Paras to safeguard economic investments. Mission creep left the Paras trying to suppress semi-political criminal activity across the whole colony."

Fontenoy opened his mouth, but Allenson was into his stride.

"Once one gang made a successful raid other gang leaders had to do as much or lose face. Losing face is terminal in gang culture. Mansingh is of the opinion that Riders are the same. He predicts we will face waves of attacks. Each success will incite escalation with more attacks on bigger hamlets."

"And when that happens the public will call for heads," Fontenoy said, adding for emphasis, "yours and mine."

"Beezlebub eventually abandoned Carmen. By the time the Paras had neutralized the gangs there were no assets left to defend," Allenson said dryly. "We can't spread ourselves out all over the Hinterlands to defend every little settlement. And we can't stop the Terrans bribing the Riders to raid us without ejecting Terra from the Hinterlands. So far our attempts in that direction have been less than totally successful. In short, governor, I can't stop the attacks."

"I am not asking you to stop the attacks," Fontenoy said carefully. "I am asking you to do something to save our heads. The government must be seen to be responding decisively. We have to do something. It doesn't have to be successful."

"Ah, in that case, I do have a plan," Allenson said.

"I thought you might," Fontenoy replied. "As I said, you are becoming quite the politician."

"We re-equip the Militia as a highly mobile Hinterlands assault force to intercept Rider clans as reprisals. It won't stop attacks but it will train the Militia."

"Yes, we must be seen to fight back. That will work. But what do you mean by re-equip?" Fontenoy asked suspiciously.

"I mean, military grade laserifles and one-man combat frames—for starters," Allenson replied. "Two-seater frames are not maneuverable enough to deal with Riders. We will also need to double or treble the size of the Militia. It's just not big enough to keep a reasonably sized force in the field."

"I don't understand. Surely you take all the troops into the field?" Fontenoy asked.

"I thought that, too, until I grasped how the military work," Allenson replied. "Putting everything in the shop window is fine for parades, defense, or even one-off emergencies. But you need three troopers to have one always available for offensive deployment on a continuous basis. At any one time, one third of the force is resting and one third is training. And that doesn't include sickness, accidents, and so on."

"I see. But where will you find recruits?" Fontenoy asked.

"According to Mansingh, the recruits will come, once refugees start pouring in," Allenson replied bleakly.

"The recruiting sergeants pray for famine in Ireland," Fontenoy said softly.

"What?" Allenson asked.

Fontenoy shook his head. "Nothing, just thinking out loud. It might be useful for my staff to draw up contingency plans for an influx of refugees into the stream. With regard to new equipment for the militia, you must be reasonable, Allenson. How am I supposed to get the expenditure act through the Assembly?"

"As I see it, Fontenoy," Allenson replied, using his name now they were apparently on informal terms. "You lay my plans before the Assembly and let them veto the necessary tax rises. Then when the inevitable disasters happen and the hue and cry starts, you present the plans again, with a warning that the delay has already prejudiced the Militia's ability to stem the Rider raids. That usefully provides us with an excuse for not being able to do the impossible. This time the Act will pass, and you will be seen as prescient and dynamic."

"And your own position and political power will be enhanced," Fontenoy said, in a "don't imagine I don't know what you get out of this" tone of voice.

"Meanwhile, I will train the Militia for their new

role and place the necessary equipment orders using promissory notes," Allenson said.

Fontenoy winced. "I didn't hear that."

Allenson rode through the Continuum at the head of a company of Stream Militia. Frames spread out in a funnel formation behind, loosely grouped around their platoon and section leaders. They rose and fell in loose conical formation, which allowed good visibility ahead to all clock numbers. However, the formation left a trail through the Continuum like an interworld ship. They had not seen a single Rider, or even the trail of a Rider, but that did not mean that Riders had not seen the Militia patrol—God knows, they stood out like a dog's bollocks.

Apart from training, the point of these exercises was to show the flag and reassure the mudtrotters. The Militia was like a watchman doing his night round. No one expected him to see, let alone catch, a criminal, but it reassured the town burghers to know he was there.

They stopped briefly at each settlement to obtain intelligence about Rider raids—and intelligence was to be had in plenty. The problem was that much of it was contradictory.

Sometimes they came across tragedy. A rumor took them to an unnamed world. Thin smoke rising from woods guided them to a settlement, or, to be more exact, the wreckage of a settlement. Allenson wandered amongst the remains of the Rider sack. It had been a pitiful place of a dozen wooden dwellings. Now they were nothing but smoking charcoal and ash.

The inhabitants had been at the subsistence-agriculture level. The under-capitalized settlement would probably have collapsed with the first crop failure, but it never got a chance to become something more. Body parts of the inhabitants lay around. The corpses were mutilated and hacked to pieces. Allenson noticed that there were no hands. He gave the order to bury what was left.

"I joined the Militia to kill savages, not to become a bloody gravedigger," said a militiaman, attacking the soil with an entrenching tool.

"Shut up, Perkins; you do what you're bleedin' well told. If the colonel says dig an 'ole, you answer 'how fekking deep,' got it?"

Allenson pretended not to hear. He could hardly blame the man for voicing what they were all thinking. He was burning with anger, but kept a stoic appearance for form's sake.

After they completed their patrol and returned home, Allenson could see the tent city of refugees around Port Clearwater had expanded. Parts were taking on the shape of a shanty town of semi-permanent buildings erected from discarded packing material.

The governor's Lictors manned a checkpoint at the entrance to the causeway to prevent refugees flooding into Manzanita City. Seen from the air, the Lictors were a thin line of purple uniforms. Armed or no, they would be ground under if the refugees rioted. No doubt Fontenoy would then call out the Militia. Allenson did not relish the prospect of gunning down desperate plebs.

New recruits were parading at the Militia base when he landed.

"God's blood, what a sorry lot of wankers! I'm supposed to turn you tossers into soldiers, am I?" the instructor sergeant asked rhetorically. "I don't rate my chances but I intend to try. One of us may die in the process, and it won't be me."

Allenson ignored the NCO's welcoming address. Hell, it was probably unchanged since the *Primus Pilum* inspected the latest batch for Caesar's army. He noticed that nearly half the recruits were women; a novelty for the militia.

"Sergeant," Allenson said.

"Colonel Allenson." The NCO turned on the spot and came to attention with a high knee parade ground stamp and snapped out a crisp salute. Some of the recruits tried to copy him.

"Don't embarrass yourselves, me or the officer," the sergeant said witheringly.

Allenson returned the NCO's salute with a casual motion and walked up to one of the female recruits.

"Why did you join, mistress?" Allenson asked the somewhat brawny woman.

"Well, it's like this. My man didn't get out of the village before the Riders came, and Mavis's man, she's my friend you see, is drunk most of the time so I kicked him out. Mavis has a chest and ain't too well so she's looking after my kids while I go soldiering to earn some money. It seemed better than going on the game."

"I see," Allenson replied, taken aback by the frankness of the explanation. He had expected pious comments about duty and patriotism.

"You say, sir!" the NCO screamed at her.

"Sorry, sir."

"Not to me, to the officer." The NCO turned puce.

Allenson decided that this was no place for a CO.
"A fine batch of men, ah, recruits, sergeant."

"Yes, sir," the sergeant said, without much enthusiasm.

"I am sure you will soon get them into shape. Carry
on, sergeant."

Allenson had learned that three-word phrase was
one of the most useful orders an officer could give.

The current strategy of fighting patrols was an
utter failure, as they never found anyone to fight.
He needed a new strategy—a game changer. Talking
his problems through with Trina helped. Today, she
had suggested he might visit a first aid center in the
shanty town funded by one of her charities, so he
was dutifully on his way.

The exit from the base was guarded, to stop refugees
stealing everything not actually syncreted in.

"You should not go out there alone, sir. It's not
safe. Let me get you an escort," the guard NCO said.

"I shall be quite all right, sergeant," Allenson
answered.

The sergeant looked doubtful, but it was not his
place to contradict his colonel. If a Rupert—Militia
slang for an aristocratic office—wanted to get mugged
then that was up to him.

The refugee camp stank of human waste and rotting
materials. Sewage pooled in the open spaces between
dwellings. Allenson was transported in his head to the
Militia fort on Larissa. He could see corpses piled
around a tent made of plastic sheeting. He shook his
head and looked again. The corpses were just sandbags, anchoring the edge of the sheeting. He had to
get a grip. There were bodies lying around the camp,

but they were still alive, just out of their minds on locally distilled rotgut.

He stood out because he was expensively dressed and well fed. Bully boys guarding a large tent eyed him up, as if they were assessing his suitability as a mug. His height, the width of his shoulders, or possibly the ion pistol holstered across his chest caused them to look away when he stared back. Maybe it was none of those things. Maybe it was more the look in the eyes of a man who saw a figure dancing in the flames.

The tent was open at the front. Inside was a makeshift bar that reeked of vomit.

The only person to approach him was a young woman clutching a baby in one arm. Her face was hollow and she still had a black eye and bruised cheek from a blow.

"Want a good time mister, only a shilling? My tent's just over there."

She gestured, losing her grip on the baby, nearly dropping it. The child was listless, head lolling.

"Where's your man?" Allenson asked.

She shrugged. "Dunno. He stayed behind to get the crop in. He was supposed to join me but never came."

She had been abandoned, or maybe her man was dead.

Allenson pulled some florins from his pocket and passed them to the woman. He palmed the coins so the bully boys could not see.

"Buy some food," he said, suspecting that much of it would probably go on tonk.

The woman scuttled away, her head down, eyes darting from left to right and back again. She reminded

Allenson of a rabbit he had owned as a child. When offered a treat, the pet grabbed it and shot off, in case the giver wanted it back or it was stolen by a jealous rival.

He located the first aid tent by the long line waiting outside. Inside, medical technicians ran basic tests and slapped on medical patches. He was not surprised to find that Trina was there, with her sleeves rolled up and pitching in. She was so absorbed in her task that she did not notice him. He waited, watching her work. She bent over, scanning a crying child with a diagnoser and waiting while the machine went through its decision-making process. It manufactured a patch, which she slapped on the child's bare arm with a click of the trigger. The child increased its howls, as if it were being tortured.

Trina straightened up, running a hand through her hair. Allenson was shocked to see despair on her face before she composed herself.

"Oh, Allen," she said. "When did you arrive?"

"Just now," Allenson replied. "How's it going?" A stupid question but he could not think of one more intelligent.

She sighed. "We are being overwhelmed. Refugees are flooding in. They are weak, malnourished, and fall easily to disease. We are getting the first cases of cholera, but there will be more. I am not doing much good here. Walk with me back to my carriage, if you please."

She rubbed decontamination gel on her hands and left the tent with Allenson. Her two bodyguards accompanied them. Allenson cast an eye over them, and was pleased to see that they met his gaze coolly.

They carried charged batons and ion pistols, and showed every sign of proficiency in their use. One walked behind and on Trina's left; the other ahead to the right. Their heads turned constantly and they looked away from their charge, not toward her. Trina seemed not to notice that she was surrounded by a moving bubble of security.

"This cannot go on. We must provide basic health care and food or Manzanita will have a plague on its hands. The charities cannot cope."

"The Council will not be of a mind to vote funds for such a purpose," Allenson said.

"The Council does not know its mind because it has not yet been properly instructed," Trina said. "I intend to rectify that."

Allenson chuckled. He suspected that the first Councillor to oppose her would not know what had hit him. The lady was formidable.

"And how have your enterprises prospered?" she asked politely.

"Not well. It is impossible to intercept Rider raids." He found himself giving her the details. Trina listened politely without interruptions.

"As I see it," she said when he had wound down. "If it is impossible to intercept a raid, then the only logical course of action left is to nip them in the bud by raiding the raiders. Fight fire with fire."

"To do that we would have to know their locations," Allenson said.

"Do you not have an intelligence officer?" she asked.

He went to see Destry. His friend had insisted on doing his bit by joining the Militia. This presented

Allenson something of a problem. Destry's social status meant that he had to be given a high rank, captain at least, but Destry was not line-officer material. So Allenson appointed Destry head of intelligence, a job of appropriate status but not in the line of command. One nonmilitary advantage of Destry's presence is that it preempted unexpected social visits from Sarai.

Allenson thought of Destry's position as a sinecure, and largely ignored his friend. It occurred to him that this was unfair and stupid. Destry was imaginative and educated. Who knows, he might come up with something. The Riders could operate from anywhere and nowhere.

"The Riders are leading us around by the nose, Destry," Allenson said. "We need to know where they will strike next so we can ambush them."

"I thought you might ask that," Destry said, "so I have plotted the attacks to look for a pattern."

He keyed his datapad to project a hologram of the Hinterlands. Red squares marked out Rider raids. "I can run the data by time," Destry said.

The red squares disappeared to reappear one at a time.

"That looks random," Allenson said, disappointed.

"Not really. Statistical analysis confirms that there are a number of aggregations," Destry said, "indicating Rider clans operating independently, so I have analyzed each clump independently." The hologram ran through each clump. "Unfortunately, it didn't help. The pattern of attacks for each clan is indistinguishable from random."

"So there is no way of predicting raids," Allenson said, getting to his feet.

"Afraid not. All I can do is pinpoint the possible location of the Rider camps," Destry said casually.

Allenson sat down again. "What?"

"The Rider clans must operate from somewhere," Destry said. "They are essentially extended families with noncombatants along. So I have worked on finding their camps. Is that useful?"

"Oh yes," Allenson said, somewhat faintly. "That could be very useful."

"I can only make statistical estimates of probability," Destry said, didactically. "Riders move their camps frequently, muddling the data. But I have used a system employed by criminal sociologists."

"Go on," Allenson said, encouragingly. He wished Destry would get to the point, but his friend had earned the right to explain his work.

"Criminals tend to commit their first crimes close to home, with later attacks spiraling outward from where they live or work—or both. The data is also skewed by communication pathways, like roads and so on, so you have to plot the data on a communication map rather than a geographic map. Also copycat crimes mean that you can have multiple centers."

"Like the Rider clans?" Allenson asked, more to show he was keeping up than because he needed an answer.

"Yes," Destry replied. "As I said, the analysis is of transient value because Riders move camps frequently."

He manipulated the screen of his datapad to show a cluster of squares indicating attacks. Another adjustment and the hologram distorted to show distances in the Continuum. Red lines tracked back from each red square, intersecting on a single point.

"But, for example, the latest attack analysis suggests that there was a Rider camp here very recently." Destry pointed to the intersection.

"And it might still be there?" Allenson asked.

Destry turned both hands palm up. "Could be," he replied, in a proper noncommitted academic fashion.

Allenson sprang up, reenergized. "Consider yourself promoted to major," he shouted at Destry as he left the office.

Allenson blessed his good fortune to have friends who were cleverer than he. He used the command channel on his datapad to link straight to Hawthorn.

"Destry has located a potential Rider camp," Allenson said.

"I'll lead a group of our best men—" Hawthorn replied.

"No," Allenson interrupted. "I want to use a standard company, partly for reasons of training, and partly because speed is of the essence. The Riders could move on at any time. And I intend to lead the force."

"In that case, we will use my company," Hawthorn said. "And I will come as well."

Three hours later, Allenson surveyed the assembled force.

"Three hours is far too long to assemble," he said.

"I agree," Hawthorn replied, grimly. "I intend to initiate a new training program when we return."

"We ought to have one company on standby, in rotation," Allenson said. He stepped forward. "Men, up to now we have taken insult and damage from an enemy that hides like cowards. Well, no longer. We know their hiding place. Who is ready to give some back?"

A roar greeted him.

"I intend to lead the company straight in and hit them on the ground where we have the advantage. The primary target is the beasts and any Rider trying to mount a beast. After that all armed combatants will be killed, but we will spare women, children and noncombatants. Any man who fails in his duty from cowardice or who shows excessive brutality will be punished to the full extent of military law. They may be savages, but *we* are civilized men. Is that understood?"

There was a mutter.

"I can't hear you. Is that understood?" Allenson asked again, raising his voice.

This time there was an answering shout.

"Mount up!"

This time the cheer was spontaneous, enthusiastic, and loud.

"Destry had better be right about the location of the Rider camp," Hawthorn said gloomily to Allenson. "The men will likely hang us if we find nothing."

"It's being so cheerful that keeps you going," Allenson replied, slapping him on the shoulder.

The company moved swiftly through the continuum. It was a long haul, but there were no stragglers, despite Allenson setting a brisk pace. The militiamen were much hardier than the force he had led to Nengue. That enterprise seemed a lifetime ago.

They made the unnamed target world in two jumps. Allenson considered overnighting close by, to give the men a chance to rest, eat, and assemble into assault teams. That would have been the textbook option, but he decided to attack straight from the march.

Rider camps were transient, so a twelve hour delay might mean the difference between success and failure. The persistent and very visible trail in the Continuum left by the company was also a factor in his thinking. That was not a problem when they were advancing toward the enemy at speed. But a delay raised the odds of a Rider spotting the trail and alerting the camp. Strategically, a "hasty attack" was the best option to exploit the surprise gained from his forced march. "Faint heart never won fair lady," he said to himself. Damned silly proverb, where had he picked it up?

He part-phased into the world's atmosphere and started a grid search, his instruments looking for signs of habitation. The company followed, flattening its formation into an arrowhead. The first anomaly detected turned out on inspection to be a natural event, as did the second. Rider camps were not exactly high tech, and so were difficult to distinguish from natural processes, like forest fires.

He was closing on a third trace, when a Rider beast shot across his bow and up. The company formation rippled as the men spotted it. Allenson ordered the company to stay in formation, using the phasing of his frame's field to signal. He did not want to see half his strength dissipate chasing after a single Rider. A stern chase was notoriously a long one.

The third time was the charm. He took the company straight into the Rider camp. He wanted his men on the ground, where they could use their energy weapons freely without worrying about getting the degree of frame power right for the field to be transparent to laser bursts but still strong enough to stay aloft. Someone was bound to get it wrong in their excitement, and a frame-field explosion could take out a whole platoon.

The Rider beasts became agitated by the appearance of the frames, clashing their crystals together and emitting monotone notes like a sound wave generator. Allenson hit the ground hard, leaping off his frame. He fired a long burst at a nearby beast, holding down the trigger and walking laser bursts across the crystals. It sang like a soprano. A long crystal spear on its flank shattered into glistening shards. The beast twisted sideways and tried to phase, flickering. More laserifle shots struck the crystals. They exploded in a flash of light, filling the air with crystal fragments and silver ash.

Troopers landed all around Allenson, spreading out to take beasts under fire. One rose into the air, attracting massed fire. It died with a shriek, emitting a noise like nails dragged down a window. Rider warriors appeared as if out of the ground. Some ran for beasts while others attacked the troopers. Allenson dropped the battery from his carbine and tried to shove in a new one. He fumbled it.

A Rider erupted from a lean-to and bounded toward him, stone ax raised high. The world slowed down. Allenson dropped the carbine and caught the haft of the ax with his right hand. It hit his palm with a firm smack. He pulled the ax toward him. The warrior refused to let go off his weapon so came with it. Allenson hit him in the face. Something broke under Allenson's fist, and the warrior went over backward. Allenson reached down for his weapon. A trooper stepped in front of him, firing into the warrior's chest.

A cry and movement from the lean-to caused the trooper to spin around, leveling his rifle. It was a girl.

She looked about ten, but was probably a year or two older. The girl lunged at the trooper who hesitated, reluctant to fire. She punched him in the groin and he fell, screaming. Bright red arterial blood poured down his legs. It pulsed in spurts in time to the trooper's heartbeat.

The girl held a long shard of plastic ground into a stiletto. Drops of blood dripped off the end when she turned on Allenson. He pushed her away, rolling her over, and very deliberately picked up his gun and pushed home the new battery until it clicked. The girl regained her feet and lunged at him.

He fired a burst at point-blank range. It was impossible to miss. Laser bolt explosions blackened her flesh. One set her hair alight. She looked as if she were dancing in flames. Allenson fired until she stopped moving. She died without uttering a sound.

He checked the trooper, but he was already dead in a pool of his own blood.

Allenson's world had shrunk until he focused only on immediate personal threats. He had lost appreciation of the wider battle and was merely functioning as another trooper. He forced himself to stop, take a deep breath, and take stock.

The battle was as good as over. It had been a massacre. Every Rider able to hold a weapon had attacked the troopers, and been gunned down regardless of age or sex. Wooden and stone weapons were no match for laserifles. Nevertheless, a few troopers were down, mostly with cuts and contusions although one or two looked bad. Troopers moved from body to body, treating their wounded and shooting any Riders that showed signs of life.

A trooper discovered infants in a lean-to that seemed to have been a crèche. He clubbed one with the butt of his rifle. The child's skull broke with an audible crunch, scattering blood and brains across the trooper's legs.

"Stop that, you bastard!" Allenson said, downing the trooper with a back handed blow that dislodged the man's jaw.

"Captain Hawthorn?"

"Sir!"

"Put that man on a charge. Make sure your men know that I will shoot the next trooper who kills a helpless child."

At that point, Rider beasts dropped out of the sky.

· CHAPTER 24 ·

Perseverance

Beasts swept across the dismounted militia, their Riders unleashing a hail of spears, rocks, and slingshots. Explosions caused clouds of thick black smoke. The bloody Riders had gotten their hands on grenades. They weren't very effective with them, but their morale impact on soldiers unused to being under artillery fire was out of all proportion to their killing power. The Militia panicked and the men ran about, shooting wildly into the sky.

Allenson fired a burst at a beast running down a fleeing trooper but missed. The Rider flung a spear that struck the trooper between the shoulderblades. He pitched forward, arms outstretched, head back. Allenson corrected his aim and fired again but the beast had already vanished back into the Continuum.

The more disciplined militiamen returned aimed fire, but the fast-moving beasts were difficult targets. They flicked in and out of phase with a smoothness that could not be matched by machines. Smoke drifted across the battlefield, hiding the attackers and degrading laser bursts. The company were sitting ducks on the ground.

A shadow that might have been a beast or a frame flickered over Allenson. He ran for his frame, firing a long burst into the smoke above, lighting it up and attracting his company's attention.

"Mount up!" he yelled.

Troopers ran through the hail of missiles and explosions, glad to have some direction. Allenson mounted his frame and switched on. He forced himself to count slowly to five to give enough men time to join him, using the old one-thousand, two-thousand convention. He reached three thousand when his face stung from a nearby explosion. He touched his cheek and his hand came away red with blood.

"Sod this for a game of toy soldiers," Allenson said, and took off.

He cleared the smoke to find the air full of frames and a scattering of Riders. A beast slid neatly across his front, forcing two militia frames in pursuit to pull up to avoid a collision. He drew his spring gun and gave chase. The beast turned ninety degrees and dropped, presumably to begin another attack run across the ground. Allenson cut the corner, gaining fast on the enemy. Taking careful aim, he fired his spring gun at close range, aiming at the Rider. The shot was low. The bolt missed the Rider, but knocked crystal chips off the beast, causing it to sheer off and phase into the Continuum.

Allenson took his hand off the control stick to cock the spring gun, his frame flying on in a straight line. A slingshot struck him on the shoulder, numbing his whole arm. His fingers lost their grip on the spring gun. He grabbed the control stick with his good hand and yanked it viciously, causing his frame to corkscrew. A spear flew through where his body would have been if he had flown on straight and level. He had a beast on each flank, attacking as a team. He would evade one, simply to run into the other. He dodged frantically, knowing his luck would run out sooner or later.

A frame burst out of the Continuum in front and above him. The pilot turned off its field and dropped under gravity. Allenson was momentarily blinded by the scattered light flash of a heavy hunting rifle aimed in his direction. An explosion rocked his frame as one of the beasts on his tail disintegrated.

He yanked back on the stick, assuming that the other frame would continue to drop. Hawthorn had cut his rescue attempt very close. He twisted his head desperately, trying to locate enemies or friendlies on a collision course. He still had dark blobs in his field of vision where his overloaded retinal cells had gone on strike.

He saw nothing. He was completely alone: no Riders, no frames, nothing.

Blinking to restore his sight, he phased fully into the Continuum. Frames flashed by in all directions, chasing a handful of beasts. The enthusiastic militiamen kept getting in each other's way. No sooner did a frame line up for a shot than it had to veer away to avoid colliding with an eager compatriot trying for the same target.

The Riders scattered and ran their beats out from the Militia like shrapnel from an explosion. Allenson blipped his fields with the recall signal to stop his command from scattering itself all over the Hinterlands where it could be ambushed in ones and twos. The Militia had, he felt, done handsomely.

The trip home was uneventful. News spread fast of their victory. The company was all heroes and they loved it, strutting into the mess for celebration drinks as if they had won the war single handed, instead of coming out barely ahead in a minor skirmish. They cheered Allenson, they cheered Hawthorn, they cheered themselves, and they started drunken fights. Morale was high.

Allenson left Hawthorn to oversee the celebrations and returned to his office to write up a preliminary report for the governor. Such a document had to be a masterly exercise in deception. Blatant lies were dangerous and to be avoided, but the full truth was equally unwelcome. The truth would focus on failures, the inability to stop the Rider raids and the way the Militia had been panicked by a handful of Riders. Truth was unpalatable, involving blood pouring down the legs of a militiamen and a girl peppered with laser bursts, hair alight—a corpse dancing in flames.

Fontenoy did not need the truth. He needed a glorious victory to show the Council and the people of the Stream. So Allenson would give him a glorious victory, something that made Streamers feel good about themselves—something that would bolster support for the Militia.

He strung together a tale of derring-do, illustrated by first and third point of view virtuals created from edited data capture. The highlight was an external view of Allenson pursued by the two Riders and rescued by Hawthorn. The voice commentary described a trooper luring the enemy into a cunning trap set by Major Hawthorn, as he now was. The laser burst split the beast into shattered crystal spears, releasing energy in white-blue pulses and electrical discharges. A red circle outlined the falling Rider. The clip would be on near continuous loop on the news reels, if Allenson was any judge. There was no need to mention that the "trooper" was fleeing for his life or that he was Inspector General and Colonel of the Militia—no need to deviate from the script.

Fontenoy's PR people would work it over again before release, but Allenson was reasonably pleased with the draft. He sent it off and settled back to write the report that mattered, the one highlighting problems and failings. He was tired, but he needed to get his thoughts down while they were fresh, before they became edited by his memory into what he wanted to remember rather than what actually happened. The raid on the Rider camp was not just a political device, but was also a test of doctrine. Such operations were only useful if ruthlessly examined with a mind stripped of illusions. You had to recognize failings before you could begin to fix them.

His desk beeped. An icon indicated that Fontenoy wanted to speak to him. Allenson keyed the icon and a hologram of Fontenoy popped up.

"You got my report, then?" Allenson asked.

"What, oh yes, that," Fontenoy replied. "But that's not why I need to speak to you."

"No?" Allenson asked, somewhat nettled by the cavalier dismissal of his efforts.

"The packet boat is in with dispatches from Brasilia," Fontenoy said. "The government has changed. Isolda's faction is out and Pretten's is in. Policy on the colonies across the Bight has changed. They are sending out a major expeditionary Force under General Levit to force back the Terrans."

"Nice of them to tell us," Allenson replied. "It would have been even nicer if they had asked our opinion."

But by then he was talking to himself. Fontenoy had gone.

Allenson looked around the meeting room. He had arranged the chairs in a circle to indicate that this was intended as a private gathering among equals, to encourage a frank exchange of views.

"Well, gentlemen, you have all read my report. The real one, that is, not the PR job," Allenson said.

"Thanks for putting my face all over the news loops," Hawthorn replied. "I can't venture out without being challenged to a fight by the local ruffians."

"I am not surprised," Destry said. "If you will flirt with their girlfriends..."

"It's not my fault women find me attractive," Hawthorn said, defensively.

Mansingh choked back a laugh.

"Your charm makes you tailor-made for the role of the face of the Militia, so I am afraid you will just have to put up with all the female adoration," Allenson said, with a grin. "Recruitment applications have increased so much that we can pick and choose among the candidates."

"The things I do for my country," Hawthorn said, putting on an expression of noble sufferance.

Allenson tapped his nails on the edge of the screen to attract attention.

"Gentlemen, majors, fascinating though Major Hawthorn's romantic problems are, we must return to the point of the meeting. Our raid was a useful morale-building exercise, but it revealed weaknesses in our doctrine. Specifically, we transit in large groups of at least company strength to magnify our impact." Allenson said.

"Strike concentrated, not dispersed," Destry said. "It's a principle from an Old Terran general."

"The problem is that we leave a wake through the Continuum that just screams our location to the enemy. This is not good if the enemy is fast moving bands of Riders. They will see us first and retain the initiative, fighting only at a time and place of their choosing. We can't win by carrying the fight to the enemy on those terms. The truth is that we were lucky on the last raid, and I mean no insult to our Intelligence Section, who performed magnificently."

"None taken," Destry said.

"Regular formations travel in convoy. Battles are set pieces and inevitably take place on or around strategic locations, so it's not an issue for Home World armies," Mansingh said. "But I can see that is not applicable to our situation. The Hinterlands is too big and our forces too small."

"It's not possible to transit dispersed and concentrate only to fight. Given the haphazard nature of Continuum travel, we could hang around for days waiting for stragglers to show up. Many of them would never arrive, for one reason or another," Rutchett said darkly. "It would not increase our mobility."

"I concur," Allenson replied. He had no illusions about the reliability of the average trooper.

"Sometimes I wonder if this concentration principle is necessarily correct," Hawthorn said.

"It is standard, tried, and tested military wisdom," Mansingh said.

"Hmm, but you know, we got in each other's way when the Riders counterattacked. I doubt if there were more than a dozen of them but they created chaos," Hawthorn said.

"In practice, we fought as individuals, not as a team," Allenson said. "That is something that I intended to bring up later, but since the matter of tactics has been raised..."

"Have you ever wondered why Riders tend to work in twelve-man groups or thereabouts?" Destry asked, interrupting his colonel.

Destry appeared to be drifting off subject. Academics like Destry were irritatingly didactic. They did not give their opinion and then justify it if necessary, like any reasonable person. They started with observations and then meandered along the winding lanes of academic discourse until they reached their destination. Allenson would once have shut Destry down, but he was inclined to let him develop his theme. Destry's intelligence coup was still fresh in his mind.

"No, enlighten us," Allenson said, encouragingly.

Hawthorn shut his eyes. Fortunately, Destry did not notice.

"It's basic human biology. When Riders split off from the human population, males hunted in packs of about twelve. Warfare was just an extension of hunting, so the same applied. Warrior bands fought in groups of twelve or less, usually led by a hero."

"And how is this relevant to our present situation?" Allenson asked patiently.

"As I said, it's basic human biology as well. Have you noticed how committees only function with twelve people or less? Any bigger and they split into sub groups. Similarly, the minimum sized unit in regular armies is usually a squad of ten. It may be less, but never much more."

"That's true," Mansingh said. "But surely it's just for administrative convenience?"

"All this is very interesting," Rutchett replied, insincerely, "but I don't see how this applies to the conditions found in modern warfare."

"Mostly, it doesn't," Destry admitted, "but there are circumstances where you find the old patterns work. Weapons may have changed, but people are the same. Do you know anything about early aerial warfare?"

"Go on," Allenson replied, starting to see where Destry was going with his argument.

"There were two types of machines," Destry said. "Large slow ones carried explosive devices to drop on cities. They would huddle together in convoys for protection from the small fast fighting machines that were designed to destroy them. The bombing machines would be escorted by their own fighters. Fighting machines faced the same issues as us. Attacking one at a time was hopeless, as the defending machines could concentrate their firepower."

"Defeat in detail," Allenson said softly.

Destry stopped at the interruption.

"Nothing, carry on," Allenson replied.

"Well, doctrine would have them attack en masse, but it took too long for these primitive machines to

take off and assemble in the air. Also, a large mass of machines was visible for many kilometers, giving the defenders warning, and they tended to get in each other's way," Destry said.

"So what was the solution?" Mansingh asked, clearly intrigued.

"They operated in groups of twelve. The warriors lived and fought together, maximizing team building. They also had an internal team structure. The twelve were broken down into 'flights' of four, which were then broken down into elements of two. One flight would protect the other two from enemy warriors so they could concentrate on the bombing machines. Similarly, in an element of two, one attacked and the other protected his rear. Twelve turned out to be the optimum compromise between firepower, stealth, and low visibility—and team building."

"I like it," Hawthorn said, in excitement. "I can see this working."

"Yeees," Rutchett agreed, "but our command structure might get in the way. Not all our NCOs and officers would necessarily function well as team and flight leaders. We can't just dismiss or demote them, as it would cause chaos and be disastrous for morale."

"That's not a problem," Allenson said. "Combat team leaders will be outside the normal chain of command that applies on the ground. They will be a new rank applicable only to Continuum combat."

"Funnily enough, the ancients used the same solution," Destry said.

"Whatever works," Allenson said. "Well, gentlemen, we have a great deal of work ahead of us."

❖   ❖   ❖

"That's not fair!" Allenson said, jabbing the air for emphasis.

Fontenoy winced and looked alarmed.

General Levit merely raised an eyebrow. She was a petite, slim woman who looked about thirty but was probably older. Her uniform, a combat suit of the Brasilian Regular Army, was exquisitely tailored but otherwise entirely standard in design—standard for a general, that is. She spoke softly, so that you had to strain to hear her. This tended to cause people to concentrate on her words more effectively than if she had yelled. In short, she was a woman who oozed gravitas.

"Colonel Allenson, that's no way to speak to—"

"What's not fair, Colonel?" Levit asked, interrupting Fontenoy as if he had not spoken.

"Using Perseverance as the main base and jumping-off point for the expedition into the Hinterlands. It will give *their* economy an enormous boost."

"And why is that unfair?" Levit asked, puzzled.

"It's unfair because the Stream has borne the brunt of the fighting up to now. It is not fair that Perseverance should reap the benefits," Allenson replied.

"Our base has to be somewhere," Levit said reasonably. "It hardly matters exactly where as far as the Government is concerned. You are all Brasilian colonies, are you not?"

"Quite so," Fontenoy said, nodding to show his agreement.

Levit and Allenson ignored him. Allenson realized that Levit genuinely could not see why he favored the Stream. The colonies were interchangeable from her perspective. He had to find an argument that would engage her intellect.

"Manzanita has certain advantages compared to Perseverance," Allenson said.

He listed them on his fingers. "First, Chernokovsky built a base on Manzanita as an assembly and jumping-off point for his expedition. It would be less effort to reopen it than start again somewhere else. Second, I take it you will need a trackway for your vehicles. Again, Chernokovsky's expedition built one for much of the way to Larissa. Third, Manzanita has experience of supplying a Regular Army expedition, unlike Perseverance. Finally, the Stream Militia is the largest and most combat experienced military force this side of the Bight, and is specifically trained for Hinterlands combat. You will want to take us along, and we operate from our base here on Manzanita. For all these reasons, Manzanita is a better jumping-off point than Perseverance."

Levit smiled, "I think I can see where this is going. But first, to answer your points, Chernokovsky's base is far too small for my force. I have heavy siege equipment. Also, building a new base will keep my troops occupied while the battlegroup is assembling. There is no port big enough this side of the Bight for the Navy transports to land the battlegroup in one go and, trust me on this, you do not want large numbers of idle troops wandering around your colonies, gentlemen."

"God, no!" Fontenoy said, shaking his head.

Levit continued, "I doubt that Chernokovsky's trackway now goes very far into the Hinterlands. Has anyone checked? No? Well, I am confident that the Terrans have decommissioned it not far out from the Stream. I would, in their place. The army's experience of using Manzanita as a supply base is one of the primary reasons for moving the center of operations to Perseverance. The army had great difficulty finding supply vehicles and spares in the Stream, because it lacks an industrial base. Perseverance has at least a degree of manufacturing capability."

Allenson opened his mouth to reply but Levit held up a hand to show she had not finished.

"Finally, there is the matter of morale. Squadies are superstitious, gentlemen, and they know that Chernokovsky's expedition was a bloody disaster. It will give them no confidence to repeat the process."

She smiled at Allenson. "I think I know what the real problem is here. All you young officers are the same, glory hunters to a man. You probably realize that my battlegroup is far more combat capable in the Continuum than Chernokovsky's light infantry."

She wagged her finger at Allenson.

"You are afraid that I will leave your Militia behind. On the contrary, I think it would be useful for your men to gain experience alongside a proper combined-arms force of regular troops. Don't worry. I will allow you to come with us so you are in at the kill."

Allenson was speechless. Sometimes, he thought he was the only one with any vision for the future of the Stream. Fontenoy was clearly relieved that the army was just transiting through Port Clearwater to dump heat and refuel. He just wanted a quiet life and the arrival of a major military force was nothing but a threat to the established order. Allenson suspected that most of the ruling families of the Stream would agree with him. It was hardly in their interests to upset the status quo, even for the greater good.

Nevertheless, it was galling to think that all his

efforts would merely go to benefit Perseverance. Once the Terrans were evicted, the trackway would act as a magnet for economic exploitation. Colonies not on the trackway, like the Stream, would become backwaters. Well, there was nothing he could do about it. Maybe he was being too parochial? Maybe he should start thinking of the Brasilian colonies across the Bight as a unitary whole? Ah well, a problem for another day. He had a war to fight.

"Very well, General Levit, we shall move the Militia temporarily to Perseverance. My men are trained to function as light cavalry. I suggest that we move outside the trackway in independent companies to scout and screen your Regulars. I must warn you that the Terrans will know where you are at all times. It is impossible to stop Rider scouts detecting something as large and slow as an army building a road."

"You use your troops as you see fit, Colonel. Don't worry about us. I will be delighted if the Terrans attack my battlegroup." She smiled. "Unfortunately, I doubt they are that stupid."

Levit offered the Militia a ride in a transport to Perseverance, but Allenson declined. Running along the edge of the Bight in squadron-sized attack formations was good practice. The squadrons assembled into company and then regiment strength each night to rest.

He made it a competition. The last company to arrive at a rendezvous had to do all the dirty jobs, like digging out the latrines. The troops christened the losing company "Tail End Tossers," and they were subject to barracking that drove home the message that it's good to be a winner. As far as possible, the

Militia lived off the land while in transit by hunting, preserving the minimal rations that could be carried on one-man frames. By the time they reached Perseverance, the Stream Militia could re-assemble a company at a distant rendezvous about as slickly as the vagaries of the Continuum would allow.

Allenson wanted the regiment to feel comfortable in the Hinterlands without being tied to supply chains. His experience with Chernokovsky's expedition had taught him that mobility was about far more than speed of locomotion. He began to understand why Regular soldiers were so obsessed with logistics. Lack of supply, and its favorite partner, disease, had killed more armies than weapons.

Hawthorn, being Hawthorn, took the training one stage further. He encouraged his squadrons to make mock-attacks on each other. The art was to sneak up on another company unobserved and then burst in on them. This usually led to a swirling duel before both sides broke off. Each night he looked at the data records and awarded virtual kills. Squadron Leaders that were continually surprised without any successes of their own were replaced. Hawthorn was forgiving of any squadron leader who showed skill and aggression but occasionally was too bold for his own good, but he refused to tolerate timidity or incompetence.

The system was so effective that Allenson made Hawthorn head of combat training and let him introduce it to the whole regiment. Transit times lengthened as the regiment's squadrons stopped moving along predictable routes where they could be ambushed and became masters of using the energy turbulence of the Continuum for cover. But Allenson was in no hurry. He knew the

Regular Army would be slow to assemble. He had time to kill and realistic training was never a waste of time. And eventually they arrived at Perseverance.

Allenson surveyed the ranks of his Militia. It was a sight that would have brought tears to the eyes of a Regular drill sergeant. He did not mind that few of the men had full uniforms and those that did were ill fitting. He did not even mind the black eyes and split lips and knuckles. They were there to fight, not look good. He did mind that many were wearing medical patches and that some even paraded with splints holding broken bones in place.

He waved his datapad at the troops. "Not a pretty picture, is it?"

There was silence.

"Well?" Allenson shouted.

Muttered "No, sirs" answered him.

"Who started it?" Allenson asked.

After a pause, a sergeant took one step forward. He was one of those men who provided living proof that human beings had interbred with Neanderthals—before wiping them out. He was not a tall man but had a barrel chest and forearms thicker than Allenson's thighs. What remained of his face bore witness to many a violent encounter, but none of the damage was recent.

"One of mine, Colonel, platoon sergeant Voskov. He's a pretty good NCO if you keep him off the tonk," Rutchett said softly into Allenson's left ear.

"And how did you start the fracas?" Allenson asked.

"Well, sir, it was like this, i'n'it. One of them Brazzies, I mean Brasilians, sir, asked me if us colonial monkeys had our tails docked to fit into men's clothes."

"I see," Allenson replied.

"So I asks him, like, if Brazzies have their pricks docked at birth or whether they're born dickless."

"And for some reason the Regular Army took exception to this comment," Allenson said, dryly.

"S'pose so, sir. Anyhows, he takes a swing at me sos I belts him with a bottle and it sort of spread, sir."

"Sort of spread?" Allenson asked slowly. "Sort of spread? I give the regiment leave for one night—just one miserable night. In that time, Union Street is burned to the ground, the civilian riot police forced to flee, and several military police hospitalized. In addition, a civilian security organization going by the name of the Jolly Boys—"

"A street gang that act as enforcers for the pimps," Hawthorn said softly into Allenson's right ear.

Allenson continued as if Hawthorn had not spoken. "—are so badly beaten that three are dead and a number maimed for life. Fortunately, the civilian police do not seem minded to investigate that incident further. Much more seriously, a number of Regulars have also suffered injury. Sergeant Voskov hardly did all this on his own. Who else in the regiment is responsible?"

As one man, the entire Militia took a step forward.

"Hmmpf," Allenson grunted. "I am at least pleased that the entire regiment has mustered as fit for duty. If you must fight, I expect you to win."

Actually, one man strategically positioned at the back of the parade was only upright because he was being supported by a comrade on each side.

"You obviously have too much time on your hands. I have therefore arranged a program of intensive training in ground combat. In addition, in case you still have surplus energy to burn, General Levit has kindly lent me Staff Sergeant Hobbs."

Allenson indicated a small thin man who stood to attention on one side of the line of officers. The creases on his uniform could have sliced cheese and his buttons and boots shone.

"Do you think you can teach them to drill, Staff?" Allenson asked.

"You can teach fleeks to drill if you work them hard enough, sir," Hobbs replied. "It's just a matter of application and sweat: my application, their sweat."

"No time like the present. Carry on, Staff," Allenson said.

For a small man, Hobbs had an astonishingly loud voice that Allenson could hear some way from the parade ground.

"Sounds like the men are having fun," Hawthorn said with a grin.

A Regular ran up, saluted, and handed Allenson a sealed note. He slit it open and read the contents.

"They won't have to endure Hobbs for long. This is from Levit's chief of staff. We ship out in three days."

Quartets of forty-seater vehicles slid ponderously along the trackway. Ten firing positions, armed with heavy spring guns on universal gimbals, ran along the top side, the other three sides being protected by carbon-fiber armor. The vehicles in a quartet were positioned in a circle, gun-side out, such that all firing arcs were covered. The troops inside were divided into ten-man watches. At any one time, one watch pedaled, recharging the powerful batteries; one was on overwatch, manning the guns; one available as replacements; and one on downtime. Quartets followed each other at set distances in a long caterpillar. Each battalion was followed by lightly manned, unarmed transports containing the baggage and heavy equipment.

The vehicles were slow and unhandy. The formation would be unmanageable in the open Continuum, but in the smoother trackway it presented a bristling defense to any attacker. Levit's army was a much more formidable force than Chernokovsky's doomed expedition. It resembled a glacier, grinding imperceptibly but remorselessly forward to the Terran base on Larissa.

Allenson rode at the head of a company of militia along the trackway, overtaking the quartets as they moved toward the lead battalion. His company was divided into ten squadrons that criss-crossed each other's trails, spiraling around the convoy and moving in and out of the trackway to check the continuum. Four companies of militia were always on close escort around the convoy. Allenson was determined not to be surprised again.

One company was pathfinders, seeking out the next system to stop and set up the next link in the trackway. At each layover, Allenson was able to present Levit's staff with a map of the Continuum ahead. His troopers began to be afforded a measure of respect by the Regulars, as auxiliaries of course. No Regular conceded that they would be of any value in combat.

The remaining five companies ranged independently into the Continuum on free-hunting missions. The militia troopers had reached such a level of expertise that this was seen as the plum mission. Allenson rotated the companies to keep the men sharp and avoid suspicions of favoritism.

The scouts reported finding abandoned Rider camps and occasional beast tracks but had no contact with Riders, hostile or otherwise. The clans appeared to be retreating from the advancing Brasilian column, not concentrating for an encounter. The militia had orders to launch an immediate company-sized reconnaissance in force at any concentration of Riders, scattering them if they could, and reporting back for reinforcement if they couldn't.

This absence of Riders puzzled Allenson, who had a higher respect for the offensive ability of Rider clans than Levit's people. They could not envision mere savages daring to assault a Regular column, but they had not been with Chernokovsky. The Riders, and hence the Terrans, must know the location of the sluggish column. Why had they not made any effort to disrupt the column's progress? They could not destroy it, but they could mount delaying attacks. The trackway looked horribly vulnerable to Allenson.

The explanation made for a stopover on a world christened Wobble by the scouts, because of its eccentric spin that progressed the seasons through a five week period. He had a message to attend General Levit "at his earliest convenience." He took Hawthorn with him.

Levit's command tent hummed with quiet purpose. It reflected the general's character: efficient, thorough, intelligent but colorless. Unimaginative might be too strong a word but it did cross Allenson's mind. He was shown almost immediately into the general's inner office.

"Colonel Allenson, come in. A fast picket has just

come in with information. What do you think of this?" Levit asked.

She and her Chief of Staff stood in front of a hologram of a map of the Continuum. Allenson did not immediately recognize the area covered. It took a mental adjustment to realize that the map was on a large scale, showing all the Brasilian and Terran colonies across the Bight and the Hinterlands behind them. He was not used to thinking at that scale. Various glowing symbols were located on the hologram, blue for Brasilia and red for Terra. The path and projected path of Levit's trackway was a blue line that linked Perseverance to Fort Revenge, as the Terrans had pointedly named their base on Larissa. At this scale, it looked to be an insignificant distance.

"What's this?" Allenson asked, pointing to a red line that originated in the colonies of New Terra, curving deeply through the Hinterlands until it reached Larissa.

"The Terran supply line," said the Chief of Staff, somewhat condescendingly.

"The red knots are the Terran chain of forts guarding strategic points," Allenson said, to show he was not entirely a halfwit, "so what's that?" He pointed to a flashing red icon.

"That's the Terran relief force," Levit said, calmly.

· CHAPTER 25 ·

Contact

"Terran relief force? What bloody relief force?" Allenson asked, shocked.

"It was always a possibility," Levit said. "The correct military response to the approach of a siege army is to send a relief force, either to bolster the defenses such that they are impregnable, or to operate in the field against the besiegers. The only other solution is to withdraw the defenders and destroy the installation."

She spoke as if modern war were a chess game of move and counter-move, something not involving actual fighting at all. We threaten their pawn with a knight, and they either move the pawn or defend it with a bishop.

"How do you know this?" Allenson asked.

"The SIS, the Special Instance Section—" said the Chief of Staff.

"I am familiar with the acronym," Allenson interrupted, fed up with the assumption that he had just fallen off a turnip truck.

"Yes, well, the SIS observed the build of the relief

force in New Terra and alerted us," said the chief of staff.

"I don't understand how they could have traveled all that way in just a few days," Allenson said, tracing the length of the red line on the hologram.

"They haven't," Levit replied. "They set out before us."

"And we have only now found out?" Allenson asked.

"Things take time," Levit replied. "The SIS operative in New Terra would have reported to his handler, who would have waited for a courier to take the data back to Brasilia, probably via an independent Home World to avoid arousing suspicion. The SIS would then have spent time evaluating the significance and importance of the data before passing it on to the Army. Intelligence is always reluctant to disclose information to other government departments in case it leaks back and compromises their operatives."

"The spooks do like their little secrets," the chief of staff contributed brightly.

Levit pointed to the flashing red dot. "That is simply a prediction based on our estimate of their speed. They're moving along the chasms that link New Terra to the Hinterlands behind our colonies, so will be making better time than us." She sighed. "We may as well turn around now if the model is accurate. They've beaten us."

"What?" Allenson asked. "We have not yet fought. How could we be beaten?"

"According to the model, they are two weeks out from Larissa. We are three weeks away, so they'll get to Fort Revenge at least a week ahead of us." She shrugged. "In which case, the siege will fail. There is little point in losing well trained troops to a lost cause."

Allenson could not believe that they had come all this way, so methodically, merely to turn around at the first difficulty. "Why not assemble a fast detachment to get to Larissa first? We might be able to take it by a coup de main or bluff the Terrans into surrendering."

Levit looked at him and shook her head. "I'm not prepared to break my defensive formation. Being outmaneuvered is one thing, the luck of the draw, but the new government cannot risk a debacle with heavy losses. The political fallout could be catastrophic, and not just for the politicians. The incoming administration made great play of the previous one's incompetence in sending out an under-resourced expedition. How would the army explain another humiliating defeat after we had been given a free hand to set the budget? Heads would roll, starting with mine. No, the Brasilian commoners don't give that much of a damn whether we or the Terrans control a piddling fort on a useless mudball that they've never heard of. The expedition can be spun as a successful flag-showing exercise, provided we have no significant losses."

She cocked her head to one side and studied the hologram. "Actually, we don't know the exact position of the relief convoy or its composition. This is, after all, only a simulation."

"Then I think we should find out before making any irreversible decisions," Allenson said.

He didn't raise his voice, but neither did he wait for a response before he turned on his heel and stalked out of the tent.

For the reconnaissance, Allenson attached himself to the Tenth squadron of Third Company. This company was largely made up of new troopers, so he wanted to see how they performed. He was pleasantly surprised by their keenness to show off their skills. Each squadron transited independently through the continuum, rendezvousing at an undistinguished world with barely breathable air due to sulfur compounds. Each of the five companies involved in the reconnaissance, half the Militia, had independent muster points along the predicted track of the Terran Relief Force. Third Company was in the center, just where the Terrans were supposed to be.

The companies operated in squadrons for the reconnoiter, to cover the maximum possible ground as fast as possible. The point of assembling first was to check all squadrons were present. In the case of Third Company, Seventh Squadron failed to make the rendezvous. Allenson refused to intervene, leaving the decision up to the company commander, a young captain called Lai-Po, who elected not to wait for the missing formation but to split Sixth Squadron into two flights to cover Seventh Squadron's zone as well as their own. On a whim, Allenson led the second flight.

He kept an eye out for Riders on the transit to the Chasm, but saw none. That was a bad sign. He anticipated that the relief convoy would be escorted by Riders, so he was not hopeful of finding the Terrans in his zone. The flight could see the chasm from a long way off. It looked like an elongate storm cloud, illuminated by flashes of lightning. It writhed and pulsed like a monstrous growth. There was no Continuum current on this scale near the Brasilian colonies. He had seen simulations, but they did not do the reality justice.

Signaling the flight to close up, he pedaled into the chasm, choosing a ninety-degree entry angle to minimize the time that the flight was in the highly turbulent zone where visibility was close to zero. His frame hit the chasm wall like a boulder dropped into a river. A splash of yellow energy lit up his vehicle. The frame shuddered, its field twanging like a vibrating wire. It hung against the turbulence and then surged through, coils of multicolored mist flowing around its field.

Allenson emerged into choppy eddies along the inner edge of the chasm wall. The frame tossed and pitched, but visibility was good. He turned his head to look behind and check the rest of the formation. All five frames punched through the chasm wall after him. It was like watching a video played backward of stone dropped into a pond. The troopers managed to keep reasonably tight through the chasm wall, but they immediately began to spread out into an attack formation after they emerged. What in heaven were they thinking?

The other shoe dropped and he looked forward, feeling remarkably foolish. A chain of dark gray tubes slid slowly past, connected to each other by a thick central cable. A single field enclosed the whole train. The front module was half the size of the others. The cars had large observation windows along their length, with mounts for crew-served heavy spring guns, but the lead vehicle had viewing ports only in the rounded bow. Presumably this was a tractor unit, supplying power to the rest of the chain.

Allenson changed course to hug the chasm side, finding an eddy stream that counter-flowed against the central current occupied by the Terran vehicles. He hoped that the small one-man frames would be inconspicuous against the flaring energy of the chasm wall. The Terrans did not appear to be taking any special precautions to watch for enemy vehicles, but there was no harm in caution.

The train of troop transports flowed by. It was followed closely by a bulk conveyor the size of two train cars. This had few observation windows, so presumably was battery powered with a small crew. The Terran convoy was carried by the main central current. The vehicles used just enough power to maintain steerage, so that the chasm itself did most of the work. It would be a nightmare trying to move such a low-power convoy cross country through the Continuum, and it brought home to Allenson the enormous advantage the Terrans enjoyed by the controlling these major chasms. Another conveyor followed, and then a troop train.

Allenson decided that they had seen enough. He signaled to his flight to close up and punched his way out of the chasm. His flight pedaled hard on the way back, making the fastest possible transport time. Allenson barely noticed his exertions. He was too busy thinking.

Levit sighed. "So the model was entirely accurate. I feared that was the case. Logistical realities make operational maneuvers in modern warfare entirely predictable. That's why there are so few battles."

"Shall we deconstruct the trackway as we retreat?" Maluoli, the chief of staff, asked. "It seems foolhardy to leave something that could be used as an invasion route into our colonies, and I doubt that we will have any further use for it."

"Wait a minute," Allenson said, before Levit could reply. "Who said anything about retreating? There are other options."

"No, there aren't," Levit said, firmly. "We've been through all this."

"I have a new suggestion," Allenson said.

The chief of staff raised his eyes to the roof of the tent, not hiding his exasperation at having to deal with ignorant colonials. Levit, however, looked at Allenson with quick birdlike eyes. "Which is?"

"Turn loose the Militia," Allenson replied. "And we will do to the Terran Relief Force what the Riders did to Chernokovsky."

Maluoli laughed condescendingly. "Oh, get real, Allenson, you can't destroy a military column with a handful of light cavalry. This won't be like the bandit skirmishes that your militia is used to fighting. These are Regular Army. You can't just shoot at one and expect the rest to run away."

Allenson kept his temper, albeit with difficulty. His purpose was to destroy Fort Revenge. To do that he had to win the Brasilians over to his point of view, not antagonize them.

"I see you have never fought Riders," he said, mildly. "But you mistake my meaning. I have no intention of trying to destroy the Terran column. I just have to delay it."

Levit's eyes defocused as she thought through the implications and probably the political implications.

"What have you got to lose, General Levit?" Allenson asked. "If the Militia fails, then it's hardly your fault, but if we succeed..."

He left the rest of the sentence hanging, tempting

Levit to imagine a victorious homecoming with cheering crowds, medals, and promotion.

"And if the Militia are destroyed in the attempt?" Levit asked.

"Would anyone on Brasilia notice, or care?" Allenson asked lightly.

Levit gave him a thin smile. "I see you have a shrewd grasp of politics, Colonel Allenson."

People kept saying that to Allenson. He was not sure if it was a compliment. He liked to think of himself as a straightforward gentleman of integrity. Political skills did not fit that self image.

"Very well, Colonel, I doubt your mission will succeed and I *advise* you not to attempt it. Nevertheless, we will continue marching on Fort Revenge, until such time that the matter is resolved, one way or the other."

Allenson noted Levit had used the weasel word *advise* rather than *order*. Politically, he was on his own. Failure would be laid at the door of enthusiastic but not overbright colonials. Success would erase the advice and it would be an army-sanctioned raid.

He remembered something from a book of quotes. An Old Earth politician had remarked that "Victory has a hundred fathers, and no one acknowledges a failure." Allenson had considered the saying overly cynical at the time.

"I will let you know when we have stopped them," Allenson said. He might as well sound confident, even brash, as he was likely to be dead if wrong, and past caring.

Mansingh was waiting for him in the outer office, and fell in behind as he left the command tent.

"Well?" Mansingh asked quietly.

"It's on," Allenson replied.

"Yes!" Mansingh punched the air, attracting curious glances. He hastily composed himself. "In that case, sir, there is someone I think you should meet."

"I don't have time to spare." Allenson warned.

"I have been talking to the major of Engineers, a chap named Josk," Mansingh said. "This way, sir." He pointed, stumbling on the uneven ground. "I went to see Josk about my leg. It's due for recalibration. I hoped that he had the right equipment."

"And did he?" Allenson asked.

"No such luck, but it's not bad enough to stop me going with you, sir," Mansingh said quickly, in case Allenson got the wrong impression. "I looked up those Old Earth combat vehicles that Major Destry described, the fighters. I mentioned them to Josk and he's come up with an idea."

"Go on," Allenson said, intrigued.

"Do you know how they mounted their guns on those antique fighters, sir?" Mansingh asked.

"Never thought about it. I suppose they hand-held the light ones and mounted the heaver weapons on some sort of gimbal and pivot mechanism, so they could swing it around," Allenson replied.

"Yes, sir, they did initially, but they needed heavier and heavier batteries of weapons and the vehicles were just single-seaters."

"So they used automatics," Allenson said.

"They did not have automatics," Mansingh said.

"Really? I thought the Third Civilization had automatics," Allenson said.

"No, sir," Mansingh said, in the sort of neutral tone one used when one's superior has lost the plot.

"Not that it matters. So how did they aim their guns?" Allenson asked, following his script.

"They bolted them to their fighters pointing straight ahead and aimed the whole vehicle, sir," Mansingh said excitedly. "Their fighters were fast and maneuverable so they simply lined up on the target. The vehicle was the weapon."

"And that worked?" Allenson asked.

"Oh, yes," Mansingh replied. "It meant that small vehicles could deploy firepower sufficient to destroy much larger targets. It also reduced parallax errors. Here we are, sir."

Major Josk was a short, stout man with a jutting chin that gave him a pugnacious air. His uniform lacked the gleam Allenson associated with Regular Army officers. When they arrived, Josk was fiddling with Mansingh's frame, with the help of a fitter. He casually wiped his hands on his uniform, before holding one out for Allenson to shake.

"Colonel Allenson, Major Josk," Mansingh did the formalities.

"What do you think?" Josk asked, gesturing at the frame.

A heavy spring gun was tied to each side of the frame's battery pack. They were mounted upside-down so the pilot could reach down and pull the triggers. A simple crosshair sight was bonded to the controls.

"It's a bit of a bodge, I'm afraid," Josk said. "Mansingh tells me it has to be a quick job, or I would do it properly. 'Fraid the ties will work loose after half a dozen shots and you'll lose accuracy, and they can only be reloaded after you land, and I can only mount two on each frame without causing too much extra drag."

Josk stopped for breath. Allenson reflected that to a proper engineer, all jobs were thrown together bodges.

"It's a brilliant idea," Allenson said, "utterly brilliant." He walked around the frame. "How many can you do in forty-eight hours?" Allenson asked.

"Well, if I train some of your people, then they can train the rest, and they can all do their own frames. It's only a bit of cement and friction ties, after all. I reckon a day should do it," Josk replied.

"All of them? And you have enough spare equipment?" Allenson asked.

"Good Lord, yes," Josk replied. "This is the Regular Army. We have enough spares to equip a division."

"I can't pay you," Allenson said.

"How would you pay me?" Josk asked rhetorically, spreading his arms. "The army has no mechanism for accepting payment, but campaigns are wonderful for losing stuff. I fully expect to have a vehicle crash in a day or so that will write off whole casefuls of spare guns—amongst other things."

He grinned cheerfully.

"And no one will query that?" Allenson asked.

"The paperwork will be fully in order," Josk replied happily.

Allenson halted all outgoing patrols until he had the entire Militia on base. He summoned the whole regiment and placed a supply box in the center of the parade, signaling the troopers to surround him. He used as little artificial amplification as practical, as he wanted each soldier to feel that he was being personally addressed.

"Fellow Streamers, I'm not a politician, so I'll keep

this short," Allenson said. A self-examining portion of his mind whispered something about a typical politician's lie. He told it to shut up.

"A Terran convoy, a relief force, is approaching Fort Revenge, drifting down the Hinterlands chasms. They think that they own the Hinterlands. I intend to teach them different."

He slid up the amplification. "Is anyone here frightened of Terrans?"

"No, sir, no colonel," came back as a series of replies.

"I can't hear you," Allenson said.

"No, sir," this time the reply was in unison.

"And Riders will be there. Anyone here have issues with killing Riders?" Allenson said.

"No, sir!" the men replied.

"I intend to lead a force of Stream Militia to smash the Terran convoy. There won't be room for the faint-hearted. Anyone who hasn't got the balls can stay here with the Regulars. So who's coming with me?" Allenson asked.

The troopers gave a huge cheer and clustered around Allenson, lifting him shoulder high. They were chanting something, something about Chernokovsky. The veterans wanted revenge for Chernokovsky's expedition and were carrying the newcomers along.

While the Militia's combat frames were converted, Allenson chaired a planning meeting with his company commanders and Destry.

"Our tactics will be to hit the Terran convoy in a stream of pinprick attacks. A stream can cut a groove in granite. We don't have to be able to destroy the Terran convoy; we simply have to delay it, or even better, turn it back. The best way to do that is to act as a constant irritant. Accordingly, we will attack in company strength on the conveyor belt principle. As one company is in combat, a second will be returning to base, a third taking off, and a fourth on standby. The other six companies will be sleeping, eating, carrying out maintenance, or hunting to eke out our rations."

"Half the regiment on active service at any one time sounds reasonable, but it will prove exhausting in the long run," Rutchett said.

"I know," Allenson replied. "But I don't think that there will be a long term. Someone will break after a few days. Our job is to make sure that it is them."

Allenson looked around the faces of his officers, wishing that he had had more time to assess and train the newbies. He would just have to trust them.

"Tactically, each squadron will operate individually. I want every Terran on that convoy to feel that he is personally under threat—that an attack on *him* could come at any time. I propose to set up a temporary base alongside the chasm being used by the Terrans. The question is where?" Allenson asked.

"Classical military strategy would be to set up a blocking position downstream of the convoy, so our logistic lines shorten with each skirmish," Rutchett said, "but I doubt we have the force to stop the Terrans bursting through our defenses."

Allenson shook his head. "I have no intention of placing the Militia in front of the Terrans and provoking a set piece encounter battle. That would be playing to their strengths and our weaknesses."

"Upstream," Mansingh said, firmly, "the base should be upstream. Our strength is mobility. From upstream we have the initiative, able to engage and break off combat at will."

"Yes, but..." said one of the newer captains, hesitantly. He broke off when all eyes turned on him.

"Carry on, Captain...Frong," Allenson said, nodding encouragingly. "The point of a council is for me to hear your opinions."

"Well, sir, frames returning from combat, possibly damaged or with a wounded pilot aboard, will have to travel through the Continuum, or in the turbulent back-eddy zones at the chasm walls. We could end up losing people to exhaustion or equipment failure."

"That's true," Allenson said, "but it can't be helped. So upstream then—anyone have any candidates?"

Hawthorn passed a file around the meeting. "I have," he said. "My company discovered a world. I believe it is suitable."

Allenson looked at the file on his datapad and winced. "I am awfully afraid that you are right. I see your people christened it Slimeball."

· CHAPTER 26 ·

Dancing In Flames

Slimeball by bloody name, Slimeball by bloody nature, Allenson thought. The planet was a water world, like Paragon, but the resemblance ended there. Evolutionary development was at an even lower level than Paragon. Life had gotten all the way to the photosynthetic algal slime level. The world ocean was clogged with the stuff. If anything fed on the slime, it was too small to see with the naked eye.

Slimeball was geologically inactive, so there were no mountains, just mud banks of various sizes rising out of the shallow seas. There was no rock, no stones, no terrestrial animals or plants. Apart from its strategic location, Slimeball was tactically suitable as a base. The single-seater combat frames could not carry much in the way of nonessential supplies and weapon reloads, so heavy equipment for building and defending forts was out. The mud bank was too small for an enemy to land and encircle them. Allenson was not going to repeat the mistake he had made at the first battle of Larissa. His only air defenses were detectors and the frames themselves, but Allenson was satisfied that they could take on anything capable of deploying onto the mudbank. But, oh God, it bloody stank.

He walked around the base with Destry, neither of them having direct responsibilities in its erection.

"Why does this bloody place smell so bad?" Allenson asked. "Is it the algae?"

"Oddly enough, no, at least not directly," Destry replied. "I wondered about that myself and did a little investigating."

"I thought you might," Allenson said, dryly.

Destry scraped his boot along the mud, revealing black organic matter just below the red-brown surface. A foul stench burst out.

"The reduced layer, just below the surface of the mud, is thick with methagenic and sulfur-reducing archaeons," Destry said.

"Indeed," Allenson said, clearly none the wiser.

"Primitive single cells," Destry explained happily, "too simple to be classed as bacteria. They have no organelles at all, just a cell wall. The feed by reducing organics to methane and hydrogen sulfide—you know, rotten-egg gas. They would have been driven down into the reduced layer of the mud after photosynthetic cells evolved. Oxygen is toxic to them.

"The source of the organic material that they feed on puzzled me," Destry said. "After all, there is no terrestrial life, but I worked it out. Algae must be washed up onto the mud and die."

"How?" Allenson asked. "The tidal range is minuscule and the planet is geologically inert, so no tsunamis. I checked before I chose the base."

Destry shrugged. "Who knows? I suspect that the

world is subject to meteorite bombardment at regular intervals. That would cause tsunamis. It would also explain why higher life never evolved and how the mud banks are formed." He beamed at Allenson like a man who had just explained the three-card trick.

"So we could face a tidal wave at any time?" Allenson asked, keeping his voice level with a certain amount of effort.

"I suppose so, but we're only going to be here a few days. We would have to be unlucky to get hit by something in that time."

Allenson filed the information under "things that nothing can be done about, so concentrate on what is tractable."

A trooper nearby sprayed stabilizer onto the mud to create a dry platform for a tent.

"At least the stabilizer will cut down the smell," Allenson said.

"Mmmm, probably not," Destry replied. "The archaeons will love it under the stabilized layer. They will bubble along happily, protected from the air. The smell could even get worse."

"Terrific," Allenson replied. He changed the subject. "I wanted to talk to you about something. I need a base commander to stay here and take control. You are the obvious choice with your administrative and evaluation skills, and you have the rank to enforce your orders on company commanders, if necessary."

Actually, Destry was the same military rank as some of the commanders but they both knew that Allenson meant his social rank.

"Stay here, and not fight with the rest of the regiment?" Destry asked.

"I discussed this, in confidence, with Hawthorn. He said you would not be happy," Allenson replied.

"Hawthorn was right. What about my honor?" Destry asked.

"No one would ever doubt your courage," Allenson said. He meant no one who mattered. "Hawthorn told me that he considers you one of the soundest fellows who ever lived. He could think of no one he would rather have alongside him in a fight."

"Hawthorn said that?" Destry asked, brightening.

"He did. Ask him if you like. He added that he has said as much to anyone who will listen, and he would regard any suggestion that you lacked courage as calling him a liar."

"Hawthorn conflated his own honor with mine?" Destry asked. "That is good of him."

"I add my own assurance to that." Allenson laughed. "Of course, as a civilized man I do not believe in dueling. However, I regret that I have never persuaded Hawthorn to that view."

"No, indeed," Destry said, grasping the point. "Very well, I will be your base commander."

Allenson let out a sigh of relief. In theory, he could have just given Destry an order but, equally, Destry could just resign his commission if he did not like said order. He meant everything he said about Destry's qualities, and he did need someone in charge on Slimeball, but he also feared for his friend's safety in a mass firefight. Destry was neither fit enough nor fast enough.

The turbulence was not too bad once they got into the main stream. Allenson's frame shook and bounced but made rapid progress down the chasm. He attached himself to Fifth Squadron of the Fourth Company, who were to make the first attack. The squadrons were well spaced so the first Allenson knew that they had contacted the enemy was when the squadron directly in front of him split off to leave the chasm. The plan was for all the squadrons to plunge more or less simultaneously onto the convoy at widely spaced points, offering minimum warning to the defenders.

Fifth Squadron reached the turn point. Allenson gritted his teeth and held on tightly as his frame smacked from current to current in the chasm wall. The frame's field compressed and distorted under the pressure, but held. He had every expectation that it would, but, well, stuff happens.

Out in the relative calm of the Continuum, the two flights of the squadron moved apart as they raced down the outside of the chasm. Allenson rode as an extra Tail End Charlie on the second flight. The flight leader rocked his frame and pointed. Orange spiral trails indicated the presence of Riders up ahead. The flight moved into the finger five formation that was their new tactical doctrine for combat with Riders.

Two beasts swung in on the left element of the flight. The pair of frames turned to the right, moving across the back of the flight leader, just as they had practised. The Riders took the bait, following the frames. The right hand element of the flight swung left, into the slot behind the Riders. The rearmost Rider noticed them and dropped away. The first element reversed their turn, moving back across the formation to the left. This allowed the remaining beast to close rapidly on them by cutting the corner. It also dragged the beast into a perfect no-deflection firing position for the second element.

Each militiaman carried four spring guns in holsters across his chest, and the second element fired a good half dozen. One bolt took the Rider between the shoulderblades, knocking him off the beast. His body disappeared in a shimmer of violet energy.

The flight leader blipped his shield and the flight reformed into a tight formation and headed for the seething coiled currents of the chasm wall. The second beast reappeared out of nowhere alongside Allenson. He cursed his lack of attention and fired a hasty shot at the Rider. It missed. The Rider ignored him and raced after the second element, obviously bent on revenge. Allenson could not keep up. He fired a second pistol without effect.

Then something odd happened. The beast swung away from the chasm wall and hesitated before renewing its pursuit of the second element. Allenson cut the corner. He drew a third pistol and resolved to fire only at point blank range. The beast wavered again, slowing. It did not want to enter the chasm. The Rider raged and struck it with the butt of his spear. The beast stopped and closed its crystals tightly, cutting the Rider from view. Then the crystals opened, spitting out a crushed body.

The flight survived the trip through the wall, emerging right on top of a transporter. The flight leader ignored it, turning down-chasm to chase the troop train in front. They slid in under the cars. At this range, the true size of the transports was apparent. They looked invulnerable, unstoppable.

Allenson maneuvered his frame to point the sight at the middle of a car's underbelly. It was so close that even he couldn't miss. He reached down and hit the trigger of his heavy spring gun. The bolt fired, recoil pulling the frame off course. He corrected, watching the bolt. It smashed into the floor of the car and deflected, breaking off a section of hull. He fired his second shot. This one hit more squarely, punching inside leaving just a small hole, but hopefully causing substantial damage to the interior.

Heavy guns discharged, the flight moved around the side of the car until they were level with the gallery windows. Terran troops leaned out, trying to see. The flight fired their spring pistols through the windows, knocking down enemy soldiers. A soldier fell upward out of a window, passing through the train's field. The seething energies of the chasm ripped his body apart before it vanished. The flight moved along the car, creating chaos. Allenson did not aim at anything in particular but just unloaded his pistols into the open windows on the grounds that they would feck up something. If there was any return fire, Allenson failed to see it.

The flight leader led them above the train, pausing so that they could reload their pistols and catch their breath. He signaled and they dropped to the other side of the car. There were met by ragged and inaccurate defensive fire. The flight weaved backward and forward to confuse the defenders, shooting all the time. More Terrans fell.

They slid under the car to find a safe place to reload once more, but defenders shot at them through gunports, forcing the frames to dodge. The flight leader decided that second flight had done enough that day and signaled a withdrawal. Outside the chasm, they reformed into a finger five and cruised home.

❖   ❖   ❖

Allenson climbed off his frame. He walked over to the command tent, trying to look officerial and not like a bowlegged mudhopper.

"How many back?" he asked Destry.

"Still a couple of stragglers and a few flights to go," Destry replied. "But from initial reports, our casualties are low. I am still assembling data to try to get a coherent picture of the battle, but it looks like a major victory."

Hawthorn's men clustered around excited Fourth Company troopers, who were no doubt bragging as only soldiers can. It was good for morale so Allenson let it go.

"We won't have it that easy in future. They will be ready for us next time," Allenson said.

"Which is why I have prepared a little surprise," Hawthorn said unexpectedly from behind, making Allenson jump.

"Your nerves are fraying," Hawthorn said, with a grin to show he meant no offense.

"Ha!" Allenson replied. He was too tired to think up anything clever in the way of repartee.

"What surprise?" Allenson asked, suspiciously. He knew Hawthorn surprises of old.

"Our friend Destry, here," Hawthorn gestured at the intelligence officer, "tells me it's called a Molotov cocktail after some Old Earth king."

"I've been looking up more archaic weapon systems, as we are specializing in ancient warfare," Destry said.

Hawthorn held a plastic bottle out for Allenson's inspection. It was filled with a light yellow clear liquid. He flipped the top and smelled it.

"It's tonk, bloody awful-smelling tonk," Allenson said.

"Well, you can't expect too much from something that uses algal slime and lubricating oil for a mash," Hawthorn said defensively.

"But where did you get it?" Allenson asked.

"From a still, where do you think?" Hawthorn asked.

"But I ordered the regiment to be dry on campaign," Allenson said.

"Oh, grow up," Hawthorn replied, in exasperation. "That just means that the men are sober on duty. You can't order them not to have a still any more than you can order them not to have impure thoughts."

"So who made the still?" Allenson asked, still annoyed.

"No idea," Hawthorn replied. "I simply let it be known to the NCOs that I needed fifty liters of tonk. Either it magically appeared outside of my tent in the morning, or I ripped the camp apart until I found a still."

Allenson shook his head. He must be tired. He was focusing on process rather than outcome, something he found all too easy when he was under pressure. What did it matter whether the men had a still, provided they did the business?

"So tell me what a Molotov cocktail does," Allenson said.

"I'll do better than that; I'll show you." Hawthorn said. "Let's go down to the water."

He fished a food heater out of his pocket. "You tape an igniter inside the neck of the bottle," he said. "Then it's simply a matter of setting a delay and throwing the thing."

"Throw it," Allenson said, disbelievingly. "What's our next secret weapon, flint axes?"

Hawthorn did not reply. He flicked the igniter

and slung the bottle out over the water, as if he were playing skipping stones. It bounced and ignited, exploding in flames that rolled across the sea, setting light to an algal mat.

"Imagine that inside a crowded troop transport," Hawthorn said, with a grin like a shark.

Allenson did not reply; he was imagining it.

Hawthorn's company mounted the third assault. Allenson accompanied them, riding with First Squadron, led by Hawthorn himself. Riders were conspicuously absent. Hawthorn's squadron emerged into the chasm in front of a troop transport. The Terran defenders were waiting. A hail of bolts greeted the Streamers. The Terrans crouched behind crenulated shields hung on the outside of the galleries. Fortunately, a fast-moving single-seater frame made a difficult target. Nevertheless, Hawthorn executed a rapid drop below the angle of fire and under the car. The rest of the squadron followed.

Allenson expected Hawthorn to fire his heavy bolts through the bottom of the car's hull, but Hawthorn continued to drop before reversing course and separating from the car to give maneuver room. Then he looped up level with the car's gallery. Terrans fired, but the range was too great for effective shooting.

Hawthorn slowed to allow the squadron to move into two lines, second flight echeloned behind the first. He gave the signal to charge. Allenson jammed his accelerator wide open, draining the small battery and pedaling furiously. This was no time for fuel conservation. He had no intention of letting anybody get in front of him. The range closed rapidly. Terrans fired wildly. The bolts seemed to be aimed wide, but whipped in close at the last minute as if they were actively hunting him. It was some sort of optical illusion but he still hunched down in his seat, trying to make himself smaller. Not an easy task, if you had Allenson's build.

The militiaman on his right took a bolt in the face and rolled off his frame, which curved gently away on its battery power. Still Hawthorn held his fire. On they pedaled. After a lifetime or so, when the troop car was so close that it hung in front of them like a castle wall, Hawthorn held his arm up high and whipped it down. The first echelon fired its heavy bolts in two waves. Some knocked down the gallery shields and some smashed through the hull, dislodging sheets of ceramic. Others flew through the gallery windows to disappear deep into the car. The defenders sought cover, ducking out of sight.

The first echelon pedaled furiously, drawing spring pistols. Two more waves of heavy bolts from the rear echelon struck, scattering the defenders. Hawthorn's flight was right on top of the car when the Terrans popped back up. The Streamers flew down the car, firing into the gallery. He drew and fired, drew and fired. Allenson concentrated on not accidentally shooting one of his own men. Experience gave him little reason for confidence in his skill with guns, but the car was a big target.

Second flight entered the fray, adding to the carnage. Hawthorn closed right up to the car until their Continuum shields nearly touched. He stood up on his pedals and tossed a Molotov through the gallery window. A fireball lit the interior. Other Streamers lobbed their bottles. It was difficult to throw with any accuracy from a frame, and most missed the windows. But many of these still exploded within the train's field, burning up oxygen and filling the air with smoke. Allenson's bottle hit the top of a heavy weapon. The fireball burst over the two-man crew, setting their clothes alight. One Terran threw himself out of the car in agony. The flames only went out when his body drifted out of the train's Continuum field.

While Hawthorn's company landed back at Slimeball, Captain Chang's waited their turn to attack. Militiamen stood by their frames. Some watched entertainments; others fiddled nervously with their equipment, rechecking everything. Allenson downloaded recordings from the third attack before he dismounted, passed it to Destry's datapad for evaluation, then walked toward the command tent with Hawthorn.

Destry met them at the door. "How did it go?"

"You have the data," Allenson replied.

"Yes, but I want your subjective opinion," Destry said.

"Very, very well," Hawthorn said. "The firebombs were a nasty surprise. God knows how many were burned and choked inside the cars." He slapped Allenson on the back. "Our friend here turned a gun crew all carboneezy, didn't you?"

"Yes, all carboneezy," Allenson said, flatly.

Outside, Captain Chang's company climbed into their frames. They had the word to go.

"We'll discuss it when I get back," Allenson said.

"Back from where?" Destry asked, with a theatrical display of puzzlement.

"Chang's attack, of course," Allenson said."I'm going with him."

"No," Destry said firmly.

"What?" Allenson asked.

"You are not going," Destry replied, enunciating each word clearly, as if talking to a retarded child. "You have already been on two attacks today, and that is one too many. There is no question of me allowing you to take part in a third."

"Allow?" Allenson asked, with heavy emphasis.

"Major Hawthorn, I am base commander, am I not?" Destry asked.

"Such is my understanding, Major Destry," replied Hawthorn.

"So what part of the title 'base commander' do you fail to understand?" Destry asked Allenson politely. He continued before Allenson could reply. "Before you suggest that you do not have to obey my orders because I am merely a major, in contrast to your own exalted rank of colonel, I should point out that I would regard a refusal on your part to obey me as tantamount to undermining my authority with the other officers."

Allenson opened his mouth to reply, but Destry still refused to allow him into the conversation. "In which case, I would feel obliged to resign my commission."

"Nothing else for it, your honor could dictate no other course," said Hawthorn sagely, nodding his head like an elderly lawyer confirming some obscure point.

"If you two clowns would stop ganging up on me and let me get a word in edgewise," Allenson said mildly, "I was merely going to say 'yes, sir.' I trust that is acceptable to everyone's honor?"

As it happened, Chang's company returned without firing a shot. The Terran convoy had grounded.

✧   ✧   ✧

Allenson was on a dark, cold plain facing writhing towers of fire. Heads poked out of the flames, screaming at him. The flames morphed in to burning people that staggered after him. He tried to run, but his legs would not work properly and the burning people surrounded him. One of them reached for him with arms of fire. It had Sarai's face.

"Steady on," Hawthorn said, ducking as a fist whistled past his ear. "All I did was give you a shake. No need to try to kill me."

"What?" Allenson asked.

He was on his bunk. Hawthorn held a torch pointed at the ground to illuminate Allenson's tent without blinding him.

"You were making quite a racket," Hawthorn said, helping himself to a stool. "Not good for the men's morale, hearing their commander scream, so I came to wake you up."

"I was having a nightmare," Allenson said defensively.

"You don't say," Hawthorn replied. "I thought you might like a drink."

He had a fire-bomb bottle in his right hand, and two glasses. Allenson looked at it suspiciously.

"Don't worry," Hawthorn said. "This is the good stuff, without the lubricant."

Hawthorn poured two glasses and passed one to his friend.

"Better knock it back in one go. You wouldn't want to actually taste it. To our wives and loved ones, may they never meet," Hawthorn said, holding up his glass and giving the old toast.

"We're not married," Allenson muttered, clinking his glass against Hawthorn's.

They downed the drink in one.

"Hell's teeth, that is bloody awful," Allenson said, when he had recovered the power of speech.

"Yes," Hawthorn agreed happily. "Fancy another?"

Allenson held his glass out for a refill. He took a sip, which was an error. Hawthorn was right. You definitely did not want to taste the stuff.

"Do you ever dream, Hawthorn?" Allenson asked.

"Oh sure," Hawthorn replied. "Only last night, in fact. I was in this bar and met this stunning girl, and she had a friend who could . . ."

Allenson listened to his friend reminisce. It was better than thinking.

"You know," Hawthorn said, some time later, emptying the last of the bottle into their glasses. "Some people are not cut out for this type of life. It's not a question of courage," he said quickly, "but of conscience. Some people feel things too deeply—care too much. Me, I just go with the flow. What's done is done." He gazed into his empty glass. "We seem to have run out. I could get another bottle?"

"No, we need to sleep," Allenson replied.

"Perhaps you're right. Goodnight, Allenson."

"Goodnight, Hawthorn, and thanks."

"No sweat. I hate drinking alone." Hawthorn paused at the entrance of the tent. "You should have an answer ready—in case Destry asks you why you were shouting his wife's name in the night. Just saying."

Destry never asked.

❖   ❖   ❖

They had half a day's respite before Streamer scouts reported that the Terrans had left their overnight camp, resuming their stately passage down the chasm. The Militia returned to the attack, one company at a time, initially using fresh troops that had not yet engaged. Allenson was persuaded to let the initial attack proceed without his presence, but he waited anxiously for their return with Destry.

"Now you know how it feels," Destry said.

"How what feels?" Allenson asked, watching the sky.

"How it feels to wait until the fighting men return," Destry replied.

Finally, the base alarm chimed, indicating that friendly frames were phasing in from the Continuum.

"There's the first squadrons," Allenson said pointing them out. He shielded his eyes with a hand from the sun's glare.

"The formations are ragged," Allenson observed. "I don't like the look of this."

Destry did not reply. More frames appeared and dropped down to the landing zone in untidy gaggles ranging in size from individual stragglers to formations of half a dozen or so.

"They are not in squadrons, or even flights," Destry said. "Something has gone wrong."

"Come on." Allenson said. His instinct was to break into a run, but that would be bad for the men's morale. It would suggest he was panicking. As it was, he walked so briskly that Destry had to half jog trot to keep up. He saw more than a handful of wounded men while looking for the company commander.

Allenson spotted a lieutenant; what was his name, Dougman or Krugman, something like that?

"Where's Captain Lai-Po?" Allenson asked the lieutenant.

"Lai-Po? He's dead. The bastards fired a bolt into his frame and it exploded. Just blew up, right in front of me." The lieutenant's voice rose as he spoke, until he was shouting.

"Attention, mister." Allenson snapped. "Have you forgotten how to salute a senior officer?"

The lieutenant straightened up and attempted a salute. The ritual steadied him and he responded much more calmly. "Sorry, sir."

"Make your report," Allenson said.

"We were ambushed, sir."

"Riders?" Allenson asked.

"No sir, Terrans. They had gunships hidden in the turbulence along the chasm walls. They turned in behind us when we made our attack run. Captain Lai-Po was hit almost immediately. We evaded, but that broke up our formations, so we attacked the convoy in dribs and drabs. The defensive fire could concentrate on each attack. The men did their best, sir, but we took casualties and never got close enough to use the Molotovs."

"Very good, lieutenant. Give my congratulations to your men for their bravery in pressing home their attack in such unfavorable circumstances. Download the data to Major Destry as a priority, and then look after the wounded."

"Yes, sir." The lieutenant saluted but did not move.

"Was there something else?" Allenson asked.

"Ah, yes sir," the lieutenant said, diffidently. "You said *my men*, sir."

"Your men, lieutenant. As of now you are acting company commander," Allenson replied.

The lieutenant saluted again and trotted toward the medical tent.

"Shall I call off the next attack until we work out a counter?" Destry asked.

Allenson was sorely tempted to agree, but they dare not lose momentum. He considered joining the attack himself, but that would achieve little other than make him feel more comfortable. It was more important to go over the data. Rutchett's company was next to go, and Rutchett was experienced.

"No, but warn Rutchett and tell him to leave the Molotovs behind. They won't get a chance to use them."

Destry shrugged. "The Molotovs don't take up much room. It might be worth carrying them just in case an opportunity arises."

"The Molotovs are bloody dangerous. Frames don't just blow up. What do you think killed Lai-Po?"

Allenson asked Hawthorn and Mansingh to an analysis meeting. Destry rapidly integrated the data from various frames to produce an accurate hologram of a Terran gunship for examination. They were flat rectangular boxes lined along each side with two rows of pylons to generate the Continuum field. Mansingh examined the model carefully. It had a crew of six that sat two abreast. The four men at the rear pedaled. The pilot sat at the right front and a gunner to his left manned a heavy spring gun on a complex pivot. It had high sides that hid all but the pedalers' heads, except at the bow.

"This isn't a Continuum combat frame," Mansingh said. "It's a light assault boat. Look, the side screens protect the pedalers from light weapons but stop them firing back. Only the gunner and the pilot have a field of fire and then not to the rear. The gunner can't even fire the heavy gun laterally to the right without the risk of killing the pilot. The convoy must have been delivering them to Fort Revenge, and they broke them out to use as escorts."

"They sprang a surprise on Lai-Po. That trick won't work again," Hawthorn said. He waved a hand dismissively at the gunship. "This thing is a sitting duck in a fight with single-seater frames." He mimicked a man potting a bird with a shotgun and flashed a cruel grin.

Hawthorn's confidence proved not to be misplaced. Rutchett's company suffered few losses and the Militia ran a series of attacks until the Terrans grounded. Allenson took part in one of the attacks. Casualties stayed low; the loose squadron formation of elements and flights was effective at detecting and driving off attacking gunships. The gunships never pressed their attacks but withdrew into defensive globes.

That night, Allenson held a council of war with the senior company commanders and Destry.

"Allenson asked me to analyze the latest Terran tactics and predict outcomes," Destry said.

Allenson smiled. Destry should call him Colonel Allenson, of course, but Destry wasn't a soldier and had no patience with military conventions. There were no disciplinary issues because everyone else took it for granted that normal rules did not apply to a Destry.

"The Terran gunships are reducing our effectiveness by disrupting attacks to a degree, but not enough to matter. That's not the problem. The problem, gentleman, is that we are losing."

CHAPTER 27

The Cauldron

Uproar greeted Destry's bombshell.

"Quiet, gentlemen, please," Allenson said. "Let Major Destry continue."

"Our casualties are light. We're eroding their numbers faster than ours, but make no mistake, gentlemen, we are losing."

"I don't understand," Hawthorn said.

"We cannot win a straightforward war of attrition. Yes, our losses are low at present, but our troops are tiring and will be exhausted long before the Terrans are. More importantly, we will run out of time. I remind you that the aim was to turn them back, not just reduce their numbers by some irrelevant amount."

Hawthorn sighed. "Perhaps we should change our strategy. Stop the pinprick attacks and gamble everything on one mass attack on the head of the column."

"There's too little chance of success." Allenson shook his head.

"I agree," said Rutchett. "There is nothing wrong

with our strategy." He shuddered. "Pinprick attacks
work. Ask anyone who fought with Chernokovsky."

"I do have a suggestion for a change in tactics,"
Destry said mildly.

They all looked at him expectantly and he flushed.

"That is, Mansingh and I have a suggestion," Destry
corrected himself with an academic pedantic precision
with respect to intellectual property rights.

"Oh no, you get the blame for this one," Mansingh
said. "All I did was act as a sounding board."

"Well..." Destry ran his hand through his hair.
"I was digging around in files on third civilization
air fighting tactics. I wondered whether there was
anything else there that we could use, since modern
Continuum combat appears to show such a striking
similarity..."

"And you found something," Allenson said encouragingly, wondering why his friend was behaving so
diffidently.

"Yes," Destry replied. "Our problem is that we
are not damaging the Terran *vehicles*. They're much
larger than those used in Chernokovsky's expedition.
We are like Riders circling a fortified settlement. We
can cause casualties, but that's all. We need to stop
the vehicles—correct?"

"Correct," Allenson said.

"Mansingh has illustrated the weak spot for us."
Destry waved his datapad and a troop train hologram
filled the command tent.

"Key to the new tactics are the power cars. Knock
one out and you stop a whole train. The batteries
and field generators would be prime targets, but we
don't know their exact position, and they may be

armored. But there is one component that is visible, vulnerable, and unarmored." He walked around the hologram to the front.

"The pilots, gentlemen. Kill the pilots, smash up the controls, and you stop the whole damn train. And I have an idea how to guarantee success—we make head-on massed attacks with *Sturmböcke* tactics."

"Sturm-whata?" Hawthorn asked.

"We strip the heavy guns off half our frames and add them to the others, giving them four-gun firepower, and we rig it so all guns fire on a single trigger."

"The overloaded frames will be clumsy and easy meat for gunships," Rutchett said.

"So we escort them with the lightened frames, one escort squadron for each heavy squadron."

"You mentioned mass head-on attacks," Allenson said.

"Sure," Destry replied. "A whole squadron attacks together in a tight formation. It lays down concentrated fire on the nose of a power car or supply transports at minimum range with a no-deflection shot. Every attack will smash in like the hammer of god, killing crewmen and wrecking the control systems. If we get lucky, the weight of fire will run the length of the car until a bolt hits a battery or something equally sensitive."

"Of course, the defenders will have a no-deflection shot back at the attacking squadron," Hawthorn said, dryly.

"Yes," Destry agreed, somewhat deflated. "There will be casualties, but the number of defending gunports in the bows of the cars must of necessity be limited. There just isn't much room." He lifted his chin. "But there will be casualties. I volunteer to lead the first attack."

"Declined," Allenson said. "You are too valuable in your present role."

"As one of the originators, I should lead the attack," Mansingh said.

"Agreed," Allenson replied, "and I will come with you."

Allenson lead a stormbuck squadron, as the men christened the modified frames, ignoring all pleadings from his senior officers. The thing was a pig, heavy on the controls and slow, requiring constant pedaling. They saw a few Riders, but the savages refused to engage the lightened escort frames. This seemed to be the pattern. Riders might pick off wounded stragglers returning from combat, but they were disinclined to go head-to-head with the Militia after the first day.

Allenson was bloody tired by the time they reached the combat zone. He doubted his troopers could make many attacks in the clumsy stormbucks.

The squadron became disorganized passing through the turbulence of the chasm wall, and time was lost reforming for the attack. The stormbucks moved up the center of the chasm toward the train. Gunships tried to intercept them, but they were pounced on by the light escort squadron.

Allenson pedaled on, sweating hard. The stormbuck squadron closed remorselessly on the power car's bow. Guns poked through opened ports to fire at them. A stormbuck was hit, dropping back into realspace.

Allenson concentrated on the job in hand, focusing his attention on the target. He could see the glowing outline of the car's field. Chasm turbulence streamed off the front of the field, tumbling down the side of the car. He lifted the nose of his frame until the sight rested on the cabin window. He could see the Terran pilot's chalk-white face staring. Allenson fired, the rest of the squadron firing more or less in unison.

He was so close that his frame's Continuum field began to glow from energy leakage from the train's field. Allenson heaved desperately on the control stick, as if muscle power could turn the frame. It lurched under him, much more maneuverable after discharging its weapons, and he slid across the bow of the power car.

Allenson rotated the frame, trying to keep the car in view. Bolts scythed into the bow, leaving splashes of energy where they penetrated the train's field. Great chunks of hull came free, spinning down.

A frame failed to pull out. Maybe the pilot was hit, or perhaps he just misjudged the distance, but his frame's field contacted the car's in an explosion of blue-white light that Allenson could still see with his eyes closed. When he opened them, the Militia frame was gone, and the power car was on fire.

The bow rose and twisted to the left, pulling the first towed car to the right. When the power car hit the chasm wall it shuddered, halted, and slid backward. The rear cars kept on coming, folding up like a concertina. The tangled mess drifted back across the chasm and stuck in the far wall, rotating about a common center of gravity. The linkage holding the rear car broke and it tumbled down the chasm.

It was the most wonderful, god-awful mess that Allenson had ever seen. His second-in-command pulled alongside and jabbed his arm down the chasm. More gunships were on their way and the light escort squadron had disappeared. The other stormbucks had also vanished. One minute he was surrounded by frames, and then there was just him and his faithful wingman. It was time to go.

The Terrans grounded again, having made little progress toward Fort Revenge. The mood among the men in the Militia camp that night was jubilant. Allenson was hailed and cheered when he walked to the command tent. He noticed Sergeant Jezzom amongst the revellers and signaled him over.

"We showed them, sir," Jezzom exclaimed.

"Yes, Jezzom, we did. I understand that the men need to party and, God knows, they've earned it, but there will be more fighting. We've won a battle, not the war. I need the men sober and ready in the morning. Can I rely on you and the other warrant officers?"

"Yes, sir," Jezzom saluted. "You can."

"Carry on, Jezzom," Allenson said.

The mood at the company commanders' briefing was more somber.

"Casualties?" Allenson asked.

"Close to eighteen percent of those engaged," Destry replied. "Most were lost, but there was the usual trickle of wounded. One man brought his wounded wingman back as a passenger."

"How did they manage that?" Allenson asked, genuinely puzzled.

"The wingman's frame was damaged, but he successfully grounded on a world with a biosphere and his element leader landed and took him off. We might find more survivors on worlds along the attack path if we mount a systematic search," Destry replied, shrugging.

"Maybe after the battle," Allenson said.

He did not bother to add "if any of us survive." His audience were neither stupid nor out of touch with reality.

"The casualty rate is worrying. Is that the result of the new tactics?" Allenson asked.

"Partly. The highest losses were in the stormbuck squadrons," Destry replied. "But I think it's also down to exhaustion. The men are so tired that they are making mistakes."

"Yes, I know," Allenson said. He felt it himself. It was not fear he associated with battle so much as total bloody exhaustion.

"I suspect some of the men are close to battle fatigue," Rutchett said. "One of my troopers couldn't take his place in the last attack. He shot himself in the foot loading his spring pistol. He claimed it was an accident, of course."

"What did you do with him?" Allenson asked, curious.

"Put him in the hospital tent with the other wounded. What else could I do?" Rutchett asked. "It could have been an accident."

"I've got men throwing up before getting on their frames," Mansingh said.

"Very well, gentlemen, I want you to remove around forty percent of your men as a strategic reserve. Form them into shadow companies to act as guards to patrol over the base. That way they won't have to enter the chasm. Select the men who are experiencing problems. We can bleed them back into the combat companies as they recover, if they recover. I think we can make one more bow attack, albeit at reduced strength, before our offensive capability is blown."

"Permission to ask a question, sir?"

"Yes, Mister Krugman," Allenson replied.

"We gave them one hell of a kicking today. Won't they see sense and retreat?" Krugman asked.

"Well, it's always convenient if the enemy do what you want," Allenson replied. "But it would be optimistic to rely on their cooperation."

Someone chuckled, making Krugman blush.

"These are Terran Regulars. They may just push on to spite us," Rutchett said.

"I don't think so," Mansingh said.

They all looked at him.

"Krugman's right, we did hit them hard today. For all they know, we have unused fresh reserves ready to do it all over again tomorrow. They don't know how close to breaking we are. I don't think they will just press on. If I were the Terran commander, I would forget about trying to swat wasps and clean out the nest once and for all."

"They will attack our base?" Allenson asked.

"I would in their position," Mansingh replied. "Their Rider allies must have located us by now."

"They we had better prepare for evacuation. Major Destry, please select a suitable world upstream and prepare a base there. You can use the reserve troops. It would be quite convenient if the Terrans followed us back out of Brasilian territory, leaving Levit to capture Fort Revenge. With luck, we may have fired our last bolt, gentlemen."

"What about the wounded?" Destry asked.

"Leave them here in a clearly marked hospital tent," Allenson replied. "We are not facing Riders, gentlemen. The Terrans are not barbarians."

❖   ❖   ❖

Neither Mansingh nor Allenson proved to be absolutely correct. Given the choice of pushing on, retreating, or making a mass attack on the Militia base, the Terran commander found a fourth option. Most of the Terran convoy stayed grounded, but three trains with two supply vehicles lifted in tight formation escorted by every gunship the Terrans could muster. The assault force traveled laboriously up the chasm.

Allenson recognized the logic of the Terran plan. They couldn't get enough men into the gunships alone to guarantee success in a ground attack on the Militia base, but adding three train troop transports gave the assault force a strength of around four thousand men. Allenson was down to about six hundred, perhaps eight if he added the walking wounded and battle-shocked. The gunships should be able to mount a close protection on just three trains. Meanwhile, the bulk of the convoy was perfectly safe on the ground behind its automated defenses.

The Terrans had come up with a perfectly workable plan, but Allenson felt a surge of excitement. The enemy had split his command in the face of the enemy, just as Chernokovsky had done at the second battle of Larissa. He had a chance to defeat the Terrans in detail. The slow speed of the Terran assault force gave him time, time to reorganize and plan an ambush.

There were no stones, flat or otherwise, on Slimeball, but Allenson spun a crust of syncrete that had flaked off the edge of the landing apron. It bounced once on the slimy surface of the sea before submarining with a plop. The viscous surface quickly damped down the resulting ripples.

"Do you have a plan yet?" Hawthorn asked, from behind him.

"Hello, Hawthorn. I didn't hear you arrive," Allenson replied.

"That's because I did not want to disrupt the Colonel's mighty thought processes," Hawthorn said.

"A plan—well; I intend to attack," Allenson said.

"I assumed that," Hawthorn replied. "The question is how."

"I considered a surprise attack on the assault force's base," Allenson said.

"Bloody suicide," Hawthorn interrupted him.

"And rejected it as impractical," Allenson said, ignoring the interruption.

"Damn right," Hawthorn said. "An attack on a base that undoubtedly has automatic defenses, while outnumbered four or five to one. Please. We're good, but no one's that good."

"So we hit them in the chasm, but not pinprick attacks this time. There are too many escorts for just three trains for that strategy to work. I intend to hit them in regiment strength in two separated waves. The first will go for the trains."

"Why the trains? Surely the escorts should be the first target?" Hawthorn asked.

"No, there are too many. We lighten all the frames and the first wave goes in against the trains in independent squadrons. I want an endless hit and run. Keep dragging the gunships after you. Make the bastards sweat. Exhaust the crews, and drain the batteries. It would be a positive advantage if you can kill some of the troops on the trains, but it is not your primary goal. Withdraw when your men tire. We can't afford too many casualties."

"So, I am to command the first wave," Hawthorn said, with satisfaction.

"Unless you can think of someone better?" Allenson asked.

"No," Hawthorn replied succinctly. Hawthorn had many vices but they did not include false modesty.

"I will lead the second wave. We will go after the escorts and kill the bastards. They will be tired and low on power and ammo, while we will be fresh. The escorts are the key to this, not the troop trains. Without escorts the trains are near helpless."

"What a disgustingly evil plan," Hawthorn said.

Allenson flushed. "If you think it stains our honor not to fight fairly—"

"Screw our honor," Hawthorn replied, cutting in. "I like to win, and it's a welcome bonus if I have a reasonable chance of survival while doing so. Fair fights are for the mentally retarded."

Allenson gave the combat companies another day's rest while the reserve evacuated the camp. By that time the Terran assault force had set up base camp on a nearby world for their supply vehicles. This meant the tired Militiamen had short transit times to the combat zone. He launched the attack when his scouts reported that the assault force had entered the chasm again.

Battlegroup Allenson gave Battlegroup Hawthorn an hour's start before phasing into the Continuum. They entered the chasm and pedaled down the main channel, encountering the Terran assault force barely an hour later. The three trains were linked into a single structure moving slowly along the eddy back currents near the chasm wall. The long line of cars snaked and rotated around a constantly changing center joint of mass, buffeted by turbulence.

Hawthorn's squadrons weaved in and around the cars, sniping at the crews. They used the chasm wall like a smokescreen, retreating through it when pressed only to reappear unexpectedly further along. Gunships chased up and down the line, trying to seal off each new incursion. From a distance the battle looked like wasps around a hive.

The first wave squadrons disengaged and withdrew when they spotted Allenson's force. Instead of retreating out of the chasm, they withdrew up the eddy channels, pursued by the bolder gunship crews. Some of the gunship crews spotted Allenson's frames and fled but others kept going, fixated on their apparently fleeing foe.

Allenson led his frames down the center of the chasm until they were alongside the pursuit. In a single skirmish line, his squadrons turned and sliced into the outnumbered gunships, who finally noticed them, and broke and scattered in all directions.

A gunship turned and attacked the element on his left. It immediately turned right, leading the enemy across Allenson's front. He slid left, crossing its rear, firing all his pistols into the hull, and then he dropped back to reload while his wingman shot up the vehicle. The gunship tried to evade by breaking hard and turning in to his wingman, who backed off from the lethal heavy gun on the bow. This presented the gunship's rear to the original element, who took full advantage of the opportunity. The gunship's turn degenerated into a spiral and it spun out of control into the chasm wall.

Allenson's flight reformed into a finger four and pulled back into the center of the chasm to reload. He checked the area for hostiles, but the flight was alone. That was something that happened in Continuum combat. One minute you were surrounded by other frames, both friendly and enemy, and the next, there was nothing. Rearmed, he led the flight down-chasm to reengage.

More flights ducked and weaved around the gunships in defensive circles. Some of Hawthorn's force had reengaged, ignoring orders. No doubt they had followed Hawthorn's example.

Ahead, six gunships formed a tight wheel that was rotating just fast enough to maintain steerage and hold formation. The wheel turned clockwise so the gunners were on the outside, giving the maximum field of fire for their main weapon. A Militia element inserted itself into the wheel behind a gunship, shooting into the backs of the pedalers. The next gunship in the line closed up and fired the multiple shot heavy spring gun into the Militia wingman in a single burst. The frame's field collapsed and it dropped out of the Continuum. Allenson hoped the pilot had been killed by a bolt. He would have an unpleasant death if still alive when he appeared unprotected in realspace.

Allenson slid below the plane of the wheel and made a right-angled attack on a gunship, aiming for the gunner, who stood up to return fire. Allenson's frame-field flared when a bolt passed through, clanging off the side of a storage unit without causing critical damage. He carried on into the center of the wheel, out of the field of fire. He checked behind. His wingman and another pair of Militia frames followed him.

He pedaled across the diameter of the circle and turned counterclockwise, running around the inside of the wheel firing at the pilots as he passed each gunship. Allenson's attack would have been suicidal if all the Terran pilots had kept their nerve, and rotated to bring their guns to bear inside the wheel, but he gambled on someone panicking and breaking formation. When they did, it was every man for himself, conditions that favored the maneuverable Militia frames. By the time he reached the third in line the wheel disintegrated, gunships breaking in all directions. The Militia pounced.

Streamer flights and elements piled in, harassing gunships from multiple sides. Gunships fled for the illusory safety of the triple train formation. Frames followed all the way, weaving and ducking. The train crews fired into the melee, more likely to hit their own gunships than the Streamers.

Allenson drew back to assess the situation. The remaining gunships, and there were not that many, hung close in to the troop trains for protection, in a reversal of roles. Streamers engaged the train crews, firing into the galleries. A Militiaman sneaked in close and tossed a Molotov through a gallery window. Allenson recognized Hawthorn's distinctive field streamers.

This was turning into a battle of attrition with the troopers on the train, something Allenson wanted to avoid. He had no replacements and couldn't take heavy casualties without destroying what remained of his own combat capability. He blipped his frame, signaling withdrawal. Squadron and flight leaders repeated the signal and the Streamers withdrew up the chasm. The demoralized crews of the surviving gunships let them go unmolested.

They exited the chasm near their old base. Destry had scouts waiting to guide them through the Continuum to their temporary base. Most of Hawthorn's squadrons had already grounded when they arrived. The base was on a rocky crag projecting out of a swampy rainforest. It was hardly ideal—there was no water for one thing—but at least they could not be overlooked or surprised.

The air around Fort Crag, as the troops christened it, was heavy with the smell of mold and fungal spores. Destry insisted that they were harmless but Allenson was not so sure. However, he anticipated a short stay. It wasn't as though they intended to live there. Nevertheless, they were still on Fort Crag two days later and nothing had happened.

"Any word from the scouts?" Allenson asked.

"No," Hawthorn replied. "The Terrans are just sitting there on Slimeball."

The Terrans had captured Slimeball unopposed. As far as Allenson was concerned, they were welcome to it.

"Why don't they come after us?" Destry asked. "They still outnumber us considerably and our men are exhausted. We're also running out of bolts, just to add to our problems. It would be touch and go whether we could force the troop transports down again."

"Yes, but they don't know that," Mansingh replied.

"The enemy is always ten feet tall. They're probably judging our combat capability on earlier battles. They must have lost two thirds of their gunships, so they probably think they risk annihilation if they lift."

"Whereas we risk destruction if we attack their camp at Slimeball. They not only outnumber us, but they have automatics on point defense. You may recall, gentleman, that we chose to put the base on Slimeball because it offered no convenient landing and assembly point for an attacker," Destry said.

Allenson felt numb. His brain refused to work. He listened to the discussion without comment, letting it slide over him like a gentle breeze.

Rutchett moved and winced. A bolt had broken his left arm in the last battle. It was rigged up in a healing pod with pain suppressors, but they did not remove all sensation. A patient could do real damage to a limb that way. The pod allowed him to move at the elbow and shoulder to keep the joints from seizing, so some degree of discomfort was inevitable.

"So we have a standoff, which suits us just fine," Rutchett said. "Our job was to stop the Terrans reaching Fort Revenge before Levitt, not to destroy them."

"True," Mansingh said, "And I doubt the Terran main force will proceed until they receive word that we have been destroyed. They have no gunships at all. The Terran commander is probably having nightmare visions of running into a massed frame attack without any escorts to protect his transports."

"So we sit and wait it out," Rutchett said. He moved his arm around until the pod rested on a side table.

"That might work," Mansingh said.

"You sound unconvinced," Rutchett said.

"Well, it occurs to me that if we are no longer attacking, the Terrans on Slimeball might conclude that they have us treed, and send a messenger to tell the main force that they can resume the trip down-chasm to Larissa," Mansingh said.

There was a long silence.

Allenson ran his hand through his hair. He was sick of the arguments. He was sick of the war. The thought that the enemy had them pinned and that it had all been for nothing was intolerable. He wanted an end, one way or the other, right now.

Hawthorn put his hands behind his head and tilted his chair back. He gave a sharklike grin.

"I dunno, all these great military strategists and none of you play Cheat," he said. "I must invite you to a real bar sometime. Bring plenty of cash. I don't take IOUs."

They gave him a blank look.

"Look," Hawthorn said, "in Cheat what matters is not what cards you have in your hand, but what cards you can psych your opponent into believing you have. We need to convince the Terrans that we are still a major threat—yes?"

"That would be good," Allenson replied.

"And we can't attack their combat base because it's too well protected, yes?"

"Yes," Allenson replied again, irritated at playing the straight man. He was on a very short fuse. "So?"

"So, why don't we shoot up the assault force's supply depot? My scouts report that it is only lightly manned by troops, although it has air-defense automatics. Most of the people there are civilians and logistic troops."

"But it's not really a military target," Mansingh said. "It's . . ." He stopped.

"Helpless?" Hawthorn asked. He shook his head. "You bloody officers and gentlemen will be the death of me. Yes, it's helpless. When attacked, they will send messengers to scream for help from the combat force on Slimeball and, if we're lucky, the Terran main force. Believe me, estimates of our numbers and ferocity will lose nothing in the telling."

Hawthorn let his chair fall back on all fours with a thud and lit up a cigarette. He shut his eyes and blew smoke rings up to the roof of the tent.

Allenson gazed at Hawthorn in admiration. Lethargy and despair dropped from his shoulders. He felt revitalized.

"We can assemble about four hundred effectives for the raid. It will only take a day to go down-chasm to get there. We will take only laserifles, chargers, and combat rations. Hawthorn's scouts will have to guide us into landing grounds that are close to the base, but outside of the point defense zone. Any questions?" Allenson asked.

"Yes," Destry said. "One way or another, this is likely to be our last battle of the war, and I wish to participate. I suggest that Major Rutchett and I swap duties, as he is wounded. He commands the base and I command his company."

"Now wait a minute," Rutchett said hotly. He half rose, winced, and sat down again.

"Major Destry's right, and you know it, Pietr," Allenson said, using Rutchett's personal name to soften the blow.

"I suppose so. But you look after my company, Destry."

"You have my word," Destry assured him.

✧   ✧   ✧

Allenson lay on his stomach and surveyed the Terran supply depot though his datapad. They had held the depot under siege for three days. The Terrans had chosen a flat prairie, presumably to give a free field of fire to the automatics. The only problem with that was that the autos had a minimum angle of depression that was well above the height of a man.

Two big supply transports sat on wide skids sunk deep into the ground, with bunkers in a circle around them. Wheeled tractors and trailers lay destroyed around the camp. One still burned, greasy smoke curling into the air. Every so often, a malfunctioning automatic identified the smoke as an attacker and fired at it, laser bolts whipping the smoke on convection currents.

The Militia were concentrated on one side of the camp where a slight incline gave them an angle of fire, but it was still under the Terran autos' field of fire. They shot up the base, killing anything that moved. After three days of laserifle bombardment, little did move. The Terrans were driven into their bunkers. The Militia shot up the tracking equipment on the autos. Allenson doubted that any of them were working properly, but it would be foolish to ask someone to find out the hard way. They shot through the open hatches on the transports, trying to set them alight. Twice they got a fire going, but it soon went out.

The Terrans abandoned the crew-served heavy weapons on top of the bunkers when the heavy rain of laser fire whittled down the crews, so the Militia shot at the weapons instead. They were a difficult target, but they were going to damage something if they fired enough rounds.

Conditions within the bunkers must be getting unpleasant. A handful of Terrans had fled into the prairie from the unguarded side. Allenson let them go. It would have suited him if the whole garrison ran away. There was nowhere for them to go. He did call massed fire onto anyone trying to leave by frame. It would have been disastrous if enemy reinforcements arrived prematurely. Escape attempts by frame stopped after half a dozen spectacular explosions. Maybe they had run out of frames. More likely, they had run out of men willing to try.

Defensive fire had dwindled to the odd pot-shot.

Allenson was tired. He was so tired that his joints didn't ache anymore from lying on the hard ground. He hadn't slept properly for days. He was dirty and sweaty, and an aromatic oil in the vegetation had set off a rash on his face and arms that itched horribly. Scratching made it worse. He had had enough.

He tried to decide if the camp had been softened up sufficiently for an assault. How could he know, except by trying? If he went too soon and enough Terrans manned crew-served weapons still functioning . . . hell, they were dead and at least he would get some rest without that bloody rash itching. Bugger it! He couldn't bloody care anymore. He just wanted it over.

He stood up and examined the base with his datapad. Lights winked at the bunkers where Terrans shot at him. Bugger them as well!

He walked toward the Terran base, rotating his gun off his shoulder and firing a short burst in the general direction of the enemy. Hawthorn, Destry, and the other company commanders followed. Man by man the Militia got up and followed without a word. Soon the whole regiment was on the move, men rising from concealment like rabbits from a warren.

Destry caught up with him, offering a cigarette. For once, Allenson accepted, pausing for Destry to give him a light. He drew a lungful of smoke and examined the blue sky.

"Going to be another nice day, Destry," Allenson said. "Do you think it ever rains here?"

"I suppose it must, sometimes," Destry replied. "Or all the plants would die."

"Good point," Allenson said.

They walked on. Terran fire picked up, becoming more accurate with every meter they covered.

A Terran shot caused a patch of grass near Allenson's foot to blacken under a hit. He noticed that it burned with blue and green flames. There must be some interesting biochemistry in the plant oils. No wonder it irritated his skin. He made a mental note to take some back for proper analysis after the war.

Hawthorn's companies dropped prone, returning fire into the bunkers. After they had gone another hundred meters, Allenson's troops dropped to give covering fire and Hawthorn's advanced through them. Allenson remained standing. He told himself that it would steady his troops but actually, he just couldn't be bothered to drop down only to get up again. It would only set the bloody itching off.

Two or three of Hawthorn's troops were hit. It was never like the theater. Shot soldiers never died gracefully or fell in acrobatic dives. They just dropped, like cutting the strings on a puppet. The actors never got it right.

At a hundred meters to go Allenson started to gently

jog, firing from the hip to intimidate the defenders. The whole regiment trotted behind him. At twenty meters he broke into a run and started to scream. He headed for a bunker. A light winked on and off in the firing slit. His world contracted until there was just the bunker, then just the firing slit, then just the flash of laserifle fire.

He put his rifle barrel though the slit and fired a burst. There was another flash and something burned his hip. He fired again, a long burst this time, swinging the barrel from side to side.

He stopped to reload his rifle. He did not want to find out the hard way when the battery was empty. With careful deliberation he ejected the old charge and rammed another home, double checking the latch.

A Militiaman pushed past him, climbing over the bunker. A second later he slid back down on his face, arms and legs loose. Another trooper fired a long raking burst into the bunker, setting something alight.

Allenson walked around the bunker, penetrating the defensive ring. Militia troopers moved in front of him, scuttling forward, bent low, guns held out like magic talismans to deflect laser bolts.

The ground was peppered with foxholes and open-topped dugouts. His troops checked a pit in front of him, pointing guns over the edge. Someone down in the dugout shouted something Allenson did not hear. The troops hesitated for a moment, and then passed on. Allenson rechecked the dugout when he reached it. Terran personnel huddled at the bottom, some in uniform, some not. None presented a threat so he left them unharmed.

The assault pressed on. Miliitiamen fired into the

next dugout. Allenson ran to join them. Three Terrans lay at the bottom of the pit, all dead from repeated laser hits at close range. One had his hand on a gun. Maybe he meant to use it, maybe he didn't. Whatever, he had doomed both himself and his unarmed companions.

The Streamers spread out, moving through the base.

A woman in civilian clothes popped out of a bunker and shot a young lieutenant.

Allenson aimed his gun. She dropped her pistol and raised her hands in the air. Allenson hesitated. A trooper shot her down with a sustained burst. She fell back into the dugout with her clothes alight. Other troopers ran to the dugout and fired down into it on full auto, raking the pit until the screaming stopped.

Allenson checked the lieutenant. A tiny wound in his forehead marked where a pellet had entered his skull. He was very dead, killed by a woman with a popgun. The round could have gone anywhere.

That was the way they cowed the camp. They spared the harmless but shot everyone where they encountered resistance. Possession of a weapon was resistance.

Allenson approached a dugout, carbine at high port. A rifle flew out. He peered carefully over the edge, gun ready. A Terran soldier lay unconscious at the bottom, the back of his head bleeding. A bloodied stone lay nearby, a woman clutching a child.

Allenson gave her what was supposed to be an encouraging smile, but she regarded him with horror. He picked up the abandoned laserifle and pushed it muzzle first into the dirt, ruining its optics.

Bodies lay unburied across the base. Most had been killed during the bombardment, but not all. Most were Terrans, but not all.

A Streamer ran up to one of the base's point defense guns with a whoop of glee. He fired at point blank range into the mechanism. Reflected back-blast burned off his face and blackened his uniform. He ran around wildly, screaming, until someone shot him. A sergeant with more sense thrust a combat knife into the automatic's innards, shorting out its mechanism in a shower of sparks.

Men ran into the nearest transport, some reappearing with civilians. Troopers pushed the prisoners down into a dugout. There was the sound of an exchange of fire from the second transport and only Streamer troopers came out.

Allenson kicked down the door of what he took to be the command bunker. An elderly, bald man in a senior officer's uniform looked at him in dismay. He had a pistol in a sealed holster on his belt but made no move to extract it. Allenson gestured him away from the signals gear. The old man soiled himself, but didn't move.

Allenson pushed him away. Backing up, he fired a burst into the communications, angling the gun so that the reflected blast went upward, setting fire to the wooden roof. A hologram of a pretty young woman with children sprang into focus above the burning equipment.

She smiled at Allenson. Was she the commander's daughter and grandchildren? Something knowing in her smile suggested that she was more likely to be his mistress. The console exploded in another shower

of sparks and the hologram winked out. He dragged
the old man out by the collar of his uniform and left
him sobbing by the burning bunker.

Smoke swirled across the camp. One of the transports was on fire. The sun lit up the tip of a silver fin
that projected out of the smoke, catching his attention. Allenson forced himself back to the battle, to
assess the overall situation. It took an almost physical
effort to do this.

The base was overrun with Militia. No Terrans were
visible—well, no living Terrans. Anything that could
be smashed had been. It was time to go before the
enemy realized that they still outnumbered the raiders two or three to one and some hero organized a
counterattack. He got out his datapad and gave the
withdrawal signal to his officers. Streamers withdrew
in small groups as they got the word, one man always
walking backward to cover the group's rear.

The precaution proved necessary when a "body" sat
up and reached for a gun. Fire from a dozen rifles
turned him back into a body. A trooper stopped to fire
another round into the corpse at close range, kicking
away the corpse's rifle, just to be on the safe side.

Allenson relaxed somewhat when they left the
enemy base. He waited to see his men safely out,
watching them stream back across the prairie. One
or two were assisted by comrades. The last trooper
had withdrawn and he was about to follow when the
hum of a vehicle caught his attention. A small transport frame rose over a bunker. Allenson lowered his
weapon when he recognized the driver. The frame
settled down beside him.

"Wanna lift?" Hawthorn asked.

"You silly sod, I nearly shot you," Allenson replied.

"You'd have missed," Hawthorn said, crushingly.

Allenson climbed aboard but did not deign to reply, not least because he probably would have missed.

"Where on earth did you find this?" Allenson asked as they lifted.

"It was dug in round the back of one of the transports. The previous owner kindly said I could have it. At least, he didn't say I couldn't."

Hawthorn gave one of his trademark innocent boyish grins.

"What have you got there?" Allenson asked, gesturing at some boxes in the loading rack.

"Who knows? Some decent plum brandy would be welcome," Hawthorn said.

They opened the boxes back where they had left their frames. It wasn't plum brandy. They had a fine selection of motivational posters extolling the might and glory of the hereditary Chancellor of Terra, a box of garden ornaments, and several cases of prophylactics.

The Streamers took their time going home to Fort Crag. They world-hopped, stopping to rest and hunt. The first stop was for several days to give the wounded and exhausted time to recover. The regiment was a spent force. Allenson himself could do no more, and he did not want to lose any of his people pointlessly in a forced march. He did not bother to do a head count to work out the casualties. The lost were lost. The mission had been successful. He told himself that was all that mattered. He also told himself that he was a liar.

They returned to find Fort Crag in an uproar. Men were openly drinking and dancing around the base. Allenson discovered a male and female trooper locked in an intimate embrace outside the command tent. A trooper shoved a bottle of something disgusting in his face. He shoved the man aside.

"Major Rutchett, what the hell is going on here..." he began.

Rutchett was with a guest, a lieutenant dressed in the uniform of the Perseverance Regiment, who threw him an enthusiastic salute.

"Dispatches from General Levit, sir," said the lieutenant.

Allenson gave him a blank look. He was so tired that he just could not bother to speculate.

"We've won, sir. Victory. The General has captured Fort Revenge, and the Terrans are retreating up the chasm," said the lieutenant.

Hawthorn stuck his head through the tent flap. "You didn't bring any plum brandy with you, by any chance?"

· EPILOGUE ·

The victory parade in the Plaza at the heart of Manzanita City ended. Militia soldiers in their resplendent dress uniforms, designed by Allenson a lifetime ago, broke into clusters surrounded by their friends and relatives in formal clothes. It was astonishing how easy it was to persuade the legislature to vote the money for dress uniforms for a victory parade, when Allenson considered how difficult it had been to get them to fund decent weapons. Everyone loved a party. Everyone loved a winner.

Vice-Governor Fontenoy presented new colors to the regiment, adorned with battle honors won in the campaign, and medals had been liberally distributed. Allenson had the Freedom of the City, allowing him to graze sheep within its boundaries if he so desired, assuming he had any sheep.

"I think that went rather well," Fontenoy said to Allenson as they watched troops leave. "What are your plans for the future?"

"I intend to resign my commission," Allenson said.

"I've done enough soldiering for one lifetime. I intend to retire from public life and devote myself to family business. Speaking of which; if you will excuse me, governor—I intend to start immediately."

Leaving an open-mouthed Fontenoy, Allenson walked briskly to join a colorful group that included the Destry family and Trina Blaisdel with her children and their nanny. He drew Trina to one side. It had taken him a great deal of nerve to initiate this conversation so he dived straight in without preliminary small talk. After all, Trina had said she liked him to be himself.

"Lady Blaisdel," Allenson said. "If you approve, I propose to send my representatives to meet yours with a view to drawing up a marriage contract."

Trina gave his hand a squeeze. "With all my heart," she said simply.

Allenson looked over her shoulder. Sarai had buried her head in Royman's chest while he tried to comfort her. Linsye looked him in the eye and nodded slightly, like one who had put her money on a promising young horse in the three-thirty and seen her judgement confirmed.

Allenson looked into the sky. The setting sun was blood red. Steam venting from an interworld ship twisted across its disc like the black shadow of a figure—a figure dancing in flame.

The following is an excerpt from:

CAPTAIN VORPATRIL'S ALLIANCE

LOIS McMASTER BUJOLD

Available from Baen Books
November 2012
hardcover

Chapter One

Ivan's door buzzer sounded at close to Komarran midnight, just when he was unwinding enough from lingering jump lag, his screwed-up diurnal rhythm, and the day's labors to consider sleep. He growled under his breath and trod unwillingly to answer it.

His instincts proved correct when he saw who waited in the aperture.

"Oh, God. Byerly Vorrutyer. Go away."

"Hi, Ivan," said Byerly smoothly, ignoring Ivan's anti-greeting. "May I come in?"

Ivan took about a second to consider the, at best, complicated possibilities Byerly usually trailed in his wake, and said simply, "No." But he'd hesitated too long. Byerly slipped inside. Ivan sighed, letting the door slide closed and seal. So far from home, it was good to see a familiar face—just not By's. *Next time, use the security screen, and pretend not to be here, eh?*

Byerly padded swiftly across the small but choice living quarters of Ivan's downtown Solstice luxury flat, rentals by the week. Ivan had picked it out for its potential proximity to Solstice nightlife, which, alas, he had so far not had a chance to sample. Pausing at the broad glass doors to the balcony, Byerly dimmed the polarization on the seductive view of the glittering lights of the capital city. Dome, Ivan corrected his thought to Komarran nomenclature, as the arcology existed under a hodgepodge of seals to keep the toxic planetary atmosphere out and the breathable one in. Byerly pulled the drapes as well, and turned back to the room.

Yielding to a curiosity he knew he would regret, Ivan asked, "What the hell are you doing on Komarr, By? Isn't this off your usual beat?"

Byerly grimaced. "Working."

Indeed, an experienced observer, which Ivan unfortunately was, could detect a distinct strain around By's eyes, along with the redness from drink and perhaps recreational chemicals. Byerly cultivated the authentic look of a Barrayaran high Vor town clown given over to a life of dissolution and idle vice by actually living it, ninety percent of the time. The other ten percent, and most of his hidden income, came from his work as an informer for Imperial Security. And ninety percent of that was just more dissolution and vice, except for having to turn in reports at the end. The residue, Ivan had to concede, could get dicey.

Ratting out your friends to ImpSec for money, Ivan had once heckled By, to which By had shrugged and replied, *And the greater glory of the Imperium. Don't forget that.*

Ivan wondered which it was tonight.

In reflexive response to the manners drilled into him in his youth, Ivan offered, "Something to drink? Beer, wine? Something stronger?" He contemplated By's boneless flop onto his living room couch. "Coffee?"

"Just water. Please. I need to clear my head, and then I need to sleep."

Ivan went to his tidy kitchenette and filled a tumbler. As he handed it to his unwelcome guest, By said, "And what are you doing in Solstice, Ivan?"

"Working."

By's open hand invited him to expand.

Ivan sat across from him and said, "Trailing my boss, who is here for an Ops conference with his assorted counterparts and underlings. Efficiently combined with the annual Komarr Fleet inspections. All the excitement of a tax inventory, except in dress uniform." Belatedly, Ivan realized By had to already know all this. He'd found Ivan, hadn't he? Because By's random social calls, weren't.

"Still working for Admiral Desplains?"

"Yep. Aide-de-camp, secretary, personal assistant, general dogsbody, whatever he needs. I aim to make myself indispensable."

"And still ducking promotion, are you, Captain Vorpatril?"

"Yes. And succeeding, no thanks to you."

By smirked. "They say that at Imperial Service Headquarters, the captains bring the coffee."

"That's right. And I like it that way." Ivan only wished it were true. It seemed barely months ago, though it was over a year, that the latest flare-up of tensions with Barrayar's most traditional enemy, the Cetagandan Empire, had pinned Ivan to military headquarters 26.7 hours a Barrayaran day for weeks on end, sweating out all the most horrific possibilities. Designing death in detail. War had been averted through non-traditional diplomacy, mostly on the part of Barrayaran emperor Gregor's weaseliest Imperial Auditor and, to give credit where it was due, his wife.

That time. There was always a next time.

Ivan studied Byerly, who was only a few years older than himself. They shared the same brown eyes, dark hair, and olive skin common to Barrayar's somewhat inbred military caste, or aristocracy, whatever one wanted to call it, and, indeed, common to most Barrayarans. By was shorter and slighter than Ivan's six-foot-one, broad-shouldered fitness, but then, he didn't have a Desplains riding him to keep up the recruiting-poster appearance expected of an officer serving at Imperial Headquarters. Granted, when they weren't squinting from the dissolution, By's eyes had the startling beauty that distinguished his famous, or infamous, clan, to which Ivan was connected by a few twigs in his own family tree. That was the problem with being Vor. You ended up related to all sorts of people you'd rather not be. And they all felt free to call on you for favors.

"What do you want, Byerly?"

"So direct! You'll never become a diplomat that way, Ivan."

"I once spent a year as assistant military attaché to the Barrayaran Embassy on Earth. It was as much diplomacy as I cared for. Get to the point, By. I want to go to bed. And by the looks of you, so do you."

By let his eyes widen. "Why Ivan! Was that an invitation? I'm so thrilled!"

"Someday," Ivan growled, "I might say yes to that old line, just to watch you have a coronary."

By spread his hand over his heart, and intoned wistfully, "And so I might." He drained his water and gave over the vamping, the face so often arranged in a vague smarminess firming intently in a way Ivan always found a touch disturbing. "Actually, I have a little task to ask of you."

"Figured."

"It's quite in your line. I may even be said to be doing you a good turn, who knows. I'd like you to pick up a girl."

"No," said Ivan, only in part to see what By would say next.

"Come, come. You pick up girls all the time."

"Not on your recommendations. What's the catch?"

Byerly made a face. "So suspicious, Ivan!"

"Yeah."

By shrugged, conceding the point. "Unfortunately, I'm not entirely sure. And my duties with, if I may say it, the unusually unpleasant people I am presently accompanying—"

Spying on, Ivan translated this without difficulty. And the company By kept was usually unpleasant, in Ivan's opinion. *Unusually* unpleasant implied . . . what?

"—leave me little opportunity to check her out. But they have an inexplicable interest in her. Which I suspect is not friendly. It worries me, Ivan, I must say." He added after a moment, "She's quite well-looking, I assure you. You need have no fear on that score."

Ivan frowned, stung. "Are you implying I'd refuse to supply assistance to a homely girl?"

Byerly sat back, eyebrows flicking up. "To your credit, I actually don't believe that's the case. But it will add a certain convincing verisimilitude for the outside observer." He pulled a small plastic flimsy from his jacket and handed it across.

The background was too fuzzed to make out, but the picture showed a striking young woman striding down a sidewalk. Apparent age could be anything between twenty and thirty standard-years, though that was no certain clue as to real age. Tumbling black hair, bright eyes, skin glowing an interesting cinnamon brown against a cream tank top. Decided nose, determined chin; either the natural face she was born with, or the work of a real artist, because it certainly didn't bear the stamped-from-the-same-mold blandness of the usual body sculpture, a biological ideal that lost its appeal with repetition. Long legs in tan trousers that hugged in all the right places. A nicely full figure. *Nicely* full. If the face was natural, might the other prominent features be, too? With weakening reluctance, Ivan said, "Who is she?"

"Supposedly, a Komarran citizen named Nanja Brindis, lately moved to Solstice from Olbia Dome."

"Supposedly?"

"I have reason to suspect that might be a recent cover identity. She did move here about two months ago, it does seem."

"So who is she really?"

"It would be a fine thing if you could find that out."

"If she's hiding her identity for a good reason, she's hardly going to tell me." Ivan hesitated. "Is it a good reason?"

"I suspect it's a very good reason. And I also suspect she is not a professional at the game."

"This is all pretty vague, Byerly. May I remind you, my security clearance is higher than yours."

"Probably." Byerly blinked in doubt. "But then there is that pesky need-to-know rule."

"I'm not sticking my head into one of your dodgy meat grinders—*again*—unless I know as much as you know. At *least*."

Byerly flung up his well-manicured hands in faux-surrender. "The people I'm with seem to have got themselves involved in a complex smuggling operation. Rather over their heads."

"Komarr local space is a major trade nexus. The place is lousy with smugglers. As long as the transients don't try to offload their goods within the Imperium, in which case Imperial Customs deals sharply with 'em, they get ignored. And the Komarran trade fleets police their own."

"That's two out of three."

Ivan's head came up. "The only thing left is the Imperial fleet."

"Just so."

"Crap, Byerly, if there was even a hint of that sort of thing going on, Service Security would swoop in. Damned hard."

"But even Service Security needs to know where and when to swoop. I am doing, as it were, a preliminary pre-swoop survey. Not only because mistakes are embarrassing, especially if they involve accusations of Vor scions with arrogant and powerful relatives, but because they tip off the real crims, who then promptly escape one's tediously set net. And you've no idea how tedious that can get."

"Mm," said Ivan. "And once military personnel get involved with, they think, simple civilian crime, they become vulnerable to more treasonous blackmail."

By bared his teeth. "I'm so pleased you keep up. One of your saving graces."

"I've had practice." Ivan hissed alarm. "Desplains should know about this."

"Desplains will know about it, in due course. In the meanwhile, try to remember you *don't* know." Byerly paused. "That caution is cancelled, of course, should my dead body turn up in a lewd and compromising position in some ditch outside the dome in the next few days."

"Think it might?"

"The stakes are very high. And not just the money."

"So how's this girl connected, again?"

Byerly sighed. "She's not with my crew. She's definitely not with the non-Barrayarans they're dealing with, though it's not outside the realm of reason that she could be a defector. And she's not what she pretends to be. What's left, I am forced to leave to you to find out, because I can't risk coming here again, and I'm not going to have time in the next few days for side-issues."

Ivan said slowly, "You think she's in danger of her

life?" Because why else would By bother to set even a side-friend on this side-issue? By didn't make his living through charity.

But he did make his living through a weird sort of loyalty. And, somewhere underneath the persiflage, camouflage, and just plain flage, he was high Vor of the highest...

"Let's just say, you would gratify me by staying alert. I should not care to explain any accidents that might befall you to your lady mother."

Ivan allowed the concern with a rueful nod. "So where am I to find this so-called girl?"

"I am fairly certain she's a real girl, Ivan."

"You think? With you, one never knows." He eyed By dryly, and By had the grace to squirm just a bit, in acknowledgement of his cousin Dono née Donna of lamented memory. Donna, that is. Count Dono Vorrutyer was all too vivid a presence, on the Vorbarr Sultana political scene.

By dodged the diversion and, so to speak, soldiered on, though the idea of By in any branch of the Service made Ivan wince in imagination. "She works as a packing clerk at a place called Swift Shipping. Here's her home address, too—which was unlisted, by the way, so unless you can devise a convincing reason for turning up there, probably better to run into her coming into or out of work. I don't gather she does much partying. Make friends, Ivan. Before tomorrow night, by preference." He rubbed his face, pressing his hands to his eyes. "Actually—by tomorrow night without fail."

Ivan accepted the contact data with misgivings. By stretched, rose a bit creakily to his feet, and made his way to the door. "Adieu, dear friend, adieu. Sweet dreams, and may angels guard your repose. Possibly angels with clouds of dark curls, sun-kissed skin, and bosoms like heavenly pillows."

"Dry up."

By grinned over his shoulder, waved without turning around, and blew out.

Ivan returned to his couch, sat with a thump, and picked up the flimsy, studying it cautiously. At least By was right about the heavenly pillows. What else was he right about? Ivan had an unsettling premonition that he was going to find out.

Tej was conscious of the customer from the moment he walked in the door, ten minutes before closing. When she'd started this job a month ago, in the hopes of stretching her and Rish's dwindling resources, she'd been hyperaware of all customers who entered the shop. A job that exposed her directly and continuously to the public was not a good choice, she'd realized almost at once, but it had been the entry-level position she could get with the limited fake references she commanded. A promotion to the back office was mentioned, so she'd hung grimly on. It was being slow in opening up, though, and she'd wondered if her boss was stringing her along. In the meanwhile, her jagged nerves had slowly grown habituated. Till now.

He was tall for a local. Quite good looking, too, but in a way that fell short of sculpted or gengineered perfections. His skin was Komarran-pale, set off by a long-sleeved, dark blue knit shirt. Gray multi-pocketed sleeveless jacket worn open over it, indeterminate blue trousers. Shoes very shiny yet not new, in a conservative, masculine style that seemed familiar but, annoyingly, eluded recognition. He carried a large bag, and despite the time, noodled around looking at the displays. Her co-clerk Dotte took the next customer, she finished with her own, and the fellow glanced up and stepped to the counter, smiling.

"Hi, there"—with difficulty, he dragged his gaze from her chest to her face—"Nanja."

It didn't take that long to scan her nametag. *Slow reader, are you? Why, yes, I get a lot of those.* Tej returned the smile with the minimum professional courtesy due a customer who hadn't, actually, done anything really obnoxious yet.

He hoisted his bag to the counter and withdrew a large, asymmetrical, and astonishingly ugly ceramic vase. She guessed the design was supposed to be abstract, but it was more as if a party of eye-searing polka dots had all gotten falling-down drunk.

"I would like this packed and shipped to Miles Vorkosigan, Vorkosigan House, Vorbarr Sultana."

She almost asked, *What dome?* but the unfamiliar accent clicked in before she could make that mistake. The man was not Komarran at all, but a Barrayaran. They didn't get many Barrayarans in this quiet, low-rent neighborhood. Even a generation after the conquest, the conquerors tended to cluster in their own enclaves, or in the central areas devoted to the planetary government and off-world businesses, or out near the civilian or military shuttleports.

"Is there a street address? Scanner code?"

"No, just use the scanner code for the planet and city. Once it gets that far, it'll find him."

Surely it would cost this man far more to ship this... object to a planet five wormhole jumps away than it was worth. She wondered if she was obliged to point this out. "Regular or premium service? There's a stiff price difference, but I have to tell you, express won't really get there much faster." It all went on the same jumpship, after all.

"Is it more likely to arrive intact with premium?"

"No, sir, it will be packed just the same. There are regulations for anything that goes by jumpship."

"Right-oh, regular it is."

"Extra insurance?" she said doubtfully. "There's a base coverage that comes with the service." She named the amount, and he allowed as it would do. It was in truth considerably less than the shipping charges.

"You pack it yourself? Can I watch?"

She glanced at the digital hour display over the door. The task would run her past closing time, but customers were fussy about breakables. She sighed and turned to the foamer. He stood on tiptoe and watched over the counter as she carefully positioned the vase—a glimpse of its underside revealed a sale tag with four markdowns—closed the door, and turned on the machine. A brief hiss, a moment of watching the indicator lights wink hypnotically, and the door popped back open, releasing a pungent whiff that stunned her sense of smell and masked every other scent in the shop. She bent and removed the neat block of flexifoam. It was an aesthetic improvement.

Ivan Vorpatril, read the name on his credit chit. Also with a Vorbarr Sultana home address. Not just a Barrayaran, then, but one of those Vor-people, the conquerors' arrogant privileged class. Even her father had been wary of—she cut the thought short.

"Do you wish to include a note?"

"Naw, I think it'll be self-explanatory. His wife's a gardener, see. She's always looking for something to stuff her poisonous plants into." He watched her slide the foam block into its outer container and affix the label, adding after a moment, "I'm new in town. Yourself?"

"I've been here a while," she said neutrally.

"Really? I could do with a native guide."

Dotte closed out the scanners and turned off the lights as a broad hint to the laggard customer. And, bless her, lingered by the door to see Tej safely free of the shop and him. Tej gestured him out ahead of her, and the door locked behind them all.

The oldest human habitation on the surface of Komarr, Solstice Dome had a peculiar layout, to Tej's eye. The aging initial installations resembled the space stations she'd grown up in, with their labyrinths of corridors. The very latest sections were laid out with separate, street-linked buildings, but under vast, soaring, transparent domes that mimicked the open sky the residents hoped to have someday, when the atmospheric terraforming was complete. Middling areas, like this one, fell between, with much less technologically ambitious domes that still gave glimpses of an outside where no one ventured without a breath mask. The passage that Swift Shipping fronted was more street than corridor, anyway, too broad for the persistent customer to easily obstruct her.

"Off work now, huh?" he inquired ingenuously, with a boyish smile. He was a bit old for boyish smiles.

"Yes, I'm going home." Tej wished she could go home, really home. Yet how much of what she'd known as home still existed, even if she could be magically transported there in a blink? *No, don't think those thoughts.* The tension headache, and heartache, were too exhausting to bear.

"I wish I could go home," said the man, Vorpatril, in unconscious echo of her thought. "But I'm stuck here for a while. Say, can I buy you a drink?"

"No, thank you."

"Dinner?"

"No."

He waggled his eyebrows, cheerfully. "Ice cream? All women like ice cream, in my experience."

"No!"

"Walk you home? Or in the park. Or somewhere. I think they have rowboats to rent in that lake park I passed. That'd make a nice place to talk."

"Certainly not!" Ought she to invent a waiting spouse or lover? She linked arms with Dotte, pinching her in silent warning. "Let's go to the bubble car stop now, Dotte."

Dotte gave her a surprised look, knowing perfectly well that Tej—Nanja, as she knew her—always walked home to her nearby flat. But she obediently turned away and led off. Vorpatril followed, not giving up. He slipped around in front, grinned some more, and tried, "What about a puppy?"

Dotte snorted a laugh, which didn't help.

"A kitten?"

They were far enough from Swift Shipping now that customer politeness rules no longer applied, Tej decided. She snarled at him, "Go away. Or I'll find a street patroller."

He opened his hands in apparent surrender, watching with a doleful expression as they marched past. "A pony...?" he called after them, as if in one last spasm of hope.

Dotte looked back over her shoulder as they approached the bubble-car station. Tej looked straight ahead.

"I think you're crazy, Nanja," said Dotte, trudging with her up the pedestrian ramp. "I'd have taken him up on that drink in a heartbeat. Or any of the rest of the menu, though I supposed I'd have to draw the line at the pony. It wouldn't fit in my flat."

"I thought you were married."

"Yes, but I'm not *blind*."

"Dotte, customers try to pick me up at least twice a week."

"But they aren't usually that incredibly cute. Or taller than you."

"What's that have to do with anything?" said Tej, irritated. "My mother was a head taller than my father, and they did fine." She clamped her jaw shut. *Not so fine now.*

She parted company with Dotte at the platform, but did board a bubble car. She rode to a random destination about ten minutes away, then disembarked and took another car back to a different stop on the other side of her neighborhood, just in case the man was still lingering out there, stalker-like, at the first one. She strode off briskly.

Almost home, she started to relax, until she look up and spotted Vorpatril lounging on the steps to her building entrance.

She slowed her steps to a dawdle, pretending not to have noticed him yet, raised her wristcom to her lips, and spoke a keyword. Rish's voice answered at once.

"Tej? You're late. I was getting worried."

"I'm fine, I'm right outside, but I'm being followed."

The voice went sharp. "Can you go roundabout and shake him off?"

"Already tried that. He got ahead of me somehow."

"Oh. Not good."

"Especially as I never gave him my address."

A brief silence. "Very not good. Can you stall him a minute, then get him to follow you into the foyer?"

"Probably."

"I'll take care of him there. Don't panic, sweetling."

"I'm not." She left the channel open on send-only, so that Rish could follow the play. She took her time closing the last few dozen meters, and came to a wary halt at the bottom of her steps.

"Hi, Nanja!" Vorpatril waved amiably, without getting up, looming, or lunging for her.

"How did you find this place?" she asked, not amiably.

"Would you believe dumb luck?"

"No."

"Ah. Pity." He scratched his chin in apparent thought. "We could go somewhere and talk about it. You can pick where, if you like."

She simulated a long hesitation, while calculating the time needed for Rish to get downstairs. Just about... now. "All right. Let's go inside."

His brows shot up, but then his smile widened. "Sounds great. Sure!"

He rose and politely waited while she fished her remote out of her pocket and coded open the front entrance. As the seal-door hissed aside, he followed her into the small lift-tube foyer. A female figure sat on the bench opposite the tubes, hands hidden in her vest as if chilly, voluminous patterned shawl hiding her bent head.

A slender gloved hand flashed out, aiming a very businesslike stunner.

"Look out!" Vorpatril cried, and, to Tej's bewilderment, lurched to try to shove her behind him. Uselessly, as it only cleared the target for Rish. The stun beam kneecapped him neatly, and he fell, Tej supposed, the way a tree was said to, not that she'd ever witnessed a tree do such a thing. Most of the trees she'd seen before she'd fetched up on Komarr had lived in tubs, and did not engage in such vigorous behavior. In any case, he crashed to the tiles with a vague thrashing of upper branches and a loud *plonk* as his head hit. "Owww..." he moaned piteously.

The quiet buzz of the stunner had not carried far; no one popped out of their first floor flat door to investigate either that or the thump, alarming as the latter had seemed to Tej.

"Search him," Rish instructed tersely. "I'll cover you." She stood just out of reach of his long but no doubt tingling arms, aiming the stunner at his head. He eyed it woozily.

Tej knelt and began going through his pockets. His athletic appearance was not a façade; his body felt quite fit, beneath her probing fingers.

"Oh," he mumbled after a moment. "You two are *t'gether*. Thass all right, then..."

The first thing Tej's patting hand found was a small flimsy, tucked into his breast pocket. Featuring a still scan of her. A chill washed through her.

She seized his well-shaved jaw, stared into his eyes, demanded tightly: "Are you a hired killer?"

Still weirdly dilated from the stun nimbus, his eyes were not tracking quite in unison. He appeared to have to think this question over. "Well...in a *sense*..."

Abandoning interrogation in favor of physical evidence, Tej extracted the wallet he'd flashed earlier, a door remote much like her own, and a slender stunner hidden in an inner pocket. No more lethal weaponry surfaced.

"Let me see that," said Rish, and Tej obediently handed up the stunner. "Who is this meat really?"

"Hey, I c'n answer that," their victim mumbled, but fell prudently silent again as she jerked her aim back at him.

The top item in the wallet was the credit chit. Beneath it was a disquietingly official-looking security card with a heavy coding strip identifying the man further as one *Captain Ivan X. Vorpatril, Barrayaran Imperial Service, Operations, Vorbarr Sultana.* Another mentioned such titles as *Aide-de-Camp to Admiral Desplains, Chief of Operations*, with a complicated building address featuring lots of alphanumeric strings. There was also a strange little stack of tiny rectangles of heavy paper, reading only *Lord Ivan Xav Vorpatril*, nothing else. The fine, black, raised lettering bumped under her curious fingertips. She passed them all up for Rish's inspection.

On sudden impulse, she drew off one of his polished shoes, which made him twitch in a scrambled reflex, and looked inside. *Military* issue shoes, aha, that explained their unusual style. 12 Ds, though she couldn't think of a reason for that to be important, except that they fit the rest of his proportions.

"Barrayaran military stunner, personally coded grip," Rish reported. She frowned at the handful of IDs. "These all look quite authentic."

"Assure you, they are," their prisoner put in earnestly from the floor. "Damn. By never mentioned any lethal blue-faced ladies, t' ratfink. Izzat...makeup?"

Tej murmured in uncertainty, "I suppose the best cappers would look authentic. Nice to know they're taking me seriously enough not to send cut-rate rental meat."

"Capper," wheezed Vorpatril—was that his real name? "Thass Jacksonian slang, innit? For a contract killer. You expectin' one? That 'splains a lot..."

"Rish," Tej said, a sinking feeling beginning in her stomach, "do you think he could really be a Barrayaran officer? Oh, no, what do we do with him if he *is*?"

Rish glanced uneasily at the outside door. "We can't stay here. Someone else could come in or out at any moment. Better get him upstairs."

Their prisoner did not cry out or try to struggle as they womanhandled his limp, heavy body into the lift tube, up three flights, and down the corridor to the corner flat. As they dragged him inside, he remarked to the air, "Hey, made it inside her door on t' first date! Are things lookin' up for Ma Vorpatril's boy, or what?"

"This is not a date, you idiot," Tej snapped at him. To her annoyance, his smile inexplicably broadened.

Unnerved by the warm glance, she dumped him down hard in the middle of the living room floor.

"But it could be," he went on. "...To a fellow of certain special tastes, that is. Bit of a waste that I'm not one of 'em, but hey, I can be flexible. Was never quite sure about m'cousin Miles, though. Amazons all the way for him. Compensating, I always thought..."

"Do you ever give up?" Tej demanded.

"Not until you laugh," he answered gravely. "First rule of picking up girls, y'know; she laughs, you live." He added after a moment, "Sorry I triggered your, um, triggers back there. I'm not attacking you."

"Dead right you're not," said Rish, scowling. She tossed shawl, vest, and gloves onto the couch, and dug out her stunner again.

Vorpatril's mouth gaped as he stared up at her.

A black tank top and loose trousers did not hide lapis lazuli–blue skin shot with metallic gold veins, platinum blond pelt of hair, pointed blue ears framing the fine skull and jaw—to Tej, who had known her companion and odd-sister for her whole life, she was just *Rish*, but there were good reasons she'd kept to the flat, out of sight, ever since they'd come to Komarr.

"Thass no makeup! Izzat...body mod, or genetic construct?" their prisoner asked, still wide-eyed.

Tej stiffened. Barrayarans were reputed to be unpleasantly prejudiced against genetic variance, whether accidental or designed. Perhaps dangerously so.

"'Cause if you did it to yourself, thass one thing, but if somebody did it *to* you, thass...thass just *wrong*."

"I am grateful for my existence and pleased with my appearance," Rish told him, her sharp tone underscored by a jab of her stunner. "*Your* ignorant opinion is entirely irrelevant."

"Very boorish, too," Tej put in, offended on Rish's behalf. Was she not one of the Baronne's own Jewels?

He managed a little apologetic flip of his hands—stun wearing off already? "No, no, 's gorgeous, ma'am, really. Took me by surprise, is all."

He seemed sincere. He hadn't been expecting Rish. Wouldn't a capper or even hired meat have been better briefed? That, and his bizarre attempt to protect her in the foyer, and all the rest, were adding to her queasy fear that she'd just made a serious mistake, one with consequences as lethal, if more roundabout, as if he'd been a real capper.

Tej knelt to strip off his wristcom, which was clunky and unfashionable.

"Right, but please don't fool with that," he sighed. He sounded more resigned than resistant. "Tends to melt down if other people try to access it. And they make issuing a replacement the most unbelievable pain in the ass. On purpose, I think."

Rish examined it. "Also military." She set it gingerly aside on the nearby lamp table beside the rest of his possessions.

How many details had to point in the same direction before one decided they pointed true? *Depends on how costly it is to be mistaken, maybe?* "Do we have any fast-penta left?" Tej asked Rish.

The blue woman shook her head, her gold ear-bangles flashing. "Not since that stop on Pol Station."

"I could go out and try to get some…" Here, the truth drug was illegal in private hands, being reserved to the authorities. Tej was fairly sure that worked about as well as it did anywhere.

"Not by yourself, at this hour," said Rish, in her *and no backtalk* voice. Her gaze down at the man grew more thoughtful. "There's always good old-fashioned torture..."

"Hey!" Vorpatril objected, still working his jaw against the stun numbness. "There's always good old-fashioned *asking politely*, didja ever think of that?"

"It would be bound," said Tej to Rish, primly overriding his interjection, "to make too much noise. Especially at this time of night. You know how we can hear Ser and Sera Palmi carrying on, next door."

"Houseless grubbers," muttered Rish. Which was rude, but then, she'd also had her sleep impeded by the amorous neighbors. Anyway, Tej wasn't sure but that she and Rish qualified as Houseless, too, now. And grubbers as well.

And that was another weird thing. The man wasn't yelling for help, either. She tried to decide if a capper, even one who'd had the tables so turned upon him, would have the nerve to bluff his way out past an influx of local police. Vorpatril did not seem to be lacking in nerve. Or else, against all the evidence, he didn't think he had reason to fear them. Mystifying.

"We'd better tie him up before the stun wears off," said Tej, watching his tremors ease. "Or else stun him again."

He did not even try to resist this process. Tej, a little concerned for that pale skin, vetoed the harsh plastic rope from the kitchen stores that Rish unearthed, and pulled out her soft scarves, at least for his wrists. She still let Rish tug them plenty tight.

"This is all very well for tonight," said Vorpatril, observing closely, "especially if you break out t' feathers— do you have any feathers? because I don't like that ice cube thing—but I have to tell you, there's going to be a problem come morning. See, back home, if I didn't show up for work on time after a night on the town, nobody would panic right off. But this is Komarr. After forty years, assimilation into the Imperium's going pretty well, they say, but there's no denying it got off to a bad start. Still folks out there with grudges. Any Barrayaran soldier disappears in the domes, Service Security takes it up seriously, and quick, too. Which, um ... I'm thinking might not be too welcome to you, if they track me to your door."

His comment was uncomfortably shrewd. "Does anyone know where you are?"

Rish answered for him: "Whoever gave him your picture and address does."

"Oh. Yes." Tej winced. "Who *did* give you my picture?"

"Mm, mutual acquaintance? Well, maybe not too mutual—he didn't seem to know much about you. But he did seem to think you were in some kind of danger." Vorpatril looked down rather ironically at the bindings now securing him to a kitchen chair, dragged out to the living room for the purpose. "It seems you think so, too."

Tej stared at him in disbelief. "Are you saying someone sent *you* to *me* as a *bodyguard?*"

He appeared affronted by her rising tones. "Why not?"

"Aside from the fact that the two of us took you down without even getting winded?" said Rish.

"You did too get winded. Dragging me up here. Anyway, I don't hit girls. Generally. Well, there was that time with Delia Koudelka when I was twelve, but she hit me first, and it really hurt, too. Her mama and mine were inclined to be merciful, but Uncle Aral wasn't—gave me a permanent twitch on the subject, let me tell you."

"Shut. *Up*," said Rish, driven to twitch a bit herself. "Nothing about him makes sense!"

"Unless he's telling the truth," said Tej slowly.

"Even if he's telling the truth, he's blithering," said Rish. "Our dinner is getting cold. Come on, eat, then we'll figure out what to do with him."

With reluctance, Tej allowed herself to be drawn into the kitchen. A glance over her shoulder elicited a look of hope from the man, which faded disconsolately as she didn't turn back. She heard his trailing mutter: "Hell, maybe I should've *started* with ponies..."

—end excerpt—

from *Captain Vorpatril's Alliance*
available in hardcover,
November 2012, from Baen Books